A Time on the Hill

Hill

BY

Allan Turner

The Steven Pinder and Ian Turner series

Book 1. A Web of Conspiracies

Book 2. A Time on the Hill

Book 3. A Seeker

The following story is fictional and is in no way intended to accuse or embarrass Governments of the UK and USA, and their representatives, both past and present. Also no intention is to be construed to implicate the former 'Imperial Chemical Industries' of any wrong doing in their processing of chemicals, nor of the treatment of their employees and residents of Haverton Hill. Friends and other names used to represent the various characters, have been changed, or are purely fictional, except that is, for Colin Hatton who's kind permission was given.

A special thanks to Ronald Long for his help.

CONTENTS

1959 THE FALLOUT

PART ONE
REVELATION

PART TWO

THE BEGINNING

PART THREE

OPERATION JERICHO

PART FOUR

WEAPONS OF MASS DESTRUCTION

PART FIVE

EXPOSUER

THE FALLOUT

IMPERIAL CHEMICAL INDUSTRIES

BILLINGHAM DIVISION

PLANT S IX. Midnight December 23rd 1959

The loud crackling sound of the plasma cutters and the blue flashing light that escaped through the tie holes of the canvas shroud was outdone only by the occasional lightening flash, which was followed instantaneously by the boom of thunder, as a storm raged directly overhead.

'What a bloody night,' Bob Fisher night-shift Plant Operator, said as he squinted through the control room window room. 'Pouring down.' His eyes strained to see if he could discern anything of the decommissioning works. 'Like sodden stair rods. .. Can't see a bloomin thing.' He muttered. 'There's no way I'm going out there to check progress.'

'You don't have to Bob, it's not our concern.' Stan Richardson responded nonchantly. Stan the only other Plant Operator on duty that night was slumped in a swivel chair which he oscillated with his leg in Bob's direction and then he spun back to face a large control panel. 'Anyway it shouldn't be necessary, these contractor guys are supposed to know what they're doing… Don't they?' He said with a hint of sarcasms in his voice.

'Hope so Stan, bloody hope so.' Bob repeated as he straightened and retuned to his seat next to Stan's in front of the control panel. 'I personally don't have a clue. Bloody strange, isn't it? …Never known a plant being shut down like this before.'

'Aye, you and I both, Bob.'

Too bloody damn quick, if you ask me. …Something's bound to happen, you mark my words Stan.' Bob nodded solemnly as he spoke. 'I can feel it in my water, something bad, mark my words.'

'I'm not too sure about your water, but something's got give, recipe for disaster if you ask me.' Bob nodded in agreement as Stan swept an arm over the array of lines and lights and switches. 'Just look at this control panel, half the flippin lights are out. How the hell are we supposed to know what's on line and what isn't?

'Yeah, and how the bloody hell are we expected to monitor anything?' Bob shook his head from side to side. 'As soon as we empty a vessel those bloody Yanks jump in,' he nodded towards the window and the flashing blue light, 'and that's the last we see of it.'

'Why don't they wait until the whole plant is shutdown and we've got rid of all the chemicals before they start tearing it to pieces?'

Again Bob shrugged his shoulders. 'Nothing's been done by the book, the whole bloody lot's been an enigma from the start.'

'An enigma, you're right there. I thought I knew a bit about chemistry and physics, but....'

'Isn't that why we're here?' Bob put in.

'Yeah for sure, but I just can't figure the composition of the crap being pumped into those pods. Not an experiment that I've come across, maybe it's some kind of secret weapon.'

'Maybe.' he said, as he surveyed the control panel. 'Got more lines than there's handrail around the 'Queen Mary' and more lights than 'Blackpool's illuminations.'

Stan smiled. 'Only when they are working, Bob, only when they are working.'

Bob gave out a sarcastic snigger. 'Aye, you're right there.' They both stared at the control panel in front of them.

After a moment Bob changed the subject. 'Doesn't look like we'll make it home for Christmas Stan.' He said sombrely.

'Nope, don't look that way, another one missed,' he mused. And they both lapsed into a state of melancholy.

It was Stan who broke the silence, as if taking his mind off thoughts of his wife and children at home in Salisbury. 'Wonder what they do with all that stainless?'

'Down the mine I hear tell.'

'No, you've got to be joking; it must be worth a fortune in scrap value alone.'

Bob shrugged his shoulders. 'Only what I heard. … What the! Bloody hell!'

The conversation was interrupted by a loud buzzing and flashing red light on the panel.

'What do you reckon?' Stan had jumped up and was tracing a finger along the multitude of lines.

'Valve on the cooling water line, - better check pressure.'

'Damn, no reading, - try to divert.'

Bob frantically stabbed at the buttons on the panel. 'Not responding.'

'Looks like I'll have to go and physically check it out.' Stan moved quickly to the lockers at one end of the room. He took out and started to pull on his white rubberised, coverall. 'Where is it?'

Bob nodded towards the window and the shrouded vessel. 'Give you one guess.'

'Hells bells, - you thinking what I'm thinking?'

'Somebody's turned off the wrong valve?'

Stan nodded. 'Hope it's that simple.' He pulled on a respirator pack and attached the breathing tube to the helmet, before heading out the door to face the storm.

He headed in the direction of the former 'Cyanide' vessel. The vessel was now shrouded inside a canvas cover and was in the process, no doubt of being cut up into small pieces.

Although he tried to hurry, his progress was slowed by the gale force wind which caught him head on and the rain lashed against the visor reducing his visibility to virtually zero. Eventually after what seemed an age he reached the shroud and began to pick at the knot in a nylon rope tied around one of the scaffolding poles which formed the framing of the shroud. No sooner had it loosed when the gusting wind took it and blew back the canvass sending it flapping uncontrollably. Stan ignored it and waved just as vigorously to attract the attention of any one of the dismantling contractors.

As if by magic the plasma cutting stopped, angle grinders ceased and sparks from acetylene cutters tailed off. All was not totally quiet, there was still the throbbing of the generators to contend with as well as some of the contractors busily going about their work with hammers and wrenches, but at least now Stan could make himself heard through his helmet. The workers in the immediate vicinity seemed to turn in unison to face the white clad visitor who looked to them like some sort of alien that had just arrived from outer space.

'Can we help you pal?' A big guy said menacingly in a Yankee drawl.

'A valve's been turned off that shouldn't have been.' Stan shouted, aware that his voice would be distorted.

'Oh yeah, and just where is this valve that's been turned off that shouldn't have been?' The big guy scoffed.

'On the pipe bridge, should be somewhere about there.' Stan pointed up at the overhead runs of pipe-work in an attempt to pinpoint the suspect valve, but despite the number of arc lights, his visor began to steam up so he couldn't see, nor did he discern the shocked look on the Americans face.

'Son of a bitch! Hey Jody, you just hang fire there, you hear boy.' He shouted up at the bridge.

'Too late boss I'm just about done the lines out and it's all cut up.'

Somewhat concerned Stan put in. 'What's happened?'

'We isolated that valve a couple of hours ago, I sent Jody up there to remove and cut up the lead in pipe-work.'

'Cut up, two hours ago! That was the coolant for the Reactor.'

'Goddamn, is that serious?'

'You bet your backside it is.'

'We're just gonna have to fab up a new piece.'

'How long's that going to take?'

'Don't know gotta see if we can salvage some pipe off somewheres and weld it in. Trouble is we don't have a welder, ceptin Jamie, but he's day shift.'

'Bloody hell!' Stan shouted through his visor and emphasized the urgency by slapping a gloved hand down on an adjacent pipe. 'I don't care how you do it, but get that water back on line like now!' Leaving no doubt as to the importance of his request. The big guy seemed to get the message and took off up the ladders to the pipe bridge to assess the situation.

No point in hanging around. Stan thought as the man disappeared, so he turned and ran back as fast as could to the control room.

Still trying to catch his breath, he pulled off his helmet and respirator and called to Bob. 'Shits hit the fan - need to get hold of Miles-Johnson, - like now.'

Bob grasped the receiver and dialled the number on the pad. It took an age before the telephone was eventually picked up.

'Black Swan.' A tired sounding female voice answered.

'Sorry to bother you so late, but I need to talk with one of your guests, Doctor Miles-Johnson.'

'He'll be asleep by now, shouldn't wonder.'

Not wanting to create any sort of panic, Bob tried to keep his voice at a calm pitch. 'I really need to speak with him on a matter of some urgency, if you'd be so kind as to wake him, I'd be grateful.'

'Okay I'll give him a knock, who shall I say is calling?'

'Er Bob, Bob Croswell.'

Bob heard the receiver clang on down, *probably on the bar* he thought. Seven minutes later he heard the rattle of the receiver being picked up.

'Hello Bob, Miles-Johnson, what's the problem?'

'Big one sir, the Yanks have cut off the cooling water feed to the Reactor, stripped out a whole section of line in the process.'

'What! What are the rods doing - do you have a thermal read out?'

'Haven't been able to get one sir, that part of the panel's out, the sensors may have been struck by lightening.'

'How long before you can get the cooling line back in?'

'No way of knowing sir, depends on how much has been removed.'

'Humm,' Miles-Johnson responded thoughtfully, 'just as a temporary measure link the line into the fire hydrant. That ought to buy us some time, if the Reactor goes more than two hours without coolant the rods will start meltdown and I have no idea what the consequence would be.'

Stan interrupted. 'Tell him the Yanks shut it down a couple of hours ago and chopped up the flippin pipe.'

'Did you hear that sir?'

'Damnation! There'll be no way we can save the rods now, uncontrollable meltdown. Got to shut it down somehow and damn quickly.' There was a long pause as the doctor ran the scenario through his mind.

Bob waited patiently, receiver pressed to his ear, he looked up at Stan, who was leaning over trying to get an ear in range of the telephone, and pursed his lips emphasized with a slight shake of his head.

'Okay Bob get the cooling water in there, won't stop it now, sounds as if it's too late, but it may just buy us a little time.' There was another momentary pause before Miles-Johnson continued. 'We'll have to assume that the rain will keep the outer shell cool. Then what we've got to do is pump in concrete, or something to encase the core. But how do we get hold of that much concrete at this time of night, - without raising eyebrows?'

Stan turned his head and spoke into the mouthpiece, without relieving Bob of the hand set. 'Gypsum sir.'

'What?'

Bob now passed the phone over to Stan. 'Gypsum sir, apparently they've got tanks full of the stuff over at the Nitrates fertilizers plant.'

'Y-e-s of course, Gypsum. That should do the trick, good thinking Stan. See if you can get hold of enough of the stuff to fill the vessel and pump it in and we need to get it in there PDQ..... I'm on my way.' At that there was a click and the line went dead.

Bob had picked up the gist of the conversation and was already in the process of scanning the internal ICI phone list. 'Extension 232.' He declared and Stan immediately lodged his finger in the appropriate number and rolled the dial. The telephone rang for about twenty-five seconds. 'Come on.' Stan muttered impatiently. Eventually it was picked up. 'Nitrates Control.' A high pitched voice responded. Stan took a leaf out of Bob's book, and tried to act composed, dismissing any signs of panic from his voice and because S IX plant was classified, he pretended he was calling from an adjacent plant.

'Hi, - Stan Wilson, Ammonia Five. Got a bit of a problem developing, any chance of getting a load of your Gypsum, urgent like?'

'Problem, what kind of problem?'

Stan thought fast, guessing at what would be a probable situation. Got a Sulphur burner running out of control, my boss is telling me the quickest way to shut the damn thing down is to fill it with Gypsum.'

'I'll need paperwork.'

'Can that wait? Need to sort this right now.'

'Sure it can, come and take as much as you want, we've got more of the stuff than we can handle, every bloody tank's overflowing. What do need wet or dry?'

'What's the difference?

'Well if it's allowed to dry, it becomes compacted and starts to set, a bit like wet sand when the tides gone out. - That's what's happening now, to the overflow, we've got keep hosing it down to stop it setting solid. It's OK while it's in the tanks; we keep it fluid mixing it with water and keeping it moving.'

'The wet stuff sounds good, any idea as to how we can get over here - fast?'

'Well if you can get hold of enough fire hose I'll pump you as much as you need.'

'Great – I'm on it. – By the way who am I talking to?'
'Joe McKinley.'
'Thanks Joe.'
Stan dropped the receiver back on to its cradle and turned back to Bob who was now trying without success to get a core temperature reading from the now defunct instrument panel. 'Looks like we're going to need about a mile of fire hose Bob.' Just then there was a loud rumbling sound coming from the Reactor area. 'And I think we're gonna need it sooner rather than later.'

'Shit, that doesn't sound good; we're not going to make it. Told you something would happen, knew we'd have bother.'

'Got an idea, I'll get the Yanks to help, - may be enough at the fire station.' Stan shot off again towards the shroud, but this time he left the helmet and respirator behind, he didn't need the hindrance.

Stan quickly explained the situation to the American Forman, and two men were sent immediately to the nearest hydrant to fix up a hose into what remained of the coolant pipe. The rest of the men were split into teams and dispatched to collect as many fire hoses as they could lay their hands on.

The moment Dr Miles-Johnson stepped out of his Ford Corsair a fork of lightening played for a long second directly over the plant, the following thunder crack was so loud that buildings seemed to shake. Despite the intensity of the gale force wind the centre of the storm had moved little and the angry looking dense blackness of the clouds rolled and swirled in turmoil over ICI Billingham and the neighbouring town of Haverton Hill.

Miles-Johnson pulled up the collar of his overcoat and grasping the rim of his trilby with one hand, hurried head down into the control building.

'What's the situation Bob?' He said, the moment he set foot inside the building, making no attempt to remove his now wet hat and coat.

'Best I can tell sir, the rod's meltdown is causing a pressure build up, we've just had one hell of a rumble, - thought it was thunder at first. The Yanks have got a hose tied into what remains of the pipe-work, but I think it's now too hot to do any good.

Stan and the Yanks are coupling lengths of fire hose to the remnants of the cooling intake.

'For the Gypsum?' Bob nodded. 'Good, let's hope we're in time.'

Unfortunately they weren't, for five minutes after Miles-Johnson had arrived at the Plant, the Reactor vessel blew up, ironically the explosion coincided with another flash of lightening and the sound was merged into a double roll of thunder.

'What can you see Bob?'
'Not much at all, sir.'
At that moment, what was formerly a ten inch diameter by two inch thick blanking plate, clattered to the ground with such an impact, the road was relieved of several inches of its tarmac.

'Goodness me, - that's off the crown of the vessel, - it must be venting.'

Evan against the dark sky and despite the strong wind, a plume of white emitted swirling and twisting from the top of the vessel. The white plume shot skyward with such force as to maintain the upward thrust close to a hundred of feet above the vessel's domed head, before succumbing to the winds velocity and bending almost at right angles, as it tailed off in the direction of Haverton Hill.

Miles-Johnson, with Bob at his side approached as near as they dare to the vessel. Debris was still falling and clouds swirling dust seemed to play with the black mass of the storm clouds as it disappeared off into the distance. Aware of contamination risk they both wore their white rubber suits and respirators. 'Rumbling stopped sir.'

'Y-e-s, but what damage I wonder?'

'Not sure, - too dark.'

'See if you can get hold of an arc light Bob.' Miles-Johnson nodded in the direction of the shrouded vessel. 'I need to know the extent.'

It was fast approaching five in the morning by the time Miles-Johnson, still clad in his rubber suit, was able the carry out an inspection of the damage to the upper section of the Reactor vessel. A whitish plume, albeit far less intense than it had been, still oozed from the fractured orifice. The plume now swirled and bent almost horizontal within feet of the vessel top, indicating to the doctor that the pressure was being reduced. But what the plume might contain concerned the doctor greatly, particularly as the indication was that it could and probably has, fallen out over the town. While standing on the gantry overlooking the reactor, he stared for a long moment in the direction of Haverton Hill, contemplating the likely problems that could ensue should any of the citizens there contract the contamination.

Miles-Johnson was in the process of heading back down from the structure when the Gypsum rumbled through the intake pipe followed by a loud hissing noise as the mixture hit the core.

Bob and Stan both in their protective suit were stood at the foot of the access stairs waiting for him. He shouted to Bob as he got near. 'As suspected it's melting, lots of debris mainly asbestos lagging from what's left of the hot lines. No one is to get within a hundred feet until I say, rope it off.' Then he turned to Stan. 'Stan, get the American Foreman to my office.'

They both waved their acknowledgement and hastily set about their tasks.

One blessing, he thought, the reactor was small scale, - experimental really.

Dr Miles-Johnson was seated at his desk when the American rapped on the door.

'Come in.' the doctor shouted and the big burly American strode into the office and sat, as the doctor had gestured on the seat opposite.

'Look, I guess I got my wires crossed out there.' He said defensively.

The doctor held up a hand. 'What's done is done - err –mister.'

'Fitzgerald - Eddie Fitzgerald.'

'Well Eddie what I want to talk to you about is how we're going to put it right.' He looked at the American, nodding assuredly and then he eased back in his chair leaving an arm extended, the fingers of which drummed rhythmically on the desk top. 'Do you know what radioactive fallout is?'

'Like the stuff that spewed out the Atom bomb?'

'Humm yes, near enough, - well what we have here is something similar spewing, as you say, from the Reactor. Or should I say was, that Gypsum we're pumping in there should contain it for a while.' Eddie nodded slowly as if he understood, but he clearly had no concept of how harmful radiation poisoning could be. *Probably just as well,* the doctor thought.

'This is what I want you to do, straight away, no delay, you understand.' Again Eddie nodded. 'Get your men togged up in protective suits, Stan will help with that. I want you to take the vessel down in one piece, no time for a shroud. Get it as deep as possible down the mine and once there cover it with lead sheet and encase the whole lot in three foot of concrete. Don't stop until it's done. I have written out the necessary requisition notes for the concrete....Ready Mix will need to be organised. Rolls of lead, you should be able to get from the main stores.'

'That bad uh?'

'Yes Eddie, that bad.'

'Okay sir, I'm on it.' Eddie stood.

'Oh, and Eddie, detail a couple of guys to return the hoses, we don't want any enquiries into this.' Dr Miles- Johnson touched the side of his nose with his forefinger. 'The fewer people who know about what happened here the better.'

'Gotcha.'

After Eddie had left the office, Dr Miles- Johnson picked up the telephone receiver and dialled zero, there was a pause before the operator's voice was heard. 'Number please.'

'International line. – America. – I'd like to send a telegram, the number is -.'

The doctor replaced the receiver and immediately brought the palms of hands to his temples and rested his elbows on the desk. *Does damage limitation really involve the destruction of a town?* He mused.

PART ONE

REVELATION

Middlesbrough Teesside. 2010

Late, one rainy October night, an old man staggered from side to
side along the pavement, catching and hanging onto, for some
respite, any convenient post. With one hand he clutched at the collar
of his dressing gown in a vain attempt to prevent the cold and wet
penetrating through to his pyjamas. The cloth slippers on his feet
were soaked and leaden from the number of puddles they had been
dragged through. Clearly in pain and gasping for breath, he forced
himself to keep moving. There was little in the way of traffic on
Marton Road that night. Any passing motorist merely took the
staggering figure as just another drunk. And the weather was so
adverse it ensured that the pavements would be clear of any potential
night crawling pedestrians.

Eventually with sheer determination and at the very point of
exhaustion, he crawled up the drive of a house in Gunnergate Lane
in Marton Village. Reaching up he grasped at the door handle and
with all the strength he could muster, pulled himself up and flopped
against the door panel. Gasping for breath he let his body rest there
for a long moment, the pain grabbed again like knife point twisting
in the side of his chest. He squeezed the door handle and bit down on
his lower lip to prevent himself from crying out. When the pain had
subsided, he lifted his eyes and a weak shaking hand to the door bell

and resting his finger on the button, pushed with the little strength he had left.

'What the-! Where, uhh'! Colin rolled over flinging an arm to the bedside table and fumbled for the light switch. It seemed to take an age for it to dawn on him that someone or something was pressing the door bell. As the light came on he squinted at the bedside clock. 'It's one thirty.' He declared as he eased himself up the bed. 'Who on earth can that be, at this time of night?'

'What's happening – what's the noise?' Colin's wife Miriam awoke in a confused state.

'Someone at the door, I think.' Colin said as he sat up and dropped his legs out of the bed, his feet instinctively seeking out his slippers.

'What are you doing?'

'Going to see who's there.'

'Do you think you should?'

'Well at this moment I can't think of an alternative.'

'Oh do be careful dear; don't open the door until you know who it is, - and make sure the chain's on.'

'Yes dear.' He said stifling a yawn, while putting on his dressing gown.

Still half asleep Colin plodded down the stairs, not really sure he was doing the right thing, particularly as there was no let up to constantly ringing door bell. 'Okay, okay, I'm coming.'

As he approached the front door, he noticed that the handle was in a downwards position. *Someone's trying to get in,* he thought. Colin cautiously turned the key in the lock and as the lever withdrew, the door sprang open and snagged against the chain with some force. Although to some extent expected, Colin was still startled by the suddenness of it and jumped back with the shock. 'Get a grip of yourself man,' he mumbled, as he approached the now ajar door with some degree of caution. He peered through the crack. At first unable to comprehend what the dark shape was resting against his door. He stared, trying to discern what or who it was, then it dawned, it was a dishevelled figure of a man slumped against the door and hanging on to the handle. As he stared, the body slid and its pale face lodged itself in the opening. This time the shock sent Colin jumping backwards clutching his chest and he give out a startled cry. 'Ahhh!'

'Colin!' Miriam shouted.

A moment passed before Colin could catch enough of his breath to respond. 'It's alright dear, - I'm fine, nothing to worry about.' He shouted back as he recovered his composure.

With a cheek still pressed against the panel, distorting his already heavily lined face, the old man uttered weakly. 'Colin- ah – it's me – ah – Ray, --- Ray Hartley.'

'*Ray Hartley who the* -. My god, Raymond! What on god's earth.' Colin exclaimed, as he suddenly realised who it was. Pushing the door closed he removed the chain and almost instantly, the limp, gaunt and soaked body slumped forward and collapsed on the hall welcome mat.

Miriam by now was standing half way on the stairs. 'Who is it dear?'

'It's Ray Hartley.—I think we'll need towels dear and could you get a blanket.' Colin said as he kneeled down next to the prostrate figure of the man. He laid a hand gently on the wet shoulder of the body. 'You're soaked Ray old chap, let's see if we can get you out of those wet things and make you more comfortable.'

Ray, still laid on the hall carpet visibly trembled and shook as the cold and wet penetrated his bones, but other than the occasional moan, did not resist Colin gently rolling him, first extracting one arm and then the other from the ringing wet dressing gown.

'Ray who?' Miriam asked as she descended the stairs with a blanket, towels and Colin's spare dressing gown.

'Hartley – an old friend.'

'Oh my, - the poor man.' She said as she took in the scene. 'I'd better call an ambulance.'

A hand comes up and with surprising strength grasps Colin's arm. 'No - ah, - need, - no - ah – time. Haverton was – ah – poisoned.' He gasped and his eyelids flickered.

'Ray, hang on in there, mate.' Colin began to rub him with a towel aiming at stimulation as well drying. 'We'll soon have you out of those wet things, warm and snug.'

Ray's hand still held firmly onto Colin's arm and Colin felt it squeeze trying to get his attention. He stopped for a moment and looked thoughtfully into Raymond's eyes. Those bloodshot, tearful eyes set within a sallow wrinkled face, stared back at him. *A long way from the Raymond I once knew.*

'Colin – ah - promise - you'll –ah - the ICI.' Ray pulled on the arm and tried to lift his head to be closer to Colin's.

'Sure I will. Let's get you out of that wet …..'

Ray gasped and the intake rattled deep down inside him, he didn't breath again, still staring wide eyed at Colin, a rivulet of dark brownie red liquid oozed from the corner of his mouth. He stiffened and then went limp.

'Hello, ambulance please.'
'No rush Miriam, he's dead.'

After the confusion of bodies, Police, Ambulance crews and the obvious questions, Colin and Miriam sat in the lounge nursing their cup of tea, both staring blankly into nothingness, withdrawn deep within their own thoughts. 'Pointless going to bed, I'm way past any thoughts of sleep, might as well get dressed.' Miriam roused herself, placed her cup on the coffee table and started to head back to the bedroom.

'Might as well dear – might as well.' Colin said sombrely as he too prised himself out of the armchair. – As Colin followed Miriam out of the lounge, they passed through the hallway and the welcome mat, with its still wet patch where Raymond Hartley's soaked body had lain lifeless. Colin looked at the mat and shuddered, in his minds eye, he pictured Ray's body lying there. He shook his head in a vain attempt to dispel the thoughts as he climbed the stairs.

'What a night, eh, don't want to go through anything like that ever again.'

'Couldn't agree more, I'm about all in.' Miriam said over her shoulder as she laboured the ascent.

'Wonder what induced him to walk all the way here in that state? – Nearly two miles, you know.'

'Who was he Colin? You never really told me.'

'A friend from way back, grew up together in Haverton Hill. We were classmates at the school, but never real buddies. Ray had his clique that he hung around with, I had mine. When they demolished Haverton and moved us all to Billingham, Ray's family became our new neighbours and Ray and I became closer friends for a time. That friendship was short lived.'

'Why, did you fall out with him?'

They were now in the bedroom, sat on the bed and Colin continued to reminisce.

'Oh no, nothing like that, we more or less drifted apart, you know, teenagers, different interests, girls.' He turned and winked at Miriam. 'Besides, he worked in the Furness Shipyard and I was with Power Gas. We both found new circles of friends.' Colin sighed. 'Strange he would think of me after all this time, must be all of thirty years.'

'That's a long time.'

'It is indeed dear.'

The funeral was held seven days later at Acklam crematorium. Colin and Miriam attended, primarily out of respect for an old acquaintance. But in reality, they were still somewhat puzzled by the events of that night and still curious as to why Raymond Hartley had chosen them to be the last people to see him alive. Also Colin couldn't relieve his mind of the promise he'd made, albeit vague, to say the least. All he knew was that he'd promised to look into something connected in some way to the ICI, which he'd assumed to be Billingham ICI as opposed to Wilton ICI. They both had grown up and lived within sight of the Billingham Plant. Colin half hoped he would meet someone closer to the latter part of Ray's life who may be able to shed some light on the matter.

After the service, the few attendees, milled around the chapel entrance, vying for the opportunity to express their condolences.

Their sympathies were directed at a lonely female standing near the doorway. She had dark hair, shoulder length and was wearing a black wool coat. *Pretty little thing,* Colin mused, but he didn't know her. 'I wonder who she is.' Colin said, but he didn't expect Miriam to respond. 'Seems to be by herself, wonder where the rest of the family are?'

'Were there any?'

'Hum, a brother that I know of.'

'Well it looks to me like she is the only representative of the deceased.' Miriam said.

Colin and Miriam edged around the outskirts of the group making small talk to the unknown mourners. Colin not wanting to distract anybody from the reason they were there, tactfully mentioned the circumstances of Raymond's demise, to a few of the gathering, and hinted at the vague promise he'd made. People just nodded and hummed their insincere understanding of the matter, but not one offered any explanation of Ray's demands.

Colin turned to Miriam. 'I've got to conclude dear, that Ray must have been rambling.'

'He was a very sick man.'

Colin nodded and decided to put the matter out of his mind. That was until, purely by accident, they found themselves face to face with the pretty little lady in the black wool coat.

'Hello, I'm Michelle Thompson, Raymond's daughter. - You are Colin Hatton aren't you? She cocked her head to one side as if studying Colin's face. Colin nodded. 'Thought so, I saw your photo in the Gazette. - I'd like to thank you for taking care of dad.'

Colin gave out a little cough to cover his minor embarrassment. 'No thanks necessary my dear, Ray was an old friend.'

'I know, I remember you.'

Colin pulled back his chin and looked somewhat puzzled for a moment. 'Y-e-s of course, how could I have forgotten, you were just a young girl the last time I saw you.'

'Yes – it was a long time ago.'

'Well Michelle it's really nice to meet you again after all this time, but I wish it hadn't been under such tragic circumstances.'

Miriam stepped forward and took Michelle's hand. 'I'm Miriam, we're so very sorry for your loss.'

'Thank you Miriam.' She turned to face Colin who had taken a step backward. 'I really need to talk to you about something dad may have said.'

'He did say something that I don't really understand.'

'Hum, thought so.'

'But we, Miriam and I are, to say the least, puzzled.' Colin paused as if to emphasize the point. 'Puzzled as to why Raymond forced himself to walk almost two mile from James Cook Memorial Hospital to my, err, our door?'

'He certainly was in no condition.' Miriam put in.

'He had your book, waved it at me, said. "If anybody, you would understand".'

'Understand what?'

'I'll try to explain, would you mind waiting until they've all gone?' She said nodding in the general direction of the mourners.

Colin and Miriam nodded in unison. 'No not at all.' Colin said.

Fifteen minutes later the small congregation at Raymond Hartley's funeral had dispersed, a hearse and limousines complete with mourners were arriving at the chapel preparing to send another departed sole into the furnace.

'Thanks for waiting.' Michelle said as she approached. 'Shall we walk?'

'Why not.' Colin said. While they walked slowly along, Colin felt he ought to broach the subject of Michelle being the only family representative at the funeral, just to put things right in his mind. 'Err, we couldn't help but notice Michelle, that you're by yourself, are you, - ahem, forgive me if I'm speaking out of turn, but I mean are you all that's left of Rays family now?'

'In short, yes. Oh I am married, but the timing of the whole thing caught us a bit on the hop, Bill, my husband had just gone back to the North Sea rigs... He didn't feel it was necessary to come back for the funeral. – Bill hasn't spoken to dad in years,' she added as an after thought.

'No family?' Miriam queried.

'Yes a son, Gary.' She pondered a moment. 'He's away at University and he's very upset about losing his Granddad. But with all the studying he has to do, I thought it best for him not to come.'

'Quite, quite, understandable I believe.' Colin said, nodding his head as he spoke. 'And what about Eddie?'

The group wandered in the direction of the remembrance gardens.

'Uncle Eddie, he's part of it.'

'Part of what?'

She paused a moment as if trying to put the memories into some sort of context. 'The last time I saw Dad, alive,' she added, 'he was really excited about his findings and what's more your book. That's when he said you would understand.'

'Understand ?' Colin screwed up his face in an expression of puzzlement.

Michelle pursed her lips. 'W-e-l-l, I think he wanted you to take over his campaign.'

'Campaign?'

'Huh huh.' Michelle nodded. 'He was obsessed with the idea that the ICI had poisoned part of what used to be Haverton Hill about fifty year ago. He was planning to ask you -.'

'Where we grew up.' Colin said in a quiet voice, talking more to himself, rather than being informative.

'Apparently, - he's got all sorts of papers and stuff back at the house, I'll need to sort them out for you.'

'For me, I – I wouldn't know what to do with, err - it-them.' Colin a little flustered, shook his head. 'No no Michelle, I'm not sure I want to be involved. – Can't you err – do whatever?'

'Dad said he wanted you to have them.'

That comment momentarily killed the conversation they strolled on in silence. – Colin's mind was racing with thoughts of how to get out of the hole he'd just landed in, but no feasible excuse other than a stern refusal to get involved, would come to mind. *I don't want to risk hurting her feelings, especially not at this time, better I listen to what she has to say.*

A place to sit and reflect on the matter was conveniently found in the form of a wooden bench donated in memory of "William Walker 1936 – 2005 beloved husband of Jean."

They sat on the bench facing into the remembrance garden, Michelle in the middle. 'I think I'd better start from the beginning,' Michelle said as she stared blankly at a pot of Geraniums, 'as much I know that is. You see, everyone popped off within such a

short space of time, no wonder dad was demented.' Then she threw
back her head and sniffed, tears weld up and pooled in the corners
of her eyes, about to start their journey down her cheeks. Colin
without hesitation took out his handkerchief and handed it to her.
'Thanks.' She sniffed, 'I'll be alright in a minute.' She sniffed
again and dabbed her eyes before continuing.

'Granddad was first, -- just over years ago, followed within months
by Grandma. Their deaths were put down to old age, but it wasn't
until sometime after that dad began to question the suddenness of
it. Then Uncle Eddie died.'

'Yes I remember Eddie, Ray's older brother.' He said leaning
slightly forward, for Miriam's benefit.

'Uncle Eddie never married, lived out in Spain, bit of recluse by all
accounts. Apparently he'd been dead for nearly a month before
they found the body. That came as a bit of a shock I can tell you,
Uncle Eddie was so fit. At that point the three of us, Dad, Mum
and me, seemed to shrink into a state of depression, we felt as if
everything had gone wrong in our lives.'

'Understandable, it must have been a traumatic time for you dear.'
Miriam said in a consoling manner as she patted Michelle's knee.

'Last year, just when we thought things couldn't get worse, Mum
suddenly started to feel unwell, - really bad chest pains.'

'Jean?' Colin queried aware that Raymond had married, literally, the girl next door, his childhood sweetheart, Jean Harrison, but was a little unsure if the marriage had lasted.

Michelle nodded. 'Within twenty-four hours she was dead. That's when Dad lost it; he went crazy, he wanted answers and when he didn't get a satisfactory explanation, started his 'campaign' - for want of a better word.'

'Sounds to me like he had good reason,' Miriam said understandingly.

'Hum perhaps. I was so upset about losing my mum. I just wanted to cry all the time.' Michelle sniffed again and let out a sigh as the memory of it tugged on her heart strings. She had a little cough to compose herself, before continuing. 'I didn't support dad, in truth; I cocooned myself with thoughts of everything being fine and distanced myself from his obsessive behaviour. What I didn't realise until yesterday, when I read through some of his notes, was that both granddad and grandma had suffered similar fates.'

'You mean they both had chest pains?'

'Not quite, I'm not sure where the pains where. But dad had noted that they had both died within twenty-four hours from the onset of their pains.'

'And your father died the same way. All very coincidental, too coincidental if you ask me. Perhaps some peculiar strain of virus, could even be something hereditary or whatever, but something definitely affected your family.'

'Dad ruled out the hereditary bit, when Mum was affected.'

'What about Mr and Mrs Harrison?'

'They died sometime ago...'

'Y-e-s I vaguely remember...Something about a coach crash...I think...That was a while ago.'

Michelle nodded. A club outing to Seaton.... Dad didn't even consider them in this scenario.

I only wish I'd listened to him, instead of shutting him out. He was probably right all along.' She shifted on the bench seat so that she could look Colin in the eye. 'Dad was convinced the ICI had put out some poisonous cloud that came down over Haverton Hill and that was responsible for the extermination of our family. His words, not mine.'

'Yes so you said, - but what I don't understand is how? I mean, what kind of poison waits fifty years to work? Haverton Hill was demolished, bulldozed. No Michelle, I just can't comprehend such a scenario.'

Michelle shrugged her shoulders. 'But you will help won't you?' Her eyes widened pleadingly.

'I, I don't really know where I would start my dear, It's not my—.' Colin fumbled for words that would tactfully reject any offer of help on the matter.

'Dad thought you would, least you can do is take a look at his papers. He left them to you anyway.'

'He left them to me?'

'Not in a will or anything official like, but there's a large envelope with your name on it.'

'Well in that case, - it won't do any harm to take a look I suppose.'

'You could count it as research for a new book, dear.' Miriam suggested.

'Err – yes, perhaps I could dear.'

'Good, that's settled.' Michelle fumbled in her little black clutch bag. 'This is Dad's address.' She handed a card to Colin. 'I'll be there in the morning. Would that be convenient for you?'

'Well err -.' Colin was still a little apprehensive.

'Yes dear, I'll make sure he gets there.' Miriam said.

Michelle stood and busied herself running a hand over her bottom smoothing the folds out of her coat. 'I'll be there about ten, - see you there then.'

Colin nodded. 'Fine, fine.' But he was still very unsure about the whole thing.

She turned and began to walk away and then as an after thought, she stopped and looked back at Colin and Miriam still seated on the wooden bench. 'You know, I never knew Dad had taken himself into hospital...Turned up at A and E...Admitted straight away... He must have known he had such a short time left.'

The next day, Colin's Rover arrived at the address in Guisborough bang on ten, only to find Michelle's Mini was already parked in the driveway.

'Morning Colin.' She stood to one side and motioned him in. 'Please, - come in.'

'Hello Michelle, not late am I?' He said as he sidled past her.

'No of course not, I've only just got here myself.' She declared as she ushered him into the lounge and motioned him to sit on the sofa. Michelle then handed Colin a thickly packed A4 size envelope. 'This is for you, - I've not opened it, it's just as dad had left it.'

'Thanks.'

'Now then, I'll put the kettle on, - what do you fancy, - tea or coffee?'

'Coffee please, - white two sugars.'

'No problem.' She disappeared into the kitchen.

Colin examined the package, his name was boldly written in black felt tip across one side. He then poked his finger into the gap on the envelope flap and prizing it open and withdrew the bulk of the papers, letting them fall on the coffee table.

The first thing to catch his eye was another smaller envelope, again with his name on it. He picked up the unsealed envelope and took out the single sheet of paper, unfolded it and gazed at the hand written message from an old friend. *Ray's handwriting was always good,* he thought as he browsed the neat italic writing.

Hi Colin, if you are reading this, then it's more than likely that I have succumbed to the ICI poison.

First of all let me apologise for involving you, but yours was the only address I could find, got it from the Gazette advertising your book, and as a former resident of Haverton Hill, I just know you will feel as passionate as I do about the whole stinking mess.

It's taken me a while, but I am now confident that some time in or about fifty-nine; there was an accident in the ICI, which caused some sort of poisonous fallout over parts of Haverton. I have progressively plotted the possible track of the fallout on the map which you will find in the envelope. I am doing this as and when I learn about deaths of former residents. As you can imagine our former friends and acquaintances are now well spread and it is difficult to assess if their deaths had been in anyway unusual, but when I can, I contact the relatives, it's of no surprise to me to find that most of the deaths were a replica of my Jeanie.--------

Some of the people I know were Havertonians, but I wasn't sure where their lived, hopefully you can fill that bit in and plot the line of the fallout and more importantly its source, their names are listed on the map. Another thing you will note is the lack of females, simply because I didn't know their married names, although I found a few by reading about the suddenness of their untimely demise. If you are doubtful about my conclusions, it's worth pointing out that in all cases deaths occurred about twenty-four hours after the onset of a variety of pain,--all the cases had the same symptoms occurred within the last eighteen months and not one case involved any person under the age of fifty.

Good hunting Colin, -- get the bastards. ------

Raymond Hartley

Michelle came in carrying two mugs of coffee; she plonked her bottom on the sofa next to him and handed him a mug, he handed her the letter.

'Been busy my dad, hasn't he?'

'He certainly has. – But I'm not really sure I could emulate him.'

'Well I think you ought to a look at everything dad has put together, before you jump to any conclusions.'

'Expect you're right,' he agreed as he picked up a large piece of folded paper, he assumed to be the plan Ray had mentioned and unfolded it. He flapped it out and spread the large hand drawn map on the coffee table. Colin was amazed at the scale and detail in the drawing of the place he spent his first eighteen years and he felt a twang of nostalgia as memories of those times flooded into his head. Michelle busied herself taking cognisance of the list of none placed names. 'Know where any of these lived?' She enquired.

Colin's mind snapped back to the present. 'Eh, hum. Let's see. Mmm.' He murmured as he studied the list one name at a time. 'Albert Teasdale, my god I didn't know he'd died, used to be a pal. He lived in Hawk Street, number twelve, there.' Colin pointed at the map; Michelle leaned forward with a pencil and marked the spot with an asterisk.

Twenty minutes later, Colin had placed most of the names on the list and it became apparent that the asterisks formed a band about fifty yards wide lying diagonally over the Haverton Hill estate.

'It would seem Ray had a point.'

'Yeah, but if that was the fallout track of some kind of poison, what direction did it come from?'

'From Billingham ICI of course.'

'What about the other direction?'

'Nothing there then, - apart from that is, the marsh, a clinker tip and a few allotments.'

'Dad seems to have point, whatever air born poison fell over Haverton Hill must have come from the ICI.'

Colin pondered for a moment. 'You know Michelle, this doesn't prove anything, you know it's all supposition.'

'But!'

Colin held a hand up. 'I've no doubt Raymond got it right, I just don't know how or what we can do about it.'

'Surely we can do something?'

Colin hunched his shoulders. 'Like what? There's nothing to prove that these deaths were the result of a fifty year old poison and again nothing to establish, if there was poisonous fallout, that it was leaked from some plant in the ICI.' Colin shook his head and looked her into her eyes. 'Sorry Michelle, but unless we could prove it, I can't see anybody believing us and even if we can, who are we going to sue anyway, the ICI no longer exists and the plants at Billingham are all but gone.'

'Maybe you're right Colin, but dad thought he could do something about it, surely we should try to prove that he was right.'

'W-e-l-l, I suppose seeing as I've made a start here, I guess I owe him that much.' Colin said reluctantly.

'Couldn't we start by checking if there was an accident in the ICI about fifty years ago and take it from there?'

'Could do I suppose, if I only knew how and not least where to look.' He turned to Michelle, 'Billingham ICI was a very big place, you know.'

'Yeah but we know the fallout must have come from one of the plants along the diagonal band on dads map.'

'Hum, think we know,' he corrected her, 'but if everything is as we suspect, then in my view we should start at what used be Synthetic Ammonia number five, that was the nearest plant to Haverton.'

'Well that's as good as anywhere, isn't it?'

Colin shook his head slowly from side to side. 'Looks like I've talked myself in to this.'

'Ah ha,' she said smiling.

'Okay Michelle you win, I'll do a bit of digging, maybe I'll find something, maybe I wont, can't promise anything.'

'Thank you Colin, I know dad would have been grateful.'

Colin headed back towards Middlesbrough from Guisborough, the car more or less on autopilot as he wrestled with the problem of where to start and look for a mythical accident fifty years ago in anyone of many ICI plants that fell into Raymond's diagonal band. *Where to start, where to start.* He mumbled tapping the steering wheel out of sheer frustration. Then it came to him, *Ken, yeah Ken Cookson my old contact at the Gazette, he may be able to help.*

When he reached the roundabout at the end of the A171, he took a right and headed to a house on Ormesby bank.

'Hi Col, didn't expect to see you. Come in ..' Ken closed the front door as Colin passed. 'Caught the piece in the paper bout that Hartley guy kicking the bucket on your carpet.....You okay?'

'Sure I'm good.'

'And Miriam?'

'Yeah she's good too.'

'Then you've gotta be after something, info for the new book perhaps, eh?'

Colin smiled. 'Something like that Ken, I need your help to sort a problem.'

'If I can, if I can. Come on into the lounge.'

They wandered through to Ken's lounge and sat down.

'Hi Colin, how are you?' Brenda, Ken's wife enquired, but before he could respond, she continued. 'Cup of tea?'

'Not for me, thanks Bren, I'm not staying long.'

'You sure?' Colin nodded. 'Alright then, I expect you guys will want to talk so I'll leave you in peace.' She said as she left the comfort of an armchair and headed to the kitchen.

'Okay Col, let's hear it.' Ken said as he plonked himself into the recently vacated armchair. Colin sat on the adjacent sofa.

Straight to the point. Colin thought, *I like that.* But he hesitated on purpose, before asking the question, just to emphasize the serious nature of it. 'Ken, I'm looking for an event, possibly something catastrophic, you know, an explosion maybe, in ICI Billingham about fifty years ago. Does that ring any bells?'

'Fifty years! Bit of a tall order Col, but anyway I can't help.'

'Can't?'

'Fraid not old chap, un written rule you see, unless anything happened that affected the outside world, any incidents in the ICI were kept internal. It was the same for the Northern Echo and the Billingham Press. Anything noteworthy probably found its way into the ICI's own rag, but as you know, their records went along with the office closures in the sixties.'

'Pity, I was kind of hoping you may have been able to recall something.'

'You know as well as I Col, there were explosions, leakages, fires and who knows what else almost every day in some plant or other. So come on, be specific, what catastrophic event has caught your interest?'

Colin pursed his lips wondering how much he was willing to reveal. *What the hell.* 'It's to do with Ray Hartley.'

'The guy on your welcome mat?' Colin nodded.

'You must have known him, you lived in Haverton.'

'Sure I do, knew Eddie better, more my age. As I recall the Hartley's lived at the end of Marlborough.'

'Yeah, that's right. Well, before Ray died, he made me promise to look into something; you know last wishes and all that.'

'Promise what?'

Colin hesitated, not wanting to over dramatise the situation, but at the same he wanting to express the seriousness. 'You may find this hard to believe, but Ray had this theory that a cloud of poisonous substance was emitted from one of the ICI plants which fell out over Haverton Hill, that's why the town was flattened, to cover up the contamination.'

'Hum, that figures.'

'You think Ray had a point?' A surprised pitch in Colin's voice.

'Sure I do... Sort of fits what I've being thinking for years.'

'And you think people were poisoned?'

'We all were poisoned Col...The shit those plants pumped out, it's a wonder any of us survived. I didn't really consider the poison aspect, but I always thought there was something dodgy about the whole thing. Don't forget I'm a few year older than you and I remember back in nineteen sixty just before they flattened Haverton.' Ken glanced sideways at Colin. 'Although I didn't know anything about that, at the time. I was courting Bren and we were thinking about getting hitched. Didn't have much in the way of dosh, not many of us did in back then.'

'And?' Colin prompted.

'And I thought I would pay a visit to the council offices and put my name down for one of the new house that were being built on the Billingham estate. I was told then that it would not be possible at that time, as all the houses had been allocated to accommodate all the residents of Haverton Hill. When I asked how come, no one seemed to know anything, that is, except for one guy who had heard a rumour that Haverton Hill was to be demolished to make way for ICI expansion. That, as I recall, I thought was very suspicious.'

'Suspicious, why?'

'Well rumour had it at that time, that the ICI had just demolished one plant, stuffed the scrap down the mine. So if they were pulling down plants and ceasing their mining operation, how come they were talking expansion?'

'I s-e-e.' Colin said slowly. 'And the scrap, why put down a mine...must have been worth something.'

Ken pursed his lips. 'Probably, didn't give that much thought. I did note that years later nothing was built on the Haverton site, which confirmed the bullshit expansion theory.

Colin nodded thoughtfully. 'Humm, this plant, the one that was demolished, any idea which one?'

'All I remember now Col is that it was a plant near Haverton.'

'Synthetic Ammonia number five, gotta be. Thanks Ken.'

Anthony Davidson MD Senior Pathologist, Teesside area, was in the 'Pot and Glass' Public House, Eaglescliffe, seated in a cosy alcove. His hands were wrapped around the balloon glass, nurturing the brandy it contained.

'Hello Tony.' A tubby man said, as he proceeded to slide his bottom onto the shiny wooden bench seat, next to Anthony. 'Don't mind if I join you, do you.'

Anthony Davidson looked hard at the intruder, but remained silent.

'I do believe we have another one for you Tony.'

The Pathologist clenched his teeth and whispered out of the side of his mouth. 'For Gods sake, leave me alone.'

'Come now, that's no way to talk to your benefactor.'

'I've told you, I don't want your money.'

'Can't stop now Tony old bean, people will notice, explanations to be made, all of them accusing fingers pointed at you. It would be far better to take the money.—Don't you agree, -- huh.'

The Pathologist tightly closed his eyes to hold back the tears of shame and slowly nodded.

'There you go Tony old chap, you know it makes sense.'

Langley, Virginia, USA

Simon Kendall hunched over the steering wheel of his battered Chevy pickup, staring blankly at the white road markings as they disappeared beneath his vehicle. His mind wandered to the football game that he watched the previous night and he became oblivious to everything except it. The flash of an overtaking car quickly jarred his attention back to his driving and same dreary tiresome roadway he used every workday for the past five years. He frowned and gave out an audible sigh followed by an outspoken thought. *'Another boring day at the office.'*

If he'd have only known at that point, that this day, unlike any of those of the last five years, would turn out to be very different, very different indeed.

Simon's Chevy turned off the major highway and drove rapidly along a tree-lined road that led to the large security gate. As on every other working day he pulled up to the barrier, which didn't lift to allow him access. *OK I'll cut the engine.* He mimicked the guard's usual patter.

He wound down the window and nodded at the first guard. 'Hi, Bill, how's it going?'

The guard peered from under the peak of his cap and examined the pickup cab. 'ID, please.' No attempt at small talk, no personal acknowledgement. In all the years Simon had being coming and going from Langley, it had always been like this.

'Pop the hood, please.'

Simon, knowing the routine, had already complied. The other guard, the one he knew only by his name tag as Steve, checked under and around the body of the vehicle as usual.

'Thank you, sir, please log in?' Steve handed Simon a clipboard.

Yeah, always the same routine, at least for me. Higher profile personnel seem to get in with a mere salute.

The barrier raised and Simon drove into the main car park adjacent to the large grey stone oblong building, several stories high, housing the headquarters of the United States Central Intelligence Agency (CIA), Langley, Virginia.

Simon, a qualified 'Computer Analyst and Programmer,' held a somewhat less enhanced position in the CIA than his qualifications suggested. He was a 'Computer Operator' grade three and as such, held a low-level security clearance. Still, he had to go through all the ritual security-checks, fingerprint scans, and ID card swipes, before reaching his work station on the second sub-basement level. There, he flopped into his chair, and booted-up his computer.

The large monitor mounted on the partition wall in front of him flickered into life.

Along with a few others, Simon worked in the 'Subversive Publications Department' (SPD), English section (because he spoke no foreign languages). His job required him to scan all publications from English-speaking countries, searching for anything that might be construed as having a detrimental or subversive effect on the USA and or its policies, home and abroad. It sounded involved, but the computer did all the work, using an elite keyword-recognition program. Not surprising, there was very little in the way of subversive material coming out of English-speaking countries. *Little wonder I'm bored.*

That afternoon, like all the others, he sat nearly horizontal on his swivel chair, legs crossed, and heels resting on his desk. With his hands clasped behind his head and one eye half-open, he stared blankly while the multiple lines of text scrolled at breakneck speed across each of the screens.

All of a sudden, an alarm sounded on the monitor. The noise together with the flashing lights, gave him such a start that he flipped backwards onto the floor. His chair shot out from under and careened with some force across the small office space, coming to rest with a bang against the partition adjoining the next workstation.

Simon scrambled to his knees and stared quizzically at the blinking, flashing, screeching object. A moment ago this was a quiet, smooth-running computer monitor, now it was a strange, threatening object. This had never happened before.

Before he could raise himself, a firm hand gripped his shoulder. 'What you got, son?'

'I . . . I'm not . . . um . . . quite sure . . . sir.' Simon spluttered, as he raised himself to his feet.

Jim Benson, deputy controller SPD, leaned forward and punched the keyboard, subduing the cacophony. Suddenly all was quiet again; no flashing lights, no noise, and no more heads peering, like a colony of alerted Meer Kats, over the surrounding partitions.

Simon recovered his composure and chair and pulled himself, now seated, up to the terminal, his fingers automatically finding the keyboard. 'Now, sir, let's see what all the fuss was about.' He started tapping away.

A few minutes later Simon turned to Jim Benson. 'Something very peculiar, sir, it appears the alarm was triggered by one innocent-looking group of words from an equally innocent-appearing book written by some English guy. By themselves, or even when five of the six occur, no reaction. But, when all six appear together, the alarms ring. They don't look like anything subversive to me, just a couple of places and some chemicals.' Simon tapped away at the keyboard, his eyes fixed on the monitor as he analysed the flashing data.

'Simon, can I take it that you will at some point enlighten me, or do I have to beat it out of you.'

'Oh yeah. ... Sorry sir.'

'Well ... I'm waiting; I'm not stood here for the good of my health.'

'Er . . . sorry, sir. The key words are: 'ICI Billingham' and 'Haverton Hill', I think these are place names. The related chemicals are, 'nitrates, hydrogen, ammonia and cyanide.' It appears they are all mentioned at some point in this book, 'Images of England, Haverton Hill, Port Clarence to Billingham,' written by Colin H. Hatton. I've no idea what it all means sir, the book is just a nostalgic look back at a small town.'

'What the fu—are we doing looking at a book of a small town in England, for Christ's sake?'

Simon shrugged his shoulders. 'Must have come in on a special order, probably sent for by some expat.'

Jim stood almost trance-like, one hand clasping his chin. 'Beats the shit out of me, son. But those chemicals don't sound too healthy. And I sure as hell never heard of those places Billingham and Haverton Hill before.'

'Neither have I, sir.'

'And what the hell does 'ICI' mean?'

'According to my reference manual, it stands for 'Imperial Chemical Industries,' a huge British conglomerate of the forties.'

'Yeah, that fits with the chemicals.' Jim prodded a stubby finger at Simon's computer screen. 'Check out the recipient, find out who ordered the damn thing and get a profile on this Hatton guy. He may have a record. Then type-up the whole scenario in a report and I'll kick it upstairs, see if any light comes on.'

'Will do, sir.'

The recipient turned out to be a guy call Graham Harrison Denham, an eminent Professor of English at the University of Michigan. He was born and raised in this small town of Haverton Hill. He checked out....Clean. As for Colin Hatton, other than being an aurther, nothing conclusive was found.

The report passed swiftly through the offices of several departmental managers. They too, scratched their heads and came to the same conclusion Jim Benson had and kicked the problem further up the command chain.

Within hours, it eventually landed on Deputy Director Jack Rosenthal's desk. Jack studied the report for a long moment. From his first glance something clicked, something from way back, something important and hazy, but what? He slumped back into his seat, one hand on his desk, jiggling a pen between his fingers, and stared long and hard at the report.

'Shit,' he muttered. Throwing aside the pen, he stuck a hand into his desk drawer and retrieved a notebook. Hurriedly he flicked the pages eventually finding the page he was looking for. He studied the page intently for a moment, mouthing the long number into his memory, before tapping the digits into the telephone. He then sat back in his chair with the telephone receiver crooked in his shoulder and resting against his ear.

The instrument purred for sometime before it was eventually picked up.

'Hello.'

'Conlan, -- Conlan Powell?'

'Y-e-s, - and you are?'

'Ah, Conlan, it's been a long time since we spoke, - it's me, - Jack - Jack Rosenthal, DD CIA.'

'Hey hi there, Jack! It has been a while, how the hell are you?' But without waiting for any response, he continued. 'What can I do for you, ole buddy?'

'Look, Conlan, I don't think there's anything to it, but our computers have dug up a bunch of key words that more than

likely relate to a meeting we had back in '92, when you were Chairman of the Joint Chiefs.'

'Hmm, sounds interesting, just what meeting would that be then?'

'It was off the record, towards the end of the Gulf war; you and I paid a visit to the home of ex-President Richard Nixon, remember?'

'Hum vaguely, but I don't remember too much about it.'

'You should Conlan, think chemical shit. And the reason we went to war again.' Jack paused, his silence inviting Conlan to respond. He didn't, so Jack continued. 'As I recall, you reacted on that information and we've had our hand in that bag of shit ever since.'

'Ah now, if I remember right Jack. It was information gathered and corroborated by the CIA that was acted on, - that was a good while after 92.'

'Yeah true, but that particular story originally came out of Iraq from an Iraqi refugee trying to get into Germany. It was always thought that this guy was double dealing, you knew that. But the thought that Sadam was producing chemical weapons came pretty damn close to what Nixon was saying.'

There was a long pause before Conlan accepted the memory of the meeting may have had some bearing on later decisions. 'You mentioned key words, what words exactly?'

'Mainly chemicals, you know nitrates, hydrogen, ammonia and cyanide. But what's more interesting are the places cited in limey land–'ICI Billingham and Haverton Hill.' Those places ring any bells?'

Over the phone lines, Jack heard his friend repeating the words slowly, as if trying to tie them to a conversation taking place nearly eighteen year before. After a short pause, Jack heard a definite gasp when Conlan's memory of that meeting came flooding back.

'So what's the damage Jack, can we bury it?'

'Bury what! The fact that the Brits actually manufactured the 'Weapons of Mass Destruction,' that you insisted Saddam was making for use against the West.'

'You believe.' Conlan interrupted.

'Which were never found,' Jack emphasized, 'despite your effort to put Iraq under a microscope.'

'Well, can you?' Conlan put in, not wanting to explain or excuse his past actions, any further.

'Yeah no problem,' Jack said reluctantly, 'I don't think anyone would want to resurrect that old potato. Except the guy who wrote the book, maybe. Name of Hatton, he's a bit of a mystery.' Jack mused. 'I'm not sure how much he knows or just how far he's dug. Could be a problem.'

'What if he somehow discovers those chemicals were used to make weapons for America? Especially if it's then discovered that those weapons were shipped to Iraq. Oh boy, that'll surely open a can of worms.' Conlan said worriedly.

'And the whole bag of shit will get dumped in our back yard...Again.'

'Yeah, guess your right Jack. Perhaps we should keep an eye on this guy. - Just in case he starts sticking his nose into things that don't concern him.'

'Leave it with me Conlan I'll have a discreet word with a guy I know in MI5, see if he can check out this Hatton guy, just to be on the safe side.'

'Thanks, I owe you one Jack.'

'For sure. - See yah, General.'

As soon as Conlan replaced the receiver, he paused momentarily before picking it up again. He dialled an international number, 00441642****** and waited while it purred intermittently, for what seemed an age. Eventually the receiver at the other end was lifted.

'Ah – h - hello.' A voice sleepily responded.

'It's me, Conlan Powell.'

'Conlan! This isn't a secure line.'

'Yeah, I know, sorry to have woken you, ring me back on my private line, and put your scrambler on.'

Moments later Conlan's phone jingled and he snapped it up. 'Is it safe?'

'Yeah Con, scramblers on, just as well you rang I have some news, I was going to call you in the morning.'

'What's the problem?'

'There's been another.'

'Is it local?'

'Yeah.'

'Then deal with it, in the usual manner.'

'That's not the problem, it's our Pathologist friend. He's getting cold feet.'

'You tell that son of a bitch he can't chicken out now, took our money didn't he?'

'Sure he did.'

'I don't care how you do it, but you've got to persuade him to continue the process, tell him it's his neck on the block and to keep his goddamn mouth shut. Shut it for him if you have to. Get me!'

'Sure, I get the picture, don't worry he'll be sorted one way or another. Now, what was it you wanted to tell me?'

'Just to be extra cautious, the CIA are now involved and maybe MI5 will be doing a little snooping, but I can't see it affecting our operation.'

'Why now? This thing's about done; we'll soon be in the clear.'

'Can't be helped, unfortunately, it seems a writer may have stumbled onto the weapons thing.'

'How?'

'It's a long story, but I doubt they'll make any connection to us. They'll be more concerned with a guy called Hatton; he wrote a book.'

'Nevertheless, with those snoopers about, I'm not keen on hanging around.'

'Just take it easy, they'll soon realise that Hatton's book is the innocent heritage writing that it purports to be.'

'Okay Conlan, I'll take your word for it, but if I get even a sniff of the cops, I'm out of here.'

The moment Jack Rosenthal finished his conversation with Conlon Powell; he turned to his computer and started to type out an e-mail to Mark Pritchard, Head of European desk, MI5, London. - He requested visual contact via the satellite link, urgent.

Considering the time difference, it meant Jack would have to wait until Mark arrived at his desk in the morning, UK time. *'Shit – gonna be stuck here half the effen night,'* he muttered to himself while he typed.

At two-thirty a.m. the video link buzzed, rousing Jack from his doze. He rolled, rather clumsily off the sofa which was against the sidewall of his office, and scrambled over to the desk. He pressed the relevant keys and while the image formed, he rubbed the sleep from his face.

'Jack, you wanted to talk to me?'

'Ah Mark, thanks for getting back. I need your help.'

'If I can Jack, what's your problem?'

'Nothing really serious, but our computers have thrown up some subversive material, involves one of you Brits. A guy, name of Colin Hatton. - Think you can set up a listening brief for me. At our expense of course.'

■■■

Poole, Dorset

Ian Turner moved the cursor to the 'log off' icon and clicked on it. The machine chimed as the screen display began to shut down and eventually went blank. He eased himself back from the computer, taking in a deep breath as he did so. He stared at the blank screen trancelike. 'Have I really finished?' He muttered, not daring to believe that the extensive task he'd been undertaking for the past twenty weeks was now complete, but just to verify to himself, he began to run the programme through his mind again. A tap on the door interrupted the thought process. 'Come in.' He called.

Maureen, his secretary entered carrying a steaming mug.

'Coffee Ian.'

'Thanks, right on queue. I've just finished.' He pushed back into his chair looked up at her and smiled like the Cheshire cat.

'Oh well done.' She said excitedly as she placed the coffee on the desk. 'Now you can take it easy, - let the others do their bit.'

'You know Maureen, I was just thinking that, in fact it's about time I had a holiday.'

'I said take it easy, not go flipping overboard.' She put a hand on Ian's brow. Feels alright,' she muttered.

'No no, I really mean it this time.'

She stood there hand on hip nodding assuredly. 'You holiday, ding – a – ling, pull the other one that ones got bells on. As I recall, wasn't that what you said last time. How long did you go away for? - Let me see if I can remember, ah yes it must have been almost an hour. Oh and the time before that, it was almost two hours.' She said, widening her eyes in a mock look of surprise.

Ian raised his hands. 'Okay I admit it; I have been tied to the desk a bit.'

'A bit,' she said giving him a sideways look, 'that's putting it mildly; haven't known you take a decent break in all the five years I've worked for you.'

'It's about time then.' Ian declared as he got up put on his coat and headed to the door, giving Maureen a little peck on the cheek as he passed. 'The ball's in your court my dear, look after the place while I'm away, bye.'

Maureen stood open mouthed as Ian disappeared out of his office. 'Your coffee. - What about your coffee?' She called after him, all the time thinking that he would stop and turn around with a huge grin on his face, but he didn't.

Ian headed to the car park making a point of not stopping to say his farewells to anyone. Not because he didn't want to, but because inwardly he knew that if he stopped he would become embroiled with their problems or he would be tempted to return to his office and start the next challenge. He also realised that should he go straight home, he would only be kicking his heels around the apartment and end up on his computer. *No this time I'm determined to get away from it all; I'll go see mum and dad.*

Twenty minutes later, Ian's car pulled up outside of his parent's house.

'Hi Dad, hi Mum.' Ian leaned in and kissed his mother on the cheek.

'Hello dear, you're a little early for dinner, didn't expect you til seven.'

'I know, couldn't think of anything to do and I didn't want to go back to the office. Probably make Maureen's day.'

Ian's mother cocked her head to one side. 'I don't understand.'

'I told Maureen I was taking a holiday and she intimated that if I did pigs may fly.'

Allan and Alice took in the pitiful look on their son's face, and they both burst out laughing. 'She was quite right.' His father said between fits of giggles. Ian's frown turned into a smile as he too saw the funny side of the situation.

It was a good few minutes before a state of normality returned to the Turner household, but before things got too quiet, Allan pointed a finger in the air as if making an exclamation mark. 'I may just have the solution. Give you something to think about other than them damn computer programmes.' Allan retrieved a book that was resting on a side table. It was a thin heritage type book titled 'Haverton Hill, Port Clarence to Billingham by Colin Hatton.' Allan opened it and began to flick through the pages. 'Do me a favour and solve this little problem for me, son.' He said as he held out the open book at a particular page. 'You could visit the author for me and while you're in Teesside you could go and see your Grandma.'

'Gran would love to see you, just what she needs a little company,' Alice chirped in.

'Yeah it would be good to spend some time with her.' Ian said while nodding approvingly.

'And you'll be able to relax, for sure, forget about all them programme things you do.'

Ian nodded, reached out and took the thin heritage type book from his father. 'What's the little problem Dad?'

'The book was written by a friend of mine, - grew up in the same place, that's him in the newspaper cutting.' Ian pulled out the folded paper from between the book pages and began to unfold it. The sheet of newspaper was taken from the Middlesbrough Evening Gazette and carried a photograph of the author with contact details, as well as a description of the books contents. Allan pointed to the opened page of the book and tapped his finger on a picture. 'This guy with his back to the camera, holding the drill, I'm convinced it's my dad, your granddad, but I'm not a hundred percent certain. I've had a word with Colin, he thinks he still has the original photo and if he remembers right it had some writing on the back. If you could get hold of this original photograph, it may just solve the matter.'

'Yeah, why not, I'll give it ago.' Ian's thoughts at that moment were centred on seeing Grandma, the book and the photograph were of lesser importance. 'I'll take off tomorrow.'

Middlesbrough, Teesside

Ian's Audi A4 turned onto the Priestfield estate in Middlesbrough, threw a couple of rights and lefts before stopping outside a familiar house. Ian let his head go back against the headrest and closed his eyes for a few seconds. A moment later he glanced at his watch.

'Hum, eight- thirty not bad. Only five and a half hours from Poole, not bad at all considering the traffic.' He said out loud.

The lounge light was shining through the gaps in the vertical blinds and as Ian approached Grandma's front door the sound of the television could be clearly heard, well she was getting a little deaf, no more than one would expect of a woman her age. He knew she would be waiting for him, she had sounded so excited when he'd telephoned to ask if he could stay for a couple of days. No doubt a meal had been prepared and the dining table set ready for him. Grandma loves to make a fuss especially of her grandchildren. He pressed the intercom at the side of the door, within seconds the sound on the television was muted and the receiver was lifted, she had probably been sitting with her hand on it. Then there came a very polite sounding.-

'Y-e-s?'

'Hi Gran, it's me Ian.'

'Woo-hoo.' She yelled, like child let loose in a sweet shop. No sooner had the receiver gone down in its cradle when the sound of the door being unlocked occurred and the door flung open with gusto. A little lady appeared, rose to all of her four foot six height, wrapped her arms around Ian's neck and pulled him down with surprising strength for an eighty-nine year old, until his face met her lips.

'Come here.' She said, as she planted a kiss on his cheek.

Ian wrapped his arms around her and gave her a big hug. 'Lovely to see you Gran, it's been ages.'

'Come in, come in.' She ushered him in, closing and locking the door behind him, as she'd been so often told to do. 'Bet you're cold, now you sit down by the fire, while I put your dinner out.'

'Thanks Gran.' But he knew that Grandma would have been so preoccupied looking after his needs, that she would not have bothered about herself. So instead of making himself comfortable by the fire, he followed her into the kitchen. 'Ah beef stew, smells good. Where's your bowl Gran?'

'Oh I'll have some later; I'm not hungry just at the moment.'

'Nonsense, I won't eat without you.' He reached over and collected another bowl from the cupboard and passed it to her. 'There's plenty, enough for the both of us.'

'Well, perhaps, just a little.'

Ian picked up both bowls and carried them into the dining area, noting that there was a basket with bread on the table but only one place setting. So he made sure Gran sat at that place despite her protests, before setting himself a place.

'You shouldn't have bothered about me; you must be tired after all that travelling.'

'So good to have you here son, it's been ages.'

'Yeah, at least five years.'

'No problems?' She asked enquiringly.

'None at all Gran just thought I needed a break. Well actually it was dad who suggested I should head north.'

'That's surprising.'

Ian nodded and smiled. 'Yeah I know, it's usually mum who comes up with the suggestions.'

'Can you remember mum buying a book for dad last time she was here, all about Haverton Hill?'

'Y-e-s I think so, from Waterman's in the town, I was with her.'

Ian nodded. 'Well, - dad found a picture in it, he's convinced it's his father, Granddad Turner. He wants me to visit the author and if I can, find out more about the photograph. I phoned this Colin Hatton, the author, just after I telephoned you. - I'm meeting him tomorrow morning in the Rudd's Arms at Marton.'

'Oh that'll be nice.'

'Yes Gran, it probably will.' Ian stood up. 'I'm fairly shattered; I think I'll have an early night.'

'The bed's all made up for you, - pink room.'

'Thanks Gran.' He leaned over and kissed her on the cheek. 'Goodnight god bless.'

'Night night god bless son. Love you.'

'Love you too Gran.'

Ian headed up the stairs to the 'pink room' as Gran defined it. Dropping his leather holdall on the floor, he flopped onto the bed and lay there for a few moments just reflecting on the past.

He was in this room, the last time he'd stayed. His eyes traced a familiar hairline crack in the ceiling plaster as he stared upward. *I was almost at the point of suicide then.*

Ian let his mind drift back to the dark days of his life, remembering the pain and the anguish of that time.

He'd lived with a girl for eight years in Cheltenham; they had a daughter, Jenny. *She will be eighteen now... It all went pair shape that night.... The night I found out.'*

Ian had been working the nightshift, in a printing works. The partner, who shall remain nameless, worked for GCHQ, doing what, he was not sure. For whatever reason, Ian got home early that night and discovered the nameless one in bed with her lover. It transpired later that he also worked for GCHQ. Following the inevitable blazing row, she took off with this guy and a still very sleepy Jenny. Apparently they were all packed and ready to do a flit. They had even applied for a transfer to a similar facility, which Ian believed was in Canada, but was never able to establish that as fact. At one point he tried to find out more by approaching GCHQ only to be fobbed off with red tape. He'd stated that he only wanted to contact his daughter, but his name had not been passed on to the child, nor did he have anything to say that he had been sharing the past eight years of his life with this woman. It became apparent they new location was protected by some GCHQ official secrets act.

After a period of being a social dropout tinged with depression, Ian got over it, thanks in no small part to Gran who had taken him in.

He had long since given up any thought of pursuing the matter and had poured himself into a new life wiping clean the slate of his past.

A thin smile formed on his face as he lay there staring at the ceiling. *Upon reflection there is some irony to the situation.* He laughed out loud.

Once he'd pulled himself together, he decided to rekindle the education which had been sacrificed so long ago. He put himself through University and did pretty well, a BSc with Honours in Computer Science. After graduating he headed south to stay with his parents in Poole. With their help, he set up his own software company 'IT Telecoms', specializing in telecommunications. The company expanded at a great rate and following the award of a government contract, the business took on the hardware package as well, offering full communication systems.

And there's the irony, - for it's Ian computer communication system together with a special software programme that are now installed in the bowls of GCHQ Cheltenham donut and covers the whole of Britain's 'Secret Service' network, enough said.

Marton a suburb of Middlesbrough

Late afternoon a dark blue Mercedes Vito van, with a dark tinted windscreen, eased to a stop at the half way point along Gunnergate Lane, in the village of Marton, a suburb on the outskirts of Middlesbrough. There were three occupants in the vehicle, the driver and another in the front and one man in the back sitting at a desk, in front of him a bank of electronic equipment.

'This is it.' George the driver announced.

'Which house?' Bill the guy in the front seat asked.

'Well according to the sat-nav, it's that one, over there, the one with the silver Rover parked in the drive.' The driver said, pointing at a detached house three doors down on the other side of the road.

'Looks like they're in.'

'Yeah, you're probably right. Try ringing Charlie.' George said over his shoulder. 'They may have gone for a walk.'

'Will do.' At that Charlie brought up the Hatton's telephone number on the computer screen and activated it.

Dring–dring–dring.

After a short wait, it was answered.

'Hello.'

Click – purr-r-r-. As soon as the female voice was heard on the speaker, Charlie disconnected. 'No such luck George, the pigeons are still in the nest.'

'What do you reckon?'

'Well we're here, may as well stick it out for while, you never know, they may go out for the evening.'

'If not, I'll nip out when it gets dark and stick a tracker on the car.' Bill suggested and the others nodded in agreement.

'What about the neighbourhood, - reckon we'll be noticed?'

'Don't know, quiet street, houses set back, but I'd lay odds there are a few curtains twitching as we speak. Better stay in the vehicle until it gets dark.'

'Well in that case, bung us a packet of crisp and the flask Charlie....Looks like it's going to be a bit of wait.' Bill said as he eased back in the seat.

'Who was it dear?'

'Don't know.' Miriam Hatton looked quizzically at the telephone receiver in her hand and pursed her lips. 'Whoever it was replaced the receiver when they heard my voice.' She put the telephone back into its cradle and headed back into the lounge, uttering as she did. 'Umm strange, - you aren't having an affair, are you?'

'Fraid not dear, not at my age I'm past all of those shenanigans.'

'Hum I had noticed, - must have been a wrong number then.'

Two hours later. 'What do you reckon George, dark enough?'

'Guess so, nobody about, ruddy ghost town.' George said as he rubbed at the misted windscreen. 'Go for it.'

Bill was out, tracker in place and back in the vehicle, within a minute. 'Job done. What now, guys?'

'S-pose we head somewhere for the night.'

'I think that we should stay on standby, until we suss this Hatton guys habits. Probably means spending the night in here.'

'What! You've gotta be joking, I'm busting for a piss and its effin freezing in here.'

'Okay okay.' George held up a calming hand. 'What I don't want is one of the neighbours reporting a strange van coming and going from the place. I suggest we leave about midnight and get back here about five, - agreed?'

'Agreed,' Charlie said, 'anyone got a bottle?'

The others ignored Charlie's plea.

'No problem as far as I'm concerned George, Bill said, 'providing we get a meal organised.'

'You'll have to make do with what's left of the sandwiches.' George said over his shoulder as he spoke to Charlie. 'Book us into the Travelodge, tell them we're in transit and will be arriving about twelve.'

Breakfast time in the Hatton household in Marton was a quiet affair, just Colin and his wife Miriam. Colin took a slurp of his coffee and clenched a slice of toast between his teeth, got up and started to fiddle with his briefcase. 'Mind if I take the car today dear?' He said as he munched on the bread.

'I do wish you'd finish your breakfast before you start messing with things, - crumbs all over the place.'

'Sorry dear,' he said stuffing the remainder of the toast into his mouth. 'I'm meeting Allan Turner's lad in the Rudd's Arms.'

'And don't talk with your mouth full.'

'Sorry dear.' Colin swallowed and took another drink of his coffee before continuing. After that, I intend to head off to Billingham to meet some friends, get some background for the supposed new book.'

She looked at him sideways. 'Yes you can take the car, - I doubt I'll need it today.' She picked up her cup and took a sip of tea and then, as if it had just dawned on her, she said. 'Allan Turner's lad?

'Yes that's the one.'

'The lad who's looking for his Granddad?'

'The mine photograph.'

'Ah yes, the photo from my dad's tin box. Did we get it back?'

Colin nodded and pointed his chin at the paperwork he was just about to sort out. 'In my file.'

Miriam wandered over to the table where Colin was transferring paperwork into his briefcase, the small black and white photograph being among them. 'I hope it is his granddad, the lad seems to have come a long way to find out.' She picked up the photograph and flipped it over to study the faded pencil scrawl.

'There's writing on the back.' Miriam screwed her eyes in an effort to discern the faded text. 'Dad worked with a Roger, - not sure about the Turner bit.'

'Yeah—well I'm convinced. Allan's father was Roger, so it's more than likely they're one and the same.'

'Hope you are right.'

'Yes dear.' Colin placed the photograph and paperwork into his briefcase, put on his jacket, leaned over and kissed Miriam on the cheek. 'Bye dear, see you later.'

'Bye love, - drive carefully.'

It was nearer seven in the morning when the Vito with its crew had rolled up to take up station again in Gunnergate Lane. Bill was on watch, the other two George and Charlie were curled up in sleeping bags, on the vans freezing floor, trying to catch up in the sleeping stakes. They had spent what remained of the night in the Travelodge, but by the time they had each climbed into the sack, it was time for them to get up, so none the three were feeling anything like fresh.

'Wake up guys! Target's on the move.' Bill shouted, as he spotted the Rover reversing into the lane. George the driver shot to his feet, or to be more precise stumbled to his feet, the lower section of the sleeping bag wrapping itself around his legs like a constricting snake. Half in half out of the bag he leaned his body over the front seat and squinted through the screen.

'Him or her?'

'Him, - I think.' Bill lifted a small pair of binoculars to his eyes and twiddled with the focus screw. 'Yeah it's him, that's an affirmative.'

'Got him.' Charlie piped in. He had managed to shed his sleeping bag without fuss and was now sat at the computer.

'What do you reckon George? Should we follow him?' Bill enquired.

'Can't bug the place while she's in there and I've just about had enough of sitting here. We'll follow him; maybe he'll stop somewhere, give us a chance to catch up with our ablutions. I don't mean to offend, but you guys sure do stink.' George climbed out of the now crumpled sleeping bag, jumped into the driver's seat and started the engine, at the same time electrically lowering the windows. The cold morning air gushed in and wiped out any vestige of warmth that was still hanging around the tin box. 'Ah, fresh air, lovely.' George declared as the van moved off in pursuit of the Rover.

'Must have heard you George, he's turned into the pub car park.'

'What pub?'

'Er the R-Rudd's Arms. Now will you shut the bloody windows, its freezing back here.'

'Shit there's nowhere to stop on this road, too near the 174 junction. I'll have to follow him into the pub car-park.'

'I wonder if we can use their facilities.' Bill said, as someone in the confines of the van, broke wind.

Ian's Audi turned into the Rudd's Arms pub car park, almost colliding with three men as they came scurrying out of a blue van, and made for the door of the pub. In their haste, they hadn't even noticed the Audi. Ian just shook his head in dismay. *'Silly buggers.* He mumbled to himself.

Ian made for the lounge bar. As he entered, he immediately recognised the author from the news paper cutting. Colin Hatton was sitting on a long curved corner seat nursing what looked to Ian like orange juice. Ian approached him, right hand extended. 'Colin Hatton I presume. Pleased to meet you, I'm Ian Turner.'

'Ah Ian, good to meet you.' Colin stood up firmly grasped Ian's hand and shook it vigorously. 'Can I get you a drink?' Colin said as he edged out of the seat and started for the bar, a hand already inside his trouser pocket in the process of collecting an adequate amount of coinage.

'Er, thanks, bitter shandy please, I'm driving.'

'Yeah me too.' Colin said nodding towards the pint glass on the table. 'Orange and lemonade.'

Colin headed to the bar and Ian settled himself next to where Colin had been sitting. He noted that apart from an elderly couple in the opposite corner, he and Colin were the only occupants in the lounge.

'Ah –ah, needed that,' George said as he shook the last dribbles of urine into the urinal.

'Me too.' Charlie said, as he tucked his penis back into his pants. Bill was in one of the closets making his own noises.

'Did you see that sign board as we came in? Full English for a fiver.

'Sounds good, but what about the target?'

'Well he wasn't in the bar as we came through, so he's probably in the lounge. If we eat in the bar he won't even clock us.'

Bill flushed and headed for the sink. 'I'm game, - I'm bloody staving.'

'No Charlie I'm not concerned about the target seeing us. I'm thinking he could just take off while we're just getting tucked in.'

'Hum... could do I suppose, but I have got this.' Charlie pulled a small remote from his pocket. 'This will let us know when he leaves. As long as it's not immediately, then there should be no panic.'

'Okay let's do it,' George said.

Moments later Colin returned with a pint shandy and placed it on the table in front of Ian before seating himself.

'Cheers.' They both exclaimed as they clinked glasses.

'I talked to your father on the telephone sometime ago. We talked for about an hour about our mutual friends and many others mentioned in my book.' Colin took a sip of his orange and lemonade concoction. 'Did you know your Granddad?'

'No, no...Died along time before I was ever thought about, Dad only mentioned the photograph to me the day before yesterday.'

'Ah yes, the photograph, the one on page one hundred and nineteen.'

'Dad is keen to find out more about it.'

'I may have some good news on that front.' He said, raising a finger into the air as if about to conduct an orchestra and then he delved into his briefcase. After a little paper rustling, Colin produced the photograph, inspected and commented on it, before placing it on the table, keeping Ian in suspense a little longer. 'You understand this photo belonged to my wife's father, Harry Walker. Not too sure who took it, but Harry isn't in the shot, so I presume it was he.'

The photograph was far clearer than the book, but as Ian had never known his granddad, he just stared at it.

'This could be the clincher.' Colin said, as he turned the photograph over, scrawled on the back hardly discernable written in fading pencil was.

Roger and Mike drilling the blast holes
'Well that's just fantastic; you know my granddad's name was Roger Turner.'

'I do now, hadn't a clue when we put it in the book, it was Miriam suggestion to mention that Harry had been killed in an accident down the Anhydrite mine.'

'That's a coincidence granddad also, I believe.
According to dad, a drilling machine, like that one I suppose, flew back and hit on the side of his head. Dad's still bitter about that, apparently the whole shift knew how badly he was hurt, but they just sent him home in a taxi. Nobody registered it as an accident, because ICI had a green flag accident free day's bonus scheme. So many days without an accident and everybody gets a bonus payout....So it was not reported and when he died from the injury, Grandma missed out on the compensation.'

'Yeah, typical.'

They both looked gloomy for a moment, lifting their glasses in unison and drinking in silence. Colin spoke first. 'The photograph's yours if you want it Ian.'

'Thanks very much, it will be treasured.'

'You're probably not aware, but I am now collecting material for a sequel. This time with more emphasis on ICI Billingham, and its impact on the people of Haverton Hill. If possible, with your permission, I would like to cite practices that existed such as happened to your granddad along with my father in laws case, as a lead in to the ICI Anhydrite mine.'

'Can't see a problem, but you'll need to run it past Dad.'
Colin nodded.

Ian shrugged. 'Lead in? Lead in how?'

'Probably of no interest to you Ian, but I recently discovered that ICI Synthetic Ammonia plant number five was demolished.'

'Not unusual.'

'Agreed, that is until you realise that the scrap, allegedly, ended up encased in concrete deep down the Anhydrite mine....Why?'

Colin drained his glass. 'The Plant was full of stainless steel; surely the scrap value alone must have made the recovery of the metals a very viable option.'

Ian didn't know if Colin wanted his input, but he chirped in anyway. 'I would say some kind of serious contamination. Radiation, perhaps.'

Colin nodded. 'Yes that, or even some kind of toxin which couldn't be washed away.' He stood up, lifting his brief case as he did so. 'Never mind, I'm sure I'll find out. Got to go now I've another meeting, nice to have met you Ian.' Colin held out his hand. 'Pass on my regards to your father.' He said as he pumped Ian's hand.

Colin turned to leave. He took one step paused and then turned back. 'Er – Ian.'

'Yes Colin?'

'This Ammonia plant issue, I'm going to meet a couple of guys now who I know worked at some point, in number five. The point is, both of them knew your dad very well. How do you fancy coming with me?'

'Sure I would, I'm not doing anything else. I have my car, I'll follow you.'

'No, no need, leave your car here. I'll drop you off on the way back.'

'Sorted.'

Ian and Colin headed towards the Rover, got in and drove off.

'Finish up lads, he's on the move.' The remnants of their full English was jammed between slices of bread and stuffed into their respective pockets. The three watchers scurried out of the Country Club and jumped into the Mercedes Vito, each headed to their respective station. The monitor was beeping indicating that the tracker on Colin Hatton's car was still within range.

'Let's go.'
'Which way?'

'He's taken a left, heading towards town.'

'I'm on it.'

The Mercedes van gunned its engine and set off to follow Colin and unknowingly Ian, at a discreet distance. The tracker had an active radius of two miles, so there was no panic.

The Rover headed down Marton Road, across Middlesbrough and picked up the A66 towards Stockton.

'Who are we going to see?'

'Well I've arranged to meet Philip Walton at his home in Billingham. Philip was in my class at school, a few months older than your dad, but they grew up together. Philip lived in 4 Drake Street, three doors away from number 10, where your dad lived.'

'And this Philip worked in the ICI?'

'Yes.'

'On this number five plant?'

'Some of the time I believe.'

There was only a moments quiet before Ian enquired. 'Didn't you say you were meeting two guys?'

'Sure, the other is Jack Fisher. Jack used to live at number 8, next door, - grew up with your dad, a little younger but nevertheless a pal. He's meeting us at Philip's, should be there by now. I've also asked another person to turn up, bit of a surprise, but we'll discuss that, if and when.'

The Rover took the slip road down to the former Newport roundabout and took a right over the Tees via Newport Bridge joining the A19 towards Billingham.

'See all this waste land on the right, that was all built up with various ICI plants, not so long ago, 1999 in fact.'

'Is that where this alleged infamous plant number five was?'

'No no, you see that chemical plant still standing, beyond the waste land.'

Ian nodded.

'That's all that remains of the ICI works now, but at other side of it, there is an even bigger area where once stood massive plants producing all kinds of chemical cocktails, plant number five being one of them. It was over there,' Colin pointed his chin and nodded in the general direction, 'on the other side of those cooling towers. It was also the nearest plant to what was once the Furness estate Haverton Hill.'

'George! You've missed the flippin turn off for the bridge.'

'Soddit, came up a bit sudden. - Is there another way Charlie?'

'About a half mile or so further on, keep in the left hand lane, we'll take the A19 flyover to Billingham.'

'Are they still in range?'

'Just, but I think we'll lose them by the time we make the flyover.'

'Damn! Damn! Damn!' George banged his hands against the steering wheel, out of anger tinged with more than an inkling of frustration. Bill said, more or less in a nonchalant manner.

'We know this Hatton fella is involved with the ICI in some way.' The other two waited for Bill to spit out what he was getting at. 'Didn't there used to be a Billingham ICI? Seems to me we're already heading in that direction, why not cruise the town, see if we pick him up.'

'Or we could head back to Marton.' Charlie chipped in. 'The missus may have gone out and we can do the place.'

George pursed his lips and nodded in agreement. 'Hum, - if she's indoors we'd be stuffed. No Charlie, I'm on the slip now. We'll stick with Bill's idea. If we don't find the target in Billingham, then we'll head back.'

The Rover pulled off A19 via Billingham town centre, then onto Marsh House Avenue and right onto Low Grange Avenue, stopping outside of a particular house.

Colin headed down the path, closely followed by Ian, to the front door and rang the door bell. The door opened almost instantly and a tall guy, at least six foot six, filled the open door frame. 'Hi Col,' he said and stuck out a big wrinkled hand. 'Come on in.'

'Hope you don't mind Phil,' Colin said as he pumped Philip's hand, 'I've brought an acquaintance.'

'So I see, - Hello I'm Philip Walton.' Philip held out a hand.

'Ian took it. 'Pleased to meet you, - Ian Turner.'

Colin interrupted. 'Allan's son.'

'Allan's son?' Philip looked quizzically at Colin.

'Allan Turner, Drake Street, Haverton.'

Then it dawned. 'Flipping heck, Allan Turner eh, - your dad, - it must be more than fifty year ago since I last saw him.' By this time the three were in the lounge meeting and greeting Jack Fisher. 'Jack this is Al's son.'

'Yes, I heard. Hi, Jack fisher, I used to live next door, grew up with your dad.' Jack said as he shook Ian's hand vigorously.

Colin and Ian were seated on the sofa, a coffee table in front of them, on the other side of which, Jack and Philip each occupied an armchair. They were in the front living room, enjoying a mug of coffee and each others company. The talk between the three older men, re-countered the nostalgia of their youth and took pleasure relating to Ian the exploits of his father and the gang.

It had occurred to Ian that Colin had not made any mention as yet about the ICI and he was beginning to wonder why.

Colin reached over, placing his mug on a coaster, on the coffee table and studied his wrist watch. And then gave out a little cough, mainly to get attention. 'Err Phillip, hope you don't mind, but I've taken the liberty of inviting another person.' Again, he glanced at his wrist watch. 'Should be here shortly.'

'To do with the new book?'

'Could be.'

'Not a problem. Anybody like another cuppa, while we're waiting?'

Before anyone could respond, the door bell rang. Colin instantly sprang to his feet and hurried to answer it, much to the bemused look on Phillips face. A moment later, standing with Colin, framing the living room doorway was an attractive, dark haired lady.

Hmm damned attractive, I'd reckon, early forties, same age as me. Ian thought.

'Allow me to introduce our special guest. Michelle Thompson. Michelle has something to say that I think you will find of interest.'

'Got it!' Charlie exclaimed. 'Take the next right, George.'
'Right you are.'
The Vito slowed to a stop about fifty metres behind Colin's Rover, parked on the road outside of a row of houses. 'Which house, do you think George?'

'Can't be sure Bill, but one thing's for certain, we won't be able to hang around here too long. We'll get noticed.'

A short while later, a red Mini came up the road and parked behind the Rover. A lady got out, approached one of the houses and rang the door bell.

'Obviously a visitor, but who is she visiting?'

Bill nodded towards the house. 'Obviously Colin Hatton and whoever else, seeing as he's just opened the door.'

George turned around in his seat. 'Charlie, run that plate and can you run the house number. – What road are we on, Bill?'

'Err—Low Grange Avenue.'

'My gut instinct tells me she is –.'

Almost instantly Charlie came back with the answers. 'The Mini belongs to a Mrs. Michelle Thompson, -- and the house is owned by Phillip Walton. Nothing on either.'

'Thanks Charlie, make a note for the report.'

'Is what George?'

'Er nothing really Bill, but I just had this feeling that we ought to be keeping an eye on her as well as the Hatton fella. Anyway

I don't think we're going to get any more here for a while. What do say to heading back to that pub we passed?'

'The Telstar?'

'That's the one.'

'I'm game, could do with a swift half.'

'Me too.'

'Michelle nee Hartley, – Raymond Hartley's daughter.' Colin announced.

Phillip responded immediately. 'Ray's daughter, I'm so sorry for your loss.'

'Please accept my condolences also. I read about your dad in the Gazette. He was a good friend.' Jack said as he came forward taking Michelle's hand in his, patting it gently.

'Thank you.' She said

Colin continued the introductions. 'This is Phil and Jack, we all knew your father rather well and this is an acquaintance of mine, Ian Turner.'

'Pleased to meet you Ian.'

'And I you.'

It was plainly obvious to Ian that Michelle had recently lost her father, but not knowing the situation, decided it was not his place to comment. Instead he vacated his seat, gesturing to her to sit, as he did so, he took a seat on a dining chair near the window. Colin completed the introductions, referring to Ian as an interested party on behalf of his father, who had also been a friend of Raymond Hartley. Ian politely nodded and turned to gaze out of the window. As he did so he couldn't help noticing the blue Mercedes Vito go slowly passed the house, only to pass again a moment later in the opposite direction.

'Perhaps you would like to tell the story, Michelle.' Colin prompted.

Michelle nodded and gave out a little cough to clear the vocal chords, with a mug of coffee now held between her hands, she sat up straight and jiggling her bottom as she did so.

'I suppose it started about two years ago, when mum took ill.'

'Kathy Harrison?' Phillip put in.

'Yes, - of course she grew up in Haverton Hill, you all probably knew her.'

'Sorry Michelle, please go on.'

'Well she developed these very severe pains, - right side, - sort of upper back.' Michelle put down her coffee and demonstrated, running a hand down her side, below her arm. Ian who was somewhat transfixed by the curvature of her ample bosoms, blurted out. 'Lungs.'

Michelle nodded. 'Yes, lungs. She was whisked into hospital for a scan and they found a growth. The Surgeon at James Cook Memorial Hospital, admitted to dad, that he'd never seen the likes of it before and didn't feel it was operable. Within twenty-four hours she was dead.

Dad was beside himself at that point and couldn't seem to get his head round what was required. This guy turned up said he represented a firm of solicitors who may be in a position to pursue a claim; I not sure how he managed it, but he took over, sorted all the arrangements. Don't know who he was, can't recollect him ever mentioning his name.' She picked up her coffee and took a sip. The blank look in her eyes, betrayed the deep thoughts of her loss. Then she gathered herself and returned the cup to the coffee table.

'It was a week or so later, - after the funeral, - when dad seemed to get it together and started to ask question. I suppose he reflected upon the untimely deaths of Gran and Granddad and Uncle Eddie. He suddenly seemed to become obsessed, tinged with more than a little anger.'

'Could hardly blame him.' Jack muttered.

Phillip turned to Jack. 'Ray's mum and dad were getting on a bit and from what I recall Eddie contracted some foreign bug.'

'Quite right Phillip.' Michelle agreed, 'but what I later discovered was that both Gran and Granddad died within twenty-four hours after experiencing severe pain. Uncle Eddie's body was unrecognisable by the time they found him, eaten away by some kind of fungus.'

'Like I said, I guess Ray had good reason to get angry. But what I don't understand Michelle, is what's it got to do with us?'

'I was coming to that Jack. - As I was about to say, dad became obsessed and began to do some checking. I must say at that point I'd distanced myself from him, probably because I had some misguided feeling of embarrassment. So it wasn't until recently that I discovered the extent of dads' research.'

'And.'

'He found another twenty persons who had died in recent years from similar symptoms as mum, Gran and Granddad, - the onset of severe pain followed by death within twenty-four hours. You can now say twenty-one deaths when dad's included.' She added sombrely

'No doubt Raymond came across some rare virus.'

'Hardly rare Phil when there are at least twenty-one cases that we know about. But I'm still puzzled Michelle as to what it's got to do with us?'

Michelle glanced over to Colin, he nodded back assuredly.

'In every case found,' she continued, 'the victims were all over the age of fifty and all former residents of Haverton Hill.'

'What! - Bit hard to believe Michelle.'

Ian had no idea what was going on, but he found the conversation intriguing, especially when Michelle was talking, he was finding her fascinating.

'Believe me Phil,' Colin put in. 'I've checked it out every which way, the bottom line is that the victims seem to been affected by some toxin which, for whatever reason lays dormant in the body for about fifty years, then a fungi grows, apparently like thin veins which rapidly shut down any vital organs they come in contact with.'

'Come on Col, surely someone has noticed the similarities?'

'Not necessarily Phil.'

'Dad thought there was a cover up.' Michelle put in.

'Yes, there's that Michelle, but you've also got to factor in the older victims, those assumed to have died of natural causes and you've also got to consider where people died. Some at home and not all in the Teesside area, some in hospital, different ones apparently and when the hospital was the same, different consultants attended.'

'A cover up - by who Michelle?' Ian queried.

'I'm not sure, something dad said –.'

But nobody other than Ian seemed to be interested in Michelle's cover up theory.

'Let me get this straight Col, are you trying to tell us, because we lived in Haverton we will catch some sort of deadly fungal growth.'

'No, no I don't think so.'

'But—.'

Colin held up a quieting hand and flipped open the lid of his briefcase with the other. 'If you recall I wanted to talk to you and Jack about a certain ICI plant.' At that Colin unrolled Raymond's drawing on the coffee table. 'Take a look at this.' Everyone including Ian leaned forward to look. 'I have managed to place a cross on the homes of all the known victims on Raymond's sketched map of Haverton.' There was a momentary pause as all five scrutinised the map. 'You will note,' Colin continued, 'these, quite clearly indicate a band of about twenty-five yards wide which is projected running diagonally across the village, - the source.' Colin stabbed his index finger on the drawing. 'I believe to be ICI Synthetic Ammonia plant, number five.'

'Hum that seems to be round about the right area,' Jack said as he studied the map intently. 'If that is some kind of poison path, then none of us should be affected, it seems to miss all of our former homes.'

'W-e-l-l,' Phillip said hesitantly, 'we don't know what it is yet and if it does represent some kind of poison trail, how do we know Colin has got them all.'

'Thanks Phil, forever the optimist.' Jack responded as he turned his attention back to the map. 'Oh dear, Stanley Gardens name, I didn't know he'd died and Richard Noble, - I never knew.'

'Colin nodded sombrely. 'Stan passed on about two months ago; Dick died much earlier, almost a year ago.'

'Yeah we all knew Stan and Dick, good pals.' Phillip said, forgetting about the presence of Ian and Michelle, at that moment.

Ian glanced at Michelle and shrugged his shoulders; she smiled back and mimicked him, shrugging her own shoulders.

'Stanley apparently had the same symptoms as Ray, as for Dick, Ray wasn't sure, but the Noble's home is smack bang in the middle of the band, so if there is any substance in Ray's theory, then it's highly likely that Richard Noble suffered the same symptoms as the rest.'

'Still can't believe nobody noted the similarity of the deaths. And another thing bothering me Michelle, if you knew all this, how come Ray's condition wasn't exposed, or was it?' Philip said.

Michelle shrugged. 'Dad reported what he knew to the police. They showed interest at first, but there was nothing to hint at anything unusual in any of the pathology reports and in all known cases at that time, the bodies had been cremated. So they dropped it. As far as dad is concerned, by the time I was informed that he had died, an autopsy had already been undertaken and cremation arranged.'

'That's not usual, is it?'

'No Jack I can't say it is.'

'Nothing mentioned in the pathology reports. That's very strange, - - isn't it?' Ian put in.

But before Michelle could reply, Jack interrupted. 'Couldn't all this be just a big coincidence? It all seems far fetched, a growth that Pathologists don't think exists, affects only former residents of Haverton and that only after fifty years.' Jack moved his head from side to side in bewilderment. 'And we are to blame the ICI. It's all a bit hard to swallow, Col.'

'I tend to agree with Jack, tragic as it for the loss of former friends, there's just nothing to say that they died from some kind of poison from the ICI, and this growth thing, if it exists, takes fifty years to kill. Really is hard to contemplate, Michelle.' Phillip said, in a rather condoning manner.

'Oh I think we can be sure that this growth exists, the loss of my family for one and as far as I know, it has only infected former residents of Haverton Hill.' Michelle put in firmly, not wanting anyone in the room to take the matter lightly. 'I do realise, she continued, 'that there's a lot supposition, but as Colin has demonstrated, the ICI is not only the prime suspect, it's the only suspect.'

There was silence in the room, nobody wanted to challenge Michelle. Phillip and Jack, clearly not wanting discuss that particular subject any further, turned their attention away from the map and seemed now to be studying the pattern on the carpet. Ian looked at Michelle and noted the pleading look in her eyes, but felt it was not his place to intervene.

Sensing it was time to change the subject, Colin retrieved a pad and a pen from his briefcase. 'I think it's about time that I took some notes. Look, I know you guys worked at sometime in this particular plant. Can either of you remember any sort of incidents that could have caused this fallout, - explosion excessive blow off, something like that?' Phillip and Jack both stuck out their lips and slowly moved their heads from side to side. 'Can't recollect anything unusual, but you know as well as us, that all the ICI plant constantly threw off clouds of foul smelling stuff.'

'Aye, - living in Haverton it was more unusual not to be subject to foul smells and tingling skin.' Jack added.

Colin nodded in agreement. 'Is there anything at all you and Jack can tell me about Ammonia plant number five?'

'Just depends, - what do you want to know?'

'I would be interested to know why this particular Synthetic Ammonia plant was demolished in 1960 and dumped in one of the tunnels of the Anhydrite mine.'

'Short answer Colin, it wasn't.' Colin was dumbfounded and Ian, who at that point was more concerned with helping Michelle and wasn't paying a great deal of attention, suddenly became intrigued by the comment.

'Aye that's right,' Jack added. 'Number five plant Synthetic Ammonia came down in about 69, along with the rest of Haverton Hill. I know because I worked on the decommissioning.'

Having quickly downed their pints, the three watchers had returned to the Vito, mainly to ensure Colin's car was still parked in Low Grange Avenue. According to the computer, it was and it had been there for some time. All three were now becoming a little impatient and the smell of the beer wafting through the doors of the 'Telstar', coupled with the sounds of merriment, didn't do a lot to alleviate the boredom. 'Been sometime Charlie, you sure he's still there?'

'According to the display he is. ... Tracker could have come off, - but somehow I doubt it.'

'I think we should drive by and check it out.'

'Okay, whatever floats your boat.' Charlie responded and Bill shrugged, 'I'm game.'

George gunned the Vito's engine and the set off again, along Low Grange Avenue.

Aware that Colin was about to burst forth with a thousand questions, Philip held up his hand. 'I think what you're getting mixed up with Col, is plant number six. That certainly disappeared in 60, we assume it was demolished.'

A puzzled look gradually formed on Colin's face, this in no way conformed to the information that he had previously collected.

'What do you mean, 'we assume?' It was either demolished or it wasn't.'

Philip shrugged his shoulders. 'As I recall at that time, everything was very 'hush hush', no ICI staff were ever involved with that plant.'

'Surely to goodness you can't have a chemical producing plant one minute then nothing the next and nobody notices. The mind boggles.' Colin moved his head from side to side disbelievingly.

'Didn't anyone think,' he waved two fingers in the air, "hello" something strange is happening here.'

'Wasn't quite like that Col,' Phillip said, 'nobody I knew took any interest in the plant, it was off limits.'

'Off limits, why?'

'Not sure, but it was rumoured at one time, that the new plant was to be an addition to five and was experimental, producing a new synthetic material without the pollution.'

'So why was it demolished?'

Phillip shrugged his shoulders again. 'I guess it wasn't viable, lots of things weren't then as I remember and nobody lost their jobs, so nobody really gave a damn.'

'So when precisely did this demolition occur?'

'Rumour has it, round about the Christmas of 59, but I don't know for sure. I recall there was talk that a specialist team, from who knows where, arrived on site, built a canvas shroud over sections of the plant. Apparently when they removed the shroud, nothing was there. The shroud would then be re-erected over the next vessel or section and when it was removed, again nothing. Eventually, I'd reckon, about mid to late 60, the area where plant six once stood was completely clear, nothing remained to say that there was ever a plant there. And as far as dumping it down the mine goes, - I haven't got a clue.'

Jack added, 'I recall hearing those rumours too, but at that time I was still in the training school. I didn't get out on any of the plants until my work experience in 62.'

As Ian listened to Jack, a blue van with darkened windows caught his eye, as it slowly passed by the window. *'That's odd.'* He muttered, mainly to himself. All four turned and looked at him.

'What is?' Colin enquired.

'Oops, sorry I was just thinking aloud.' Everyone turned their attention back to the subject in hand. Colin was in a way glad of Ian's interruption, as it gave him the opportunity to dive in and bombard Philip with a multitude of questions he'd been itching to ask and could no longer resist doing so.

'What kind of plant? If it wasn't Ammonia why call it number six? Where was it? And how long was---?'.

'Whoa there.' Philip broke in. 'Just give me a mo and I tell you the whole thing, well as much as I know, that is.' Colin sat back and looked intensely towards Philip, pen poised on the pad.

Phillip coughed a little nervously before he decided to speak. 'You've got to remember in 1960, I was still serving my apprenticeship. Plant number six as I recall was constructed in 56-57, I know that because I'd only just left school, Easter 56 and the plant was under construction then. I spent the first couple of years in the ICI Training School learning to be an 'Instrument Artificer'.'

'Glorified name for a Fitter.' Jack put in rather curtly.

'You should know, your dad was the training officer.' Phillip retorted.

'What about the Training School?' Colin pressed.

'The Training School was next to the railway line and just past the new rail spur that they used that to bring the materials onto site. I used to watch the long 'low loader bogies' carrying whole or part pressure vessels, shunt by the class room window.' Phillip paused to recall the moments. 'Anyway, I remember it was 'William Press Ltd' that did the erecting, haven't a clue who did the fabrication, except it wasn't one of the usual companies. Everybody referred to that plant as number six, I think that was because that's what was shown on the erection drawings. Philip paused again, this time to take a sip of his coffee. Still holding his cup in both hands, he seemed to stare blankly, off into the distance, no one interrupted, not even Colin, everything fell silent allowing Phillip's memory to wander back, undisturbed.

'I suppose I must have only been about seventeen when it happened,' he suddenly drawled out.

'W- wha-.' Colin just managed to stop himself interrupting. Phillip oblivious, continued. 'I was on my first work experience, the first and only time I encountered plant six. I didn't know you see. Didn't know that I wasn't supposed to be on or anywhere near that plant.'

The others, as one, leaned forward, intrigued by Phillips revelations.

'I was assigned to help the Maintenance Fitter working on Synthetic Ammonia plant number five, I remembered thinking at the time, 'is this where the smell comes from' due to the proximity of Haverton.' Philip hesitated, wondering for a moment if he should divulge some long forgotten event. 'I've never mentioned this to any one before, one of those incidents you want to forget.'

The other four now, even more curious, seemed to physically edged forward in their seats, in anticipation of the mystery incident Philip was about to disclose.

'Must have been a day in late December 1958, every thing was freezing, that I remember. Due to the holidays, the maintenance department were short staffed. Nobody expected any problems, so I was asked unofficially to do a standby shift on plant five, on my own. As an Apprentice that should not have been allowed. But the Charge-hand wanted Christmas at home with his kids and I wanted the double time pay. So a blind eye was turned. Later that day, I got a call from an Operator, to say that one of the valves on the Ammonia feed line to plant six was not responding, could I check it out? - No probs, or so I thought, but when I tried isolated the valve, I found it was frozen solid, stuck in the open position. By that time feed levels were becoming critical, couldn't get a blank in, couldn't think of what I should do, panicked a little I suppose.' Again Phillip paused a moment to reflect. 'I thought the best thing to do was to follow the line along the pipe bridge to the next valve and shut it off there, so I did. Found it at the head of a Stainless Steel pressure vessel, I hadn't realised at that point that the pipe bridge had conveyed me over the security fence and onto the new plant.'

'Number six.' Colin interrupted, unable to contain himself any longer.

'Yeah number six,' Phillip continued. 'I didn't know it was out of bounds. Anyway, that's when the proverbial hit the fan.' Phillip gulped the memory of what he was about to divulge was still a concern. 'As I was about to shut off the valve, I was grabbed from behind, manhandled and carried by four blokes, one to each limb. I assumed they were blokes, couldn't tell really, each wore white plastic suits that covered them from head to toe, with a corrugated tube which ran from below the visor to a pack on their back.'

'Breathing apparatus,' Jack put in.

Phillip nodded. 'I thought I was been attacked by aliens and I almost wet myself. The four of them lifted me bodily from the pipe-rack and carried me into the control area, - they literally threw me into a shower, fully clothed.' Phillip paused momentarily to express distain of his shock horror treatment, with glared eyes. 'Someone,' he continued, 'must have gone back to finish the job. A short time later my tools were returned.' Philip stopped talking for a moment, obviously letting the memory flow through his mind. 'Didn't report that incident, I was scared stiff, I'd get the sack for being on my own, let alone being on that plant. Besides I got a right rollicking off Jeremy Miles-Johnson.'

Colin repeated the name as he wrote it down. 'Jeremy----Miles---- Johnson, - who was that then?'

'The guy whose office I was bundled into after I'd towelled off and got dressed, in the white jump suit they provided. It said 'Director' on the office door and his name plate was on the desk, I can still see it clearly, after fifty odd years. Oh, and I remember the letter, had my head down, you see, staring at his desk top as the fusillade of verbal abuse rang around my ears.'

'And,' Colin rotated his hand in encouragement.

'It was there, a letter or a report, I don't know, I just concentrated on reading the upside down heading, as my way of not listening to this Miles-Johnson reading the riot act. It read, 'Porton Down Research Laboratory'.'

At long last Ian found a point on which he could make a contribution. 'Porton Down, that's a government facility, not too far from where I live. I just may be able to trace this person, if he's still alive.'

Philip just shrugged his shoulders. 'Must be in his nineties, if he's still batting.'

'Well if he isn't, I may be able to access his data from government records.'

The other four turned in unison to stare at Ian, but not one of them felt compelled to ask how he could access government data, - for fear of showing their ignorance. Instead they each omitted a humming sound and nodded their heads in agreement.

'Yeah, - why not, can't do any harm.' Phillip said.

'As soon as I get back home, I'll make a point of tracing the guy, you never know he just might be able to tell us something about the fallout.'

After a long silence Colin slapped the palm of his hands on his thighs and made to stand.

'Well I think that just about does it Phil, s'pose we'd better be heading back.'

'Yeah okay Col.' Phillip stood and shook Colin's hand. 'Good to see you, thanks for the chat, very interesting.' Then he turned, reached out and took Ians hand as he got to his feet. 'My regards to your father and if you do come across this Miles-Johnson bloke, I would be interested to hear what he has to say.' Phillip just nodded in the general direction of Michelle as she backed towards the door.

Jack seconded Phillips comment. 'Please let us know if you manage to find out anything.'

'For sure.' Colin said as he, Michelle and Ian headed out.

As they walked to the cars, Ian turned to Colin. 'Well that was interesting, thanks for bringing me along.'

'No problem.'

'Er Colin, would you mind if I say something, as a complete outsider, you understand?'

'Not at all young Ian, be glad of your input.'

'Getting back to this mystery growth, that we can't prove exists, because there are no remains to examine. Seems to me, we need to find out why it was not spotted and who is responsible. Who did do the examinations in these cases? Was it one person, if so, could we assume the possibly there is a dodgy Pathologist. Then Michelle's cover up theory would have some credence and I for one think we should investigate the possibility further.'

'If you want to spend your time looking for a needle in a haystack, feel free, your prerogative.'

'Any idea Michelle who the pathologist was?'

'No idea, - nor for that matter, who the Solicitor guy or whatever, was.'

'How did he get involved?'

'Don't know Ian, he must have been tied in with the police or something. By the time I found out what was happening, this guy had set up the autopsy and arranged to have dad cremated.' Michelle held up a hand. 'Yeah, I know things don't happen like that, but believe me there do. I was flabbergasted when I was told that my Solicitor had sorted everything on my behalf. Now I recall that dad had had a similar experience when mum died.'

Ian paused for a moment at Michelle's car door; Colin was in the process of getting into the Rover. 'Tell me Michelle, have you by any chance got a computer?'

'Y-e-s, why?'

'You may be able to view the Solicitor lists, perhaps get a clue as to who this guy is from there. Failing that, you could try to access the Coroners reports; see which Pathologist performed the autopsy, and just how many of the others did he do. I suspect we could be looking at the same guy.'

'I'm not sure I'd know what to do.'

'Well I'm going to be in Middlesbrough for a couple of days, what do you say to me helping you?'

'Sounds good, - what about tomorrow morning, at my house?' Without hesitation she reached into her car and took out a pen and a post-it pad. 'This is my address.' She said as she scrolled on the yellow pad, - detaching the top sheet and handing it to Ian.

'Sure, why not.' Ian touched her arm, in some sort of gentlemanly attempt to assist her into her car. 'See you tomorrow then.'

'Ten o-clock would be good.'

The journey back to Middlesbrough was undertaken in relative silence, but Ian could tell that Colin was itching to say something. Eventually in a quiet slightly high pitched voice, preceded with a little clearing the throat cough, he said. 'This access to government data, ahum....er....how will you do it?'

'Best for you not to know, you know the old adage. 'If I tell you, I'd have to kill you.'' Ian smiled in an attempt to make light of his comment. Colin was not really sure how he should take it, so he just shrugged his shoulders and replied. 'Whatever.'

When the car approached the junction on Marton Road and Ladgate Lane, adjacent to Stewarts Park, the traffic lights were on red, as the car stopped Ian decided to get out. 'I think I'll walk from here Colin, I really need the exercise, been sitting about all day. I'm leaving my business card on the dash and I've got your number, I'll be in touch. Thanks again for a great day.'

'Cheers Ian.' At that the lights turned to green and the traffic moved off, he watched as Colin's Rover disappeared up Marton Road. Ian then set off to walk heading in the same direction. When he got to the traffic lights he had to wait for the green man, but once across the busy junction he began to step it out at a good pace to put some use into his aching muscles. *That's odd.* He said to himself, as a blue Mercedes Vito van, with darkened windows, went by him towards Marton.

Elm Tree Estate, Stockton-on-Tees

Ian's Audi, eased to a stop outside of a house on the 'Elm Tree' estate Stockton. Ian lowered his head and looked through the nearside passenger window, checking that the house number corresponded to that on the yellow piece of paper, now adhered to the Audi's dash board. It did. Michelle must have been watching for him, for as he approached the house, she appeared on the front door step.

'Hi Ian, glad you could make it, please come in.' She led Ian in the direction of a small room at the back of the house. 'I use this room as an office.' She explained.

'I half expected to meet your husband.' Ian said coyly.

'He's at work, on the oil rigs North Sea, - and my son's away at Uni. so I've got you to myself.' She said, gesturing with raised eyebrows.

Ian blushed. 'Only joking.' She said laughingly.

A lit up, switched on computer stood on a desk top. 'I've been 'surfing,' if that's the right expression.'

'And?' Ian said as Michelle sat down in front of the screen.

'I've searched Coroners reports, didn't manage to get anywhere.'

'Hum, o-k-a-y, then we'll just have to try another tack.'

'That was, until I put mums details in and found the name of the Pathologist who did the autopsy.'

'You little devil, you almost had me going then. Now we've got somewhere to start, we should run the same search again. See if this guys name crops up with any of the other known victims, -- and if it does, we're in business.'

'And if it doesn't?'

'Let's cross that bridge only if we need to.'

'But I'll have to find the victims first, not all of them had autopsies. Could you pass me dad's list please, it's in that envelope over there, with Colin's name on.'

'Sure.' Ian reached over to a corner unit, retrieved the envelope and handed it to her.

Michelle extracted the list, and selecting the names she believed had died locally, tapped away at the keyboard, Ian stood looking over her shoulder. Two minutes later the same pathologists name appeared on the screen. *Anthony Davidson MD FSSoc.*

'Bingo, - got him.'

'Should be no problem getting an address and telephone number; we could even take a look at his home on Google earth. Just in case we need to pay him a visit.'

'Don't you think I need to check out more victims?'

'Won't hurt, to be sure, but I've a sneaking feeling this is one bent Pathologist. Probably in league with that Solicitor chap.'

'Hmm I've checked the law society lists looking for anything to give me a clue to his identity.'

'And?'

'Nothing so far, I'm afraid.'

'Hum, -- I think we should concentrate on the Pathologist.'

'If he is, as you say, bent.' She smiled, turned her head to the side and the tip of her nose brushed lightly against Ian's cheek.

Although Ian was attracted to her he hadn't even contemplated that the feeling could be mutual. He turned his head to meet hers, their lips met and out of impulse, he kissed her. Michelle stood, wrapped her arms around his neck and returned the favour with vigour. They embraced passionately and any constraints that may have existed in respect of a married woman were quickly dismissed from Ian's mind. He slipped his arms around her waist and automatically ran the zip of her skirt down her well rounded bottom. Her hand came back and pressed against his, holding there for a moment. *To hasty he thought, - shouldn't have pushed my luck.*

Michelle pulled her mouth from his. 'Not here, let's go upstairs.' She gasped.

She literally dragged him up the stairs and into what Ian perceived to be the son's bedroom. As soon as she let go of his hand she began, without any prompting, to strip. Ian followed suit and it became a race to see who could disrobe first. Michelle won and stood facing Ian in all her glory. Ian froze, his trousers around his ankles and gazed in awe at the sight of this beautiful body. He slowly stepped out of his trousers and approached her, taking her gently in his arms they embraced again. As he lowered her onto the bed, he let his lips caress her neck and move slowly down to discover and caress the rest of her body. She sighed as he spent some time in the erotic area before sliding his body back up hers. Now with mouths once more joined, they made love.

They lay side by side in their nakedness, staring up at the ceiling. 'Wow Michelle that was good; I, I never meant for anything like this to happen.'

'But you're pleased it did.'

Ian nodded. 'Oh yes.'

'Me too, that's the best sex I've ever had.' Ian opened his mouth about approach the husband factor, but she pre-empted him. 'I love my husband Ian, it's just that he's been working away a lot and what with dads funeral and all the stress, I was feeling a little low, then when I met you at Phillip Walton's house, my heart skipped. I'm not naïve, I know this feeling I have for you is just pure lust.'

'Well I definitely fancy you, call it lust or whatever, but I never intended to take advantage of you.'

She turned her head towards him and smiled. 'Let's just enjoy the moment, - keep it special between us.'

Ian headed down the stairs, tucking his shirt back into his pants as he went. Michelle shouted from the bathroom. 'Put the kettle on Ian, we'll have a cuppa.'

Eventually Ian had managed, after a lot of cupboard door opening and draw pulling, to produce two mugs of tea which he carried gingerly into the study. Michelle was now sat at the computer tapping away at the keys. Ian put a mug down on the desk near her and again leaned over her shoulder to view the screen.

'Any joy Shell?'

'I, I think so, ah yes, Anthony Davidson Pathologist. That makes six Ian.'

'Looks like our suspicions are not unfounded.'

'If dad was right about this fungal growth, why didn't this supposed eminent Pathologist spot it?'

'Like I said, bent, but I can't imagine why he's falsifying autopsy reports on he's own volition, surely he has nothing to gain. No, the more I think about it, the more I convinced someone's behind him, but … why … what for?'

'Surely to cover up whatever caused the problem in the first place.'

'Hum possibly, but I can't help thinking there's more to it. If there was, as we believe some sort of disaster about fifty years ago, what's the big deal, keeping it covered up after so many years?'

'Don't know.' She drawled her eyes still fixed on the screen and the Pathologists name.

'Let's assume that someone is paying this Pathologist to omit certain facts from the autopsy reports.'

'Could it be a government cover up?' She put in, as the thought popped into her head.

'Perhaps.' Ian responded thoughtfully. 'But I'm not convinced on that score. Anyway it doesn't change the fact that if someone is paying the Pathologist, we're going have to find out whom. And that my love will involve subjecting this Mr. Davidson to a little pressure; see how much he's willing to tell.' Ian nodded to the screen. 'Can you key in telephone numbers, Teesside area, should be able to get his number?'

'Sure, just a mo.' Michelle tapped away, after a few moments she declared. 'Got it, its an Eaglescliffe number.' She scribbled the number on a pad and slid across the desk to Ian.

'Great, can I use your phone?'

'Feel free.'

Ian keyed in a set of digits to withhold the number before entering the Pathologist's home telephone number. 'Hope he's home.' purr-purr-purr- click.

'Hello'

'Ah, Is that, Mr. Antony Davidson, Teesside Authority Pathologist?'

'Y-e-s, who's speaking, please?'

'My name is Ian Turner. I'm writing a joint article for the 'Lancet' and 'The Science of Criminology.' I was hoping that you could give me an insight into the analysis of Autopsies.'

'Why me? Surely there are more eminent Pathologists, you could talk to.'

'I'm sure there are. And I do intend to take a consensus of opinions and practices.'

'I'm a very busy man; I don't think I could spare you the time. Goodbye.'

'A moment sir, if you please. If I told you that I have already talked to some of your colleagues, who have expressed differing views. Would that in any way tempt you to put forward your own views on any autopsy subject?...Eh, or would you just be prepared to accept another's findings, be there ever so different from you own, when the article appears in the 'Lancet?''

'I cannot conceive that differing views would apply in the factual world of Pathology.'

'Believe me sir, discovery and perception of the facts, are not always the same. I would really appreciate your comments. Would it be possible to come to your home, this afternoon say?'

'I can spare you half an hour, no more, at three.'

'That's fine sir, see you then. Bye.'

Antony Davidson stared bemusedly at the telephone for a long moment, before returning it to its cradle. He'd allowed his curiosity and perhaps his ego, to cloud his judgement. Picking up the telephone again, he keyed in 1471 and listened to the recorded message.

You were called today at - 12.20 -. The caller withheld their number.

What a nerve.' Michelle said, as Ian pressed 'end call' and
replaced the telephone to its socket. He smiled thinly. 'We now
have to do a little shopping. You wouldn't happen to have a
'Yellow Pages' would you?'

Michelle placed the heavy yellow telephone book on the desk. Ian
began to thumb through it. 'Ah, - found one, - Linthorpe Road,
Middlesbrough.'

'One what?'

'You'll see.'

They set off in Ian's Audi via the A66 towards Middlesbrough.
Forty minutes later, at the far end of Linthorpe road, Ian found the
shop he was looking for, with a rather handy parking space
adjacent. 'I shouldn't be too long.' He said as he headed to the blue
painted door of a shop. A sign hung in the blacked out window
read, 'Security and Surveillance Systems.'

Ten minutes later, Ian climbed back into the Audi, holding a
plastic carrier. 'Did you get what you wanted?' Michelle asked.
'No not really, spy stuff isn't that easy to get hold of and what you
can get costs a small fortune.' He rummaged around the carrier,
taking out the items. 'So we'll just have to improvise with this lot.
A tape recorder, two hand held, two-way radios charged ready to
go and a roll of duck tape.'

'What's the plan then?'

'You come in with me, acting as my assistant. While I distract him, you hide this radio as near as you can to the phone, we'll tape the button in the transmit position.

Davidson's house was quite large, detached, constructed of grey stone, set in landscaped gardens and overlooking the river. 'I bet this takes some looking after.' Ian said nodding at the surroundings, as he pressed the door bell. 'I wonder if he's married.'

'Guess we'll find out soon enough.' A few moments later, a shuffling sound followed by the groan of the many time painted hinges, as the large door swung slowly open.

A tall thin man with greying swept back hair and wearing a brown lose fitting cardigan with brown corduroy trousers, framed the opening.

'Mr. Davidson?' The man nodded. 'Ian Turner, I rang earlier.'

Ian, held out his hand, it was took, somewhat begrudgingly. 'This is my assistant Michelle Thompson.'

'You'd better come in then, though I must stress, - I do not intend to spend more than half an hour, answering your questions.' At that he turned and headed back into the house and along a fairly long passage closely followed by Ian and Michelle.

'Big place you have here Mr Davidson, must take some looking after.'

'Guess it does.' The pathologist said over his shoulder without elaborating any further on his status, marital or other.

Antony Davidson then entered an unkempt room which had a noticeable musty smell. The books piled high and magazines scattered about seemed to fill every nook and cranny. At one end of the room stood a desk, the surface of which was cluttered with papers. Adjacent to the desk, was the only bright spot of the room, a French door, the view from which took in the lawned garden which ran down to the bank of the river Tees. Ian deemed this room to be the Pathologist study, as it was evident from the collection of dust that this was a male environment rarely touched by a feminine hand.

Davidson seated himself behind the big old fashioned Walnut desk and stared blankly at his visitors. Ian casually removed a stack of magazines from a nearby chair, letting them drop into a pile on the floor; he then placed it and himself on the other side of the desk opposite the pathologist. Michelle likewise removed some books from what was once a dining chair and edged it close to the telephone side of the desk, being careful enough not to get too close as to encroach Antony Davidson's space. The room was full of old artefacts, having little in the way of what could be termed modern trappings, other than a telephone and if there was a computer and surely there must have been one, it must have housed within one of the walnut cabinets.

'Well! What is it you wish to know?' The Pathologist snapped.

Ian opened his briefcase and without regard or request, placed the tape recorder on the desk, immediately depressing the record button as he did so. Unhurried he extracted two sheets of A4 size paper and a pen placed them neatly on the desk. Ian picked up the pen poised over the paper before he slowly lifted his head and eyes to meet those of the pathologist before putting his question. This was just a ploy by Ian in an attempt to unsettle Davidson.

'I'd like to start by asking about an autopsy you undertook on Jean Hartley, in March 2007.'

'Goodness me, you don't expect me to remember a cadaver I autopsied over two year ago?'

'No no Mr. Davidson, of course not. But I would like point out the peculiar circumstances of that case. Jean Hartley, formerly a healthy and active sixty-four year old, suddenly developed severe chest pains. Within twenty-four hours, she was dead.' Ian let the words hang.

'Very tragic I'm sure, but like I said, I don't remember the case.'

Ian held up a hand. 'Allow me to refresh you. The Coroners report, ie your analysis, states the cause of death was lung cancer, tobacco related.

Antony Davidson shrugged his shoulders. 'If that's what I found, then that's my findings. Where are you going with this Mr. Turner?'

'She never smoked.'

The Pathologist slapped his hands on the desk and stood up pushing his chair back as he did so. 'I think you've said enough, I'd like you to leave. Now!'

'Okay, okay, I'm sorry Mr. Davidson, I don't mean to challenge your integrity,' Ian said apologetically. 'Let's discuss a more recent case, one I'm sure you will remember.' The pathologist slowly lowered himself back into his chair. 'Last week,' Ian continued, 'you performed an autopsy on a sixty-seven year old male. Again you state the cause of death as tobacco related lung cancer. Incidentally, this man never smoked either and ironically his symptoms were exactly the same as Jean Hartley's. Only before his twenty-four hours were out, he was admitted to James Cook Hospital, were he had a MRI scan. The Surgeon reported a web like growth in the lung, the likes of which he'd never seen before. Oh and by the way the man's name was Raymond Hartley, husband of Jean.'

At that point, the Pathologist, clearly lost control. He jumped to his feet, red faced and angry, he screamed at Ian. 'Get out!'

Emphasizing the point while jabbing an outstretched arm, finger extended, in the direction of the door.

'We are leaving now Mr. Davidson,' Ian said calmly, 'but it would seem that you need to remind yourself, what smoking induced lung cancer looks like.'

'Get out! Get out now!'

Ian and Michelle headed back to the Audi, each resisting the urge to burst out laughing. 'What do you reckon Shell?'

'Well he definitely lives alone; no woman I know would tolerate that deco, not to mention the dust.'

'What about the gardens, neat looking lawns?'

'Gardener, once a week I'd guess.'

Ian just nodded as he slid into the car and picked up the other handheld radio. 'You did well Michelle, I never saw you plant the other set.'

'Let's hope he didn't.'

'I think I had his full attention.'

'I'll say you did, you really got him going, - hope he reacts.'

'Oh I think he will and when he does, I'm ready.' Ian held the recorder next to the set, a finger poised over the record button.

They didn't have to wait long; a clicking sound could be heard behind the static buzz.

'Is that the telephone?'

Ian nodded. 'Get ready for a one sided conversation.'

Antony Davidson shakily picked up the telephone, balls of perspiration formed on his forehead. He wiped the back of his hand across his mouth, swallowed and then took in a deep breath in an attempt to calm himself down. He taped a number into phone and waited with trembling anticipation for what seemed an age, before it was eventually picked up.

'Y-e-s.'

'It's me Davidson, - they know!'

'Get a hold of yourself of yourself man. Who knows?'

'A man and woman have just been to my house and they know everything.

'What do you mean – everything?

'They know that I falsified the autopsy report on the Hartley case. And no doubt they'll find the others if they start digging.'

'Slow down, think about it. What could they possibly know and what could they possibly prove. Whoever they are, they are just guessing, it's all supposition.

'But he seemed pretty damn sure.

'He, he who? You got names?'

'He said his name was Ian Turner, and he was writing an article for the 'Lancet.'

'I very much doubt that.'

And the woman's name was Michelle Thompson.'

'Michelle Thompson! Michelle Thompson is Hartley's daughter. But who the hell is Ian Turner?'

The daughter! That's it. I want nothing more to do with this.'

'Calm down! Just brazen it out; you're already in this up to your neck.'

'And the next time?'

'There may not be a next time, and besides if there were then you should remember that you don't have a choice.'

'Oh yes I do, you can stick your money. ....Never wanted it in the first place.'

At that point there was a crack followed by silence. Ian looked at Michelle. 'Sounds like he's hung up.' He said as he hit the stop recording button. 'I doubt we'll get anymore.'

'Whoever he talked to knew I was the daughter.'

Ian nodded. 'The Solicitor got to be.' Michelle nodded. 'And one thing's for sure, Davidson is clearly being paid for falsifying autopsy reports.'

'Clearly.' Ian agreed.

'Do you think it's time to put Colin in the picture?'

'Damn right I do.' He said lightly tapping the tape recorder.

Washington USA

Conlan Powell rolled over in bed and sleepily threw an arm over the bedside table in an effort to lift the telephone receiver and quell that damn noise. He raised it and held it hovering above the cradle for a moment. Then it slowly dawned, perhaps he should answer it.

'Ahh – Powell.' He yawned.

'General, - it's me, we've got ourselves a problem.'

'Like what?'

'Our Pathologist asset, he no longer wants to play ball.'

'Oh yeah, any reason?'

'Feels he's been compromised.'

'Has he?'

'Possibly.'

'By whom.'

'A guy called Ian Turner says he's a writer.'

Not another one. Conlan Powell mumbled his thoughts.

'What did you say?'

'Err nothing. .. I take it, we've covered all the angles, there's no proof?'

'All cases cremated, all records adjusted.'

'Then the only problem is the asset.'

'You're forgetting CIA and MI5 are still sniffing about.'

'True, but I doubt they'd affect our operation.' Conlan hesitated, 'Still, you may have a point, can't afford to take the risk of any interference at this stage, from anybody, including this Turner guy.'

'There can't be many more fungal deaths to come. Perhaps it's time we got out, call it a day.'

There was a thoughtful pause before Conlan responded.   'Y-e-a-h, you could be right....Okay, shut it down. Clean everything, get rid of anything incriminating and transfer what remains of the capital into the Swiss fund. While you're doing that I'll make all the necessary arrangements for your return. Oh and one other thing.'

'What?'

'Dispense with the asset.'

Rudd's Arms, Marton

The Mercedes Vito was parked in the pub car-park. George was on station at the consul; Bill and Charlie were having lunch in the bar. George responded to the telephone conversation he'd just picked up from Colin Hatton's house phone. He thumbed Charlie's number into his mobile. Charlie had the phone on the table next to him and responded to the purring tone immediately. 'Yeah George?'

'Got a telephone call, target's expecting a couple of guests, in about half an hour. What do you reckon, think we should eyeball?'

'Any idea who?'

'Guy called Ian and someone called Michelle.'

Charlie looked at Bill and they both looked at the large mixed grills that had just been planted in front of them. 'Don't suppose it'll be anyone important George, just make sure you get everything on tape, we'll analyse it later.' At that he clicked off the phone, picked up his knife and fork and set about the Cumberland sausage with some gusto.

Ian and Michelle gathered in Colin's lounge, Ian set the tape going and they all listened intently.

'Well Colin what do you make off that?' Ian said as he reached out and switched off the tape recorder. Colin shook his head in dismay. 'You know, just a couple of weeks ago I was all set to write a sequel book, covering the positive aspects of the ICI and the advantages it brought to the people of Haverton Hill. And in that short time I've had to come to terms with discovering the loss of many former friends. Now I'm faced with the probability that their deaths are the result of poisonous fallout over the town believed to be from the ICI. And for whatever reason someone seems to be going to a lot of trouble to keep it covered up.' Colin fingered his chin thoughtfully. 'It's evident that this Pathologist was taking a backhander from someone, but what we really need to know is, from whom and why?'

'The solicitor guy.' Michelle put in. 'It's got to be someone who knew I was the daughter and he's the only one I can think of.'

'You're right Michelle, but who the hell is he?'

'Solicitor or not, unless we are able to find him, we will never know why he is trying to cover up a fifty year old incident.' Ian said. 'And the only way I can think of finding this guy is to keep the pressure on the Pathologist, he may just crack, and tell us all.'

'I agree, but how are you going to play it?'

I'm not Colin, you are. Call him up, make some accusations. - Let him know you're a writer, another one. He's bound to think his secret won't be secret long and he'll start to panic. After that I'll have another go, offer him some immunity from print in return for some facts.'

'May work.' Colin picked up the phone and dialled the Pathologist number. There was a long pause. '*Answer machine.'* Colin mouthed.

'Leave a message.' Ian mouthed back.

Please leave your message after the tone – peep. 'Err....Hello, er Mr. Davidson, my name is Colin Hatton, er I'm a writer and I've just come across some disturbing news regarding the falsifying of autopsy reports. I wonder could you give me a ring back on 01642 ******. Thank you.

George thumbed Charlie number on his mobile. 'I hope you guys are finished, cause I want your arses back here PDQ, something real tasty has just turned up.

The three of then sat in the van listening intently to the recording.

'Very interesting, don't you think?' George said.

'I should cocoa.' Bill confirmed in his usual offbeat manner.

'Better send it in.'

'On its way.' Charlie responded as he tapped on the computer keys.

MI5 Headquarters London

Mark Pritchard listened to the recording. He found the whole thing somewhat of a mystery, but he was sure his CIA associate would find it interesting. However after careful consideration he felt transmitting the audio in view of the time difference, may be a security risk, so he set about typing a transcript on e-mail and sent it for the attention of Jack Rosenthal CIA Langley.

Langley, Virginia USA.

It had been over a week since the excitement of the computer hysteria in Simon Kendall's work station, now everything had reverted back into the familiar boring routine. They say the devil makes work for idle hands, or in Simon's case an idle mind.

It all started out quite innocently, the initial intent being to relieve the boredom of the every day daily routine. Simon thought it would be an interesting project to determine why his computer had reacted the way it did, that day. So he started to analyse Colin Hatton's book, reading it from cover to cover. He even copied and read the newspaper promotion page for the book, giving all Colin's contact details. The fact that there was nothing at all sinister in the narration only served to intensify his curiosity.

He became more and more preoccupied with Haverton Hill and the towns relationship with ICI Billingham. And it wasn't long before this preoccupation turned into an obsession. He scanned the pages of the book underlining each of the chemicals on every instance they were mentioned, cross checking each reference in various permutations. Unable to make any logical sense of why a few chemicals and a couple of place names could have sparked such a reaction, he started to wonder why the Deputy Director had found his report of interest, were others had treat the matter with indifference.

Simon furtively looked about him; nobody was in the immediate vicinity .*Good.* He meshed his fingers together and flexed them. *'Right, let's see if I've still got the touch.'*

He was about to undertake a little bit of computer hacking, into no other than the DD's system, an offence, if caught, would undoubtedly at best, lead to him losing his job. He preferred not to think of the consequences, in a worst case scenario. 'Why was he even considering undertaking such drastic action, knowing what could and probably would happen to him if he was found out. *For the thrill, the adrenalin surge, all that goes with bucking the system, breaking the rules and knowing you were one of the few that could do it.*

His fingers danced across the keyboard with speed and dexterity. Very few of the other personnel in the office would find the need to venture by, or into Simons work station, so he felt relatively secure. For the benefit of those that would have occasion to visit him, he would prepare pages of innocent text to fill the screen at a touch of a key.

What harm could it do, I've no intention of divulging anything I discover about Haverton Hill, or anything else for that matter, - to any one.

He uttered in an attempt to convince himself that his actions were justified.

For any hacker, it would be virtually impossible to break into the CIA computer systems from outside the network, but Simon had the advantage of being on the inside of the same network. The CIA has a central main frame computer which is set up to take signals from a dedicated satellite, the signals are automatically decoded and the information distributed to the user's port. *The trick,* Simon thought, *is to persuade the main frame computer to accept his port as an extension of the Deputy Directors port, easy for a man of my calibre. All I need do then is to time my access to coincide with the DD's. A pop up will appear for a few seconds on both screens when the DD's system goes on line, hopefully.* Simon thought. *The DD is old school and with a bit of luck, he won't even realise.*

A hand came down firmly on Simon's shoulder, the shock of which literally sent his bottom two inches above his seat.

'You got problems, here son?' Simon was gob smacked, his mind raced, desperately seeking some logical reason that would cover the existence of the lines of digital text on the computer screen, but nothing would come.

'Err, err, no problem sir, I'm fine.'

'What's all this garble?' Jim Benson said, waving a finger at the screen. Fortunately for Simon and his slow response, Jim continued before Simon could come up with an answer. 'Where's the book from Oxford, I sent to your station half an hour ago?'

'Sorry sir, the programme crashed, I'm just in the process of re-booting.'

'Now you know son, your supposed to call maintenance for that kind of thing, there's a whole bunch of guys just sat there scratching their butts.'

'Just about there, sir.' With that Simon moved the cursor and clicked the mouse a couple of times and the Oxford text appeared on the screen. 'Okay, I'm in.'

'Good, I want that Oxford publication sorted, like now, any more problems, get maintenance, you hear me son.'

■■■

'Yes sir.' Without more to do, Jim Benson turned and walked out of Simon's station.

Phew, that was close. Simon took out his handkerchief and mopped his brow.

The Oxford book took but a few minutes to analyse, after which it was back again to the same boring routine. Once again Simon's thoughts drifted back to Haverton Hill and Colin Hatton's book. *What the hell.* He thought as he eased himself out of the chair and peered over the top of the dividing partition. He could see Jim Benson was in his office behind a glass screen on the other side of the building. Now feeling relatively safe, he lowered himself back down into his seat and began to rattle the keys on his computer keyboard.

It was a short time later when a pop up appeared in the bottom corner of the screen. ***User 296 logged on.*** Simon, sat bolt upright and began to tap in codes that hopefully would put his computer in tandem with the DD's. And it worked, no need to find the password he would just stay connected, taking note of anything relevant that the DD received and or transmitted, but he would not be able to record or print without the prompt showing on the DD's screen.

He read the transcript as it rolled down his screen at a speed controlled by the DD, so it was slow enough for Simon to take in the full context of the message. He was both shocked and confused at the same time and he panicked, stabbing his fingers on the keyboard and shut the system down.

Middlesbrough, UK.

The telephone trilled for sometime before the noise had registered with Mrs. Flynn and she picked it up. 'Hello.'

'Ah – hello, I'm trying to contact Ian Turner. Have I got the right number?'

'It'll be my grandson, you'll be wanting. Just a mo- I'll go and get him.' She pressed the receiver to her bosom and shouted. 'Ian! There's someone on the phone for you, it's a lady.'

Ian, who was in his bedroom upstairs, packing things, ready for the journey back to Poole, headed down the stairs. 'Thanks Gran.' He said, as she handed him the telephone.

'Hello.'

'Oh Ian, at last.'

'Michelle. What's the problem?'

'Not really sure there is one, just my intuition I guess.'

'Okay I'm intrigued, tell me more?'

'Found a letter this morning, must have been pushed through my letterbox during the night. It's from Antony Davidson.'

'He must have got your address from your dads file; he has no doubt found the radio.'

'Yes, but there's more. Ian, I feel this guy is thinking about suicide.'

'I'm on my way, -see you in about half an hour.'

Michelle was standing on the doorstep, looking clearly anxious, as Ian arrived.

'Hi Ian, I'm so pleased you're here.'

'You know me, anything to help.' He gave her a reassuring smile. 'What have you got?'

She handed him the letter and folded her arms in front of her in an attempt to show constraint. 'I can't help feeling concerned, what do you think?' Ian read the note out loud.

'Michelle Thompson, I have found the radio that you no doubt left. I dare say you and your partner, Ian Turner are now convinced that I falsified your parents autopsy reports. All I can say to you is that I'm so sorry. I don't expect you to understand why I would jeopardise my professional integrity; suffice to say that, at the time, I thought I was doing the right thing. I can now assure you that this situation will not occur again. I have decided that I will not perform another autopsy.

Antony Davidson.'

'Hum, see what you mean, looks like our pathologist has developed a conscience at last. But I don't think he's contemplating suicide, probably wants to get out of the situation he's in and decided to take early retirement.'

■■

'What do you think we should do?'

'Well now that I'm here, I don't think it would harm to pay him a visit and hope your feelings are wrong.'

'Shall we take your car?' Ian nodded. 'Hang on I'll get my coat.'

Ian's Audi took the back road out of the Elm Tree estate and headed west down Oxbridge Avenue and onto the Yarm Road to Eaglescliffe.

As Ian and Michelle made their way up the pathologist drive, they could see the smoke escaping from beneath the garage door. They broke into a run and could hear the throb of the car engine.

Fearing the worst Ian pulled the bottom of his tee shirt up over his face as he flung the door open. The acrid carbon monoxide fumes penetrated through the thin material, hitting him in the throat and eyes. He fumbled and felt his way along the side of the car squeezing between it and the garage wall, until he found the car door handle, which he yanked open, blindly feeling for and turning off the cars ignition. Then Ian staggered back out of the garage coughing and sputtering, eyes streaming.

'Is he in there, - is he alive?'

'Augh- ah....Don't know, couldn't see a thing, but I guess if he is.....I doubt he's survived. Give me a sec and I'll check. You'd better call for an Ambulance and the Police, just in case.'

As Michelle made the 999 call, Ian had decided that the fumes cleared sufficient enough for him to head back in. As he eased in he noted the car window on the now ajar door was down. *Of course it would be, should have realized instead of wasting time searching for the handle.*

At first he didn't see the Pathologist and he got a momentary feeling of elation that all was well. But that was not to be, the body was slumped over the gear housing with its head and shoulders resting on the passenger seat. Ian leaned into the vehicle and felt the neck for a pulse, at the same time confirming the body as that of the Pathologist Antony Davidson. Not feeling any throb from the main artery in the neck, he placed an ear on the pathologist's chest. More in hope than anything else, he pulled the body so that its back was flat against the passenger seat and then he thrust the heel of his hand into the chest, placing his other hand on top and began cardiac massage. After twenty presses he again placed an ear on the chest. No response, Ian straightened and declared. 'We were too late Michelle, he's dead.'

'I can't help feeling a little sad for him irrespective of the way he's covered up the facts, but whatever there goes our only proof, so what do we do now?'

'Did he fall or was he pushed?'

'What do you mean?'

'Precisely that, if I wanted to commit hari-kari that way, I would make sure the garage door was locked on the inside and the position of the body doesn't look right.'

'How do mean?'

'You alright taking a look?'

the handbrake's off.' Michelle said, Ian nodded and noted her observation. 'That figures.'

'How come?' She queried.

'This.' He took hold of the dead mans foot lifted it and examined the heel of his shoe. 'As I suspected, scuff marks. I believe our Pathologist friend was dragged across the drive. My guess is he was then dumped in the car while it was parked outside; probably the car was then pushed into the garage with the engine running. That means our man has been murdered.'

'No prizes for guessing who.'

At that the sound of sirens could be heard. 'I think we'll have to tell all Michelle, as far as the police are concerned, this is now a crime scene.'

'Got it, but we don't want to be found standing over the body, do we?'

At that they backed out of the garage in time to meet two Para-medics

She nodded. 'Yeah, no probs after what I've been through a lately.'

'Come on I'll show you.' At that Ian headed back into the garage.

'See the car door won't open fully because of the wall and although I've turned the top part, it still looks to me as if Antony Davidson's body has been dumped in the car and his legs pushed in after, you just wouldn't sit like that.' I agree he'd find it difficult to start the car in that position and running down the path.

Ian held up a hand. 'No rush guys, he's dead.'

'That's our call sir.'

'Not in this case, we think the victim's been done in.'

The medics looked at each other and then back at Ian, momentarily speechless.

'I've checked for a pulse, tried cardiac massage, - nothing.' Michelle stood at Ian's shoulder nodding in agreement.

'I still think we ought to take a look for ourselves.' One of the Medics protested and was about to push past Ian as two Policemen arrived on the scene. The Police listened to Ian before they and the Medics edged into the garage, eventually concluding that Ian may have a point.

Five hours later following their statement and individual interviews, Ian and Micelle, were still sat in the waiting room of Stockton Police station.

A man briskly walked in and headed towards Ian, hand extended. 'Detective Inspector Baker,' he said. 'Sorry to have kept you waiting Mr. Turner, Mrs. Thompson,' and he proceeded to

the handbrake's off.' Michelle said, Ian nodded and noted her observation. 'That figures.'

'How come?' She queried.

'This.' He took hold of the dead mans foot lifted it and examined the heel of his shoe. 'As I suspected, scuff marks. I believe our Pathologist friend was dragged across the drive. My guess is he was then dumped in the car while it was parked outside; probably the car was then pushed into the garage with the

as if Antony Davidson's body has been dumped in the car and his legs pushed in after, you just wouldn't sit like that.' I agree he'd find it difficult to start the car in that position and

....

engine running. That means our man has been murdered.'

'No prizes for guessing who.'

At that the sound of sirens could be heard. 'I think we'll have to tell all Michelle, as far as the police are concerned, this is now a crime scene.'

'Got it, but we don't want to be found standing over the body, do we?' At that they backed out of the garage in time to meet two Para-medics running down the path.

Ian held up a hand. 'No rush guys, he's dead.'

'That's our call sir.'

'Not in this case, we think the victim's been done in.'

The medics looked at each other and then back at Ian, momentarily speechless.

'I've checked for a pulse, tried cardiac massage, - nothing.' Michelle stood at Ian's shoulder nodding in agreement.

'I still think we ought to take a look for ourselves.' One of the Medics protested and was about to push past Ian as two Policemen arrived on the scene. The Police listened to Ian before they and the Medics edged into the garage, eventually concluding that Ian may have a point.

Five hours later following their statement and individual interviews, Ian and Micelle, were still sat in the waiting room of Stockton Police station.

A man briskly walked in and headed towards Ian, hand extended. 'Detective Inspector Baker,' he said. 'Sorry to have kept you waiting Mr. Turner, Mrs. Thompson,' and he proceeded to

The medics looked at each other and then back at Ian, momentarily speechless.

'I've checked for a pulse, tried cardiac massage, - nothing.' Michelle stood at Ian's shoulder nodding in agreement.

'I still think we ought to take a look for ourselves.' One of the Medics protested and was about to push past Ian as two Policemen arrived on the scene. The Police listened to Ian before they and the Medics edged into the garage, eventually concluding that Ian may have a point.

Five hours later following their statement and individual interviews, Ian and Micelle, were still sat in the waiting room of Stockton Police station.

A man briskly walked in and headed towards Ian, hand extended. 'Detective Inspector Baker,' he said. 'Sorry to have kept you waiting Mr. Turner, Mrs. Thompson,' and he proceeded to

the handbrake's off.' Michelle said, Ian nodded and noted her
observation. 'That figures.'

'How come?' She queried.

'This.' He took hold of the dead mans foot lifted it and examined
the heel of his shoe. 'As I suspected, scuff marks. I believe our
Pathologist friend was dragged across the drive. My guess is he

was then dumped in the car while it was parked outside; probably the car was then pushed into the garage with the engine running. That means our man has been murdered.'

'No prizes for guessing who.'

At that the sound of sirens could be heard. 'I think we'll have to tell all Michelle, as far as the police are concerned, this is now a crime scene.'

'Got it, but we don't want to be found standing over the body, do we?' At that they backed out of the garage in time to meet two Para-medics running down the path.

Ian held up a hand. 'No rush guys, he's dead.'

'That's our call sir.'

'Not in this case, we think the victim's been done in.'

The medics looked at each other and then back at Ian, momentarily speechless.

'I've checked for a pulse, tried cardiac massage, - nothing.'
Michelle stood at Ian's shoulder nodding in agreement.

'I still think we ought to take a look for ourselves.' One of the Medics protested and was about to push past Ian as two Policemen arrived on the scene. The Police listened to Ian before they and the Medics edged into the garage, eventually concluding that Ian may have a point.

Five hours later following their statement and individual interviews, Ian and Micelle, were still sat in the waiting room of Stockton Police station.

A man briskly walked in and headed towards Ian, hand extended. 'Detective Inspector Baker,' he said. 'Sorry to have kept you waiting Mr. Turner, Mrs. Thompson,' and he proceeded to shake hands with Ian and Michelle. 'Would you like to come through to my office?'

'Read your statement, very interesting concept, I must say.' He said as he eased back in his chair. 'But let's not concern ourselves with the poisonous fallout theory, for the moment. I'd prefer to deal with the Pathologists demise right now.'

'Whatever.' Ian responded.

'You say, Mr. Turner that you opened the car door.'

'Yeah, automatic really, couldn't see a thing.'

'And you didn't touch anything else?'

'No, don't think so, apart from the ignition key and Mr. Davidson that is.'

'Y-e-s, that figures, just checking.' DI Baker paused for effect. 'Yours were the only prints we found or should I say meant to find. Strange isn't it?'

'Very, not even the Pathologist's....I suppose he decided not to touch anything as he launched himself into the car.' Ian said sarcastically. 'I would have thought that the most obvious and logical explanation is that someone else, presumably the killer, wiped everything clean.'

DI Baker smiled. 'That's what we thought, so we were chuffed to buttons when we found a print on the window opening switch, not the same as the ones on the door, yours, or in fact the victims. No match as yet,' he said pursing his lips and nodding thoughtfully, 'but I'm betting my pension, when we do get a match, we'll have the perpetrator.' To emphasize the point DI Baker held out an open hand and slowly clamped it shut. 'Yes by god, we'll have the son of a bitch.'

Ian and Michelle headed back the Elm Tree estate, feeling very tired and somewhat at a loss.

'What do we do now?' Michelle said yawningly.

'I don't expect the Police to come up with any answers with this fallout situation and we both know it's connected to the solicitor guy, whoever he is.'

'So we're stuck unless we can find this guy.'

'Not necessarily there's always plan B.' Ian said.

'Plan B?'

'Ah ah, plan B, I've got to look for this Miles-Johnson chap, if he's alive, it's our only chance of finding out what really happened fifty years ago, and who would be likely to have a special reason for keeping it quiet.'

'Perhaps you're right, but what if he's dead?'

'Then, to put it bluntly and somewhat crudely, we'll be up shit creek without a paddle. No more toxic fallout theory. End of.'

Michelle nodded as if to accept Ian's reasoning. 'So we will just have to hope and pray Miles-Johnson is still compos mentis.'

The Audi came to stop outside Michelle house. 'Coming in for a cuppa?'

'Getting late, I thought I might head back to Poole tonight.'

'Ah well, another lonely night, here on my lonesome. Not to mention this murderer on the loose.'

'Put like that, how can I refuse?'

A smile spread across Michelle's face.

Ian was sitting on the settee staring blankly at nowhere in particular, obviously deep in thought. Michelle sat down next to him tucking one leg under her bottom as she did, so she was facing him. She gently removed the now empty mug from his grasp. 'Penny for them?'

'Oh nothing really, I was just contemplating what is so special about this situation that involves murder to stop the secret being exposed.'

'And?'

'Don't know, - can't figure it.'

She placed the cups on the coffee table. 'Let's just forget it for now.' And leaned in and nestled her nose in his neck. Ian took that for what it was, a come on signal and reacted in the appropriate manner, enfolding an arm around her, nudging with his cheek so that her lips came up to meet his and he kissed her.

'Do you want to stop the night?' She murmured.

'What about the neighbours?'

'I'm not asking them.'

'No, you know what I mean a strange car parked outside your house, all-night.'

She laughed. 'Shucks, big deal, besides I hardly know them.'

'Not an issue then?'

'I guess not,' she looked up and smiled, 'I'm going upstairs, you coming?'

'Guess so.'

Poole Dorset

By the time that story of the pathologist's demise had made the papers, Ian had returned to Poole. Intent on finding the answers from the only remaining probable source, Jeremy Miles-Johnson, he had headed straight to his office in Tower Park.

As he arrived he was greeted by some of the staff, in particular Maureen his secretary. 'Didn't expect to see you back so soon, everything's fine Ian, no problems.'

Ian held a hand up. 'It's okay Maureen, I've just come in to look at something, I'm not planning on stopping.' He sat at his desk and started up his computer tapping the requisite keys which would give him access to the electoral registers for 1956 through to 1961, purely as a first step, scanning the areas of North Yorkshire and Durham, looking for any reference to the man. He didn't find any, nor had he expected to. He had a feeling that the mysterious men described by Phillip, were working in Billingham on a rotation basis, possibly out of Porton Down and their family homes would more than likely be in the South. One piece of luck, Ian thought, not too many people around with a name like Miles-Johnson. Surprisingly there were a few, in the South of England, but there was only one family of that name living in the Salisbury area at that time. 'Got to be him.' Ian declared triumphantly.

The family home was listed as 'The Waterside, South Street, Broad Chalke' and a check of the current lists, indicated that was still the case.

Now for the big brother stuff, he mumbled to himself, *let's check out the private lists, if Jeremy was employed on government secret work of any kind, there will be a dossier on him, probably the full works down to the spots on his bum.'*

An hour later Ian sat back in his chair, he was reading and holding a single sheet of A4 paper that had just been ejected from the printer. 'I'd better give Colin a call; he's going to find this very interesting, very interesting indeed.' Ian mumbled.

He found Colin's number and punched it into the telephone.

'Hello.' A lady answered who Ian assumed was Miriam, Colin's wife.

'Oh, hello, is Colin there?'

'Yes, - who shall I say is calling?'

'My name's Ian Turner.

'Ah yes Ian, we talked about your granddad and my father working together.'

'Yes, thanks for the photograph.'

'You're very welcome. Just a moment, I'll go and get him.' There was a bump as the receiver was laid on a table and Miriam's distant voice calling for Colin. A moment or so later the receiver was picked up.

'Hi Ian, have you heard, the Pathologist's dead? Suspicious circumstances, the papers are saying.'

'Yeah know all about it. I take it you haven't spoken to Michelle?'

'She called yesterday, left a message on the answer phone; I've not had chance to get back to her.'

'Part of the reason I'm calling you. Seeing as how we've lost our potential source into this mystery, I'm back in Poole following up plan B.'

'What's plan B?' Colin said with a puzzled tone in his voice.

'Miles-Johnson.'

'Oh, forgot about him. – And?'

'Pin your ears back sunshine, I think we've hit pay dirt. For starters he's still very much alive, well maybe not very much, but alive and appears to have had a very interesting life. It seems Miles-Johnson was a doctor.'

'Doctor, what kind medical?' Colin interrupted. 'Sorry Ian, do go on.'

'Yes well, I'd better not say too much on the telephone, - not really secure. Have you got a fax machine?'

Colin was a little taken aback by Ian cutting off the conversation, just as it was getting interesting. He took the receiver away from his ear and looked at it quizzically. 'Y-e-a-h but.'

'Better you read it.'

'Oh, if you say so, it's the same as the telephone number, but ending with a seven instead of a six.' He was still wondering why Ian didn't want to continue the conversation, when he heard the click as the line went dead. But then again he didn't have Ian's intimate knowledge of telecommunications and Ian was not about to take the time tell him.

The Mercedes van was now parked in Stewarts Park, a good distance away from Colin's home, but still within range of the listening devices which had been placed in various discreet locations about the Hatton's home.

'Did you get that Charlie?'

'Every word.'

'What do you reckon Bill?'

Bill pursed his lips. 'This Ian Turner sounds like the Ian we recorded the other day. If it is the same guy then this Miles- Johnson fella must also be involved in the situation they discussed. We've got to assume there are connected in some way with our ICI remit, and call it in.

'You know my feelings on assumptions, when you assume -.'

'Yeah we know, - you make an ASS out of U and ME,' Charlie piped in.

'Besides,' George continued, 'our brief is to keep this Hatton fellow under surveillance and report any unusual occurrence.'

'Define unusual.'

'Can't Bill, but our friend Hatton was surprised at the inference that this Miles-Johnson was a doctor and that concerns me.'

'Yeah me too, but I don't - .'

'Could be Bill, the doctor bit refers to some sort scientific status, you know, not a medical doctor, in which case it could be feasible for this guy to be tied in someway with the ICI and all that chemical crap.'

'Hum, got a point, I suppose, I agree with Bill, we call it in, just to be on the safe side.'

'Will do,' Charlie responded.

The facsimile machine tinkled and Colin took himself to his study to stand pensively by until the single sheet of paper was disgorged. It read.

Dr Jeremy Miles-Johnson

D.o.B. 9th April 1914, Guildford

Family

Father, Colonel George Henry Johnson. Dragoon Guards. Lived together (unmarried) with the Mother Sarah Anne Miles. The Colonel was Killed in Action 1918 (Battle of the Somme). Mother Sarah Anne Miles passed away 12th June 1972.

Jeremy Miles-Johnson married, 4th June 1940

Wife, Elizabeth Fielding born 15Aug 1918

Gave birth to one child,-

Son, Henry Miles- Johnson born 2nd March 1944

Education / Career

Jeremy Miles-Johnson graduated Cambridge 1935

Continued studies to doctorate 1939

Doctor of Bio-Genetics and Molecular Synthesis.

Seconded into military service, honorary rank of Major posted to Porton Down Wiltshire to head research group. Purpose; Classified.

Post Script

Wife and son Henry were killed in a motoring accident 21st November1983, Dr Miles-Johnson suffered spinal injury and is confined to a wheel chair.

Colin, his interest now rekindled, picked up the telephone and punched Ian's number. The connection was almost instant as Ian picked up.

'Hi Colin, what do you think?'

'Very interesting, could be more to this than I first thought.'

'I agree, probably worth while me paying the old man a visit, he doesn't live that far from me.'

'Yes it probably would.'

'Okay I'll let you know what I find, if anything.'

'Yeah that would be good.' Colin said, but didn't really know why he'd said it. *Oh dear,* he thought, *perhaps we should be leaving well alone.* He was beginning to get this feeling that he'd gotten in too deep, particularly in the event of the Pathologist death. *'Somebody's already paid with their life.'* He mumbled to himself as he replaced the receiver and wandered aimlessly into the lounge. *'I wonder just how much Ian had to do with it.'*

'Is everything alright dear, you're looking very thoughtful?'

'Y-e-s, fine dear, just a feeling I'm getting into more than I bargained for.'

Charlie nodded towards George and removed the earphones, 'I think it would be prudent to send the whole transcript in George, I've got a feeling that there could be more to this than meets the eye.'

'I agree' George pursed his lips, thought for a moment and then concluded. 'Right let's do it, send in everything we've got, make sure we cover our arses, let someone else make sense of the conversations.'

Langley Virginia

Shortly after Colin had replaced the receiver in Marton, at three pm UK time, Simon Kendall's computer in the CIA Langley showed a pop up incoming icon, for a few seconds accompanied by a double chime, fortunately for Simon, nobody seemed to notice it.

Washington USA

Conlan Powell picked up the receiver of his secure telephone and keyed in Jack Rosenthal's number at Langley. 'Just read the transcripts Jack, very interesting. We need a face to face; there is something I think you should know.'

'Well I've no objection, but I'm fairly tied up at the moment.'

'Jack its urgent.'

'How urgent?'

'How quick can you get here?'

'If it's that urgent I'll grab the Lear, be with you in about three hours.'

'Oh – it's urgent alright.'

Jack Rosenthal was waiting by the Lincoln Memorial, when Conlan Powell joined him.

'Hi Jack, glad you could make it.' They didn't shake hands, didn't want to look too familiar in case a telescopic lens just happened to be pointed in their direction.

'This better be good, left a stack of shit paperwork, to get here, hope you aint pulling my dick.'

Conlan shook his large head from side to side. 'I aint about to pull your dick Jack, I'm in deep shit and sinking fast, I need a favour.'

'I guess we're still talking Haverton Hill and those chemicals here, are we?' Conlan nodded affirmatively, Jack shook his head in a disbelieving manner. 'Okay let's hear what you've got.'

'Let's walk.' And they set off at a slow, but silent pace.

'Well?' Jack said.

'Conlan studied the shine on his shoes as he walked. 'You ever heard of a guy called Ed Dawson?'

'Nope, can't say as I have.'

'Neither had I at one time, a 'no-hoper,' but permanent White House staff. Just like they thought I was, because back then black guys like me didn't do so good in politics.

'Do me a favour General; spare me the ethnic shit.'

Conlan Powell held out his hand in a calming gesture. 'Okay I'll get to the point. That meeting we had with Nixon, - I knew all about it long before.'

Jack stopped and looked disbelievingly at Conlan. 'What....the Sincyathatate shit?'

Conlan stopped turned to Jack and nodded. 'That and a little more,' he said after a moment's hesitation.

'And the Jericho thing?'

Nope not that, nor the Iraq business, the talk with Nixon was the first I'd heard of that scenario. They started to walk again, before Conlan decided to continue. 'It's the Haverton Hill thing that's the problem.'

'I'm all ears.' Jack said, prompting a response.

Conlan sighed and pursed his lips before continuing. 'Back in fifty-nine, there was some sort of cock up in Billingham ICI Sincyathatate plant; apparently an explosion sent up a cloud of poisonous gas and debris into the air which, as it turned out, came down on this Haverton Hill town. Eisenhower panicked, didn't want anything at all known of our involvement with the ICI. So to cover our arses he ordered the Sincyathatate plant and Haverton

Hill to be flattened, wiped of the face of the earth, just as if there had never existed.'

'What about the people and this fallout, where there any casualties?'

Conlan held up a hand. 'I'm coming to that Jack. Ike had a conscience, and did an under the table deal with the Brits to get the people re-housed in Billingham.

Jack nodded. 'Sounds reasonable. And the fallout?'

'You've got to remember Jack; Ike was washing his hands of the situation, so everything had to be handled with discretion, no comebacks, no US involvement.' Conlan stopped, looked at Jack and cocked his head to one side. 'You get what I'm saying.'

'I'm starting to get a stiff feeling up my Jacksee and I'm not sure I like it.'

Conlan started to walk again. 'Ike decided he had to determine if there was or would be a problem with this fallout. There were no reports at all, of the incident, of casualties, nothing. That's where Ed Dawson comes in, Whitehouse staffer, not married, insignificant really. Apparently Ed took some soil samples from Haverton Hill and had them analysed.' Conlan momentarily studied the shine on his shoes again, before continuing. 'Some of the samples developed a tiny dot of white fungus. That's when Eisenhower fearing the worst gave Ed carte blanch to set up a huge secret fund for payoffs to any of those who became affected.'

'How big is huge?'

'Ah um,' Conlan coughed, 'fifty million bucks.'

'Wow'!

'Ed Dawson was to set up an office in the UK, to monitor and administer the situation.'

'So nothing happened and all's well and this guy Dawson is a damn site richer.'

'Not quite Jack. Yes nothing happened, and after years in the UK, Dawson came home to die, but not before he handed me the batten.'

'Aw shit, this has something to with that Pathologist scenario, doesn't it?'

Conlan nodded. 'Sort of. When I took the job, felt kinda important, you know, just out of service and seconded to the Pentagon, thought that my career had peaked and I was on the downward slope to retirement. But then things started to happen to my political life.'

'Chief of Staff and all that crap.' Jack interrupted.

Conlan nodded. 'So I put a guy over there, to look after the office. Took a while before we decided we could make good use of that money.'

'You stole it!' Jack interrupted.

'To steal it Jack, it had to belong to someone, this money had been disowned, just floating around waiting to be claimed.'

'And you made godamn sure it was you doing the claiming.' Jack said angrily.

'Well it wasn't our intention to take any of the money, but we had to periodically access the account just to keep it active. Initially it was a case of reinvesting the interest in a Swiss numbered account.' Conlan motioned his head from side to side. 'Soon escalated I'm afraid, wasn't long before we started to dip into the fund.'

'Who's the we?'

'An accountant, name of Joe Nicholson. Funny, the more we took out, the more we wanted. Soon the fund became so depleted. Oh there's still quite a bit left, but I doubt there'd be enough cover a significant number of compo claims, you know how these things can escalate.

'Don't tell me, let me guess. You bribed a goddamn Pathologist to falsify report so you didn't have to fork out.' Conlan didn't have to say anything it was written all over his face. 'You're right General, you're in deep shit, but I'm not your fuckin lifebelt. Find yourself a bucket and start baling.'

Conlan, now head down continued in spite of Jack's outburst. 'The fungus, all of a sudden after almost fifty years, decided to grow at an alarming rate. We started to hear about former Haverton Hill residents dying strange deaths. We now realised, if people got wind of what was happening, there would be mass hysteria.'

'Massive claims you mean, which no doubt, you couldn't pay, because you'd gone and spent the money.' Jack shook his head. 'If I didn't considered you a friend, I'd run your fat greedy arse out of town.'

'Yes massive claims, no doubt Jack, but also the realisation would invoke an enquiry and the whole can of worms would be opened.'

'You mean the finger will be pointed at America producing all that chemical shit and probably put two and two together as to your 'weapons of mass destruction' saga. Don't bullshit me Conlan, you're in the frame for that as well,' Jack shrugged his shoulders, 'but hell, why care about your reputation when all that cash is at risk.'

Conlan nodded solemnly in acceptance of Jack's comments. 'Whatever you say Jack, but let's face it, if we can nip this thing in the bud, everything will be okay, let sleeping dogs lie, so to speak.'

'And your bank balance remains buoyant.'

There was a moments silence as they both contemplated the situation, then Conlan said. 'To be frank, we used a lot of the cash as bribes to keep the situation under wraps. And so we did, cover it up, as we thought. That was until a week or so ago, when this Ian Turner started to poke his nose in and he's getting mighty close to exposing the whole bag of shit.'

Conlan Powell turned to face Jack Rosenthal, a pleading look on his face. 'Jack, I implore you; we just can't let that happen. The US will feel it just as hard as I—.'

'Oh yeah so you expect the state to pull you out of the shit.'

'If you could only help me with the Turner problem I'm sure that would suffice.'

'Just run this by me again Conlan,' Jack said sternly, 'you were filling your pockets with US bucks when we met Nixon?' Conlan nodded. 'So you influenced the ceasing of hostilities in the Gulf, not for the protection of our troops, but to prevent anybody finding out that you've had your dirty little paws in the cookie jar.' Again Conlan nodded guiltily. They walked on, nothing was said; Jack was obviously running the whole scenario through his mind. 'Okay,' he said, 'so why stir the shit with this 'weapons of mass destruction' stuff and the Iraq war?'

'That's easy Jack, once Saddam had zapped the Kurds with that nerve gas, I saw an opportunity to get rid of the Sincyathatate stuff and accuse the Iraqi's of manufacturing it.'

'And thereby leaving the way clear for you to rip off the rest of the bucks.' Jack stopped in his tracks and stared long and hard at the man he'd formerly considered a friend. 'Now if this Ian Turner discovers the truth about Haverton Hill and what you've been up to, you're dead meat, right.'

'That's what I'm saying.'

'Conlan you're a bastard, a greedy one at that.'

'Just think Jack the problems that could ensue for America if this lot gets out, the fungus, the war, the losses, the costs.' Conlan said despairingly as they started to walk again. Jack slowly moved his head from side to side, before concluding the inevitable.

'Okay okay, so you want me to arrange for this guy to get zapped?'

Conlan nodded and Jack just shook his head in dismay. 'So be it.'

Langley

The next day, during Simons shift, the DD went online. Simon noting the pop up sat bolt upright and quickly tapped in his access code. He then slowly raised himself to check over the partition for any signs of interruption, before settling back to watch the words from the DD's computer form on one of his screens, which read.

M.P MI5   Re op Trilby watch;

Following your last report, you must prevent any meeting taking place with Dr Jeremy Miles-Johnson. We cannot allow him to divulge any info on Billingham ICI or Haverton Hill, to anyone, in particular this Ian Turner. It is now considered necessary to use drastic measures to secure the information in Miles-Johnson's head. Should you suspect that he has already passed on information to Ian Turner then he too must be terminated.

J.R CIA

The enormity of the situation began to dawn in Simon's mind. Firstly he realised from the timing of the incoming message, that his little game, for it was only a game to him, may have been spotted. He hurriedly checked back for any previous incoming messages, hoping there hadn't been deleted. He found transcript of the conversation between Ian Turner and Colin Hatton and realised that it had come in to the DD's port during the early morning. He had booted up the screen and had taken himself off to do his ablutions and to pick up a coffee, he had been away from his station when it was received. Now panic set in, had the pop up been spotted, probably not, otherwise he would now be in some padded cell getting the shit kicked out of him. If it is even suspected that he was privy to this message, his life expectancy would be dramatically reduced. In somewhat of a panic, his fingers worked furiously over the key board erasing all trace of the complicated programme.

'All done,' he said to himself and slumped back into his chair in an attempt to relax and slow his heart rate. A few moments later his thoughts turned to Dr Miles-Johnson and of Ian Turner's intended meeting with him. *'Someone is about to get hurt here,'* he said to himself, *'was it his business, should he try to prevent it, if so how?'*

He pondered the question for sometime, telling himself that it was not his problem and he should not have got involved with the DD's business in the first place. He tried staring at the roll of text from another insignificant publication, scrolling down the screen, but all he saw was word *terminated,* flashing through his mind. *'For what, - writing a tourist book,'* he muttered to himself, *'it just aint right.'* After sometime he concluded, *'I'll have to find some way to warn them, give these guys a chance.'* He recalled the transcript of Ian Turner's conversations with Colin Hatton, Simon had noted that the last digit of Colin Hatton's telephone number needed changing to get his fax number. He hastily found the Newspaper cutting and wrote down Colin's telephone number. Now that he had determined the number, he would send Colin Hatton a warning fax. Obviously this would have to be sent from somewhere off base as all fax transmits out of Langley are recorded. After wrestling with the problem for some time, he decided that a severe migraine attack was imminent. He made his way gingerly to Jim Benson office, wrapped on the door and walked in. Expressing as best he could the pain he was feeling in his head and behind his eyes, he asked to be excused for the rest of his shift. Jim Benson was not wholly convinced by Simon's acting, but as this was the first time Simon had ever made such a request, he reluctantly granted permission for him to go home sick.

About forty miles west of Langley, Simon's pickup pulled up in a parking lot adjacent to a small office block. He crossed the street to the office and casually walked into the reception area, a pretty blonde lady with bright red lipstick seated behind a counter type desk, smiled at him.

'Can I help you sir?'

'Yes Mam, I sure do hope so.' Simon leaned on the counter and looked into her eyes. 'I really am desperate, stuck on the road between clients with no means of communication, battery flat in the lap top and there's no goddamn signal on the cell.'

'Well err.' The young lady glanced around her desk at the array of communication devices, as she turned back, Simon held up a five dollar bill.

'Have you got a fax I can use?'

'Of course,' she said nodding her head toward the corner of the desk, at the same time extracting the note from Simon's hand.

The note on an A4 sheet was already prepared and after a brief pause, clicked its way through the machine. 'Thank you.' Simon said. 'Now you have a nice day.' At that he disappeared out of the door.

Poole UK

Ian replaced the telephone receiver after talking to Colin and pondered a moment, deciding it would be better to leave the journey to see Miles- Johnson, until tomorrow. *Lunch time would be good.* He thought. He pushed himself away from his desk and computer, *'I'm going to spend the night in my own bed and dream about Michelle.'* He mumbled as he headed out of his office.

The next day just after noon, Ian jumped into the Audi and set off for Broad Chalke a small village a few miles southwest of Salisbury.

Three quarters of an hour later the Audi made a right turn off South Street and through an un-gated opening. A white painted sign on one of the pillars read 'The Waterside.' *'This is the place.'* Ian said to himself as he saw a large house at the end of a long driveway. The driveway was tarmac laid roughly, sometime ago by the looks, over the original shingle. *Probably to suit a wheelchair.* Ian thought.

A Nissan Micra was parked in front of the house which Ian assumed it belonged to a visitor as he doubted Miles-Johnson was capable of driving. He then turned his thoughts to gaining access.

What am I going to say? Lie through my teeth that ought to do it.

He rang the door bell. A few moments later the door was opened by a rather large lady wearing what Ian took to be a nurses uniform. 'Can I help you?'

'Ah yes, I would like to see Dr Jeremy Miles-Johnson, is he at home?'

'Oh yes most definitely, hasn't left this place for years. May I enquire who you are and why you're calling?'

'My names Ian Turner, I'm doing an article for the Times magazine covering forgotten heroes of the war years.'

'Better come in then, this way if you please.' She waddled off in front of him, continuing the conversation over her shoulder. 'Didn't know he was a war hero, then again, don't know much about him. Seldom talks you know, I've being living in for the past five year and he's hardly spoken a dozen words to me, still you're welcome to try. Here we are.'

She pushed open the door to the drawing room, at one end was a pair of glazed doors leading into the conservatory, where, in a wheelchair with a tartan blanket over his knees, sat a small figure, gazing out into the garden.

'A visitor for you,' she shouted. 'He's a little deaf you will have to talk loudly if you want any response at all, but I guess that's no more than you'd expect from someone of over a hundred.....Best of luck, eh.'

She backed out closing the door behind her. Dr Jeremy had made no effort to react to his presence, but Ian had a sneaky feeling the old man was fully aware of him as he entered into the conservatory. Not put off by this lack of acknowledgement Ian plonked himself into a wicker chair virtually opposite the old man.

The wizened bespectacled head raised just enough to take in Ian, and a smile cut across the thin lips.

'Henry my boy I've been waiting for you to come.'

'I'm not Henry.' Ian tried to say, but the old man was having none of it.

'Take me into the garden, Henry please, down to the river bank. It's been such a long time since I was last there.' Ian hesitated not sure if he should insist that he was not the son who had died so long ago, or to go along with the old man's fantasy. *Why*

'Come on son, push me.' The old man said while gesticulating with a hand in the direction of the conservatory doors. *Why not if it'll make him happy.* Ian took a hold on the handles of the wheelchair. 'Okay sir, your wish is my command.' Pushing it out of the conservatory and down a long winding garden path, to the river bank. They gazed for sometime into the seemingly endless rush of the water as bubbled and swirled around the various boulders strewn over the river bed. Ian was still standing behind the wheelchair, he thought it prudent to remain silent and let the old man enjoy the moment.

'Is it more money you're after son?' Ian was taken slightly aback by surprise, after waiting so long for any comment.

'Err, err, no sir I don't want any money from you.' The old man rested his chin on his chest and closed his eyes. *'Patience,'* Ian said to himself, give him time. After a good five minutes the old man raised his head again. 'Then what do you want?' Any sign of affection had now gone from voice.

Perhaps he realizes that I'm not his son. 'I wish sir, to explore your past and record for prosperity your work and contribution it made to the welfare of this nation. For so many years your achievements have been cloaked in secrecy, now after fifty years, in accordance with legislation, all can be revealed.' Ian was hoping that the old man had lost all recollection of time and indeed of any legislation. He felt sure that the small man in the wheel chair once a chemist of some repute had a story bottled up inside him; he only hoped that he'd said enough to remove the cork.

'Fifty years, -- is it really, -- well I never.'

A smile cut across the old mans thin lips and Ian thought he caught a glimpse of a twinkle behind the spectacles in the old mans eye. 'Push me back; we'll have a cup of tea, shall we?' As they neared the conservatory door, he bellowed loudly. 'Nursey! Some teas, on the double, chop chop.'

Ian had noticed the nurse in the conservatory, obviously keeping an eye on her charge. He also saw her scatter when the command rang out.

They settled themselves in the conservatory, Ian again seated in a cushioned wicker chair, the old man opposite, and an occasional table between them with the tea tray already set.

'May I use this sir?' Ian said as he placed a tape recorder on the table.

'What is it?'

'It's a recorder; it will tape everything you say.'

'I know what a recorder does, I was using one before you were born.'

'Well do you mind?'

'Not at all, let's get on with it.' The old man waved his hand impatiently in Ian's direction.

It was almost 8pm when Ian left 'The Waterside.' The old man had fallen to sleep with a contented look on his face, in the telling of his story. Right on cue the nurse appeared and pushed Dr Jeremy into, what was now used as a down stairs bedroom. At that point Ian took his leave. As he got into the Audi he caught sight of a black car, driving very slowly past the entrance. Reflecting on the information he had just acquired from the good doctor, perhaps he was being, just a little bit over cautious. His mind went into overdrive when he arrived at the gate, he'd half expected to see the black car parked in the narrow village street, but it wasn't. *Getting a little paranoid, aren't we.* He said to himself, as he pulled the Audi out onto a clear road and headed home in the direction of Poole.

Later that evening, a man alighted from a dark coloured vehicle, which was parked in an unlit area behind the village hall. In the darkness he walked quite casually to the un-gated entrance of 'The

Waterside,' hesitating for a moment to check the house at the end of the drive. Satisfied that all was quiet, he made his way down the drive, avoiding the front entrance, he opted for a means of entry around the back. The conservatory doors presented little difficulty; he opened them with consummate ease, making sure he relocked them once inside. Stealthily he moved around the ground floor of the house, until he found where Dr Jeremy Miles-Johnson lay blissfully snoring. Picking up a pillow he pressed it firmly against the old mans face until all the signs of life were extinguished. Without sentiment, he neatly rearranged the pillows and the bedding, so that it looked as if the old man had peacefully passed away in his sleep. Slipping the latch on the front door, he quietly let himself out and disappeared into the darkness.

Colin was just in the zinging stage prior to falling into a deep sleep, when the chirping of the fax machine echoed around the house. Coming fully awake, his hand found the switch of the bedside table light, turning it on. 'Goodness me, it's after midnight.' He said as his eyes eventually focused on the clock. 'Hum-m, what is it dear.'

'The fax machine, I think, I'd better go and check.'

'Can't it wait until morning, I was just dozing.'

'It may be Ian with something important.' He hauled himself out of bed, stretched and yawned. Finding his slippers and dressing gown he made his way down the stairs, arriving at the machine in time to retrieve the single sheet of paper as it finished printing.

Your house and phones are bugged, possibly your car as well, take care. Steps are being taken to prevent Dr Miles-Johnson divulging information to Ian Turner. Please warn him that they are planning to terminate the doctor and if necessary him also.

A well wisher.

Colin was ashen faced as he wandered back into the bedroom and over to Miriam. 'Whatever is the matter, you look as if you've seen a ghost?' Colin lifted a finger holding it to his lips, as he passed her the sheet of paper. She gasped when she read it and mouthed. 'What are you going to do?'

Colin went back down the stairs and picked up a small notebook from the downstairs telephone table, flicked through its pages and made a satisfactory nod when he'd found what he was looking for. As he passed through the kitchen on his way to the back door, he picked up the mobile telephone from the table and headed for the shed at the bottom of the garden.

Bill was on duty in the Vito, the other two were curled up snug and warm in some hotel room. He was cold and tired and almost on the point of dozing when the noise of Colin Hatton's fax machine was picked up in the headphones. He also heard what he assumed was Colin moving about the house. '*Another one who can't sleep.*' He said to himself as he removed headset and pulled up the corner of the sleeping bag until it encased his head. Within seconds he was snoring.

'Ian, are you all right?' Colin shouted into the mobile after it had rang for what seemed an age.

'Y-e-a-h, you've just woken me.' Ian replied holding back a yawn as he spoke.

'Can't explain now, are you at home?'

'Yeah.'

'Just get yourself out of there. I don't care where, just get away. When you are sure you haven't been followed, ring me on this mobile, - err -.' Colin fumbled with the torch holding the notebook open with the same hand. '07988844267 get that?'

'Err yeah, but -.'

'No buts, move!'

Colin was sitting in a dark shed at the bottom of the garden, letting his mind run amok as he gazed at the moon through the window. It's over an hour since he made the call to Ian and he was becoming very concerned that something could have happened to him. He had such a start as the shed door creaked open.

'What the!' But it was only Miriam with a piping hot mug of tea.

'Only me dear, are you alright? You've been out here a while.'

He pattered his chest. 'Made me jump then. Oh lovely, thank you dear.' He said as he took the mug. 'Yes I'm fine, starting to get a little concerned about Ian though, hope he's alright, if only.'

'I'm sure he'll be fine dear, now drink your tea and stop worrying. It's a little chilly out here, are you warm enough?'

'Hadn't thought about it, but now you mention it my feet are freezing.'

'I'll get you a blanket.' And she headed back to the house only to return a few minutes later with a blanket which she wrapped around her husband tucking it in where she could.

'Thank you dear.'

'I'm sure he's alright.' She said patting his shoulder.

'I know, I know.' He said unconvincingly as he laid a hand on top of hers. 'You get yourself back to bed, I won't be long.'

'Okay.' She said and reluctantly left.

After Miriam had returned to the house, Colin returned to gazing at the moon, all was quiet, and then he jumped again, startled as the mobile phone lit up and trilled out the start of 'Colonel Bogey.' In somewhat of a panic, he fumbled for the green key and pressed it.

'Hi Colin, you there?'

'Thank god,' he said as he heard Ian's voice.

Ian had been wise enough to leave the apartment via the back staircase deciding, for some unknown reason, to leave the bottom fire escape door ajar. He headed towards his car, but changed his mind at the last moment. *Better not,* he thought, *could be compromised.* And he set off to walk about two miles to Ham

Common, a patch of heath land near the Marines base in Hamworthy. It was there he'd switched on his mobile to talk to Colin, he only hoped GCHQ had not received any instruction to target him.

'Where are you? No don't answer that. Are you safe?'

'Yes I think so, what's the problem?'

Colin read out the fax message he'd received.

'I thought I was being paranoid.' Ian said. 'The first time we met I thought we were being followed and I've just had the same feeling as I left the doctors house. If you hadn't called I would have probably let it pass.'

'Thank goodness I got to you in time.'

'Colin, we need to talk, but not now, not on the phone. Knowing what I know about such matters, if someone is targeting me, then this call has probably compromised both of our positions and put 'a well wisher' in the frame. Destroy the sender's number and turn off your mobile, now. - I'll contact you later.' There was a click and almost at the same instance Colin pressed the red key turning the mobile off.

Ian carefully checked the car park area on Ham Common to ensure that he hadn't been followed, and then he made his way to his parent's house. He kept his finger on the door bell until he saw the hall light come on, through the glass door panel.

'What the- Ian, is everything alright? Come on in son.'

'Yes Dad everything's fine, sorry it's so late, but could you do me a favour?'

'Well err- yes, if I can.'

'Lend me your car.'

'Is that all, had me going there for a minute. Sure you can, no probs.

'I just need to sort out a thing or two.'

'Whatever, dare say you'll tell me what's going on in your own good time.' Allan turned and went into the kitchen to get the car the keys, without waiting for any further explanation. A moment later he appeared in the hall way, key in hand. 'There you go son.'

'I'll get it back to you, hopefully tomorrow.'

'Ah don't worry,' Allan said flapping a hand at Ian, 'it's not a big deal; we've always got our bus passes, if we need to get into town.'

'Is that you Ian? - Is everything alright?' Alice called from the bedroom.

'Yes Mum, there's no problem, sorry to have woken you.'

'You would tell us if you needed any help, wouldn't you?'

'Yes Mum, don't worry I'm fine, I'll explain everything to you later, but now is not the time.'

'Drive carefully son.'

'Thanks Dad, see yah.'

Ian decided that he must determine if he was under surveillance of some kind before he could figure out his next move. So he drove his dad's car back to his apartment, discreetly checking the surrounding area for any unknown vehicles and or anyone looking suspicious. Nothing. He remained vigilant checking out the car park area as he parked up. *'Hope the fire door's still open.'* He muttered. It was, he entered and cautiously edge up the back staircase of the apartment block. Once inside his apartment he remained cautious giving the entire place the once over, before concluding that nobody had been in there. Everything seemed to be as he'd left it, but Ian was wise enough, or paranoid perhaps, to realise that that was no guarantee, the place hadn't been infiltrated. Thoughts that someone may be listening and or even watching him caused him to edge stealthily from room to room collecting various items. When he was about to leave, probably because he'd seen it done so often on the movies, he pulled the door closed, plucked a hair from his head and with a little spittle secured it across the gap.

He left the building the same way as he'd entered, by the back stairs, jumped into his dad's car and headed to his office. This was a large two storey block on the other side of town. Where again, he cruised the area looking for anything out of place and double checked that he was not being followed. Relatively happy that all was as it should be he pulled the car up to the main gate of the company car park.

'Can I help you sir?' The security guard said, at the same time shining his torch into the vehicle.

'Yes, I like to go into my office.' Ian said, flashing his identification pass, which the guard took a cursory glance at, looking first at Ian and then at the card, a motion he repeated several times. Then he checked the vehicle, against a paper secured to a clip board. 'Don't seem to have your car registration here sir.'

'You're the new guy.' The guard didn't say anything. 'This is my father's car, so it won't be logged, but if you care to scrutinise my identification, I think you'll find that I'm your employer.'

The guard looked again at Ian's pass before exclaiming. 'The Mr. Turner?'

'The very same, now will you let me into my office?'

'Yes sir.' With that the guard unlocked the gate and swung open one leaf of the steel structure. Ian drove by, and slowed when adjacent to the guard. 'No one else, under any circumstance is to get into this place, tonight.'

'Understood, sir,' and gave his employer a salute.

To gain access into the office block involved a procedure of unlocking an outer door with a key an inner door with a digital code and a confrontation with Ted, who was stood waiting for him. 'Evening sir couldn't sleep could we?'

'You don't know the half of Ted.'

Ian went to his office on the ground floor, gaining access with another digital code and a palm scan. Picking up a sheet of paper he scribbled a note loaded it into the fax machine and sent it to

Colin, whom he'd expected, after all the excitement, would still be awake.

He wasn't wrong; Colin was seated in an arm chair in front of the gas fire and was just about to drop off into the land of nod, when the trill of the fax startled him awake, again. He literally ran to the machine, grabbing the sheet of paper as it ejected, it read.

To assure me of your freedom, please answer the following and return to me. Further instruction will follow on receipt.

What was my Granddads name?
Where was he in the photograph?
What was he doing?
Where did we meet Phillip and who else?
NB there is a time limit, if you have not answered within 10mins, consider contact broken.
I.T

Colin browsed the note. *Crafty bugger.* He thought. *I could have been asleep in bed, what then for your ten minutes.* Then he smiled to himself. *I guess he knows me.* He quickly filled in the answers, put the paper back in the machine and tapped in the return fax number.

Ian's response was just as immediate.

Ring me from my Grandma's on her phone tomorrow at 11am. Ensure you are not followed and don't use your own car.

I.T

PS destroy facsimiles, remember numbers.

Ian took the cassette out of the recorder and placed it in a twin player/recorder. With a blank tape in the other compartment, he selected tape to tape high speed dubbing. That done he placed one tape in his safe and put the second in an envelope marked FAO Colin Hatton, but he used Phillip Walton's address.

'Now then, let's see why somebody wants to have me eliminated.' He made his way to the secure test area on the first floor, in the core of the block, this was an area surrounded with a solid wall, windowless and accessed by a single steel door, requiring a digital key code and a retina scan before it could be opened. That door only gave access to an antechamber where clean coveralls were to be donned together with head and shoe coverings.

Ian selected the coveralls and other items from a locker and proceeded to put them on.

Beyond the inner door was a sterile zone. The room lighting was subdued and air conditioners throbbed away relentlessly, maintaining the room at an ambient temperature, all incoming air was passed through a number of filters to prevent the ingress of any particle of dust. Inside the room standing like soldiers on parade, were neat rows of two foot square towers, floor standing and almost reaching to the ceiling. Each tower was serviced with masses of wires coming out of various orifices and each had banks of slide in trays running the full height. The trays were formed in box fashion rather like tall chests of drawers, a series of lights flashed at each tray level and each tray contained row upon row of printed circuit boards. At the far end of the room was a large computer terminal, which was linked into the circuitry of the towers.

Ian was probably the only man in the UK, if not the world, outside the government secret agencies, that had the knowledge and equipment to, if he so wished, listen into, the Secret Service Network and the Government listening station GCHQ. Until this very moment Ian had never had the inclination or even contemplated the betrayal of the oath he'd taken at the outset of the communication contract. However the life threatening circumstances he now faced, through what he initially thought was an innocent enquiry, compelled him to react in his own defence. *'Where needs must the devil drives.'* He said to himself as he crossed the floor and headed towards the computer. He sat at the keyboard and punched in a series of commands, the screen flashed and reams of script rolled over it.

Colin approached the door and pressed the intercom button.
'Hello, who's there?'
'My name's Colin Hatton, your grandson Ian Turner, suggested I come here.'
'What's my son in laws name and where did he live when he was a young boy?'
Colin smiled. 'You know Mrs. Flynn, you have a very clever grandson, and his fathers name is Allan and as a young boy he lived at 10 Drake Street, Haverton Hill.'

'Are you by yourself?'

'My wife's in the car.'

'Just a minute love, I'll open the door.' The door opened and Mrs. Flynn looked Colin up and down. 'You look like Ian said you would. Don't just stand there, tell your wife, come in, come in the both of you. I'll put the kettle on.'

'Thanks.' Colin said, motioning to Miriam to follow.

'Come on the pair of you, sit yourselves by the fire, I'll go and make a pot of tea. Oh and Ian said you are to ring him at his parents home as soon as you get here.'

'Err thanks, but I don't know—.'

Mrs. Flynn had turned and was heading towards the kitchen; she didn't hear Colin's mild protest. 'The numbers by the phone, it's all ready for you. Do you both take milk and sugar?'

'Yes both white two sugars,' Colin called after her as she disappeared through the door.

The moment the telephone rang Ian picked it up. 'Hi Colin.'

'Hello Ian, funny business this, isn't it?'

'Guess so, how are you coping?'

'Er , you know, it's a bit nerve racking. Miriam I know is finding it all very stressful.'

'I know it won't be easy, but try not to let it bother you, just be a little careful, with what you say.'

'I really don't understand what's going on, what have we done to cause all this?'

'Oh I think I can guess, but I'd better be careful what I say on the telephone.'

'What about this call, do you think it's Okay?'

'Providing you weren't followed, calls between these numbers are a regular occurrence, shouldn't prompt any suspicion.'

'Don't think so, I drove to my daughter's home and swapped cars, nobody followed, but just in case I took the long route by the town centre.'

'Should be okay.'

'Ian, do you think this is really happening, I mean, could it be somebody's idea of a wind up?' The fear was apparent in Colin's voice and Ian could detect a slight tremor as he spoke. 'We're just every day normal folk; this kind of thing doesn't happen to normal folk. Does it?'

'I would really like to think it doesn't Colin, but knowing what I know now, I think the fax from 'the well wisher' may have just saved our lives, mine in particular.'

'The fax was sent from America, I've destroyed it, set fire to it actually, same with those you sent.'

'I take it you committed the number to memory?'

'Sure did.'

'The well wisher being American makes sense, I picked up some traffic between the CIA and MI5.' Ian made no attempt to offer any explanation into how he knew such things, and Colin was wise enough not to ask.

'Unfortunately it was too late for Dr Miles-Johnson.'

'Oh no, you don't mean, they've killed him?'
'Fraid so.'
'The poor man, can't help feeling it's all our fault.'

'Perhaps Colin, and don't forget the Pathologists demise. Someone doesn't want us to unearth the truth.'

'Well I guess we'll never know now, after all this trouble, I'm not even sure I want to.'

'Oh, so you'll not want to listen to the tape recording of my meeting with Miles-Johnson?'

'You got to him first!'

'Sure did, but this is really serious information. I'm not sure you should have it, I've no doubt it will put your life at risk too.'

'You know Ian, I think it already has, after all it was me who asked you to go and see Miles-Johnson in the first place. It must have been that conversation that triggered this whole scenario.' Colin paused, and looked across to Miriam for support. She understood and nodded her approval. 'I'm of the opinion that I may as well get hung for a sheep as a lamb, - send me the damn tape.'

'Thought you'd say that, it's in the post, sent to Phillip's address marked for your attention.'

'Good thinking, I'll look forward to hearing it.'

'And Colin, I think you'd better get Michelle involved in this.'

'Yes of course I will.' Colin lingered for a moments thought, anticipating what might be the implications of the tape. 'What do you reckon are our chances Ian?'

'I don't know Col, as for me, well its definite elimination, on the basis that I may have talked to the doctor, but what I can't quite fathom, is why their computers are systematically scanning every Ian Turner north of the Tees, when they had a direct link to me through your mobile.'

'I don't have a mobile, can't stand the things. It was my daughters; she'd accidentally left it on the kitchen table. I'd put
it handy so that I remembered to take it to her. Turned out to very convenient eh!'

'So that's why they haven't fingered me yet, or maybe they have.'
Ian paused momentarily, running the situation through his mind.
'Colin, I think you and Miriam had better spend a few days away.'

'Already planned to, I've cleared the house of all notes and faxes relative to this project, just in case they break in.'

'Very wise, I suppose I should disappear for a while too.'

'Ian.' Colin spoke in a very quiet, sheepish voice.

'Do you think there's a way out of this mess, other than been eliminated, I mean.'

'Hum, possibly, but the only thing I can think of at the moment, is exposure, local and National press coverage, the whole thing out in the open. You'll know what I mean once you've listened to the tape. Y-e-s, that ought to do it....I think.'

PART TWO

THE BEGINING

CHAPTER EIGHT

The Doctor Jeremy Miles-Johnson Story

The old man put his head back and closed his eyes. A smile slowly creased his wrinkled face and stretched his thin lips, almost to snapping point, rather like a perished rubber band. It was some time before he actually spoke, and the suddenness of it gave Ian quite a start.

'I was the only one you know.'

'The only one what, sir?' Ian said as he fumbled for the record button of the tape recorder.

'The only Biological Chemist, I was the first. I discovered, studied and wrote a paper on, 'Molecular Synthesis.''

'Molecular Synthesis sounds interesting.'

The Old man brought his head forward and squinted at Ian through his watery bespectacled eyes, to assure himself that Ian was taking him seriously. Reassured his head went back and he again closed his eyes.

'Lots of them at it now, of course,' he said, 'all following in my wake.' He pursed his thin lips as he seemingly reflected in his mind, on his own genius.

'You see, I discovered that every biological or chemical molecule is made up of microscopic cells whereby each group of cells perform a particular function, for example smell, colour, toxicity and so on, rather like a DNA chromosome, but way smaller.' A shaking hand escaped from the sanctuary of the tartan blanket on his lap and with effort he held it up squeezing together the bony thumb and forefinger to express the small.

The hand then dropped under its own weight, disappearing again under the blanket. His speech was slow and quiet, but the words were formed and delivered with a rehearsed assurance.

'I considered the possibility of combining all the toxin molecules into one hybrid solution.'

'Sounds fascinating sir, but for what purpose?'

'Ultimately, for weapons.'

'Oh, that's why the army grabbed you, to make chemical weapons.' The words slipped out of Ian's mouth and he knew as soon as the last syllable left his lips, that he should have kept his big mouth shut.

The old man lowered his head, opened his eyes and stared at Ian. 'Not quite,' he drawled, as he let his head go back and closed his eyes. This started another period of silence which lasted for five minutes. Ian had stopped the tape and sat pensively poised finger on button ready to restart the moment the old man decided to speak. *'At this rate I'll be here all night.'* Ian said to himself.

Then again without any hint or warning the old man started to speak, although his head remained back against a pillow and the eyes remained shut. Ian hastily pressed the record button.

'Hardly grabbed, I volunteered my services.....And they were keen to have me.'

Another long pause, Ian literally bit his bottom lip to prevent himself from speaking. After a few moments the old man decided to continue.

'My father, your grandfather, was killed by German mustard gas in the trenches. I suppose in some way, it was a kind of revenge for that that gave me inspiration for my work.'

He still has me down for his son. As the old man's words ran through Ian's mind. What a stroke of luck.

'My studies and findings into Molecular structure were at the forefront in its field, you know.' He momentarily opened one eye and took a sneak peep at Ian, again to check if he was still paying attention and showing interest at the level of the old mans achievements.

'At the time, I was considered to be the worlds leading authority on the subject. Not bad for a mere twenty-four year old, - if I do say so myself. I had students, you know, part of the trouble I suppose. A couple of the brightest were German.' The old man paused again, but this time Ian somehow knew that the delay was only to get facts clear in his head.

'At the outbreak of the Second World War 1939,' he began, 'I was approached by a government official. He told me that he had it on good authority that Hitler had seconded these very students into a special facility to develop their knowledge of biological and chemical matter, which they had learned from me.....For use in warfare. That's when I volunteered. I was given the rank of Major and posted to Porton Down. My instructions were, to set up two facilities, one to develop a protection against such weapons. This was to be the priority, in case of imminent attack. And the other facility was to develop our own biological and chemical weapon, to be used against the Germans.'

'Obviously, not knowing what kind of chemical would be dumped on the populous was a bit of a draw back, but we produced rubber coveralls, gas masks with flexible air filtration backpacks and an anti most toxins vaccine, which had to be injected into the blood stream. Satisfied as much as we could be with the protection facility, we turned our attention to developing our own biological weapon.'

'And did you?'

The old mans head came forward and he glared at Ian and spoke in low drawn out tone. 'Oh yes, indeed we did. We produced a most formidable weapon, that had it ever been used, I've no doubt the course of the whole world would have been altered.' He paused for a long moment considering the implications of what he was about to say. 'Oh yes a most formidable weapon, something that had never been done before....And to the best of my knowledge, since.' He added.

'Oh I remember it so well....It all really started that summer's day, way back in 42.'

CHAPTER NINE

June 1942

Porton Down, the government secret laboratory facility, consists of a number of insignificant looking single storey brick buildings, most of them windowless, surrounded by high security fencing and is nestled on the Downs, Northeast of Salisbury.

Two Jeeps, each carrying four armed Military Police, one in front of the camouflaged coloured Humber Vogue, the other at the rear. The car was also flanked by four motorcycle riders, two each side. The motorcade turned off the country road and along the drive that led to the Porton Down facility outer perimeter security gate. As the vehicles pulled up at the gatehouse there was increased activity by the on duty security staff, lots of double checking paperwork, frantic saluting and a somewhat uncertain attitude as how best to deal with the situation. Finally the MP guards with their Jeeps and motor cycles were allowed into a parking area inside the outer perimeter fencing, and between the two security gates. The Humber with its passengers was allowed to continue through to the inner fence second gate and into the facility. As soon as the Humber cleared the first gate, the duty sergeant had placed a call to the admin block causing much panic and scattering of the staff. One female receptionist had the presence of mind to request someone to go and find Dr Miles-Johnson.

'He's in number two lab, in the isolation chamber. Can someone go and get him, like now! They'll be here any minute.'

As the young lab technician ran across the road to number two facility, the Humber was just coming to a stop outside the administration building.

The front seat passenger got out of the car first, looked around pensively, before opening the rear door. The driver almost simultaneously repeated the same operation at his side of the vehicle. The two passengers got out of the car and as they came together at the entrance steps, the female receptionist arrived at the door, flinging both leafs open, she rather calmly announced.

'Good morning gentlemen. We were not expecting you, the commanding officer should be with you shortly, if you would care to follow me.' She confidently turned and headed back into the building. The visitors turned to each other and nodded.

'Shall we.'

'After you, sir'

The receptionist led them to the conference room and made them comfortable. 'Would you like tea or coffee?'

'Tea for me please,' the Prime minister said and is it okay to smoke in here?'

'Yes sir, I'll bring you an ash tray.' At that she turned her head towards General Eisenhower.

'I'd like coffee, black please.' He then proceeded to light up a cigarette, blowing a cloud of smoke into the air.

'Any idea how long we will be waiting for the Major?' Churchill asked, whilst he proceed to clip and light his cigar.

'Shouldn't be too long, sir.' She said, giving out a little cough as she caught a mouth full of the smoke, she turned and quickly made her way out of the room.

'Major, I thought we were seeing some kind of Scientist or chemical doctor?'

'One in the same, Ike, during war time this facility is controlled by the armed forces. All personnel here have been recruited via the army.'

The young lab technician knocked on the glass screen of the observation room. The doctor was completely covered. He was wearing white coveralls, a linen hood that covered all of the head, except for the eyes and a clear visor that moulded to the contours of his face and sealed itself against the linen hood. He had his hands inside rubber gloves which were fashioned into the glass panel on a sealed work station.

With the gloves on, he controlled a hypodermic syringe which he manoeuvred deftly to extract and transfer the cells at the base of a very powerful microscope.

The knocking on the glass alerted the doctor and he lifted his eyes away from the double lens microscope. He slowly turned and nodded his acknowledgment to the young technician on the other side of the glass screen, at the same time removing his hands from the rubber gloves. He then made his way to the decontamination room, where he would shower and change before emerging into the prep room, where the technician eagerly awaited him.

Several minutes passed as the young technician paced the floor biting his nails like an expectant farther waiting for an over due birth. As soon as the doctor appeared, the technician excitedly blurted out the news.

'Sir, sir, the Prime Minister Winston Churchill.'

'Yes, yes I know who the Prime Minister is.'

'No, no sir,' the young man flapped excitedly, Mr. Churchill and General Eisenhower are here to see you. They've been here ages.'

'Have they indeed, well I'll be blowed, where are they?'

'Doreen, err Corporal Watts, I mean, has put them in the conference room. They must have been there for a good half hour now.' The young technician said anxiously.

'Tough, can't be helped, I should have been informed they were coming.' Then the doctor mumbled, more to himself than to the technician, who at this point was jumping up and down desperately trying to instil some urgency into the situation. *What do they want, I wonder? They must be aware that my work is not complete.*

'Ah, - good morning Prime Minister.' The doctor marched into the conference room, hand extended and nodded in Eisenhower's direction. 'Good morning sir.' Both the Prime Minister and the General had got to their feet and in turn shook the doctor's hand whilst exchanging greetings.

'I'm Major Miles-Johnson, head of this facility.'

'Yes we know.' Churchill mumbled as he shook the Majors hand.

'Please, be seated gentlemen.' Major Miles- Johnson motioned to his guests.

'This gentleman,' Churchill said, turning to his companion, 'is Dwight D Eisenhower appointed American Commander General, European theatre.'

'Yes Prime Minister, I do believe I read an article in the Times on the subject. I'm very pleased to meet you General.'

'You're much younger than I expected.'
'If that's a compliment sir, then thank you.'

'Please call me Ike, more informal.'

'May I ask what brings you gentlemen to Porton Down?' Although he had a pretty good idea.

Winston Churchill rummaged through a leather brief case and removed a manila file marked 'top secret.' He didn't open the file, there was no need. He just tapped it with his finger, sending the ash of the cigar he was holding, across the table.

'I've a report here that tells me you have produced a biological weapon of astronomical magnitude. I, hum, we,' waving the cigar butt in Ike's direction, 'would like to hear all about it, from the horses mouth, so to speak.'

Dr Miles-Johnson sat back for a moment's contemplation before commencing his oratory, if only to express his research in terms that the layman would understand.

'Well gentlemen, I'll be as brief as I can. 'Bacillus anthraces' a relatively rare bacteria, very harmful especially to animals, you will probably be more aware of this bacteria under its better known name of 'Anthrax'.'

The doctor noticed the shocked look on both of the statesmen's faces, pausing for effect before he continued. 'I've managed to grow my own strain of the bacterium and have broken down the molecular structure of each cell. Over the course of time I have achieved identification of each chromosome and in so doing I have been able to combine all the most toxic elements into each cell, producing a hybrid bacteria of most devastating toxicity.' He hesitated momentarily before continuing in a slow woeful drawl. 'That the thought of one minuscule of this lethal concoction escaping from my lab, frankly scares the hell out of me.' He paused again for a moment, to see if the gravity of what he was saying was having any affect on the visitors; it didn't seem so; so he continued. 'The bacteria are airborne and can be absorbed on contact, through the skin, or inhaled. Once infected the bacterium goes to work immediately attacking the blood and the nervous system. It would take about three days of agony before the victim dies, but not before the bacterium infects anyone within touching distance. As far as I can determine the bacterium is still prevalent in the corpse for some time, perhaps

years and is still capable of passing itself on to another host. These bacteria can spread so fast that within a few days it would reach epidemic proportion. According to my calculations, should, a small vial of less than an hundred gram be dropped on one point of a populated area, within three days, the citizens of a city say the size of Birmingham, would be contaminated and eventually wiped out.'

'It sounds to me Doctor, that's just the thing we are looking for, something to stop the Germans in their tracks, probably shorten the war by years.'

'With all due respect Prime Minister, there's no telling what the full extent of this bacteria is. Before we can even think of releasing this on the Germans, or the world for that matter, we need to develop some antidote and some means of controlling it.'

Churchill hummed and puffed, leaned forward and flicked through the pages of the report.

'Hum, say's here, you have developed an antidote vaccine, is this not correct then eh?' And he slumped back into the chair, taking a drag on the still smouldering cigar, the wisps of smoke escaped from the sides of his mouth polluting the air as he glared at the doctor through the smoke.

'Against Anthrax as the world knows it, probably if administered immediately after infection, but against this hybrid, I very much doubt it.'

'You doubt it?' Eisenhower queried.

'All we have established Ike, is that this vaccine is able to stop the Anthrax cells dividing and multiplying, but does not counter the toxicity or contamination effects.'

'I don't quite understand Major, is it an antidote or isn't it?'

'Let me explain Ike, I developed a general vaccine as an antidote against most known toxins. That was before I embarked on the Anthrax programme. I now know that this vaccine will halt Anthrax spreading, but it will not necessarily save the life of anyone infected.'

'Better than nothing, Major.'

'True Ike, it would be better than nothing, but I haven't any idea of how the vaccine would react against this Hybrid.'

'Surely it would have the same affect.'

'Maybe.'

'In that case young man, isn't that the means of controlling the bacteria?' Churchill put in.

'Well sir, I suppose if we were able to vaccinate every victim and potential victim then it may be theoretically possible to contain the bacteria and isolate the whole contaminated area.'

'Good enough Major, that's all we needed to hear. You will prepare a vial of this hybrid Anthrax for testing in two week's time.'

'But sir, the consequences!'

'Please save your protests Major;' Churchill drawled, 'we have it on good authority that the Germans are very close to hitting us with their own biological or chemical weapons. And we cannot allow them to do that, can we?'

'We must hit them first Major, don't you agree?'

The doctor slowly nodded, it seems he had no alternative but to comply with the Prime Minister's demand.

'Everything is prepared, there is a small island called Gruinard, off the coast of Scotland that will be the test area. All that's left on the island now are few hundred head of sheep; they will be our test victims.' Churchill pulled out an envelope from his briefcase. 'Here are your orders; I would remind you Major that time is of the essence.'

CHAPTER TEN

Northwest coast of Scotland

Early July 1942.

Three camouflaged caravans forming mobile laboratories together
with accommodation units and a number of army vehicles, were

gathered in a field on the headland due east of and the nearest piece of the Scottish mainland to the island of Gruinard. The island was the designated 'Test Area' for the Anthrax biological weapon.

A Wellington bomber over flew the island at height, as it passed a small white burst could just be discerned at about three hundred feet above ground level.

Six Scientists and a unit from the Royal Army Service Corps were all clad in rubber protective suits. The leader, Major Miles-Johnson was standing as close as possible to the waters edge, looking through the lens of a powerful telescope set on a tripod. He was observing and surveying the devastation occurring on the island about one mile across the Gruinard bay. Without lifting his rubber covered head and taking his goggle protected eyes away from the telescopes lens, he began to describe the scene to the other five Scientists that were grouped behind him. His voice was somewhat distorted, having been projected through the respirator tube attached to mouth piece of the head covering.

'Hardly an hour since the drop and I can clearly see the effects it's having on the flock on this side of the island. All of the fifty are rocking unsteadily; some have fallen and are struggling to get up.' He paused to refocus the telescope, clearly struggling to achieve clarity through the goggles to the lens. 'We've got to check the flocks on the other side of the Island.'

'The Marines have a boat ready and waiting sir.' One of the scientists said.

'Has there been any contamination on the mainland?'

'Nothing reported so far, sir.'

'Good.' He let his eyes come away from the telescope and straightened, turning to face the group. 'John and James come in the boat with me, the rest of you can start collecting soil and sea samples from around the bay, you all know what's required. Let's go.'

Hamish McIntyre, the former Shepherd of those parts, that is before the army had moved him and his flock to another valley, made his way up a crag to the crest which overlooked his former croft and Gruinard bay. He didn't realise that by taking such an overland route that he had inadvertently avoided the army check points and patrols. He was more concerned about one of his dogs, Jess, who had gone missing. Hamish had thought she may have headed back to the croft and so he had taken the moorland track, up and over the crag to the old place to look for her. As he straightened at the crest, his mouth dropped open and out of shock, he instinctively threw himself behind a boulder. Now bewildered his head slowly appeared over the rock to survey the scene of these thing's moving around the bay. *They must be Germans.* He thought, for he had no idea what a German should look like. *'Aye Germans alright,'* he said to himself, 'we're being invaded.' All thoughts of Jess gone from his mind now, and with some degree of panic he turned and ran down the crag as fast as he could. He tumbled head over heels several times in the attempt, but each time his legs continued their momentum engaging with the land as they came down.

It was some time later an exhausted Hamish stumbled into the post office come general store in Little Gruinard, about two miles south of the beach at Badluachrach. He stood for a moment in the doorway, bent double hands on his knees.

'Whatever is the matter Hamish,' Mrs. McKenna the proprietor asked.

He straightened slowly. 'I fear we're being invaded Mrs. McKenna, aye for it is I'm sure the Germans that I've just seen landing on yonder beach.' At that Mrs. McKenna being the owner of the only telephone in the area, decided the best thing to do was to call the newspaper office at Inverness, as that was the only number of any significance she had.

The Scottish Herald first printed the story and within days of its start, the tests on Gruinard Island became public knowledge, to a degree that is, very few would ever know that it was a hybrid Anthrax stain that was being tested. Nevertheless the cry of outrage was so strong that the test had to be abandoned, the Island was ringed with barbed wire and notices warning of the danger, should one set foot upon the place.

CHAPTER ELEVEN

After a long moment of silence, Ian reached over and switched off the tape. The click was enough to encourage one of the doctor's eyes to open and stare in his direction. Then with a grunt it closed again and the good doctor started to talk again, at which point Ian switched the tape back on.

'It took nearly fifty years, two thousand tons of seawater and close to three hundred tons of formaldehyde you know. Before the Island could be declared safe.'

'And was that the end of your work?' Ian said trying to probe for anything in connection with Haverton Hill and ICI Billingham.

The doctor didn't open his eyes, but another smile formed. 'For then it was, the Germans along with most everybody else declared their condemnation of such weapons, so Churchill felt bound to comply with the consensus of opinion and cancelled our research.'

The smile on the doctors face broadened to such an extent, Ian felt sure the lips would snap at any moment. 'Thank goodness the Americans didn't hold the same views.'

'The Americans?' Ian said enquiringly, but realised that he'd stopped the flow of the old mans story, again, when a confused look appeared on the old mans face. 'I'm sorry, please continue.'

It was clear that the old man needed to tell the story in his own way, the same way as it had replayed in his mind so many times over the years, and his head dropped again as he took another moment to compose himself.

'At the end of the war in 1945 our research into Biological and Chemical warfare was abandoned altogether, Porton Down reverted back to a government facility looking into all manner of things from smoking to tablet tests and waste disposal. Then in 1951 Mr. Churchill became Prime Minister again.' The doctor brought his head upright; with a finger he pushed the thin wired spectacles back up the bridge of his nose. 'Shall we have another cup of tea?' He said, but before Ian could respond, the doctor yelled. 'Nursey, more tea!' Ian was more intent on hearing the story than drinking more tea, so he prompted the doctor to continue.

'You were telling me that Churchill was Prime Minister again, why was that significant?'

'Because soon after he had been re-elected, he made another impromptu visit to Porton Down, this time he had a secret service guy with him. The upshot was that I should restart my Biological and Chemical agent research, in complete secrecy. Churchill himself would arrange funding and all progress reports should be for his eyes only. - By the end of 1954, I had found the breakthrough I'd been looking for.'

At that moment the door from the house into the conservatory, opened and the nurse came in. 'Time for your check,' as she lifted his wrist and at the same time deftly stuck a thermometer under his tongue.

'Never mind that, we want tea,' he attempted say as he twitched and shrugged in a vain attempt to free his arm.

'In a minute,' she said while still counting to herself, and then she whipped out the thermometer and checked it. 'Fine,' she declared, picked up the tray and disappeared back into the house.

'So in 1954 you completed your research?' The old man nodded and Ian got ahead of himself. 'Was that when you went to Haverton Hill?'

The doctor visibly flinched. 'Haverton Hill! What do you know about Haverton Hill?' His voice was so loud that the nurse came back into the room.

'Is everything alright?' She asked. The doctor settled down and waved his hand at her. 'Where's our tea, eh?'

'Just coming.' She turned and gave Ian a hard look. 'You mustn't tire him or I shall have to ask you to leave.'

Ian nodded. 'Sorry.' But she was already on her way out of the room. Ian hadn't expected the old man to react in that way, and was a little taken aback; however the nurse's intervention proved timely, giving him a chance to concoct some sort of response.

Hinting at a father son relationship, Ian responded. 'Why sir, I believed you made mention of Haverton Hill to me some time ago, it must have stuck in my mind.'

The doctor sat forward and gave Ian a long hard stare. 'Did I Henry?' His eyebrows wrinkled and his bespectacled eyes narrowed. 'Hum well I suppose I must have.' Then he relaxed back into the wheelchair closing his eyes again and letting his head go back. 'Fancy me forgetting that, hum.' At that point the nurse returned with the tea.

They drank their tea in relative silence, that is except for the rattle of the cup to saucer in unsteady shaking hands and the slurp made as those thin lips sucked in the liquid. Rather shakily the old man leaned forward almost dropping the crockery onto the coffee table.

'Nursey! A bottle.' Ian tried to be nonchalant and ignore the situation, choosing to fiddle with the recorder and check the tape, while the nurse placed the bottle under the tartan blanket ensuring the doctor's penis was inserted into the neck of the vessel. She stood there until the tinkle of the urine had stopped.

'Finished, have we.' She said, as she removed the bottle and blotted him with a tissue.

'I want to go outside, Henry take me down to the river, its years since I've seen it.' Ian was about to correct him, but then thought. *What the hell.*

'Yes sir, anything you desire.'

Ian again chose to stand behind the wheelchair, while they both stared trance like into the babbling water. The recorder was in his hand, poised ready should the old man decide to continue the conversation, but after sometime Ian thought it would be prudent to proffer a prompt. 'You were telling me sir, about the completion of your research back in 1954.'

The old man slowly emerged from his trance. 'Was I?'
'Yes sir.'
'1954 eh, hum, what was I saying?'
'You were telling me about your research into Biological and Chemical weapons during and after the war.'

'Was I? That's top secret information, can't tell you that.'

'Its okay sir, the new legislation is allowing more openness so that the work and effort made by people like you can be appreciated.'
It was a while before the doctor decided to talk again, strangely he picked up the conversation from where it had been left in the house.

'Now where was I, ah yes, 1954, I'd solved it,'
'Solved what sir?'
'The chemical formulae for the mutation reaction to the biological hybrid bacteria.'
'Pardon?'
The old man gave out a little 'tut tut' and shook his head.
He's in his element. Ian thought. *Probably waited years for this opportunity to brag about his achievements and I'm going to get the lot, now how lucky is that.*

'It's like this,' the old man began. 'What good is a weapon that not only kills your foe but your friends as well? What good is a conquest if you have wait fifty years before it can be claimed?' He didn't wait for Ian to respond. 'I'll tell you, no bloody good at all.' The old man held the moment, just as he'd practised this oration many times in his head. 'But,' he said, 'what if after just a few days, this weapon killed itself? Just think of the scenario, you fly over your enemy's city and release a few drops of this weapon at the centre. In a day or so every living thing within that city would be dead or dying and in a few more days the weapon itself would be dead. Your armies could march unopposed into that city and find the infrastructure still intact, even the water would be drinkable.'

Ian could not contain himself any longer. 'That's absolutely disgusting, all those innocent people, all of the corpses, for what, another's dominance.' Ian felt sick at the thought. 'How one could conceive a scheme of such wickedness defies belief.'

The old man was clearly not impressed by Ian's reaction. This was not the accolade he had dreamed of.

'Don't preach to me about the horrors of war young man, I have lived through those times, you have not. The human race through all of time has suffered mans inhumanity to man, it will not change. Oh yes we all hope for peace, but we must also be realistic and accept the fact that somewhere in the world there will always be conflict, unfortunately that is, I'm afraid to say, human nature.' Ian nodded, he didn't particularly agree with the old mans views, but he realised antagonising him would be counter productive.

'I take your point sir.' He said. 'Please continue.'

For a moment the old man seemed reluctant to go on, he had closed his eyes and laid his head back into his pillow, again. Thankfully from Ian's point of view the doctor's ego within the old mans head needed to express this long held secret. Quietly out of the corner of his mouth he uttered. 'If the need should ever arise for a weapon such as mine, better that than the devastation and destruction of an atom bomb and better still than a long protracted conflict with mass destruction and deaths on both sides.' Ian wanted to argue but held his tongue, opting for an agreeing nod instead. No matter the old man didn't see him, he was within himself living the past and Ian would just have to wait until he was ready to talk again.

After about fifteen minutes of silence, except for the bird song and the water flowing that is, Ian decided to push the wheelchair back into the conservatory, perhaps the movement would wake him. After a further ten minutes sitting in silence, Ian got to his feet and headed towards the door, but just before he got there, the crafty old bugger began to talk.

'I concocted a chemical'

'A chemical?' Ian enquired, as he returned to sit opposite the old man in the wheelchair and switched on the recorder.

'A chemical cocktail derived from a number of elements. It took years to find a combination that would do the job.'

'Job sir?'

'Haven't you been listening?' The old man snapped back, again Ian had to remind himself, to keep his mouth shut.

'Ingenious of me really, I discovered a number of chemicals that would react adversely with the hybrid Anthrax. Breaking down each of their molecular structures, I removed and divided the cells selecting the most reactive and toxic particles. I used the same technique as I had on the bacterial cells. I isolated a

number of cells from a number of basic chemicals, and then I experimented combining the different cells into one nucleus until I found the reaction I was looking for. I called it Sincyathatate Nine.' The old man nodded for a moment and then stared blankly at the glass wall behind Ian.

'Another silent moment.' Ian said to himself. He decided bite his tongue and wait as long as it takes. He waited patiently for what seemed an age, but the old man's attention was fixed somewhere beyond the realms of the conservatory walls. *Sod it, got to say something to get him back on track.*

'Excuse me sir, but wouldn't this Sin- what's its name, be just toxic as the Anthrax?'

'Sincyathatate.' He responded immediately. 'Oh indeed yes, by itself it would kill quicker than and just as efficiently as the hybrid Anthrax, but unlike the bacteria the chemical cells don't reproduce.'

'Sorry sir, but I don't quite see the advantage.'

'Probably because you do not perceive the way of implementation and the unique nature of this chemical.' The old man hesitated probably to emphasize the point.

'Perhaps I should explain in simplistic terms.' He said.

'First select a target, say a city the size of Birmingham. Then you disperse a vial, say 100ml of the hybrid Anthrax over the centre, wait a week or so and then aerial spay the whole area with Sincyathatate. Within a few days the area would be clear. You see the chemical and the bacteria molecules are magnetically drawn to each other, the cells lock together in an embrace that neutralises both.'

'What if this sprayed Sin-stuff doesn't catch all of the Anthrax?'

'Sincyathatate.- It's highly likely that it won't, but the area would be sufficiently clear for the clean up operation to commence, any isolated pockets of Anthrax still intact could be dealt with using hand held sprays of the Sincyathatate Nine.'

'Hum, I see, very clever sir, but why the nine?'

'Simple, I used nine elements including the hydrogen gasses to formulate Sincyathatate.'

Ian sensed he was now getting close to the Haverton Hill issue, so he prompted the old man again. 'Nine elements broken down and then combined into one soup mix, must have been one hell of process, how on earth could production on such a large scale be achieved?'

The old man laughed. 'You do have a way of putting things Henry, always had.' It was time again for the doctor to dig into his memory bank. 'Production, y-e-s, as I recall it was a bit of a headache, but unbeknown to me at that time, there was a whole bunch of people following my progress and considering just that problem.'

'I thought your work was secret, for Churchill's eyes only.'

'So did I.' He smiled as he remembered the scenario. 'Churchill was ousted in 55, and I was quite concerned at the time, what would happen to my project, and where was I going to find the funding to continue. Strangely the cheques kept coming, nothing changed, the instructions came as always, by courier and my report updates were collected at the same time. It was not until later year that I discovered who my real benefactor was.

CHAPTER TWELVE

Ian took a deep breath and settled back in preparation for another long drawn out saga. *If only he would get to the Haverton Hill bit.* He thought, but the old man had a story to tell and tell it he would in his own way in his own time.

'Apparently,' the old man began, 'at that time the country was in a bit of mess financially, the government had made several attempts to extract money from the USA. Without much success, I gather, but I'd never given the matter much thought. That was until I received the invitation.'

'Invitation sir, from whom?' Ian put in.

'From the Prime Minister Anthony Eden, a car would be sent to collect me, all very hush hush.'

'It was to be a secret meeting?' Ian said, not sure of the old mans phrasing.

The old man nodded. 'My life was one big secret, it drove your mother wild,' he tittered like a naughty boy, 'she never knew what I was doing or when I'd be home, if at all.' Then his expression change instantly, much more serious now he continued. 'I missed an awful lot of your growing up.' Tears welled up in his eyes, without a word, Ian passed him a tissue. With shaking hands he pushed up his spectacles and dabbed at the liquid, then with a sniff, he continued the story.

'I wasn't quite sure where I was taken, but I think it may have been some secret service place. Whatever, in this office waiting for me was, the PM Anthony Eden, the Chancellor Rab Butler, err - the Minister for Defence Harold MacMillan, one man I took to be a Civil Servant and two others whom I took to be Secret Service.'

'Gentlemen allow me to introduce our guest, Dr Miles-Johnson.' The Prime Minister said. Discernable nods and mumbled hellos ensued from the bodies around the table, but the introductions were only one way.

'I suppose you are wondering why you're here.' The PM said.

'The thought had crossed my mind sir.'

'To be quite frank, I'm not really sure myself. Rab would you like to put the doctor in the picture?'

The Chancellor gave a little cough picked up and rustled a sheet of paper, which he didn't read from, but used it as a distraction in an attempt to disguise, what I later came to understand as a little embarrassment.

'Apparently Dr Miles-Johnson we, that is, the Cabinet Office, have recently been informed of an arrangement that you had with our secret service.' He glanced towards the two men at one end of the table. 'And the former Prime Minister, Mr. Churchill.' He looked at the paper as if assessing its content, before continuing. 'Also, it would appear that the Americans are privy to this arrangement. We,-' he gave out another clear the throat type cough, '- are not. Would you care to enlighten us?'

'With all due respect sir, the arrangement, as you call it, was between Mr. Churchill and me, surely he or your secret service agents should be advising you on the matter.'

'Quite so, quite so,' the Prime Minister put in, 'but things are not as clear cut as one would envisage. You see the situation Doctor, as we know it, is that MI5 passed all reports, or so they say, unopened to the CIA. Mr. Churchill is presently indisposed and the Americans are telling us all will be revealed in due course.'

'Excuse me sir, but isn't that your answer?'

'Yes Doctor I suppose it is, but it's also the reason you're here.'

The Chancellor spoke again. 'You may or may not be aware Doctor, that we have been pursuing the Americans for their help, financially. They have finally agreed, on condition,' he waved the paper, 'that you, Dr Jeremy Miles-Johnson accompany our delegation to Washington tomorrow.'

Washington USA

Following the formalities at the airport, Rab Butler together with an entourage of civil servants were taken by limousine to the Capital Building, first for a meeting with John Foster Dulles

Secretary of State and George Mason Humphreys Secretary of the Treasury and then to present Britain's case to a Congress select committee. The limousine carrying the Minister for Defence Harold MacMillan and the Doctor, took them directly to the White House.

As they entered a large room, a familiar figure bounded towards them hand extended.

'Harold, good of you to come.' He said as he politely shook MacMillan's hand.

'Y-e-s, er, didn't expect to.'- But before MacMillan could explain his surprise at being there, the host had turned to greet the doctor.

'Doctor Miles-Johnson, it's been a long time, glad you could make it.' He grasped the doctor's hand and shook it vigorously.

'President Eisenhower. A very long time indeed, I'm pleased to meet you again sir.'

'Come over here son, meet the team.' The President put an arm over the doctors shoulder and steered him towards a large mahogany table in the centre of the room, MacMillan looking rather bemused tagged along. Seated around the table were a number of men, who stood in turn and shook their hands as they were introduced.

'This is my Vice President Richard Nixon, Secretary for Defence Neil McElroy, your opposite number Harold.' Eisenhower said over his shoulder.

'Yes I've had occasion to talk with Neil, pleased to meet you in the flesh.' MacMillan said, as they shook hands.

The President continued the introductions, 'Chief of Staff Henry Peterson, Admiral John Collingwood, General Paul Thurrock.' They moved on around the table, 'our Deputy Director CIA Kermit Roosevelt, and our Consultant Design Engineer Douglas Kinnelly. Doctor you sit here next to Doug and Harold this is your chair, next to me.'

Everyone settled down, a little squeaking of chairs, one or two coughs and paper rustling, before the President spoke.

'I suppose I'd better kick this thing off, aside from our guests, I think we all know why we're here and I don't doubt you have a fair idea Doctor.' The President tapped a stack of papers, which the doctor immediately recognised as transcripts of his reports and he nodded his head in affirmation.

'I do now, Mr. President, but I'm perplexed, to say the least.'

MacMillan shook his head. 'Quite frankly sir, I do not have a clue.' There were unsure mutterings from some of those seated around the table; clearly not every one was in the picture. The President raised a hand, requesting silence. 'Okay, for the benefit of our English friends and those among us who are not fully informed, I shall explain.'

Eisenhower stood and began to pace the room as he commenced his oration. 'During 1942 I, along with Winston Churchill and the

Doctor here,' Eisenhower placed a hand on the doctor's shoulder, conducted a secret test of a biological weapon. Unfortunately news of this test got out before it was complete and we faced world wide condemnation, not least because at that time we had no way to neutralise the bacteria.' Again he motioned toward the doctor. 'No fault of the doctors, Winston and I were intent on shortening the war at any cost and rushed the test through. The sceptics had their way and most of the world, excluding the USA, banned the use of such weapons. All research was shelved, and we got back to the business of fighting a war by conventional means, another three years and thousands of lives later, before it was over.' The President hesitated for a moments thought, which allowed MacMillan to interject.

'Excuse me Mr. President, but why didn't America continue the research, or did they?'

'No Harold we didn't, in 1942 America was to busy playing catch up, fighting a war on two fronts and besides back then, we didn't have a Dr Jeremy Miles-Johnson or anyone like him. At the end of the war in 45, Churchill and I wanted to start the ball rolling again, but it turned out that Atlee was one of the sceptics and would not tolerate any talk of Biological and Chemical weapons research. Truman on the other hand had committed the budget to H bomb research and was still going through the motions of defending the atom bomb use against Japan. When Winston became Prime Minister again in 51, he and I got together and decided to restart the research, this time in complete secrecy; the US would provide the funding.'

'How in the hell did you manage that?' Nixon put in.

Eisenhower held up a hand. 'Now's not the time Richard.'

'So you provided the funds, it all becomes clear now.' The doctor said.

Eisenhower returned to his seat and again tapped the pile of reports. 'So gentlemen as of today the doctor's research is complete, we have the initial biological bacteria weapon from forty-two and now a means of neutralising it, a highly complex chemical called 'Sincyathatate Nine'.'

General Paul Thurrock felt it was time to have a say in the proceedings. 'Mr. President, I would like to discuss the capabilities and the deployment of these Biological and Chemical weapons.'

'This is not the venue General, we can sort these matters later, no need to burden our guests with such things.'

The President turned to the doctor and Douglas Kinnelly. 'We want you to start producing Sincyathatate right away. Doug has studied your reports and figured out most of what you'll need, in terms of processing vessels; you two can put your heads together and sort out the rest of the details.'

'I take it Mr. President that you have established the volume of Sincyathatate you want and calculated the size of the production facility needed?'

'Yes doctor, Doug's looked into all of those aspects,' Doug nodded in affirmation. 'We'll build everything you need here in the States and ship it to England,' Doug said.

'Why England?' MacMillan exclaimed.

'Because Harold,' the President put in, 'there's a specific site in the UK, recommended in the doctors report and for reasons of secrecy which I'm not prepared to go into right now, England is the most suitable place....Besides, it's part of the deal'

'What deal would that be?' MacMillan queried.

'Let's just say Harold, your Mr. Butler and the Congress committee on Capital Hill, are just going through the motions at the moment. A substantial loan is already approved, subject of course to this facility being built in England.'

'Hum, I see, it would seem that we have little choice but to comply. Where in England did the good doctor suggest?'

Dr Jeremy Miles-Johnson gave out a little cough to get their attention before he spoke, at the same time Douglas Kinnelly started to remove the rubber bands from a large roll of paper.

'The site I thought would be most suitable is in Northeast England, an Imperial Chemical Industries facility at a place called Billingham.'

At that Doug unrolled the paper and spread it on the table. 'This is an aerial photograph of the site,' everybody in the room stood and gathered round for a better look.

'What's so special about this Billingham site?' Richard Nixon asked the doctor.

'Well sir, it's the only place in Britton where I can source most of the nine elements used in Sincyathatate.'

'And what would those be?' Kermit Roosevelt interrupted. The doctor had no intention of revealing the full components of his chemical compound, so he casually fobbed off the reply, 'Well, the likes of Ammonia, Cyanide, Hydrogen gasses and various Nitrates.' Kermit nodded as if he understood the relevance, but he clearly hadn't a clue. While the doctor was talking, Douglas had taken a highlight pen and began to mark out the proposed site on the enlarged photograph. 'This area here on the southeast corner of the site is large enough for our purposes, it's secluded from the other ICI plants and would offer reasonable security, and just here,' he scrawled a line on the photograph, ' we can put in a rail spur from the main rail line, that would enable us to deliver most of the equipment direct onto the site and no doubt use it to extract the product'

Henry Peterson turned his head in the Presidents direction and said. 'Them there houses sure do look pretty damn close to the site, just on the other side of the railway embankment.' He raised an enquiring eyebrow. 'Do you think they'll be safe?'

'Yeah they do seem damn close,' the President agreed. 'What is that place Doug?'

'I believe it's a small town called Haverton Hill.' Douglas Kinnelly responded.

'Any problems with proximity, for those Haverton Hill folk, Doctor?'

'I, - I really can't say Mr. President, it's an aspect of the process that I haven't yet considered. The filtration and distillation processes will vent waste elements from time to time, so there will be some fallout undoubtedly over the town, dependant upon wind direction. However I cannot envisage this fallout, at the worst, being more than just of low toxicity and no more than a mild irritant to the skin.'

'Mild, how mild?'

'I would consider that some of the vented waste product may cause a rash and a mild burning sensation. If and only if,' the doctor attempted to play down the risks, 'there was direct contact.'

'And the long term effects, should someone get caught?'

'Unlikely to be lasting.'

'Hum-m,' the President massaged his chin thoughtfully, and then pulled a cigarette from a packet, lit up and paced the floor for a few moments. He stopped and pointed the two fingers that clamped the smoking cigarette, at the doctor. 'You sure Doc?'

'As sure as I can be, at this juncture.'

'Well I guess we have no choice but to suck it and see, if any problems do develop, we'll just have to move the folk out of there.' He took a long drag on the cigarette and blew out forcibly as if to dispel the thought of any problems out of mind, along with the smoke. He wandered back to the table and sat down. 'Please remember gentlemen,' he said in a low and solemn tone, 'this operation is still top secret. I hope I can count on each of you to keep it that way.'

At that moment the CIA Deputy Director slipped a hand inside his pocket and switched off a miniature recording device.

CHAPTER THIRTEEN

'And were there any ill effects to the folks of Haverton Hill?' Ian asked.

The old man took time to return his mind from the past, but after a few moments he continued. 'To tell the truth we never completed a long term appraisal of the fallout effects over Haverton Hill. Samples analysed from catchments dotted about the town, indicated fairly high levels of contaminates, and at one or two spots these were toxic. But I must point out that other ICI plants were pushing out a huge variety of contaminates into the air over Haverton Hill....Part of the problem, I suppose.'

'Problem, sir?' Ian instantly put in. The old man's chin dropped to his chest, his speech was hesitant and Ian realised that this was a part of the story that the doctor was not keen to relate.

'Ahum......W-e-l-l, for some unknown reason, I received an order direct from Eisenhower.'

'And?'

'I was to shut the plant down with immediate affect, I was told a team would be sent to dismantle and dispose of the whole facility. Nothing was to be left to give any clue that there was ever a Chemical plant there.' The old man paused, pursed his thin lips and teardrops filled the bottom rim of his spectacles. 'Do you realise,' he said, 'just how complicated a shut down procedure can be?' Ian just shook his head; he knew the doctor was not expecting him to respond. 'The number of process's in various stages of production, I could not conceive the cocktail that would be produced. Nor could I perceive of a way to dispose of the chemicals, safely.' He added almost as an after thought. He paused again for another long moment and Ian thought he was about to clam up. But the old man needed to complete the story no matter how painful the telling and it was

painful to him, Ian could see that in his face. 'It occurred during the night, I was not on duty, I didn't know.'

'What did?'

'The explosion.'

'Explosion!'

'That night there was a storm, the pressure override on the Reactor vessel was struck by lightening, no problem under normal circumstance, but cooling waters had already been turned off as part of the 'shut down' process.'

'Reactor! You mean in the likes of 'Nuclear'?'

The old man nodded. 'To a lesser degree, radiation was a process I used to breakdown certain chemical elements.'

'A Nuclear explosion?'

The old man shakily withdrew a hand from under the blanket and waved it floppily in Ian's direction. 'Not that bad,....apparently. The noise was taken as thunder and the column of debris was quickly dispersed by pouring rain.'

'What kind of debris?'

'Asbestos mainly, from the vessels lagging and extracts of various fractured chemical lines that I was unable to determine.'

'All falling on Haverton Hill?'

The old man nodded. 'Most of it, I gather.' And then he fell silent again. After a long five minutes, Ian decided that there was more to this than the old man was letting on. So he gave him a little push.

'What did you do Doctor, when you learned of this disaster?'

'I arranged a sealing operation and a clean up. What else could I do?'

'No- I mean with regards to the people living in Haverton Hill.'

'I made an assessment as to the likely content of the chemical cloud.'

'And?' Ian prompted.

Again he hesitated. 'I ....I informed the Americans that it was highly likely that 'fallout' from cloud of poisonous gas, would have a detrimental affect on the residents of Haverton Hill.'

At last. Ian mumbled. 'And what did they say?'

'To me, not a lot, but I was aware, that it was decided to demolish the place. At that time Billingham Council were in the process of building new houses to cope with the labour influx for the expanding ICI. A Government donation ensured the number of dwellings being built would be increased to cater for the citizens of

Haverton Hill. It was sometime later in 1960, I think, or was it 61. - I'm not sure,' the old man hesitated trying to relate a memory to a date, he couldn't, 'it must have been about then when they started to ship them out. About the same time as the demolishment of the plant was complete. Apparently it took about ten years to complete, although I can't be sure. As far as I know once the people had been accommodated their houses were bulldozed to cover up the contamination, although by that time I was long gone.'

'Long gone, sir?'

'Yes long gone,' the old man sucked his thin lips back into his cheeks, 'no reason for me to be around. I'd produced all the Sincyathatate the Americans wanted; the plant had completely gone, never really existed, officially.'

'That must have been plant number six,' Ian said almost without thinking.

'Number six! What on earth are you talking about?'

Ian just stared back at the old man as he realised that he'd just dug himself a hole from which he could see no way out. The old man stared back, a hard look on his face and silence once again prevailed. Suddenly the old mans face lightened. 'Ah h, of course.' He said, throwing his rather shaky hands in the air. 'I see what you mean.'

Thank goodness. Ian thought. *I'm glad you see what I mean doc, personally I haven't a clue.*

'You see the plant in Billingham ICI was, S9, S for Sincyathatate and Nine for the nine elements. I now recall that the American Engineering and layout drawings, expressed the nine in Roman numerals, hence S-IX.'

The old man, once great doctor of Bio-Genetics and Molecular Synthesis, closed his eyes and visibly relaxed, it seemed that the burden of those long kept secrets were now removed from his mind in the telling.

Ian got up slowly and headed for the door, not to disturb or encumber the old man any more, he left the Waterside residence without a goodbye or a thank you, but somehow he felt the old man would understand.

ENLIGHTENMENT
CHAPTER FOURTEEN

Billingham 2008

Colin reached over and switched off the recorder, blowing out as he eased himself back into his seat. 'Wow.....Well I guess that answers a few question.'

They were at Phillip's house sat around the coffee table, Colin with his wife Miriam, Jack, Phillip and Michelle.

Guess it does.' Phillip said. 'As I understand it, Haverton Hill was subject to a 'fallout' of irradiated particles, mainly asbestos, combined with an unknown concoction of chemicals, from this and more than likely every other plant in Billingham ICI.'

'That's the way I see it.'

'I agree.' Jack put in and there were affirmative nods from the others.

'Not forgetting that my father was right, this concoction what ever it is lays dormant for years, then suddenly grows so rapidly that it kills its host.'

'I'm not disagreeing with you Michelle, but unfortunately that's only supposition, we have no way of proving it. That is, unless there is another fatality we can have examined before it's cremated.' Colin added.

'And my dear, if Michelle is right then you, Phillip and Jack could be at risk.' The three men contemplated for a moment on Miriam's comment.

'Probably not.' Michelle said. 'None of you lived on the diagonal line my father defined.'

'That's true.' Jack said, unable to hide the relief in his voice.

'If nothing else, we now know why someone is prepared to kill to keep this secret, the problem is, how do we prevent it?' Colin said.

'And save Ian.' Michelle put in.

'Come on now, why should anyone go to such lengths as to kill someone just to keep a fifty year old incident covered up, it doesn't make sense.' Phillip put in.

'Yeah I'm with you Phil, there's got to be more to it.' Jack added.

'Could be massive compensation to payouts. Doesn't take much imagination to know what'll happen round here when the story becomes public knowledge. The compo claims would come in thick and fast, along with claims solicitors jumping on the band wagon.'

'Got to be more to it Col, bear in mind f-i-f-t-y years,' Phillip emphasized the fifty to get his point across, 'nobodies going to be left to make significant compensation payments a problem worth killing for.'

'Hum-m, perhaps your right.'

'There's got to be something else.'

'I agree, but what concerns me right now is, what happened to the Anthrax and the Sincyathatate produced.....And what happened in 60 to make the Yanks pull the plug? Maybe there's something they don't want the world to know about these weapons and that's the secret they're prepared to kill to keep.'

'Good point Jack; - I wonder what really did happen to those weapons and is that the reason for the cover up.'

'Surely it's the toxic fungus that killed my folks they don't want discovered.'

'Yes Michelle, maybe it's all those things,' Colin said, 'but whatever it is, knowing isn't going to help get the killer off Ian's back.'

'No it isn't,' Michelle agreed, 'the only thing we can do is in fact what Ian's suggested, that we send copies of this tape to the media; bring the whole thing out in the open. Unless someone can think of something better.' Michelle looked at the others in turn, they were silent.

'Then we should do it.' Miriam broke the silence.

'Yeah, let's tell the world.' Colin declared.

PART THREE
OPERATION JERICHO
CHAPTER FIFTEEN

October 1959

The Whitehouse

Douglas Kinnelly quickened his step in an attempt to keep up with the young Marine escorting him along the corridors in the Whitehouse basements. Their stopped outside a familiar door, the Marine knocked and immediately pushed it open and ushered Douglas in.

'Ah Douglas, come in. You know everyone, don't you?' Eisenhower quizzed.

Douglas looked around the table and nodded towards the six men seated around the table. Vice President Richard Nixon, Secretary for Defence Neil McElroy, Chief of Staff Henry Peterson, Admiral John Collingwood, General Paul Thurrock and the Deputy Director CIA Kermit Roosevelt.

'Yes sir.'

Douglas was not invited to sit, so he stood and waited for
Eisenhower's directive, which never transpired. 'Er Douglas,'
Eisenhower prompted, 'would you please advise us on the current
state of Sincyathatate?'

'Yes sir, I received a communiqué just this morning from the doctor.
He is forecasting that by the end of the month 40,000 pods would be
ready for shipment.'

Eisenhower turned to face the others. 'What do you think Paul?'

'Should be enough, based on the doctors original calculation, but we
can't be sure how much we'll need, if any at all.'

'I tend to agree with the General.' Admiral Collingwood chirped in.
'It's not as if we're planning to move in.'

'No it's not, but can we risk not having a fallback?' Henry Peterson
asked.

'If we don't Henry ole boy and the Ruskies find out, then it's WW3
and we'll get toasted.'

'Enough, it's decided.' Eisenhower declared and swung around in
his seat to face Douglas, who was standing like a lemon in the centre
of the room. 'Douglas I want you to arrange for these pods to be put
onboard a Freighter, have the ship sail across to Holland and have it
stand at anchor outside of Amsterdam. I also want you to send a
team of Engineers to England, with the purpose of shutting down
and demolishing of the plant in its entirety.' Douglas made an

attempt to protest, but was cut off, as Eisenhower continued with the instruction.

'B-u-t.'

'Furthermore and most importantly Douglas, the work must be compete by April next year. Not a trace is to be left, you understand, to say that such a plant ever existed. You may leave us now, thanks for your time son.'

'At that, a somewhat perplexed Douglas Kinnelly left the Whitehouse basement room.

23rd December 1959

Eisenhower paced the floor of the Oval office, one hand anxiously massaged his chin, and the other held a telegram from Miles-Johnson.

EXPLOSION. REACTOR. DAMAGE MINIMAL. CONTAINED. FEAR DEBRIS COLUMN IS RADIOACTIVE AND CHEMICALLY CHARGED. CLOUD COLUMN FALLOUT ON HAVERTON HILL IS NO DOUBT TOXIC.

MILES-JOHNSON.

The knock on the door snapped his mind back. 'Come.' He shouted and almost immediately Ed Dawson a Whitehouse aide walked in carrying an envelope file.

'I have some papers for you to sign sir.'

'Ah, thanks Ed, leave them on the desk if you will.'

Ed dropped the file on the desk and headed back to the door. 'Er - Ed,' he called out before Dawson had managed to get out of the door. 'Ed do I recall that you are a Yale graduate?'

'Sometime ago, sir.'

'Know anything about chemistry?'

'Did a bit of lab work during one semester, but I actually majored in Law.'

'Hum, that'll do, how do you fancy an overseas posting?'

Ed shrugged his shoulders. 'Never really thought about it sir, but I've no objection.'

'That's sorted then, here's the deal.' Eisenhower passed the telegram to Ed. 'We have a facility, nothing for you to be concerned about, but it looks like we've had a bit of an accident, an explosion.'

'I see sir.'

Eisenhower leaned over Ed's shoulder and tapped the telegram with his forefinger. 'This facility's in England near a place called Haverton Hill in the Northeast.' Ed stared blankly at the paper he was holding and for whatever reason and without much forethought, he found himself saying. 'Yes sir, anything I can do to help.'

'I want someone I can trust to get over there and assess the situation, you know take soil samples and whatever. All top secret you understand.'

'Understood sir, but I'm not really sure what I'd be looking for.'

'Don't worry on that score, I'll get some data from Miles-Johnson; it'll give an indication of what you'll be looking for and how to handle it.'

Ed studied the telegram again. 'And if I find any thing harmful has fallen on this Haverton Hill place?'

'Organise evacuation and demolition of the town, wipe it off the map.'

'And it's residents?'

'I understand that there is a new town under construction a couple of mile away, in a place called Billingham, I'll have someone talk to the British government and arrange re-housing.'

'And if there are casualties?'

'I would expect you to handle any situation with discretion. If needs be we'll set up a trust fund to offset any probable claims. It is imperative that no reference or association is made with the facility, which by the way no longer exists, or indeed the explosion. You understand we have never had a facility there and we know nothing about any explosion, toxic cloud or whatever. Got me.'

'Cover it up, sir.'

Eisenhower nodded. 'No expense spared, Ed.' He said solemnly.

CHAPTER SIXTEEN

January 1991
CIA Headquarters, Langley

The secure telephone on the corner of Deputy Director Jack Rosenthal desk rang. As only a limited number of special people had access to that particular line, Jack, shot bolt upright, more out of surprise than anything else. He immediately began consider the few people who had access and what possible motive they would have for ringing him. He concluded in his own mind that it could be no other than the President, so snapped up the receiver and responded. 'Sir!'

'Jack, it's me, Conlan Powell.'

'Oh, - hi there Chief, what can I do for you?' Jack let himself relax back into his chair.

'Bit of a strange one Jack, I've just had a message from ex President Richard Nixon, something to do with Gulf war.'

'That's your ball game Conlan, the CIA have nothing in there.'

'I know, but Nixon is insisting that you and I should visit him at his home. You are to access and bring with you, a transcript of file number 10772 ref September 7th 1955, Conference Room, White House.'

'Come on Conlan, that's highly irregular, and you know it.'

'Sure I do, but Nixon says the file is relevant to information which he wishes to impart, information he says is of National importance.'

'Are you prepared to authorise this?'

'Sure, why not.'

'Okay, send me the fax, I need to cover my butt.'

'It's on its way.'

'Where do we meet?'

'Take the company's Lear, arrange takeoff for nine in the morning, I'll meet you at LaGuardia about twelve. Oh and make sure you have that file.'

'Just fax over your authorisation and I'll take care of it.'

The Lear touched down at La Guardia and taxied to an isolated hanger on the west side of the apron. In the hanger a black stretched bulletproof Lincoln Continental limousine was waiting. As soon as the steps were in place and the air tight door opened, Jack quickly descended and made his way across the concrete to the Lincoln. The chauffeur alighted and opened the rear door, without hesitation Jack slid into the seat next to Conlan.

'Hi Jack, got the file.' Jack pattered the briefcase which was handcuffed to his left wrist. Always on the left, leaving the right free to pull out, if needs be, his 38, which was slung under his left armpit. Conlan Powell and Jack Rosenthal in the screened off back seat, left LaGuardia airport and headed west towards Park Ridge New Jersey. 'Do you think we ought to take a look at that file Jack?'

'I already did, suppose you'd better take a peek.' With that Jack Rosenthal rotated the numbers on his brief case combination and snapped the locks open, the case was still handcuffed to his left hand so he used his right hand to remove the file marked 'top secret' and passed it to Conlan.

He'd just finished reading it when the limo turned into the drive of a large detached house. 'Looks like we made it.'

Conlan looked up. 'Just about done.' He said as he shuffled the papers back into the file and handed them back to Jack. The limo stopped at the steps that ran to the front door which was surrounded by a Romanesque portico supported on two pillars.

'Quite an entrance, feel like I'm on an MGM set.'

'Always was one for making a statement, I just hope he isn't up to something devious, dragging us way out here.'

Before they had had a chance to ring the door bell, Nixon's wife Patricia opened the door wide and invited them in. 'Good afternoon gentlemen, thank you for coming. 'Can I take your coats?'

'Yes of course,' they both responded, Jack had to remove the cuff from his wrist before he could slip off his overcoat, but immediately clicked the cuff back on again once his overcoat had been removed.

'Thank you,' she said, taking the coats and scarves, 'I'll hang these in the closet, if you would like to head towards the study,' she gestured with her head in the direction of a door at the end of the hall. 'He's been waiting for you, go right in.'

Nixon was sitting in a high backed chair, looking old and pale, not a well man, the years of pressure and scandal had clearly taken their toll. A coffee table was in front of him already set up with three glasses, a decanter of scotch and a soda siphon. He nodded toward the table, 'I know it's early, but what the hell, you'll join me?'

'Sure, why not,' Conlan responded and Jack gave an affirmative nod.

Richard Nixon rather shakily began to pour the drinks and gave each glass the briefest of soda splashes. 'Please sit down gentlemen....Is that the file?' He said, eying the briefcase shackled to Jack's wrist.

'Yes sir it is, but I'm not sure that you still have the authority or the clearance to view top secret data.'

'Relax young man, I already know what's in it, the important thing is do you guys?'

'Read it in the car on the way here sir,' Conlan responded.

'Then you must have a fair idea why I've asked you to come here.'

'Not quite sir, I can't see that our use of such a chemical weapon would be an advantage in the Gulf, the Iraqis are retreating, and we are winning.'

'Yeah and I just can't imagine how the CIA are tied into this,' Jack put in.

Nixon sat back, took a swig of his whiskey and stared at his guests for a long moment before he spoke. 'Mr. Rosenthal, you are here because you could access that file with the minimum of fuss. Mr. Powell you are here because I wanted you to see that file, and I want you to listen to what I am about to tell you. After you have heard what I have to say, I am counting on you as chairman of the joint chiefs, to use your influence and stop our advance into Iraq.'

'That may be easier said than done Mr. Nixon.'

'Well we've made the trip, guess the least we can do is listen to what he's got to say,' Jack chirped in.

Conlan nodded, 'Okay you've got our attention, let's hear it.'

'That file you have in your case is a transcript taken from a recording of one meeting concerning the 'Jericho project.' I can tell you that there were others, none of which were taped or written up, so I reckon I'm probably the only living person who knows what went on at those other meetings.'

'What was the Jericho project and has it got anything to do with this Sincyathatate chemical shit?'

Nixon held up a hand, 'all in good time, you first must understand the full consequence of what we were dealing with.' Nixon gestured towards the briefcase. 'If you've read that file then you must understand that Sincyathatate is a deadly chemical weapon which we had the Brits produce for us. It's in a liquid form pressurised in gas cylinders, when released it's a very fine mist, the smallest droplet touching the skin would induce the blood cells to react against each other and the nerves to go into spasm, in most cases resulting in a slow and painful death. After a day or so the chemical would disperse, evaporate or whatever, leaving just the dead to bury. Quite a weapon to have in ones arsenal, don't you agree?'

'If we have that capability sir, I can assure you we have no intention of using it.'

'Please,' Nixon held up his hand again, 'let me finish.'

'Yeah Conlan, give it a rest man, I think I know where Mr. Nixon's coming from.'

'I think you must have gathered from the transcript,' he nodded at the briefcase, 'Eisenhower makes it clear that Sincyathatate was never designed as the weapon. For a start it required low level delivery, rather like crop spraying and you would need one hell of a lot to make it count..... No the real weapon, hinted at, and also in the transcript, was the biological concoction developed by that English guy Miles-Johnson.'

'Yeah we picked that up.' Jack put in, but Nixon went on just in case they had not grasped the significance.

'It was a hybrid Anthrax, a few drops would wipe out a city and it would keep growing, making it virtually impossible to take over any infected area. That's why he developed the Sincyathatate, to kill the bacterium.'

Conlan and Jack just nodded as the power of such a weapon began to sink in.

'You see Eisenhower had this thing about the Ruskies, he thought the Commies would finish what the Nazis' started, and apparently Churchill was of the same opinion. Back in the fifties the cold war was at its height, the Warsaw pact had amassed a huge army along the Polish and East German borders with more tanks and infantry than the allied nations could ever hope to contend with. Should they have decided then to make the first strike, we all probably would be speaking Russian now.' He paused so that his guests would appreciate the enormity of the situation. 'Gentlemen, world war three was imminent. That's when we devised the 'Jericho project.' This was a plan to strike at the Communist forces without actually going to war, address the balance so to speak,' he gestured with a rocking hand movement as he spoke. 'We believed Jericho would severely hamper any Communist first strike incentive, and their capability, hopefully without them knowing they had been attacked.'

Jack looked both surprised and shocked at this revelation, mumbling under his breath. 'Fucking hell.' He turned to Conlan and noted he had the same surprised expression on his face. Nixon looked directly at Conlan Powell. 'You think laser guided bombs are new, not so. Back then while the Brits were producing the chemicals, our boffins were looking at ways to deliver the Anthrax to an exact spot without being noticed. Umm, by stealth, we learnt a lot about that since....Anyway, I digress. Where was I?' Before either Jack or Conlan could respond, Nixon continued. 'Ah yes, the boffins had come up with this spherical bomb about the size of a baseball which if dropped from altitude would travel down a high frequency projected laser beam to the target and burst open precisely at one hundred feet above ground zero. The contents of the bomb, which only a selected few knew, would be spread over the target area.'

'Garry Powers,' Jack put in. Conlan looked bemused, Nixon just nodded.

'If memory serves, that was a CIA operation,' Jack said.

'Let's not get too far ahead of ourselves. Yeah that's where the stealth bit comes in; we developed the U2 aircraft, not just a spy plane as the world believed, but specifically to deliver this bomb. We thought it would fly so high as to be invisible to radar.' Nixon took a moment to ponder. 'And it probably was, from ground radar that is, but the mission was compromised from the word go. That's when we discovered we had more Russian spies in this country than you could poke a stick at, but that's another story.

The primary mission of the U2's, as you are no doubt aware Jack, was to photograph Russian ICBM sites from high altitude. For such a specialist job the camera equipment needed to be state of the art, with a laser guidance system.' He stopped to let the information register with his guests; raising an eyebrow, he said. 'See where I'm coming from. The Russians weren't that concerned about the spy in the sky; they knew we would never locate all their silos and even if we did, we could do little to combat the situation. The only thing we could do was to tip the balance of who had the most missiles, in our favour. No, they knew alright, according to our sources they watched the first U2 take off from the supposedly secret air base in Pakistan, cross into Soviet air space and allowed it to complete its photograph collecting mission and land in Norway, with only a token gesture to try and stop it. On the other hand, three weeks later Garry Powers was given the task of a similar photographic mission, but that in effect was a decoy. Jericho was initiated and Powers was instructed to deliver a laser guided bomb to a large deployment of Soviet troops amassed on the Polish border. As soon as Powers crossed into their air space they were waiting and opened up with everything they could, in an attempt to stop him dropping that package. Because of the altitude the U2 was operating, Soviet fighters attempts to intercept failed. Which we knew would happen. We also knew the only feasible way to bring it down was to get lucky with a SAM.... And because we knew, the first mission photographed and located all SAM sites along the planned route, Powers for the main part was able to avoid most of them, he got three quarters of the way to the target before they were able to anticipate and get a mobile unit in place, they got lucky with one hit out of a fourteen missile salvo. The rest is history, the Russians recovered part of the plane and the camera, thankfully the missile must have hit the housing where the sphere was housed, nothing of the bomb was found, well as far as we know, it wasn't. America suffered the embarrassment of being caught spying and although America Soviet relations worsened, we were not accused of any aggressive action.'

'Pardon me Mr. Nixon, I find the new slant on the spy plane incident, very intriguing, but hardly relevant to the current situation and does not warrant me making the long journey to hear it.'

'Well I'm intrigued,' Jack said. 'The CIA transcripts made no mention of that scenario.'

'Nor would they Jack, as I said Jericho was known only to a few. Powers for example only knew his target mission just before takeoff, he had no idea what the bomb was or what it contained.'

'Okay, I'm with you so far, but if we were just after reducing the strength of the Ruskies with the Anthrax and had no intention of an invasion follow up, why were the Brits making all that Sincyathatate?'

'Simple Jack, the Sincyathatate was merely a precaution should the Anthrax bacteria get out of hand, don't forget Eisenhower had been there before, he did not plan on going there again.'

'Good to know, very informative, we are now leaving Mr. Nixon, thank you for wasting my very precious time.' Conlan stood as if to leave.

'Mr. Powell, please sit down, I promise you, what I have yet to tell you is in the National interest and does have a huge bearing on the Gulf conflict.'

'Yeah Conlan, sit down, let's hear what the man's got to say.'

Conlan reluctantly sat down. 'This better be good Mr. Nixon.'

'Oh I think you will find it interesting Mr. Powell.' At that point Nixon decided to recharge his glass and take another sip before continuing, noting that his guests had hardly touched their drinks, he did not offer a refill.

'After that incident, Eisenhower dropped the Jericho project like a hot potato, deciding to distance himself and America from any involvement with Biological and Chemical weapons. The Anthrax bombs were, I believe in Badaber, that's the airbase in Pakistan, but they were moved to another location and I don't know where. All I know is that there were six spherical bombs, now five of course, contained in a cushioned aluminium case, about the size of a briefcase. On the other hand, the Sincyathatate, about 40,000 cylinders of the stuff, was stored in containers onboard a freighter standing off Amsterdam. When the mission failed, the ship was ordered to sail to the Gulf and unload the containers, in Iraq.'

Conlan sat bolt upright as the situation dawned. 'I had an inkling that's where this was heading,' Jack said.

'So you see Mr. Powell, I know Saddam Hussein has 40,000 cylinders of Sincyathatate at his disposal and probably the Anthrax as well. I also suspect that he has a few aircraft in reserve to deliver this cocktail on the allied troops when they pursue the retreating Iraqi forces. I think he's pulling the old Indian trick, 'look we done for, we're on the run.......Pursue them at your peril Mr. Powell.'

Saudi-Arabia

Gulf war zone, coalition headquarters Riyadh, Saudi Arabia, mid February 1991. The Commanders of the main coalition forces, America, United Kingdom and Saudi Arabia were meeting to plan the final assault into Iraq and the complete annihilation of the Iraqi forces.

Half way through that meeting a faxed message was delivered to the Commander in Chief General Norman Schwarsckof. It was from the US President George H W Bush and the Chairman of the Joint Chiefs Conlan Powell. It read,

Ensure all Iraqi troops have been evicted from Kuwait and are heading towards Baghdad. Secure the borders and desist from pursuing the enemy. Consider this your victory and cease all further hostilities.'

The General angrily balled up the paper and threw it across the room. 'Goddamn it, we had that son of a bitch right there.' He held out his hand, palm up, imagining that Saddam was in his grasp and squeezed tight upon the thought. 'What the hell am I going to tell the hordes of reporters hanging around here for a tale of glory?'

Khalid Bin Sultan, Commander of the Saudi forces, spoke. 'Perhaps Norman, I could be of assistance on that matter. As you may know King Fhad considered Saddam Hussein a friend, but not only that, he sees the Iraqi leader as a stabilising influence between the Islamic factions, the moderate Sunnis on the Arabian peninsular and the extremist Shia of Iran. I feel that if you express the ceasing of hostilities as been the Kings wishes, then all will be satisfied.'

'Sounds good enough to me Norman.' Said the British Commander, Brigadier Peter De La Billiere.

PART FOUR

WEAPONS OF MASS DESTRUCTION

CHAPTER SEVENTEEN

Early May 2003

Iraq

British forces 7th Armour Brigade mechanised units under the command of Brigadier Julian Freed, made their way north along the main highway from the mouth of the Euphrates. They were part of a pincer movement, aimed at taking the Iraqi city of Basra. A unit of four scout cars and three armoured personnel cars, pushed on ahead of the main armoured force. They encountered little or no resistance, that was until they came upon a force of Iraqi National Guards, entrenched around the small town of As Saybah. The ensuing fire fight lasted for sometime, with heavy machine gun fire, mortar and rocket grenades being exchanged.

Brigadier Freed reluctant to use his supply of heavy ordinance that would undoubtedly be needed for the 'Charge of the Knights' operation, decided that the enemy within the town were contained and were only hampering the main objective. He could not allow any more delay or he would fail to meet up with the forces attacking from the west. So he ordered the bulk of the mechanised force, consisting of tanks, armoured cars, field artillery and mechanised guns to make a detour and continue the push towards Basra.

A detachment of Guards from the Royal Horse Artillery with a scout car, four armoured personnel cars and two Chieftain Tanks, under the command of Major James Hartford, were left to finish the job. When he had subdued the resistance, he had orders to proceed with his unit to Basra, with all haste and join back up with the rest of Freed's force.

The Brigadier had grossly under estimated the strength of the enemy and Major Hartford made little or no progress, at best it could be said that the enemy were being contained. Major Hartford considered sending in the tanks to blast through the buildings sheltering the Iraqi's, but thought he could lose his asset to anti tank rockets at close quarters. So he kept the tanks back allowing them to shell the points of resistance in the town, from a distance.

Once it became apparent to the Iraqi force that they faced only a relatively small British force, with two tanks, they decided to bring out their own previously dug in and hidden armour, four Russian T55 tanks.

Major Hartford caught the swirl of dust mixed with exhaust smoke, in the lens of his binoculars and picked out the first tank emerging from what looked like a sand pit.

Further scanning of the town from his position in the turret of a scout car, he said into the mike attached to the pans on his ears. 'I count four of the buggers Sergeant Major, any chance you can pick em off?'

'Sure sir, we can take out two no probs, but we are within their range and getting real low on ammo, we couldn't sustain a battle.'

'Okay, let's draw them out see if they'll come out of the town into the open. All personnel and equipment will fall back to the road.'

The Iraqi Tanks positioned themselves in and around the derelict buildings on the outskirts, but made no attempt to leave the town.

Major Hartford's scout car hovered just about out of range of the exploding tank shells, while the rest of the unit pulled back. Still sticking out of the turret with the binoculars fixed to his eyes, he mumbled to himself. 'They aint pursuing, why?' Catching a momentary glimpse of a vehicle movement in the town, he adjusted the glasses. 'Mobile launcher, probably SAM, better not call for RAF support.'

Now on the main road and out of range from the Iraqi tanks guns, Major Hartford's small force regrouped and took stock of their situation and remaining ammunition. If and when he could catch up with Brigadier Freed, he would be of little use without a resupply, so he radioed the base and was told he would have to wait his turn.

'For crying out loud we're facing a large enemy force here with nothing to throw at them but sticks and stones.'

'Sorry sir, bit hectic here I've got three fronts to look after, you'll just have to wait till I get round to you.'

'Excuse me sir,' the Sergeant Major said, 'mind if I have go?' Major Hartford shrugged his shoulders and handed the mike to the Sergeant Major. 'Wattsy you old tow rag, it's me Jim Harper. Over.'

'Hi Jim, how yah doing old son. Over.'

'A lot better if I had some thirty-eights to throw at this lot. Over.'

'Okay, okay, Jim see-n how's it's you, I'll do my best, just might get you a wagon load in about an hour. Can you hang on that long? Over.'

'Just about Charlie, thanks. Out.'

'Guess you know the Quartermaster, Sergeant Major?'

'Sure sir, ole Charlie Watts and me, we go back sometime. I take it, we can hang on for an hour sir?'

'Well as long as the Iraqi Tanks and troops stay in As Saybah, we don't have a problem.'

'I wonder why they aren't kicking our arse, sir.'

'Beats me Sergeant Major, beats me.'

A soldier comes to attention and salutes to the Major.

'Sir.'

'Yes Corporal, what can I do for you?'

'Field Gun, single mechanised unit sir, coming down the road, sir.'

'Is there be-damned..... I wonder.'

The Major stood in the middle of the road hand held high palm facing forward inviting the lumbering caterpillar tracked vehicle with it's enormous gun barrel bobbing up and down, to stop. – Which it did, just a matter of feet from him.

'Where are you going soldier?' The Major said to the driver whose head was protruding from a small hatch at the front of the vehicle. He didn't get chance to answer as a Corporal with three others emerged from the rear.

'Beggin your pardon sir, but who are you and--?'

'Corporal Jenkins! Forgotten how to salute an officer, have you lad?'

'Sergeant Major.' And the Corporal together with the other three gun crew came smartly to attention and saluted Major Hartford.

'Sorry about that sir, - can't be too careful.'

The Sergeant Major came to the Majors side, 'Corporal Ginger Jenkins Royal Artillery, sir, I was with him on exercise at Salisbury; they are supposed to be part of the 'Charge of Knights' op.'

'That so Corporal?'

'Yes sir, 42nd battery RA on attachment to 7th Armour. Had a breakdown sir, the REME guys took an age to get us going.'

'At ease men. Tell me Corporal, how are you for ordinance?'

'Full to the brim sir.'

'Good, good.' The major casually draped an arm over Ginger Jenkins shoulder. 'You don't suppose you could spare five rounds, if I give you the coordinates?' The Major raised an eyebrow.

The Corporal looked at him and then at the Sergeant Major and then back to the Major.

'No problem sir, haven't fired a shot in anger yet, we're all desperate to get some action.'

The large gun set itself in the direction of As Saybah; Major Hartford positioned himself again just out of range of the Iraqi

Tanks, and centred a computer controlled laser guided range finder telescope on the first tank target. Reading off the coordinates, he relayed the information back to the Artillery unit. These coordinates were transferred to the gun targeting computer. The barrel elevated, steadied and instructions shouted.

'Target set! – Load! – Firing!' The big gun recoiled with a terrific bang as the round left the barrel and impacted on the target with an explosive force.

Five rounds later all that remained of the Iraqi tanks and SAM launcher were hunks of smoking steel and clouds of debris.

Job done, the mechanised gun trundled off to catch up with the battle for Basra. As it headed northwest, a large army lorry arrived from the southeast, stacked high with cases of ordinance.

'Right lads,' the Sergeant major hollered, let's get this lot sorted.

The two Chieftains rolled up to within three hundred metres of the town and began a systematic bombardment taking out any signs of Iraqi troops and vehicles. The unit of Guards positioned themselves behind the Tanks readying themselves to follow the massive steel bulk of the tanks into the town for the 'hand to hand' mop up.

After about an hour of relentless shelling, the Major ordered a cease fire while he surveyed the town, again through the binoculars. A few minutes passed before the smoke and dust had cleared sufficiently for him to ascertain the full affect of the bombardment.

'Well I'll be blowed.'

'What is it sir?'

'They're pulling out, or at least what's left of them are.'

He studied the area thoroughly, moving the glasses up and down and from side to side.

'Nothing Sergeant Major, - can't see any activity whatsoever, - I think they've buggered off, - the place is deserted.'

'Shall I send the men in sir, finish off any resistance?'

'Er, no, can't see the point, I'm reluctant to waste any more time on this shit hole. Have the men mount up we're heading to Basra, see if we can get among the action.'

The clean up operation of As Saybah, was to be left to following troops after the 'Charge of the Knights' operation to secure Basra, was complete.

It was one week later when a squad from the Royal Engineers rolled up to the southern out skirts of the now deserted town of As Saybah. They had heavy equipment in the form of bulldozers and mechanical diggers, armoured personnel cars, support vehicles and two three ton truck loads of Iraqi civilians.

Lieutenant David Thomkinson, fearful of any mines or booby traps that may have been left by the fleeing National Guards, surveyed the area through his field glasses from the front seat of the Land Rover. He was concerned, something was not quite as it should be, but he just couldn't put his finger on it. The plan was, that they would clear an area, allowing the Iraqi labourers to remove the dead, identify and box them up for mass burial, any weapons would of course be collected by the British soldiers.

A sergeant alighted from the Land Rover, stood with arms akimbo and studied the situation. The smell of rank rotting flesh hung in the air, he had smelt that smell before, but still found the foulness of it pushed him to the edge of vomiting. More out of pride to demonstrate the role his rank afforded, he stood firm pushing back the feeling of nausea from his mind, it was then he detected the faint underlying aroma of ammonia. At first he wasn't sure if his senses were playing tricks, so he turned to the lieutenant, who still had the binoculars to his eyes.

'Do you smell that sir?'
The lieutenant lowered the glasses and sniffed the air. 'Rotting flesh?'
'Behind that, sir.'
The lieutenant sniffed again. 'Ammonia?'
'That's what I'm getting sir.'
'Something's not right here Serge. I think you'd better take the column back down the road a ways. Set up camp. I'm going to take a look.'

'What about mines sir?'

'Too much devastation, I doubt any mines have been planted, but I'll take care.'

Corporal Blanes who had followed the Sergeant Jones from the Land Rover and was now standing at his side watching the lieutenant picking his way slowly over the rubble and into what was once a street in As Saybah.

'Off on his own then, is he Sam?'

The sergeant nodded without turning his attention away from the slow moving figure.

'Can you smell ammonia Bill?'

The corporal sniffed the air and tried not to let the foulness of it affect him, 'You know Sam, I think I can, that's not usual is it?'

'No Bill, it's not.'

The sergeant pondered for a moment before turning back to the corporal. 'Let's get this lot out reach of this stench and have a brew.'

Lieutenant David Thomkinson's progress was slow and cautious, besides the arduous task of scrambling over the rubble and avoiding the craters, he found himself checking for mines, trip wires, even snipers, but at the back of his mind he was confident those hazards were non existent. '*I would have expected, if there were any mines, to have found them on the perimeter, - I didn't,*' he mumbled.

He scrambled over piles of rubble that were once houses on the edge of the town. Houses that probably held defending troops, for among the rubble he came across several bodies of Iraqi soldiers. These were easily found by the myriad of buzzing flies around the decaying corpses. The remnants of blood stains around the area, the wounds and the scattered limbs, led David to conclude that these men had taken a direct hit. He held a hand over his mouth and nose and fought back the urge to vomit.

Similar scenes were apparent as he picked his way through the small town. He soon realised that the town was bereft of civilians. *'Only soldiers,'* he said, talking to himself, *'why? What were they doing here?'*

As he made his way to the Northern edge of the town, he noticed tops of containers projecting above what appeared to be a surrounding concrete wall about twelve feet high. He made a quick count, announcing the numbers out loud, because he found that countered the strange feeling of nervousness. 'If they are standing double-decker, then there's got be about a couple of hundred.'

As he drew closer, he noted a couple of containers had been hit with artillery and that the smell of ammonia was now considerably stronger. He instinctively decided to slow his progress, and moved more cautiously, now covering his nose and mouth with a handkerchief, sinister thoughts running through his mind. There were many more bodies of soldiers now, but all of these were complete corpses, no loss of limbs or signs of any wounds. These must have been the bodies he was looking at through the binoculars and he still couldn't put his finger on whatever was bothering him. As he neared the wall the body count increased dramatically. 'Was it the containers, they were guarding, if so what's in them?'

Although, he already had an inkling what it was, but hoped that he was wrong.

His suspicions were confirmed when he moved in for a closer inspection of one of the bodies. It was contorted from what must have been a traumatic experience and was lying in a pool of dried up vomit and bodily fluids. Then he realised what was bugging him, - the absence of flies.

'Nerve gas!' He exclaimed in a loud voice as if to warn anyone near, forgetting that at that moment he was by himself.

CHAPTER EIGHTEEN

Lieutenant David Thomkinson had had a no go zone around the perimeter of As Saybah set up. Loops of barbed wire had been strung out with signs at every fifty or so metres depicting the skull and cross bones with the word mines written both in English and Arabic. Hopefully that would be sufficient to keep away any Iraqis heading into the town looking for plunder, but the smell from the decaying flesh alone should be enough to deter most. He also set up a field camp and communication centre in some abandoned buildings about a kilometre from the town and adjacent to the main road. The Iraqi labourers had been returned to their homes in Basra, and the initial small squad of engineers had been increased to company size under the guise of forming a checkpoint for Iraqi vehicles using the road to and from Basra.

Although some of the more seasoned troops may have guessed what the situation was in As Saybah, the lieutenant had said nothing to anybody in the command, even to the extent that his communication with headquarters had been undertaken in private.

Five days after the discovery in As Saybah, a Land Rover entered the field camp; four occupants alighted from the vehicle and headed towards the lieutenants make shift office in one of the more stable looking houses.

'Major John Peterson army intelligence, pleased to meet you Lieutenant,' he said as he approached David with an outstretch hand. 'I've been sent to take over this As Saybah thing, hope you don't mind.'

'Not at all, bit of a relief really, now you're here, ...weight off my mind, so to speak.'

David warmly shook the Majors hand, and proceeded to welcome the other three in the same manner.

'Good, now let me introduce you to Captain Ian Porterfield and Sergeant Mike Cotterall from the bomb disposal unit and finally our civilian, Dr James Metcalf a bio-chemist from Porton Down.

Introductions over with, the major decided to get things moving. 'I think we should get on with the matter in hand without any further delay, let's go and take a look, shall we, care to lead the way David old chap.'

'Sure, have you guys got everything you'll need?'

'Everything's in the back of the Land Rover. Haven't brought a great deal, thought we'd do a recci first,' Captain Porterfield said.

The Lieutenant led the way over the bumpy unmade road in his Land Rover, closely followed by the new team in theirs. The two vehicles edged around the outskirts of the town heading northwards in an attempt to get the vehicles, equipment and personnel as close as possible to the compound and the containers within. After passing through a pulled back section of barbed wire, the vehicles came to a stop within about twenty-five metres of the compound where the containers stood. Lieutenant David Thomkinson alighted from the lead vehicle holding a handkerchief to his mouth and nose and edged his way back to the other vehicle; this was the first time since he discovered the situation, whatever it may be, that he had been back to within the compound area and he didn't relish the moment. The feeling of nausea from the putrid smell of decaying flesh had not abated and he struggled to maintain his composure. 'I think this is near enough gentlemen,' he said as he poked his head through the Land Rovers open window. 'I think we should get into our suits.'

'I agree David, does pong a bit, could do with a gas mask.'

'No need for masks here,' the doctor said sticking an instrument shaped like a hand held microphone attached to a portable radio, through the open window. 'Low toxicity reading.' He declared. Despite the doctors low level reading they all got togged up in rubber suits, just as a precaution.

Sergeant Cotterall, however also put on a full cover helmet with a respirator and a fitted radio transmitter. A pollution monitor was strapped to his wrist and he was armed with a pair of bolt croppers, as he alone headed off towards the concrete walled compound.

The other four remained in the back of the Major's Land Rover and gathered around the two way radio console, all windows now closed to eliminate the odour.

'I'm entering the compound via what seems to be the main gate. It's unlocked, can't see any wires or trips, easing the gate open now. – Okay that's fine, I'm in.'

A long silence ensured while Sergeant Cotterall took in the contents and layout.

'Is everything alright Mike,' Captain Porterfield spoke into the microphone. 'If you see any thing at all resembling trip wires, get yourself back here and get togged up with a blast shield.'

'Will do sir, but everything is fine so far. The compound looks to have been constructed purely for the containment of these containers. I've counted fifty in two rows, double stacked, a couple of which appear to have taken direct hits from heavy ordinance and are still in parts looking wet.'

Dr Metcalf reached over to the console, hitting the transmit button. 'What's your monitor reading?'

'Wow doc, it's in the red.'
'Okay sergeant another ten minutes then get yourself out of there.'
'As you say, doc.'
The doctor turned to the lieutenant, 'David do you think we can get some water and possibly some detergent up here fast, we will need to scrub the sergeant down as soon as he emerges.'

'Yeah, no problem I'll get on the radio in my Landy and get a tanker up here.'

As the lieutenant headed back to the other Land Rover, the doctor said to no one in particular. 'The concrete wall must be retaining the liquid, therefore whatever it is, it's probably delivered in a spray form not a gas. That could account for most of the victims being in the proximity of the compound, the explosion must have carried the spray.'

'Come in Captain.'

'Go ahead Mike.'

'Right, I'm just heading to the nearest container, all of which, as we guessed, are padlocked. For the record, lots of bodies here, including dead flies and the occasional rat.'

'Anything else in the compound that we should know about Mike?'

'Nothing unusual.....There is a large motorised lifting crane for moving the containers, a couple of fork lift trucks and what looks to me like a concrete bunker building in one corner.'

'Anybody in there?'

'We'll have to check later sir, although I doubt it, the door is wide open.... I'm cutting through the padlock. Arrr.' There was an audible snap. 'It's off. Opening doors now.'

A further delay as the sergeant's heavy breathing accompanied the squeak of dry unused steel hinges.

'What we've got sir, are hundreds of cylinders, I'd say, the same size and shape as the pods that fit on the underside of aircraft. – They are set in timber frames, one-two-er- um....ten to a pallet. Hang on sir, got some writing on the pallets, -- hard to make out through this visor, -- Okay got it, it says.

'Sin-cy-ath-at-ate .....I-X .... ICI Billingham.''

'Sincyathatate – where have I heard the name before? The doctor mumbled as he probed his memory for the answer. 'My God! Sincyathatate Nine.' He suddenly declared as the he recalled a moment from his past. 'Get out of there, now Sergeant!'

'Problems doc?'

'Y-e-s, you could say that Major, what we have here is a one off lethal concoction developed by my mentor and original Bio-Chemist, Dr Jeremy Miles-Johnson.'

'One off, you mean this stuff isn't made anymore?'

The doctor nodded thoughtfully. 'I only know it's name and effects from a paper written by 'the man', I had no idea that the stuff was ever produced and as far as I'm aware the formulae was never revealed, so I've no idea how to neutralise it.'

'Shit!—what are we going to do?'

'Lock the place up, contain it if we can and I'll ask 'the man' what we should do.'

'He's still alive!'

'Oh I sincerely hope so, I hadn't been at Porton long, when he left, late seventies....Retired early....Had a bad accident as I recall.

Anyway the last I heard he's still batting, although he must be getting on now.'

Sergeant Cotterall emerged from the compound at the same time, the water tanker arrived. The driver under the Lieutenants instruction jumped down and sprayed a hose pipe washing the Sergeant.

The Major nodded thoughtfully, thinking about what the Doc had just said and he turned to the others. 'Okay lock it up.'

CHAPTER NINETEEN

The head of British Intelligent Secret Service, Sir Peter Thompson-Smythe was sat with his elbows resting on the desk top and his hands balled up to support his chin. Between his elbows lay the 'As Saybah' report which he was reading. As he perused the report, the internal telephone rang and without diverting his attention from the paperwork, reached out with his right hand and depressed the intercom button. 'Yes Marj.' He said without looking up.

'The Prime Minister's here, Sir Peter.'

'Oh good. Er,- give me a minute, then send him in please Marj.'

'Hello Peter.' The Prime Minister entered the office with hand extended, Sir Peter stood took it and shook it warmly.

'Morning Tony, do have a seat,' he said, gesturing towards a Chesterfield armchair.

'What've you got?'

'Well, quite a bit.....Dr Miles-Johnson took a little persuading, but fortunately he remembered Dr Metcalfe and eventually opened up. He explained a lot about Sincyathatate and an idea how to treat it, but what's more important is the reason it was developed in the first place.'

'And?'

'Would you believe, to counter the affects of a hybrid Anthrax biological agent, he'd developed for use as a weapon during World War Two.'

'Anthrax!? My word, this is worse than I thought. If the doctor developed an Anthrax weapon some sixty odd years ago, where is it now?'

'Haven't a clue, the doctor is playing that info close to his chest, all he would say that this hybrid Anthrax is potentially the most devastating weapon ever produced and is virtually indestructible.'

'My goodness.' The Prime minister uttered almost under his breath.

'Apparently, one tiny drop of this Anthrax released into the air, kills and keeps on multiplying and killing, apparently out of control. The doctor took years before he was able to develop Sincyathatate, a chemically based agent, to stop it.'

'So this chemical by its self is nothing to worry about?'

'Unfortunately it is,' Sir Peter screwed up his nose, 'just as deadly as the Anthrax in fact, if it gets on your skin, but it's a liquid delivered by spray and just like any other chemical after a few days it evaporates, apparently any residue that remains will be toxic but as such would very difficult to contract, unless one was to, let's say rub at the staining with a wet finger. However on the other hand, the Anthrax......Well that's something else.'

'I wonder now, did Saddam have the Anthrax as well as the Sincyathatate?' The Prime Minister mused.

'It's a possibility, but there's no knowing, all we can do is to inform Peterson of the situation and have them check out the compound, and if necessary, all of As Saybah. Let's hope we find it.'

'Y-e-s, let's hope.'

'One thing's for sure Tony; either agent could be termed as 'a weapon of mass destruction.''

'Yes, but not the WMD the Americans are seeking? Conlan Powell is looking for the chemical agent Saddam used on the Kurds and we know that was Sarin.'

'Then the Sincyathatate and the Anthrax are weapons the Americans don't know about?'

The Prime Minister nodded slowly. 'It would appear so.'

'That would figure,' Sir Peter hesitated momentarily. 'The doctor did let slip that Churchill was involved.'

'Churchill! Bugger!'

Sir Peter interrupted before any further expletives could ensue from the Prime Minister. 'I have had some listening devices installed in his home and I've stationed an agent to act as a nurse and companion. Hopefully when Miles-Johnson is ready to tell the full story we will be on hand to listen.'

'Bloody hell Peter, Chemical weapon concocted by an English guy, manufactured in England and requested by a British Prime Minister. And no doubt he was responsible for shipping to Iraq in the first place.....What a bloody mess.'

'Quite,' Sir Peter muttered

'Hum, so what do we do now, eh?' The Prime Minister rubbed his chin thoughtfully. 'How I wonder, would be the Americans react when they discover that it was us Brits that not only made the stuff, but it was Churchill who gave it to them?'

'Perhaps it may be prudent Tony, not to tell them....In fact, probably best all round, if we keep this under our hat.' Sir Peter lightly tapped the side of his nose with a forefinger.

CHAPTER TWENTY

Back at the field camp, in Lieutenant David Thomkinson's make shift office, the four army officers and a civilian doctor of Chemistry just returned from a visit to England, perused the information as it had been gleaned from Dr Miles-Johnson.

'Well I guess we all know that we have to keep the lid on this.' There were affirmative nods from the other four. The Major, sat with his bum narrowly resting on the corner of a trestle table and began to set out a plan of action. 'David we'll need a couple of dozen of your guys to pick up and box the dead, most of them will be well overripe by now. I trust they'll have some form of protection?'

'They all have NBC suits, we'll use them.'

'Sounds good, - probably the best thing for the job. What about boxes?'

'Should be enough, - the Iraqis left a load.'

'We'll need to remove the bodies from the compound ourselves, make sure the men are aware that area is off limits. Put your diggers to work digging the graves, we'll try to give the poor buggers a decent burial.'

'The quicker we get the bodies in the ground the better, the stench is becoming unbearable.'

'What does Miles-Johnson say about the burying these guys, doc?'

'Well for those of you that are not already aware, he suggested that by far the best option would be cremation, but that may cause friction with the relatives. As an alternative he recommends we burn the clothes and douse the corpses with formaldehyde, a shipment of which will be with us shortly. Then we will need to place the coffins on a layer of lime in the grave. I take it David your men have been briefed.'

'For sure Doc, it's all in hand.'

The Major shifted to rest his other cheek on the table's corner. 'We've all read the instructions; we now have another problem, finding this damned Anthrax, any idea what we'll be looking at Doctor?'

'Not really, though I would hazard a guess that the bacterium spores would be in some sort of sealed unit say a glass vial or sealed test tube, that kind of thing and more than likely the spores will be suspended in a liquid or a jelly.'

'Hum, only small then?'

'That's my opinion.' The doctor said nodding his head.

'Needle in a haystack,' Ian chirped in.

'Yes, probably but our orders are to search for the stuff before we do anything else.'

'Could be it isn't here, never was, how are we going to know?'

The doctor was the first to respond. 'In all probability David we won't, but from what Miles-Johnson told me, these two agents go together, if Saddam has the Sincyathatate the likelihood is that he has it as an antidote against the Anthrax.'

'Yeah,' Ian put in, 'I doubt Saddam ever had the means to deliver that Sincyathatate onto an attacking invasion force, in my opinion he's got to have the Anthrax somewhere.'

'Well that's what we have to assume,' the Major said, 'but where?' He slid off the table and straightened. 'I guess only likely place has got to be the compound. Anyone got another suggestion?' All was quiet. 'No, okay then let's get cracking.'

Although more in hope than expectation, the five of them clad in rubber suits with hoods fitted with respirators, began the search of the compound for the illusive Anthrax. As they did so, they took stock of the amount of Sincyathatate pods stored within each container. Perhaps had commonsense prevailed, the group would have headed straight for the concrete bunker building at the other end of the walled area, as probably being the most logical place to store a substance like Anthrax. But in truth not one of the party had any expectations on the recovery of the biological weapon, although not mentioned, each knew its discovery, if it was discovered, would prompt more questions than answers.

Namely, would they have found all of it and what on earth would they do with it, if they should by chance find it?

Eventually all five came together at the large open steel door of the bunker and gingerly made their way inside. For no other reason than the fear of booby traps, Captain Porterfield entered first, followed closely by Sergeant Cotterall who furtively swung the beam of his torch into the darkened recesses of the room.

Major Peterson turned his body fully around so that he could physically see Lieutenant Thomkinson through his visor. 'We'll need some lighting in here, see what you can do David,' he said though his hood microphone.

'I'll go take a look outside; there must be a generator of some kind.'

'No need sir.' Sergeant Cotterall said as he swung his torch beam to the left side of the room. 'We've found it.' The beam picked out a large machine which seemed to fill the whole of that side wall, 'must be the generator house sir, not a bunker.'

The sergeant approached the machine, examined it with the torch beam from every conceivable angle. 'Better stand outside gentlemen, just in case.'

As the others departed, the sergeant counted to ten to give them a little distance and then he pressed the green start button. There was a slow churning noise accompanied by a weak flickering of the over head lights, before the roar as the engine caught and settled into a steady hum. As the lights came on the others made their way back into the confines of the now brightly lit concrete building.

It became instantly clear that the concrete building housed more than the generators, for directly in front of them was the stainless steel access doors of a lift.

'Let's go for it,' Captain Porterfield said as he pressed the call button. The doors opened instantly, indicating that the car was stationed at that level before the power was cut.

'Why cut the power? If there were evacuating in a hurry why stop to punch a red button.'

'I guess we'll find out David.' The major hit the only other level on the indicator panel, 'level 0' and the lift car descended for what must have been ten- twelve metres.

The doors opened on to a huge open plan area equally as big as the compound above with glass screened rooms around the perimeter. There were a number of bodies laying just inside the room, adjacent to the lift door.

'There's your answer David, those lucky enough to get into the lift probably panicked and feared contamination, probably thought something had gone wrong down here.'

Dr Metcalfe nodded in agreement as he pushed the probe of his analysis meter in the direction of one the corpses. 'Umm— traces of Sincyathatate, must have come through vents, although levels are somewhat low now.'

The open plan floor was set with a number of desk and benches covered with typical chemistry equipment, glass bottles, vials, containing various amounts of various coloured brews, Brunson burners and microscopes.

'It looks like they were trying to analyse the chemical weapon.'
'Or reproduce it doc.'
'Yes whatever.'
'I suppose we'd better check the place out, David you and the doc check out the rooms from that end, Ian and Mike take the rooms this end and I'll check out this area.'

The rubber suited figures set off in the different directions each checking and looking for something unusual, but what exactly, no one really knew. A short time later the doctor called everyone to one of the rooms.

'What is it Jim?'

'Don't really know John, but this room seems to be the only one that is locked, I've looked through the slats of the blinds and I can see a number of isolation tanks, you know the type with internal gloves and microscope.'

'Alright doc, we're there. David, Ian, Mike....Did you get that?'
'Affirmative, we're on our way.'
It took Sergeant Mike Cotterall ten minutes to smash the lock off the toughened glass door using a metal bar and screw driver he found during the search.

There were five separate glass screened boxes set into the wall; each contained a single metallic sphere about the size of a tennis ball.

'What do you make of them doc?'
'I'm not sure ---.'
'That's a bomb,' Captain Porterfield declared as he looked over the doctor's shoulder.
'You sure Ian?'
'Sure I'm sure, not much of a bomb I'll grant you, but a bomb nevertheless......Do you concur Mike?'
'Aye that's the detonator with a pressure switch.'

'A what?'

'I agree Mike. Yes John a pressure switch, quite dated in its construction, but nevertheless a pressure switch.'

'You've got the floor Ian, explain please.'

'I'll try; see the small dial on the outside of the casing.' There were discernable nods from the others. 'Well that, I think is an altimeter, once that little primer button is depressed, then the altimeter becomes the trigger which fires the detonator at a set height. The RAF used a similar device in the Gulf war, where cluster bombs are spread over a large area from a casing exploding at a set height above the ground.' He looked to the Sergeant. 'Agree Mike?'

'That's the way I see sir.'

'Any way of taking the thing apart, let's have a look at what's inside?'

'Sure doc, I'll have a go, want to stand second Mike?'

'Sir, I'll take these guys back a pace.'

After about ten minutes Captain Porterfield had the little spherical bomb unassembled and the component parts set out neatly in the bottom of the inspection tank. At the core of the sphere was a glass tube, sealed at the end and set within a steel securing frame, inside the glass bubble was a greenish liquid, the consistency of which, looked to be jellified.

'Want to take a look John, it's disarmed? Not much in the way of explosives. Probably just enough to split the casing and shatter the glass.' Captain Porterfield said over his shoulder as the Major came to his side.

'Hum, you thinking what I'm thinking Ian?'

The Captain nodded. 'Anthrax?'

'That's what I'm thinking, better let the doctor take a look.'

He turned and waved the doctor forward. 'You'd better take a look at this lot Doc.'

Although nothing was said, each of the party had the same idea of what was contained within the metal sphere. The doctor, with the other four now gathered around, spent a little over a minute, examining the liquid content of a glass tube through the microscope.

'I will need much more time to undertake a full analysis, but my suspicions are that what we have here are what Dr Miles-Johnson hinted at.' He paused and said sombrely.

'Anthrax spores and lots of them.'

CHAPTER TWENTY-ONE

The next day, back at the Lieutenants HQ, the group gathered again to take stock of the situation.

The doctor had spent most of yesterday in communication with Miles-Johnson via Porton Down Administration. However the old bugger had refused to divulge anything further on the matter. It wasn't until Major Peterson made a telephone call to London and the resultant visit by Sir Peter Thompson-Smythe to the Miles-Johnson's home, that the doctor's resolve waned. He offered Sir Peter something in the way of advice as to the amount of 'Anthrax' he produced and how it could be disposed of.

Major John Peterson again plonked his bottom on the corner of a trestle table, acting as the lieutenant's makeshift desk, the other four were seated on fold up wooden chairs scattered around the room. He studied the notes he'd made and then began to set out the plan of action as he perceived it.

'We'll need a hand David, a couple of guys you can trust.'

'I know just the men, Sergeant Sam Jones and Corporal William Blanes, both been with me a number of years.'

'You think this'll work Doc?'

'Well Dr Miles-Johnson thought it would and that's good enough for me.' Doctor Metcalf was sitting legs crossed balancing a clip board on his knee with a pencil and a calculator poised over it. 'Although,' he said, the calculations aren't balancing.'

'How so?'

'Well from Miles-Johnson's account, there should be more Anthrax spores somewhere.'

'Perhaps it would be prudent to consider the old mans memory and maybe his sanity, aren't what it used to be. Apparently Sir Peter remarked that he had had to remind the Doctor several times, what it was, they were discussing.'

'Yes Major, I don't doubt a man of his age has not got all his chairs at home and will get mixed up about many things, but I can't imagine for one minute that the Doc's calculations would be wrong.'

The Major raised an eyebrow. 'Perhaps it would be in all of our interests to assume the Iraqis have used some.'

'Perhaps,' Doctor Metcalf responded.

There was a moment of silence while the doctors concern was brushed aside, nobody, the doctor included wanted to cogitate on the prospect of unfound Anthrax.

'You're sure Doc; both areas are in the clear?'
'Absolutely, we can all leave our rubber suits at home today.'

'Good, good, well er, I guess we're all set, let's do it shall we.' Either by luck or design the steel door into the concrete building was large enough to accommodate a forklift truck, as were the lift doors and the lift itself was large in size and capacity.

'Made for the job, serge.' Lieutenant Thomkinson said, stood arms akimbo, with Sam Jones and Bill Blanes. They were watching Sergeant Mike Cotterall drive a forklift into the lift, followed by the doctor and the two officers.

As soon as the lift door slid shut, David turned and issued his orders, 'Okay let's get started. Bill get the other forklift, we'll start with this container.'

The size of the lift allowed only half of each of the containers contents to be loaded, so as the lift car descended, Bill began to unload the rest of the containers pallets just inside the steel door. All in readiness for the next load of the bomb like pods to be sent down into the bowels of the earth. To where and for what, Bill didn't have a clue. He had guessed that he was dealing with some kind of chemical weapon, but thought it best to keep his mouth shut and follow orders, mumbling to himself under the noise of the forklifts engine. 'Ours is not to reason why, ours is but to do or die.'

David was driving the motorised container lifting crane, with Sam rigging the slings onto the containers. As Bill emptied one, it was removed and another put in its place.

While the activity was going on at ground level, three of the four people in the underground room were equally busy stacking the Sincyathatate pods. The doctor spent most of his time in the isolation area analysing the Anthrax, or trying to.

Four very long days later, the Sincyathatate pods had all been transferred to the below ground complex. The now empty containers had been neatly restacked and those damaged, washed out to remove all traces of the chemical.

The doctor had arranged for a number of dead goats to be brought down and placed in the centre of the room amid the now re-sited glass tubes of suspected Anthrax spores. The tubes had been set with a small explosive charge, as had the necks of one hundred Sincyathatate pods. The pods were positioned and set to explode open, allowing the chemical to spray the whole room. Just four hours after the charge on the Anthrax tubes had been detonated. That was based on the doctor's calculation that the supposed Anthrax spores would need some time to mature and multiply upon the goat carcases. However nobody would actually know if his calculations were correct, as once the timed charges were set, concrete was poured into each ventilator shaft and as the team left the underground complex, the access opening was walled closed. And once the team were at ground level, the lift was sent back down, the lift access door at ground level forced open and thirty cubic metres of concrete was pumped into the lift shaft, to ensure the underground complex would be sealed for eternity.

PART FIVE

EXPOSUER

CHAPTER TWENTY-TWO

Late March 2008

London

'What the hell is going on!' Prime Minister Graham Brown declared, as he threw the large sheets of flapping paper that were the 'Daily Telegraph', across his desk with such force that it joined the collection of the other tabloids, now littered over the floor of the cabinet office.

'Perhaps you may wish to talk with Sir Peter on the matter sir.'

George Jenkins Permanent Secretary to the cabinet office, suggested.

'Sir Peter, -- Sir Peter who?'

'Sir Peter Thompson-Smythe, head of the British Intelligence Secret Service.'

'The what! Never heard of him or them.'

'I do believe I informed you of BISS and Sir Peter, when you took office.'

'Did you? Umm, perhaps you should run it by me again.'

'Very well Mr. Brown,' Jenkins uttered condescendingly. 'Sir Peter, no disrespect to your position Prime Minister, is probably one of the most powerful men in the UK. He is the head of a little known secret service organisation, specifically appointed by the Crown but supported by parliament, a position which allows a certain amount of influence, in a discreet way of course, to decisions made in this office.'

'Does he by god?'

Jenkins nodded slowly.

'Then perhaps I'd better have a word with him.'

'If you wish I can make the call on your red phone.'

'Oh the red phone,' Prime Minister Brown mumbled as he watched the Permanent Secretary pick up the special red telephone and tap in a number, seemingly from memory and held out the receiver to the PM.

'Ah, err, Sir Peter, this is er, Prime –.'

'Yes Prime Minister Brown, good morning. I had been expecting your call, the newspaper headlines I take it.'

'Y-e-s, but, but how?' The Prime Minister stuttered.

'Oh I have a digital readout that tells me which office the call is being made from.'

'Well Sir Peter, I, I have it on good authority that you can offer some enlightenment on this situation?'

'Yes of course. No doubt we'll need to have a chat, preferably face to face.....My office, I think.' Sir Peter glanced at his wristwatch. 'Shall we say half an hour.'

'Well err I don't know where –.'

'Don't worry Graham; it is alright to call you Graham isn't it?'

'Yes of course.'

'Good, I did sort of pre-empt this situation and have taken the liberty of sending my driver for you, he should be with you shortly.'

The Prime Minister replaced the receiver, stared blankly at the wall opposite and uttered disbelievingly. 'I'm being sent for.'

'Of course you are sir.' George Jenkins said, as a broad grin spread across his face.

The chauffeur driven Jaguar made a short detour around Victoria before returning via the Mall and turning into Queen Anne's Gate. As the car approached the corner of a particular building, an electrically operated roller shutter door began to open allowing the car to access a large below ground level car park.

The Chauffeur opened the rear door advising the Prime Minister as he alighted to visit security for further direction. He was escorted in the lift up to the seventh floor and ushered towards Marjorie Fawcett's desk.

Marjorie, Sir Peter Thompson-Smythe's PA had her desk Sir Peter's outer office. She looked up as the Prime Minister gave the outer door a little tap and gingerly poked his head around the door jamb. 'Ah am I'm looking for Sir Pet---.' He began to say, but Marjorie had already depressed the intercom button and was speaking into it.

'The Prime Minister has arrived Sir Peter.'
'Very good Marjorie, wheel him in.' Came the response.
Prime Minister Graham Brown entered Sir Peter's office, rather cautiously, he had no idea why, but he had this feeling, somewhat like a naughty child who had been told to report to the headmasters study.

'Ah Graham, do come in.' Sir Peter said gesturing to a Chesterfield armchair for the Prime Minister to be seated. Graham Brown edged into the office and sidled, as instructed, over to the armchair.

'I'm just about to have a brandy, care to join me?'

The PM nodded and mumbled. 'Er- er- please.' Sir Peter had two balloon glasses at the ready and a bottle of Courvoisier poised over them. He poured out a measure and handed it to the PM, filling his own glass before taking a seat in the opposite armchair.

The Prime Minister took a sip of his brandy and relaxed. Now somewhat more at ease, he was first to broach the subject. 'What's it all about Sir Peter?'

'Just Peter, please Graham.'

'Okay Peter, all this hullaballoo in the papers. Is it true? Did the Americans produce chemical weapons here and poison a town with fallout from an explosion in the plant producing it? Was the town then demolished to hide the truth? And did we kill that old man to keep the secret?' The Prime Minister shook his head in dismay as he spoke.

Sir Peter held up his hand. 'It would seem the answer is yes, yes, ahem yes and yes.'

The Prime Mister's jaw dropped, Sir Peter continued. 'The Americans did indeed, with the help of a British Scientist and no doubt the then government, built a special plant in Billingham ICI for the production of a chemical weapon. And from what I gather there was an accident, some kind of radioactive explosion during the de-commissioning of the plant.'

'So the papers are correct.' Sir Peter pursed his lips and nodded. 'Apparently. All of the tabloids have repeated the full context of the tape without any notable omissions.'

'The tape as submitted by this Hatton guy, how do you know?'

'Because we have the same tape. I've had Dr Miles-Johnson's home bugged, both audio and visual, since 2003.'

'Dr Miles-Johnson, the British Scientist?' The PM interrupted. Sir Peter nodded.

'Yes, Miles-Johnson, I've been hoping that he would reveal all he knew about the Anthrax and Sincyathatate. I even took steps to place a Nurse in his residence to be on hand twenty-four seven. But instead he chose to tell the story to one Ian Turner. By the way Colin Hatton was only a conduit, responsible for forwarding the tapes to the media.'

'It seems to me, much of the story is supposition and can't be proved. Haverton Hill for example, there's no substance in the allegation that the town was demolished in an attempt to cover up the contamination.'

Sir Peter nodded thoughtfully. 'Well the town was demolished and I would doubt there'd be any mileage in trying to deny the reasons for it. In my opinion we should leave that particular scenario to conjecture at this stage. Besides I dare say even as we speak, someone will be taking soil samples for analysis from the former Haverton Hill site and no doubt they will find traces of something which could be construed as originating from toxic contamination.'

'What about the old man, - this scientist chap, Miles-Johnson. Did we kill him?'

Sir Peter nodded. 'Apparently a joint venture between MI5 and the CIA, which, I'm afraid I was not informed about.'

'A joint venture!' The Prime Minister exclaimed. What a bloody mess Peter.'

'Indeed it is Graham, but there can be no doubts, I have it all on tape. I even have a transcript of the instruction to the contractor.'

'Bugger! Is there any way we can cover it up?'

'His death, oh yes, I think so. Miles-Johnson was an old man, natural causes, that sort of thing.' Sir Peter took another sip of brandy, swallowed and eased himself back into the chair. 'However there is something that I feel you should be aware of, not mentioned on the tape.'

The Prime Minister interrupted. 'You're going to tell me what happened to these concoctions, I hope.'

Sir Peter looked sideways at the Prime Minister, he wasn't used to being interrupted or second guessed. 'Y-e-s,' he said slowly, 'the concoctions as you call them did not end up in America as all the papers pre-supposed.'

'I'd figured that, I mean why go to all the trouble of producing them overseas, just to have them shipped back to you, didn't make sense to me.'

'Quite.' Sir Peter took down a swallow of brandy, then after a moment's thoughtful pause he began. 'Yesterday, when the story hit the worlds press, I took the opportunity to contact an old friend of mine, a chap by the name of Jack Rosenthal, Deputy Director CIA. We had quite an enlightening conversation and Jack filled in some of the blanks. Apparently it was Eisenhower who instigated the manufacture of the Sincyathatate and it was he who had it shipped to Iraq.'

'Iraq! Bloody hell.' The Prime Minister gulped at his brandy in an attempt to counter the shock, having swallowed he sat forward resting his arms on his knees, his hands cradling the balloon glass. 'So if the Sincyathatate is in Iraq, then Saddam Hussein did have a Chemical weapon and the Americans must have known. That's why they had us all looking for the 'Weapons of Mass Destruction.' The Prime Minister blew out a faint whistle as he eased himself back into the chair. 'No bloody wonder Conlan Powell was so adamant.' He shook his head in dismay. 'And what about the Anthrax, what happen to that?'

'The Americans don't know what happened to the Anthrax.' Sir Peter hesitated momentarily. 'But we do.'

'We do?'

Sir Peter put his head back and contemplated the ceiling, a ploy to keep the suspense in the conversation. 'Oh yes.' He said matter of factually, bringing his head back so he looked the Prime Minister in the eyes. 'And the Sincyathatate. We found them both.'

'We found them!?' The Prime Minister exclaimed loudly.

Sir Peter held out a hand in an attempt to subdue the Prime Ministers outburst, before he calmly continued. 'Yes Graham, we the Brits, found them.'

'W-w- where when?' The Prime Minister stuttered, clearly flabbergasted by Sir Peter's revelation.

'In the small town of As Saybah, near Basra. And we found them when we invaded Iraq of course, 2003 wasn't it?'

Sir Peter paused for a sip of his brandy, smacking his lips as the liquid slipped down his throat. 'No doubt now, as it's turned out. These were the 'Weapons of Mass Destruction' the Americans were looking for, but we didn't know that at the time.'

'So why didn't we tell the Americans we'd found them? - Or did we?'

'No, we didn't.'

'Why not? - Tony was being crucified by public opinion at that time for taking the country to war under the guise that we were looking for these weapons. Everyone concluded that was false pretences.'

'At one point we considered it, but then thought discretion was the better option at that juncture. You see, the pallets carrying the chemical pods were clearly marked, --- Sincyathatate IX – ICI Billingham. Clearly 'Made in England', that set the alarm bells ringing, couldn't risk any kind of recrimination could we. So we, Tony and I, thought it would be prudent to do some checking before we announced to the world what we had found.' Sir Peter took down another swallow and drained his glass. He got up and went to his desk for a refill. 'Top up Graham,' he said as he hovered the bottle over the Prime Minister's glass, he nodded.

'Thanks, you were saying?'

'Ah yes, that's when we learned about Dr Jeremy Miles-Johnson and the potency of the biological and chemical concoctions we'd found. And believe you me, these it would seem are the most deadly concoctions ever to have been produced.' Sir Peter paused, more for effect than any other reason. 'You must bear in mind Graham, at that time we knew nothing of America's involvement, all we knew for certain was what Miles-Johnson was prepared to tell us. Which was not very much, other than the fact that he developed both strains, with Churchill's help and the Sincyathatate was produced in Billingham ICI. You can no doubt see why Tony and I decided to keep this information to ourselves.'

'Quite, quite,' the Prime Minister said thoughtfully, 'but surely the Americans must have known.'

'Not necessarily, from what Jack told me yesterday, Conlan Powell and he were the only ones, aside from Richard Nixon.'

'Ex President Nixon?'

'The very same, - when the Gulf war had just about ran its course and the Allies were preparing to pursue the Iraqis back to Iraq, Nixon insisted on a meeting with Jack and Conlan Powell. Apparently the purpose of this meeting was to highlight certain extracts taken from a meeting with Eisenhower, the joint chiefs and among others Dr Miles-Johnson. The discussion was centred on the production of Sincyathatate, Anthrax was also mentioned. It was Nixon who informed them that the Sincyathatate had been shipped to Iraq.'

'So Conlan Powell knew what was produced in Billingham ICI and knew that it was Sincyathatate that was shipped to Iraq.'

Sir Peter nodded. 'Correct, he also knew Saddam had Sarin nerve gas because he'd used it on the Kurds. I figure he couldn't use the Sincyathatate as a reason to invade, for obvious reasons, so he hinted at the Sarin as being the WMD.'

'Whatever, Peter.' The Prime Minister raised an eyebrow at that juncture, deciding that a swig of brandy was in order. Then he looked thoughtfully into the balloon glass for a moment before giving the golden liquid a swirl. 'I take it Bush knew?' He said.

'No, not according to Jack; - Bush didn't have much of a clue about anything. He was just eager to back Powell's WMD theory, in the belief he would get his hands on the Iraqi oil.'

Sir Peter paused and took a sip at his brandy, nursing the balloon glass against his chest.

'What did happen to the Anthrax and the Sincyathatate?'
'All taken care of Graham, I doubt we'll ever see then again.'

It was a minute or so later when the Prime Minister decided to pursue the matter further. 'Why now Peter, why go to the trouble of killing an old man and raising all these issues?'

'Someone was trying to keep a secret, why, I'm not really sure.'

'That after all this time does seem a good enough reason, to take someone's life.'

'I tend to think, there was more to this than meets the eye. And that brings me to the current problem.'

'Which is?'

'The MI5 contract killer, who terminated the doctor, is still on the loose with instructions to assassinate the man the doctor told all to, a young man called Ian Turner.

'Can't you just cancel the contract?'

Sir Peter shook his head. 'No Graham once in motion these contracts can't be revoked.'

'Hum, then perhaps we should just let things take their course, distance ourselves from the situation.'

'Not that easy Graham, this particular Ian Turner is, ahum, let's just say, of some importance to BISS.'

The Prime Minister nodded thoughtfully, 'Okay, this Ian Turner is your business; I'm going to pretend that I've never heard the name before. But what's to do about these news reports, can't deny any of it now.......Can I?'

'I would suggest Graham that you make an immediate announcement that you are appointing an independent body to look into the whole affair. That ought to buy us some time before the floodgates open.'

'Floodgates?'

Sir Peter nodded. 'It's fair bet when the independent report is complete, it will be found that toxic chemicals were discharged over the town of Haverton Hill. The floodgates will open with thousands of claimants coming forward, who may or may not have had any connection with the town during that period.....And I think it's going to prove to be a very expensive exercise.'

'Perhaps I should be inviting the Americans to contribute.'

'Perhaps you should.'

The Whitehouse

President George Milton Bush snapped at that morning's 'Washington Post' with such vigour that paper's front sheet tore down its centre. 'Godamn! Son of a bitch!' He shouted so loud that the Manservant about to serve him breakfast physically jumped and sent the pancakes sliding across the table.

'What on earths the matter dear.' His wife Elizabeth enquired.

He ignored her and continued to shout across the dining room to the nearest Aide. 'Get me Rosenthal. Like now!' He roughly removed the napkin that was tucked into his shirt front and threw it hard on to the table in a vain attempt to vent his anger. 'I'll take it in the office.'

He stormed out of the dining room and headed to the Oval office. As he reached the leather chair behind his walnut desk the special telephone rang and he snatched it up. 'Jack.'

'Sir'

'You see the papers?'

'Yes sir.'

'What the hell is this shit?'

'All true I'm afraid sir.'

'What the! Why was I not informed?'

'It goes way back sir.'

'Not the fact that you've had someone killed.'

'In the National interest, sir.'

'Don't give me that shit, you have no right to take a life for such a trivial excuse as to keep a fifty year old secret that I'm sure nobody gives a damn about.'

'Except the people of Haverton Hill, I'm sure there'll be a few of those that won't be too pleased that they were poisoned for the benefit of Uncle Sam.'

'Don't get clever with me Jack, you're out of line and you know it.'

'Yes sir, but on that issue, I hear the Brits are doing a pretty good job of covering it up.'

'Quite.' The President paused for moments thought. 'I guess this is going to cost us a fair bit.'

'I would think so sir.'

'Jack.'

'Sir'

'What did happen to all that chemical Sin – what's-its-name – shit and the Anthrax?'

'I honestly don't know sir.'

'Could this have been the stuff that Conlan Powell was getting so hot up about in Iraq?'

Jack thought it would be prudent to keep Conlan Powell out of the frame on this one, otherwise it would be another bucket of shit and he was already knee deep. 'No sir, I'm sure he was concerned about the Sarin nerve gas that Saddam dumped on the Kurds. Conlan was convinced Saddam was making the stuff on a huge scale.'

'Hum, I guess I ought to get the wheels in motion to sort this lot out.....Oh and Jack, I want a full report my desk by tomorrow.'

'Yes sir.'

CHAPTER TWENTY-THREE

The three guys in the Mercedes Vito assigned to watching and listening brief on Colin Hatton, had now taken up residence in the Rudd's Arms, well two of the three had. The third member, whosever turn it was, stayed in the van on 'listening watch' awaiting Colin's return from where they had initially thought he'd gone, his daughters home in Guisborough. The resultant surveillance of the Guisborough house revealed that the target, Colin Hatton, appeared to have swapped cars with his daughter and had subsequently disappeared.

Bill and George were in the Dining room just finishing breakfast. 'Your turn George, to relieve Charlie,' Bill said as he picked up the morning paper.

'Okay, on my way.' As George headed to the door, Bill glanced at the headlines and the lead story hit him with something of a shock: 'Haverton Hill' and 'ICI Billingham.' He sat up straight the paper held out, arms extended and quickly scanned the full article. His suspicions were confirmed when he saw Colin Hatton's name. He got up and hastily headed out into the car park. Charlie was just about to get out of the van's sliding door when Bill appeared frantically waving a folded newspaper. 'Better get back in Charlie, I've something to show you.'

Charlie scrambled back into the vehicle closely followed by Bill. 'Clock this lot,' he said, placing the newspaper on the consul in front of George. George started to read the article while slowly removing the headset and pulling the cups away from his ears, at the same time Charlie read the piece over his shoulder. 'Well that's a turn up, what do you reckon Charlie?'

'I'll call it in,' at that Charlie picked up the mobile and tapped in the emergency number he'd been given.

Mark Pritchard got up from his seat in the Directors office, at the same time retrieving the humming mobile from his jacket pocket. 'Excuse me sir.' He said to the Director, as he pressed the receive call button. 'Hello.'

'Trilby-watch sir.... These Newspaper reports, are they relevant sir?'

Mark Pritchard sheepishly moved to a corner of the office and hopefully out of earshot of the Director, who was in the process of discussing the same matter as a prelude, no doubt, to a severe rollicking he was about to dish out. Mark brought up a hand in an effort to reduce the volume of his conversation. 'Shut it down and clean up you've never been there. Understand?' He closed the phone without waiting for a reply and casually returned to his seat. 'Sorry about that sir, something that needed my attention. You were saying, sir?'

'Ye, ye, yes sir, I understand.' Charlie stuttered to the now dead line. And then he cut the connection and sat for a moment, contemplating the rudiments of the brief conversation.

'Well Charlie what's the SP?'

'Yeah what gives man?'

'Op's aborted, but we've got a clean up problem, bound to be press hanging about the Hatton's, somehow we've got to get our gear out of there. Instructions are, we have never been here, understand.'

'Got it, Charlie. A bit of luck then as it's turned out, the Hatton's not showing up,' George said.

'Aye, let's hope they stay away a while longer.' Bill chipped in.

'If it stays that way, we'll go in at midnight.'

Stockton-on-Tees

There was a knock on the door, Michelle pushed her chair back from the computer and went to answer it.

'Michelle Thompson, daughter of Raymond Hartley?' A small lady said as Michelle opened the door.

'Y-e-s, and---?'

The lady appeared to be quite old with silver hair and a pronounced stoop, so much so she was supporting herself on a sturdy looking walking stick clasped in her right hand. She was wearing a dull pink gabardine coat a large cloth bag hung over the crook of her arm, and she clutched a daily newspaper in her left hand.

'I knew your father very well; my name is Mavis, Mavis Gardiner. I wanted to talk to you about this article.' She said as she pointed the newspaper at Michelle.

Michelle realised that her name had not been disclosed, so why then was this woman approaching her. *Only one way to find out.*

'You'd better come in.' Michelle led her into the lounge and sat her on the settee. 'I'm a little confused, Mrs Gardiner, what makes you think I know anything about any article?'

'Mavis, you can call me Mavis. You see Michelle there's a connection.'
'No I'm afraid I don't see.'
'Oh dear, I had hoped.'
'Hoped, I.... I 'm sorry Mavis, but-.'

Before Michelle could finish, Mavis Gardiner continued, 'Your father came to see me just after my husband Stan died.'

Oh I am sorry,' Michelle sympathetically put in.

Mavis sighed and shrugged at the memory of loosing her husband and then she took a deep breath and carried on. 'Your father told me that fallout from the ICI was responsible and he was going to take them to task. He hinted that compensation could be due. And then I read in the paper that he had also died.'

Michelle nodded. 'I still don't know how I can help.'

'This article in the Daily Express is all about the fallout, just like your father said. I thought this Colin Hatton could help me get what's due to me, but he's not answering the phone. Then I thought, just a chance, mind you that your dad may have talked to you about it? And besides I've known you since you were a little girl.'

Have you now don't know you from Adam. Michelle thought.

'I'm sorry Mavis but I just can't place you.' Michelle lowered her head in a vain attempt to disguise her feelings of hurt and loss she had just been inadvertently reminded of. 'Y-e-s my father, may have told me something of what he'd discovered about the ICI, but unfortunately I didn't listen. Sorry Mavis, I don't think I can help you.'

'But surely.' Mavis said pleadingly.

Michelle paused momentarily. 'Well, perhaps you could help me.'

'I don't....'

'With something that may have happened when your Stan died.'

'Well, I'll try, if I can.' Mavis sounded somewhat confused, she had come looking for help and never expected to be giving it.

'Did you get a visit from a short gentleman, smartly dressed, thinning grey hair, steel rimmed glasses and a little on the chubby side?'

'You must mean Mr. Nicholson, the Administrator.' She said assuredly. 'He came to see me, told me Stan had an insurance which would take care of all the arrangements, with a little bit left over for me. Kind gent, I didn't have to do a thing, he even dealt with the registration and death certificates.'

'And no doubt the funeral arrangements.' Michelle said with a touch of sarcasm. 'You wouldn't happen to know anything else about him, would you?'

'Got a business card here, somewhere.' Mavis said as she rummaged in her oversized handbag. 'Ah, here we are, just his name and telephone number I'm afraid.'

Poole

Ian Turner had spent last night in the spare bedroom of his parent's home, still conscious of the possibility that he still may be being hunted by a contract killer. Dad had just returned from his ritualistic walk to the local newsagent.

'Got the Daily Mail son, I think you just may want to take a look.'

'Sure dad thanks.' Ian took the newspaper and glanced at the headlines, a smirk instantly cut across his face. 'Great,' he mumbled, 'that should get Colin off the hook.'

'I thought you'd find that interesting.' His dad said a knowing look. 'You wouldn't happen to have been talking to my old acquaintances by any chance?' Ian nodded the devilish smirk. 'Expect you'll tell me all about it when you're ready.'

'No time like the present.' Ian put down the paper, looked up at his father. 'Better sit down; it's quite a long story.' Ian's mum Alice, who seldom misses a trick, sidled in and quietly sat down next to her husband. They both listened intently, without interruption, to Ian as he recounted the events of the previous week.

'What do you make of it all, Dad?'

Allan Turner stood up, put his hands in his trouser pockets and sauntered over to the patio door. He gazed through the glass and out into the garden, but he wasn't looking at anything, other than back within his mind to the memories of so long ago. 'Funny how you put things out of your mind. After all these years, I thought I'd forgotten, but deep down it's all still there.' He said sombrely, talking to no one in particular, but himself. 'The foul smells, the yellow plumes of smoke and the acid rain that made your skin tingle and itch.' He sighed, his mind drifting into the shadows of the past. Without turning he uttered. 'Someone should pay, who knows how many good lives were shortened, by that foul poison.'

Eventually he confined the thoughts of his youth and Haverton Hill back into the archives of his memory and turned away from the patio door to face Alice and Ian, the sombre look now replaced with a smile. 'Sorry, I digress, now to the matter in hand. This hit man, is he still looking for you?'

'Don't know, I can't be sure that's why I spent last night here.'

'You stay for as long as you want son.'

'Thanks Mum, but I really think I should get well away for a while, until the whole thing blows over.'

'There's the house in Spain, yours for as long as you want it.'

'Thanks, could be an idea, but if someone is pursuing me, it wouldn't take them long to discover that my parents had a place in Spain and then where would I go? No on second thoughts it may be best not to get you involved, thanks anyway.'

'See your point, what about the business?'

'No problems there, that should tick over for a few months now without my input.'

A trilling noise alerted Ian to an incoming text on his mobile. Retrieving the unit from his coat he pressed the 'read' key.

Ian can you call me back me back on the land line. Michelle
Ian closed the mobile. 'Can I use the phone please?'
'Yes of course.'

'Hi Michelle, what's the problem?'

'I've got a name and a telephone number for the phantom solicitor. Haven't a clue where Colin is.'

'Don't worry I'll sort it, what have you got?'

'J P Nicholson, 01642 876347.'

'Okay Michelle, I'll find an address and ring you back. On second thoughts.... I'll bring it myself.'

Ian closed the call, then immediately pressed in his office number. 'Hi Maureen, could you crank up the computer for me? What I'm after is an address in the Teesside area which matches this telephone number 01642 876347, probably registered to a J P Nicholson. Can you text it to my mobile.'

'Will do.' Maureen responded.

Ian closed the line and replaced the wire free telephone back into its holder. 'Dad, any chance you could run me home, please.'

'Sure.'

Ian let himself into the apartment noting as he did so, that the hair was still in place on the door frame. A cursory check just to ensure all was well, before packing an overnight bag and collecting the keys for the Audi. As he left, he re-fixed the hair across the door and frame before heading down the back staircase to the car park.

Ian didn't think to check the car over before getting in; the undisturbed hair had boosted his confidence, falsely as it turned out. As Ian drove the Audi out of the apartment block heading northward to Teesside, a beep accompanied the moving dot on the screen of a tracking device in a black BMW.

Stockton on Tees

It was just a little after five in the evening when Ian arrived at Michelle's house. She was waiting for him with excited anticipation. 'Ian, did you get it?'

'Hi Shell, I'd love a cuppa.'

'Kettles on and I've made you a sandwich. But did you get it?'

'Great.' Ian said as he followed Michelle into the kitchen. He sat on the bench seat next to a kitchen table and began to consume a ham and salad sandwich, while Michelle poured the tea.

'Well.' She said.

'Well what.' He said and received a playful punch on the arm.

'Don't mess about; you know what I mean.....Did you get the address?'

'Of course I did, it's a house in Billingham.' Ian swallowed the last bite washing it down with a mouthful of tea, smacking his lips, he said. 'Fancy paying him a visit.'

'Now?'

'No time like the present.'

'Shouldn't we call first? Make sure he's home.'

'Or not, - hopefully.' Ian said, rubbing his chin thoughtfully. 'If Nicholson is our man, I wouldn't mind having an uninterrupted nose around, see if I can find anything to incriminate him.'

'Bit risky isn't it?'

'Sure, but if I go that route, I don't want you to get involved. You can stay in the car.'

'Think again sunshine, where you go, I go and besides I know what he looks like, you don't.'

'Good point.' Ian said, holding up his hands in mock surrender.

Michelle picked up the phone and keyed in the number that Mavis Gardiner had given her. She held the instrument to her ear for a good thirty-second. 'No response sounds as if it's been disconnected.'

'We may be too late, better check it out, like now. You coming?'

'You bet.'

The Audi headed out of Stockton along Norton Road, over the A19 and up Billingham Bank. 'The house is on South View, just along here on the right. That's the one.' Ian said

'I can't see any lights.'

Ian slowly drove by. 'Seems quiet.'

'Turn left here Ian, go around the green and come back in the other direction.'

Ian did so bringing the Audi back in the other direction and parked on the verge outside of the house. They sat there for a few minutes looking over the house. All the curtains at the front were closed and there was no sign of any light. 'You think all the publicity has scarred him off?'

'Maybe, the house certainly looks as if unoccupied.' Ian said, tilting his head to see out of the near side passenger window.

'What do you think, shall we check it out?'

'Let's do it.'

Ian and Michelle made their way along the dark path up to the front door. Ian pushed the flap on the letter box open and peered though the slot. 'Can't see anything, the house seems to be all in darkness. Let's try the back.' Cautiously they edged around the side of the house, found a boarded gate, thankfully not locked, opened it and made their way to the back of the house, where it was even darker. 'Wish I'd have brought my torch.' Ian found the back door and automatically tried the handle fully expecting the door to be locked. Surprisingly it wasn't, the door creaked open. 'Shall we?' Ian tossed his head to one side.

'Do we put the light on?'

'May as well, can't look for evidence in the dark. Let's start in the lounge.'

'Michelle fumbled around until she located the light switch turning on the kitchen light. 'Power's still on, door unlocked, maybe Mr. Nicholson hasn't de-camped.'

'Or maybe he left in a hurry, why bother turning things off if you've no intention of coming back.'

'Aye, good point.' Ian agreed.

More at ease now, convinced that the house was unoccupied, Ian and Michelle made their way to the room at the front of the house. Ian felt for the switch and flicked on the light.

'Welcome.... Mr. Turner I presume and the lovely Michelle. Do come in make yourself comfortable.' Joseph Nicholson was seated in an armchair, legs crossed and resting on his knee was the silencer barrel of the pistol he was holding.

'You're not serious, are you?' Ian said nervously, his eyes transfixed on the now gesturing weapon, as he nervously edge into the room closely followed by Michelle.

'I assure you Mr. Turner; I'm deadly serious.' Beads of sweat formed on the fat mans brow, but that was down to his unfit overweight condition, not his mood of deadly intent. Ian and Michelle shuffled further into the room following the waving movement of the barrel and flopped onto the sofa opposite him.

'I guess our theory was correct.' Ian said. 'You were the guy on the other end of the Pathologists telephone conversation and probably the one that did him in.'

Nicholson sat there a smirk on his face. 'Oh we have been a busy boy haven't we, going around sticking your nose where it doesn't belong.'

'You did, you killed him because he wouldn't falsify any more autopsies for you.'

Nicholson nodded, the smirk still set on his face. 'I am aware Mr. Turner that you talked with Antony Davidson and I also suspect that it was you that got to Miles- Johnson.' Nicholson threw, with some degree of anger, a copy of the Daily Mail in they direction. It missed them, but they got the message. 'You couldn't leave it could you, now there'll be an enquiry and it won't take too long for police to join the dots. Just one more day and I'd have been home free.' Nicholson chin dropped to his chest and he sighed heavily.

He wants to talk. Ian sensed and he glanced at Michelle, who was still visibly shaking. 'What dots Nicholson and why the big deal?' Nicholson seemed to drift off into a trance like state, no doubt turning over past events in his mind. Ian sensing that Nicholson's mind was elsewhere, eased himself up with the intention of grabbing the fat mans gun away. But he had hardly lifted the cheeks of his butt off the sofa when Nicholson looked up.

He squinted at the man now half stood. 'Sit down! Sit down! I say.'

Slowly Ian lowered himself back down to join Michelle, who he noted was still shaking. 'Come on Nicholson; tell us about the dots.' Ian said feeling a little more cocky. 'What was so secretive that you found it necessary to take a life to protect it?'

'You don't know, do you?' Ian just stared at him and said nothing. There was silence as Ian's eyes bored into those of the diminutive fat man holding the gun, the intention clear, to unnerve him and it was working. 'Don't mess with me son I will not hesitate to use this.' And he shakily pointed the weapon at the couple.

'Why, 'the sit in the dark' routine and for how long?'

'Ah, the truth is I wasn't, not that is until you came by. I was upstairs about to close the curtains when your vehicle slowed. Suspicions confirmed when you came back parked out front and then I saw Michelle, knew it had to be you that was with her. I thought you'd turn up sooner or later. I was kinda hoping you'd show before I took off. Score to settle, loose ends to tie, that sort of thing. All those people reading this story,' he jabbed the barrel in the direction of the Daily Mail now strewn on the floor, 'would soon realise that their former Haverton Hill relative probably had died as a result of this toxic fallout shit, even if they hadn't. All kinds of claim and accusations will no doubt follow. I now need to cover my tracks, tie up the loose ends-.'

'Was the Pathologist a loose end?' Ian put in, hoping to keep Nicholson talking.

'What do you think? How long before the police singled him out, once all the relatives started comparing notes? I'll tell you, not long, not long at all. So I rubbed the wimp out.'

'And how long do you think it would take the police to tie you in with these deaths, eh? If I were you I'd be expecting them to be banging on my door sooner rather than later.'

'They'd be too late, if you hadn't of shown up I'd have been gone.'

'Then I've just got to keep you here. Ian thought. Why don't you tell us the reason why? You've got nothing to lose now, have you?'

Nicholson put his head to one side and scrutinised the couple. 'Ahh what the hell, you're not going to be able tell anybody anyway. You see, I don't intend letting you live long enough.' Michelle gasped.

'Well it won't harm, will it?' Ian said coolly.

'Nope, guess it won't.' Nicholson replied smugly.

'I don't suppose it'll count for much if I was to tell you that I didn't ever expect things to turn out this way. But what the hell,' he shrugged his shoulders, 'that's life, or in your case death.' He chuckled to himself no doubt amused by his sick attempt at humour. 'I came over from States, about fifteen years ago. I replaced a guy, an accountant, part of the problem, I suppose.' Nicholson paused momentarily to gather his thoughts. 'Fifty year ago it was thought that that fallout crap would start bumping people off. The US invested a huge amount to cover the expected compensation and cover up costs. Nothing happened, can you believe that?' Ian shook his head. 'All that money just sat there, growing. So I figured I was entitled, know what I mean.' Ian again just nodded. 'When folk did start kicking the bucket fifty years on, that's when the shit really did hit the fan. Oh boy did it. I had to somehow convince the deceased relatives that the deaths were natural, because there wouldn't be enough left in the kitty to cover the mass compensation it was initially invested for.'

'And you enlisted the Pathologist to help.'

'Him and others, they believed they were containing an epidemic. In actual fact it was Antony Davidson who was the first to spot the fungi and figured it was a result of something toxic. Just as well I got to him when I did. I convinced him that the government were trying to contain the situation and that he needed to keep it quiet.'

'It all becomes clear now, my father, my mother, - you bastard.' Michelle suddenly found her voice. But her outburst only served to annoy Nicholson.

'Enough! Enough! He jumped to his feet, crossed the floor and stuck the silencer gun barrel into Michelle's face. 'You!... On the floor. Now! On your stomach.' He shouted at Ian and Michelle whimpered as the gun was pressed harder against her face. Ian hesitated, contemplating giving this little squirt a right hand to the chin, but seeing Michelle's head jar with prodding from the barrel, he complied without further ado. 'Hands behind you!' A thin cord was produced from a pocket; it already had a loop on a slip knot, like a lasso, which Nicholson snared around Ian's neck. He then deftly stuck the gun into his belt and whipped the cord into a hitch around Ian's wrists. Michelle tried to take advantage of Nicholson's distraction and she jumped at him, nails extended. 'Son of a bitch!' Nicholson shouted as he swung back his left arm wildly in Michelle's direction. His fist caught her with some force behind the ear and sent flying backward. He turned his attention back to Ian who was attempting to turn over in an effort to help Michelle. Nicholson stamped hard on Ian's spine knocking the wind out of him. 'Feet up! Feet up you bastard.' The blood from Michelle's clawed gouges ran down his cheek and dripped on Ian's Jeans. The cord was whipped around Ian's feet and tied tight. Ian was now well trussed up, any movement of his hands or feet and he would pull the cord around his neck tighter. Michelle recovered enough to launch herself at Nicholson again. But this time he was ready and had whipped the gun from out of his belt and which he swung with much force at Michelle's head.

Ian didn't know what had happened to Michelle other than hearing a dull thud. 'Michelle!' He shouted, but the shout only increased the choking affect of the cord.

Ian didn't know it, but Michelle was lying unconscious on the sofa, the blood was oozing from a gash on the side of her head were she'd taken a blow from the gun barrel. Nicholson was systematically going through Ians pockets. 'Where's your fucking car keys.' Ian couldn't answer even if he had wanted to and he received a frustrating kick in his ribs, to add to his discomfort.

A few minutes passed, from the rustles, Ian assumed he was tying up Michelle, which he accepted with some relief. *She must still be alive.*

'Right you prick; you're only alive because I say so.' And he gave Ian another kick just to emphasize the point. 'But how long you live will depend upon how still you stay. Personally I don't think you'll last the night. Goodbye Mr Turner, sweet dreams.' Again he chuckled as he turned out the light and closed the living room door.

Joseph Nicholson left the house by the front door, turning the key to lock as he exited. He then tossed the key into the long grass of the unkempt garden. Smiling to himself as he patted the weapon stuck in the waist of his trousers. He walked down the path swinging small holdall in his left hand, the extent of his possessions. In his right hand he held, pointed and pressed the key fob in the direction of Ian's Audi. Smiling smugly as the amber lights flashed, accompanied by a click as the doors unlocked.

Nicholson got into the vehicle and spent a brief moment to familiarise himself with the layout, before slipping the key into the ignition and firing the engine. A smirk of satisfaction cut across his face as he pushed the gear stick into first and eased away. *Stroke of luck getting Turner's car, I was all set to catch a train to London.* The car headed down Billingham bank towards the A19.

Unfortunately for Nicholson, that was the point at which he realised that the brakes didn't work. The smirk instantly changed to a look of horror as he pumped and pumped at the brake pedal. The car was moving faster and faster and out of shear panic he pulled at the handbrake, nothing other than the dramatic increase in speed. Evan more panic now as the steering failed to respond. The decent of Billingham bank seemed to take an age, but in reality it was a matter of seconds, Nicholson screamed and threw both arms across his face. The Audi bounced up and over the roundabout at the bottom of the hill, across the road at the other side, into and though a brick wall that was the bridge parapet and tumbled down into what was once the river bed at Billingham bottoms.

The lights on of the black car parked in the shadows at the bottom of Billingham bank came on. The engine started up and it motored slowly passed the scene of the accident, confirming the extent of the destruction. It then picked up speed and turned onto the slip road to the A19 heading south. The driver laughed out loud. 'Ha, ha, ha, rest in piece Mr. Turner.'

Ian heard the sirens, but there didn't have any significance for him, he was more concerned about Michelle, who he couldn't see and couldn't hear. 'Michelle.' He croaked, but she did not respond. *What the hell have I gotten us into. .*

The blue strobe lights flashed eerily in the night, casting dull light and dark shadows around the accident scene, to the extent that the blueness of the light reflected off the tangled mass of metal that was a motor vehicle. The metal was bunched up and embedded in the embankment of the former river some fifteen feet below the road level. The two policemen, first on scene, stood at what was left of the bridge wall, looking down at the wreck.

'I've coned the road off Steve.'

'Good, what do you reckon Pete, how many in the vehicle?'

'I think it's only the driver, but I can't be sure it's in fairly smashed up. The Medics are on standby down there, but they can't get near him until the Firemen arrive to cut him out.'

'Poor Bastard.' At that the patrol car radio began to chirp. 'I'll get it.' Steve walked over to the car and put his hand through the open window and picked up the radio mike. 'Two-three-nine, - receiving.'

As Steve headed back to the bridge wall, the Fire and Rescue vehicle turned up and was in process of reversing up to the hole in the brickwork. Floodlights now shone on the wreck, a man had scrabbled down the bank and was in the process of attaching a line to the rear tow point. Another was holding what looked like a giant pair of tin snips which he aiming at what was left of the wind screen,

'Got a make on the reg. The car belongs to a Mr. Ian Turner from Poole in Dorset.'

'Bit far from home isn't he? Don't rate his chances; better make moves to contact the next of kin.'

'Already done.'

It took twenty minutes to winch the wrecked vehicle up the bank, another ten for the Firemen to cut the door off and to extract the body. Two Medics moved in and began to go through the pointless motions of revival. Within minutes one of them looked up and solemnly shook his head. And then almost immediately the Medic called to the Policemen. 'Better get down here Sergeant and take a look at this.'

'Here we go again, Steve. What have they found now?'

Steve and Pete put on latex gloves and began to search the body which was a bit mashed up blood soaked and not a pretty sight. With two fingers Pete extracted the pistol and carefully placed it in a polythene bag. 'Begs a few questions Steve, what's this guy doing so far away from home with a gun?'

Steve had extracted the wallet and an American Airlines ticket Heathrow to JFK. 'Not so far from home Pete, according to this, his names Joseph P Nicholson and he lives, or lived in South View just at the top of the bank. It also looks like he was making a getaway, one way ticket to JFK. What the fuck was he doing in Ian Turners car.'

'Oh shit, better put the NOK call on hold at least until we've checked out this address. I'm somewhat concerned, seeing that gun and where's the cars real owner?'

'This may be Ian Turner,' Steve said nodding his head in the direction of the corpse, 'he may be using a false ID.'

'Aye maybe, but we'd check it out ASAP he may have left a wife or something up there.'

As a matter of course, Steve picked up the radio microphone as they got into the patrol car and called in their findings, the response was almost instant.

'Control to two three nine, comeback.'
'Two three nine receiving.'

'Ian Turner's next of kin had not been contacted, repeat, have not been contacted. Over.

'Two three nine to Control. 'Bit of a relief on that. Over and out.'

Pete put the car in gear and headed for the bank. They were just cruising up to Joseph P Nicholson's address on South View. 'Control to two three nine. Come in.

'Two three nine receiving, go ahead.'

'Sorry Steve, just heard we were too late to stop the NOK, victims. Scratch that, the not so sure victim's father, is on his way.'

'Very funny, two three nine, out.'

The police car threw a u-turn at the top of the bank and pulled up opposite the house. 'This is it.' Pete said.

'All in darkness.'

'What would you expect?' The two officers headed down the path. 'No bell.' Steve said, as he used the but of his torch to hammer on the door. 'Don't seem to be anyone at home.'

'Shush Steve.' Pete said frantically waving a hand at his colleague. 'Hear that?'

They both put an ear to the glass pain of the living room window. 'It's a mobile. Think it should be answered?' Steve nodded and brought the but of his torch heavily against the window. It didn't take long before the Policemen were climbing through the window and into the living room. The beam of Steve's torch picked out Ian's now unconscious trussed up body and immediately after, Michelle's body. 'Bloody hell, I think we got a murder scene.' Ian's moan could be just heard above the still trilling mobile in his pocket.

'Get an ambulance PDQ, he at least is still alive.'

Ian started to come round, but before he could force his eyes open, he felt the hurt and the soreness in his throat and his neck felt as if it was wrapped in barbed wire.

Allan Turner was stationed at Ian's bedside looking at him intently, waiting for any signs that would indicate consciousness. When Ian's eye lids flickered, he hesitated momentarily before he spoke. 'Awake at last, thank goodness.'

'Oh-hi-Dad .....Where the hell......am I?' Ian struggled to say.

'Better leave the talking to me son, you're neck still looks a little sore. You're in North Tees Hospital, been here a couple of days now.'

M-i-c-h-e-l-l-e....wh--.

The lady they found with you? Michelle Thompson I believe her name is.' Ian nodded.

'Well she had a nasty gash above her ear, took five stitches and marks on her face where that bastard beat her. He must have tied her the same way he tied you, but as she was unconscious she didn't move, so didn't strangle herself.'

'H-o-w'--? Ian attempted to ask.

'Don't worry son, she's fine. She asked me to give you her love. Her husband came to take her home. Apparently she's given the Police the full rundown of events, as much as she knows, that is. Although the Police still have a couple of points they want you to clear up.' Ian's eye's widened, but Dad continued without reiterating. 'Just as well I let your mobile ring, the Police tell me that's how they found you.' Ian blinked his eyes in acknowledgement of his dad's intuition. 'In strange sort of way, that Nicholson fella, did you a favour.'

'Favour, - he - was - going - to – shoot – us.' Ian managed to croak.

'Of course, you don't know, do you? The gun wasn't loaded, so he couldn't have shot you, although I suppose you wouldn't have lasted too long if the cops hadn't broken in. Anyway if he hadn't of taken your car, it would have been you and Michelle ending up in Billingham bottoms.' The shock was evident on Ian's face. 'That's what the Police want to talk to you about, while your car was parked outside of Nicholson's house, someone made a pretty good job of cutting through the brake pipes and steering cables. 'Ian's mouth dropped open. 'That and the fact that they found some sort of tracking device secured under the back wheel arch.'

'W-o-w!' Was all Ian could manage to croak.

'As soon as we get that out of the way we'll head home son.'

CHAPTER TWENTY-FOUR

Three days after the ordeal in the Billingham house, Ian was sitting in his dad's car heading back to Poole, Allan was doing the talking as Ian was still finding the experience difficult. Although his throat felt a lot better, the black and blue bruising around his neck still looked horrific.

'While you were laid up son, I had a chat with a DI Baker, told me he knew about the fallout situation and to tell you it was Nicholson's prints he found on the Pathologists car.' Allan shrugged his shoulders. 'He said you would understand.' Ian just nodded, put his head back and closed his eyes.

Eventually just about at the half way mark, junction 15A on the M1, Ian woke, croaking thoughtfully. 'D-a-d.'

'Yes son.'

'Nicholson—stole—the—money—meant—for--- compensation.'

'Yeah, so I believe.'

'Where –is—it?'

'Ahh, - been through this with the police. It turns out the guy had a Villa in the South of France, boats and cars a plenty. There's no doubt a bank account as well, Swiss they believe, but the police have drawn a blank on that. Anyway it looks like Nicholson only came to the UK on the odd occasion, probably to transfer funds. Apparently he used a rental car when he was here to get about, that's why yours came in handy.'

Ian nodded. There but for the grace of God.

Allan allowed a little time for reflection, before continuing. 'According to neighbours, the Billingham house was purchased about three years ago, but they hardly saw Nicholson until this pasted year.'

Another long period of silence occurred before Ian croaked again. 'D-a-d.'

'Y-e-s.'

'Someone's – trying—to—kill—me.'

'I know.'

Allan paused a moment to negotiate his access from the A43 onto the M40. 'With all the media coverage, you'd think MI5 would be attempting to recall the assassin. No point in trying to keep the secret any longer.'

'Maybe—they—can't.'

'Maybe, but until they do, you're going to have to lie low for a time.'

Ian nodded, closed his eyes again, slipped down in the seat and dozed.

When he awoke, dad was just turning the car into his drive in Poole. 'I – should—head –to—my—apartment.' He croaked.

'You're going nowhere son.'

The next morning Allan took a mug of coffee into Ian's room. 'Morning... How are you feeling?'

'Lot better, not so sore.' Ian said as he eased himself up into a sitting position.

'Good.....Er, I was just thinking, why didn't Colin Hatton tell the media it was you who got the story?'

'Ah, Colin's a published author, thought it would give more credence, if these facts had come to light as a result of Colin's research for a sequel. Which, as it happens, isn't too far from the truth.' Ian took a sip of his coffee, it soothed as it slipped down. 'Colin in turn thought, if he kept my name out of it, those who wanted me killed, may have second thoughts. You know; if I wasn't involved, why kill me.'

'Well we now know that didn't work.'

At that moment Ian's mobile trilled. Allan retrieved it from Ian's coat pocket. 'It's a text.'

To learn something of benefit 2 u, meet me outside Lord Nelson Poole quay at 3. A friend.

'Hum, I wonder. What do yah reckon?' Ian held the phone so that Allan could read it.

'The quay, busy area, but I doubt that would be enough to deter an assassin.' Allan shrugged his shoulders.

'Yeah, thanks for that Dad.'

'Perhaps, whoever sent that text is your friend, who else would be privy to your mobile number?'

'You could be right Dad, yeah, you could be right.'

Allan made to leave the bedroom, turning back to look at Ian when he reached the door. 'You take it easy, get some rest, this afternoon I'll run you by the quay and we'll take a butcher's.'

'Thanks Dad'

An old man tottered shakily along Poole Quay towards 'Dolphin Quay Marina.' He hesitated for a long moment to study the array of sailing craft that were gently bobbing on their moorings in the marina. He then turned to survey the area in search of some shade from the sun's rays. Directly behind him, on the other side of the road, was an apartment building, part of the front of which overhung the walkway. '*Perfect.*' He muttered to himself and waved his walking stick in the air to fend off any approaching vehicles. Almost bent double, he ambled slowly one foot shakily in front of the other until he eventually made it across the road and took up refuge in the shadow. The overhang not only covered the pavement, it also formed a canopy over the main entrance door to the apartments. The old man found himself staring through the glass door into the lobby. At the end of the lobby a young lady Sales Receptionist sat behind a desk, twiddling a pencil between two fingers, her chin supported by a hand the elbow resting on the desk, looking bored stiff. From time to time the old man glanced furtively in her direction, and then he quickly averted his eyes as she returned his stare. After a few minutes she decided that the game of stare back was also boring, and decided a visit to the loo was necessary, or perhaps she would go and make some tea in the kitchen, but for whatever reason, she decided to leave her post. The old man eased the outer glass doors open and entered the building. Bent almost double as one of a good age, he slowly ambled over to the lift door and pressed the call button. The doors opened, he stepped in and hit the top floor button, the receptionist had still not returned to her post. The lift doors opened on the fifth floor, the old man stuck his head from out of the orifice and peered down the corridor in both directions, quickly swinging his head from one side to the other. Satisfied that nobody was about, he tottered down the corridor squinting up at the numbers on the doors. On reaching number five-two-one, he used his stick to rap lightly on the panel and waited for an answer which he knew would not be forthcoming. When as expected nothing happened, he glanced around to make sure that he was in no way being watched, before extracting a large bunch of keys and levers from an inside pocket, deftly selecting one, he pushed it into the Yale, jiggled it and turned it, and just like that, the door opened. Again the old man furtively checked the corridor ensuring that all was still clear before entering the apartment and closing the door behind him. Once inside the apartment, he straightened, checked the surroundings and then he unscrewed the top of his walking stick and removed a disc about the size of a coat button. After careful consideration he selected the large central coffee table in the lounge and secured the device to its underside. On leaving, the old man stoop was adopted again and he headed for the escape stairs that he had noted at the end of the corridor.

At ten to three in the afternoon, Alan's car cruised slowly along Poole quay. 'Quite a few people about son, that's good.

'I hope so. Drop me here dad, I'll walk on to the Lord Nelson.'

'You sure?'

'Yeah, you take off, head home. If I feel I need you, I'll give you a bell.'

'If you think.'

'Yeah, pointless dragging you into this.'

'Okay, but I'll drive around the block just to check you're alright.'
Ian nodded in agreement as he closed the car door and set off to walk
the hundred metres, or thereabouts to the Lord Nelson public house.
Outside the pub, the pavement was railed off to enclose a number of
picnic type tables with attached bench seats for customers who
wished to drink their beverage out doors. Ian found one table vacant
and slid his bottom onto the bench seat; part thinking as he did, that
he should have purchased a drink before sitting down. There was a
pip from a car horn as Ian's dad motored slowly by. Ian instinctively
waved in acknowledgement not really knowing if he was going to be
okay or not. As he turned back a pint of beer had appeared in front of
him and sitting opposite, nursing what appeared to be a glass of red
wine, was a beautiful brunette with brown eyes, the spit of Audrey
Hepburn. Ian was bedazzled.

'Did I get that right?' She asked. 'He did say your preference was
bitter.'

'Err, Y-e-s, bitters' fine, but--.'
'What am I doing here?' pre-empting his question.
Ian, dumbfounded, just nodded, he was finding it difficult to see past
her beauty, rather than be concerned about the reason he was there in
the first place.

'I've been asked to give you this.' She said as she fumbled in her
handbag, extracting a small brown envelope.

'What's this?'

She leaned her head to one side and shrugged her shoulders. 'Haven't a clue, I'm just the messenger.' Ian took hold of the envelope, but made no attempt to open it, mainly because he was unable to take his eyes off her. She took a drink of her wine, placing the still nearly full glass on the table, and attempted to stand, but was somewhat restricted by the bench. 'Got to go, bye now.'

'Hang on,' Ian protested, 'please, please sit down; I need to talk to you.'

'I don't think.'

'Finish your drink, at least.'

Hesitantly, she eased her bottom down on the bench, picked up the glass and took a drink. Ian chose the same moment to take a gulp of his beer, timing his swallow to coincide with hers, all the time taking in her beauty. Ian noted her stare, no doubt noticing the bruising and he emphasized the point by lightly toughing his neck. 'Had a run in with a guy who had a rope.' He smiled as if to make light of the matter.

'Hum didn't really notice.' She said. 'Well.'

'Well, what?'

She pointed with her chin. 'The envelope, aren't you going to open it?'

'Oh err, I was kindda hoping you would tell me what's in it.'

'I've already told you, I'm just a messenger, I don't have clue about any of this other than, whatever it is, is not illegal and that it's of interest to you.'

'But how.'

'How did I get involved?' She pre-empted him again.

'Yeah how?'

'Simple, I've just completed my Master's and I'm in the circuit looking for a placement in IT.'

'Interesting,' Ian interjected, with visions of her working with him, flitting vividly through his mind.

'I had a one to one with my tutor yesterday, in Oxford,' Ian pursed his lips and let out an audible. 'Hum.' *Oxford.* He thought.

'He told me to visit this particular IT company down here,' she slid an address card across the table, 'and while I was in Poole, I could do him a favour and deliver this envelope to you. That's it really apart from a couple of irrelevant questions.'

'Hum, so just how did you know me?'

'Easy, I was given your photograph.'

'Photograph! Ian exclaimed. 'Please show me.'

As she once more rummaged in her handbag, thoughts of how anyone could have his photo, flashed through his mind and he took another gulp of his beer in an attempt to mask the anxious expression he was sure had registered on his face. 'Here it is,' she said and slid a slightly creased 5x7 black and white photo across the table. Ian let the beer glass come away from his mouth and slowly placed it on the table next to the image now glaring up at him. *It was him alright about to get into a silver car, -- Colin's car, Rudd's Arms car park, -- how on earth ---.* 'By satellite.' He said out loud without thinking.

'Pardon.'

'Oh nothing and you were given my name?' Ian said nonchalantly, expecting an affirmative.

'No, to me you are just 'this guy.'

'And you travelled down here from Oxford, to meet a stranger and to attend a fictitious job interview?' She paused for a moment to study Ian more intently and to compose an answer.

'I did have the two-hundred pound incentive of course and the promise of a non fictitious job interview with a Mr. Ian Turner of IT Telecoms, Poole.' She reached across the table and tapped the address card with her fore finger. 'All arranged by my tutor, a very eminent Oxford Professor.' She smartly lifted her glass and took a drink.

'Well, that I don't doubt, I don't doubt at all.' Ian said thoughtfully. He glanced down at the photograph and the still unopened envelope, and then he fixed his eyes on the thing of beauty sitting opposite. *This is a set up.* He thought.

Still deep in thought he decided that the best course of action was to get away, some place where he could think it through.

'May I ask your name, after all you did buy me a drink and you have come all this way to see me?'

She smiled. 'Yes of course, I'm Amelia, Amelia Pendleton,' she reached out a hand, 'and you are?'

Ian took her hand and gently held onto it. 'Oh I thought you may have guessed its Ian, as in Ian Turner,' and he now tapped the address card with a fore finger. She looked dumbstruck and seemed to open her mouth but omitted no sound. It was Ians turn to pre-empt the doubt which was about to ensue, releasing her hand he reached into the back pocket of his jeans and extracted his wallet. He flipped it open and flashed his driving licence. 'The same Ian Turner who is about to interview you for a very lucrative IT job.'

'W- wha, what.' She stuttered, a look of perplexity on her face.

'But I would prefer the interview to be conducted in more private surroundings.' Ian said as he stood, threw a leg out over the bench seat and made to walk away, stopping only to grasp the envelope and the photograph, which he stuffed into a back pocket. Amelia half stood with her long legs cranked inside the bench seat, hesitant, not really knowing what she should do.

'Are you coming?'

'Where?'

'My apartment, it's just there, Dolphin Quay.' Ian pointed to the new apartment block directly in front of them and standing on the former site of the famed Poole Pottery factory. Noting her look of concern, he added. 'Don't worry Miss Pendleton; the receptionist on duty will confirm who and what I am.'

'Well I suppose in a way my tutor has recommended you.' At that she hitched up her tight skirt and eased a long shapely leg over the bench, much to the delight of a group of lads occupying the adjacent table, who gave out an appreciative cheer. She almost broke into a run in an attempt to catch up with Ian, who was by then, about five paces in front.

'Afternoon Mr. Turner.' The Receptionist said looking up from whatever she was reading under the desk.

'Hi Melanie, do me a favour would you?'
She nodded. 'Well er, for you anything.'
'Would you please reassure this young lady,' He turned to face Amelia, 'that I am who I say I am?'
'And who would you be today sir?'
'Melanie!'
'Only kidding.' The Receptionist smiled and turned to Amelia Pendleton. This is Mr. Ian Turner, MD, IT Telecoms; he has a very nice penthouse apartment on the fifth floor and is a very eligible bachelor.'

'Ah hem.' Ian attempted to cut short Melanie's appraisal.

She winked at Amelia. 'Good looking too.' And then she added as Amelia made to follow Ian to the lift door. 'You're one lucky lady.'

They reached the door to Ian's penthouse suite. Ian fumbled for his keys and was about to unlock the door when he suddenly noticed, or to put it another way, didn't notice the hair that he'd taken the trouble to secure across the gap. It could only mean one thing, somebody had entered the apartment and for all he knew, that somebody could still be in there. He hesitated poised with the key adjacent to the keyhole.

'Anything wrong Mr. Turner?'

'Er- er no, on second thoughts Miss Pendleton, perhaps it may be prudent to interview you at the office.'

'Well, if you think.'

'You have your car?'

'Y-e-s, but.....'

'Is it handy?

'It's in the multi-story, but.....'

'Good, we'll use yours, let's go.' Ian turned and headed off at pace towards the back fire escape stairwell, Amelia, mildly protesting under her breath, chased after him. It wasn't until they reached the ground floor parking level that she shouted loud enough to stop in his tracks. 'Would you please stop? I don't know what's going here, but I'm not taking one more step until you offer some rational explanation for your peculiar behaviour.'

'Okay okay.' Ian held up his arm in a 'stop the traffic' gesture. 'I promise as soon as we get to my office I'll explain everything, but right at this very moment I think it would be wise to get out of here, like now.'

Ian headed for the exit door, Amelia reluctantly followed.

CHAPTER TWENTY-FIVE

Ian punched in a code to unlock the outer door followed by a card swipe to release the lock on the sets of inner doors. As he progressed to his office, closely followed by Amelia, he was met with greeting calls from the staff and one or two wolf whistles no doubt aimed at his companion. A hand in the air as he walked on by was the only acknowledgement he was prepared to give. That was, until he reached the outer office and his secretary's desk.

'Why Ian, I thought you were taking a couple of weeks off.'

'Slight change of plan Maureen, but I haven't yet decided what I'm doing.'

'What on earth's happened to your neck?'

'Oh it's nothing, had a bit of an accident that's all.' Maureen didn't believe him, but she knew he would tell all eventually.

'So shall I bring you up to speed?'
'Not just now, Maureen.'

'You're the boss, whatever. But as you are here now, I'll need you to sign off a bunch of invoices.' Maureen said as she began to rummage through her in tray. 'I can tell you that all your business mail has been dealt with, no private stuff.'

'Thanks Maureen, I'll deal with them later. This is Miss Pendleton.' He said turning to Amelia. 'I'm about to interview her for a position in Programming.'

'Nice to meet you.' The secretary said as she took Amelia's hand. 'Can I get you a coffee?'

'Oh yes please, white with sugar.'

'Usual Ian?'

'Please Maureen, -- oh and could you get me a copy of this mornings newspaper, any tabloid.'

Ian pushed open his office door and made his way to the chair behind a very large desk, signalling with a hand gesture for Amelia to sit in the chair opposite.

'Well Miss Pendleton, where shall I begin?'

'You can start by calling me Amy and opening that damned envelope which I've gone to so much trouble to bring you.'

'The envelope, clean forgot.' Ian rummaged in the pocket of his jeans until he managed to extract a screwed up paper mass combining the envelope and the photograph, bunched together as if in a progress of mating. 'Here we are.' He said as he separated the items. Laying them on the desk top he proceeded to iron out each of them with the palm of his hand. 'By the way.' He took a moment to look at her. 'You can call me Ian.' And then he proceeded to open the envelope with a paper knife, extracting a single sheet of paper. The note was type written and brief.

'Well I've opened it.'

'Private I take it; err sorry I shouldn't have said that, after all it's none of my business.' She shrugged her shoulders as if to emphasize her disinterest.

'You wanted an explanation of my behaviour, this is part of it.' Ian turned the note through 180 degrees and slid it across the desk.

The contract is in place, awarded to Zest Inc and cannot be terminated, however we will look out for your future interest.

She read the note out loud and then raised her head to look at Ian. 'Straight forward enough, although I didn't realise the Professor was involved with awarding contracts. But why would he send me all the way down here with a message, surely it would have been easier for him just phone you?...And why lead me to believe I was coming here to attend an interview, even to the extent of giving me two-hundred pounds to cover my expenses?' Amy screwed her nose. 'It doesn't make sense.'

Ian held up a hand. 'More sense than you know let me explain.'

At that moment there was a brief tap on the door and Maureen walked in balancing a tray in one hand. 'Your coffees.' She announced.

'Thanks.'

'And the Daily Mail, its David's. Oh and could he have it back when you've read it, he hasn't finished the crossword.'

'For sure.' Ian said a broad grin cut across his face. 'Five minutes ought to do it.' Maureen waved a hand in a *don't bother* manner as she backed out of the door.

Ian flicked over the paper sheets scanning the pages as he did so. 'Ah here we are.' He passed the paper to Amy. 'I'd like you to read that story, page four column one.'

Amy took the paper and scanned the column headline. 'You mean this story about the Americans producing a deadly chemical weapon in the UK and a town was wiped out?'

'Haverton Hill.' Ian said.

'Heard about it, the story's been running all week, it was even on the news on the car radio as I travelled down here.'

'So you're aware that the sudden death of Dr Jeremy Miles-Johnson was, if nothing else very convenient.'

Amy nodded. 'If you say so.'

'He was murdered, to stop him from talking.'

She sat back. 'Oh come on, he was an old guy, surely he died of natural causes.'

'They didn't know it at the time, but they were too late, and now the same assassin is out to get me.'

'You've got to be kidding.'

'Wish I were.'

'But why you?'

'Because, the afternoon before his death, the doctor told me the whole story.'

Amy pondered for a moment to let what Ian had just said, sink in. 'But, but it says something about a Colin Hatton.'

'Yeah, a friend of my dads, he's writing a book on Billingham ICI and the benefits it was supposed to bring to the area. I was able to help him by interviewing the doctor. ...Only I learned more than I'd bargained for. I sort of hoped that if the story was no longer a secret, there would be no point in having me iced. That's why I asked Colin to release the story to the press.'

'How do you know it didn't work and whoever you say is trying to kill you, no longer is?'

Ian touched his still bruised neck and contemplated the cut brake pipes on the Audi, and then he looked at Amy. 'That note.' He said as he pointed his chin at the single sheet of paper on the edge of his desk.'

'But the note was—.'

'From your Professor,' Ian put in, 'who is no doubt well known to someone of high standing within the secret service.'

'I can't imagine Prof Atkins being involved with a secret service, I - I mean, what makes you think he is?'

'I know for sure it was MI5 who hired the assassin, I also know they acted without authority and another secret service is trying to remedy the situation. How else would your Professor have my mobile number and how else does he know that the contract to terminate me cannot be revoked.'

Amy shook her head disbelievingly. 'Sorry Ian, I'm just not sure what I'm doing here, I don't want to know anything else. This morning I was looking forward to an interview, now all I am is confused and maybe a little frightened.'

Ian shrugged his shoulders. 'I'm sorry Amy. Didn't mean to frighten you, but I have to know why.'

'Why what?'

'Why your Professor, Atkins you called him, sent you with the note. Why didn't he come himself? Or did he send you along as my guardian angel? Are you?'

'Fraid not, in fact I'm finding the whole thing very un-nerving, I- I don't think I should be here anymore.' Amy started to get to her feet.

'I don't think you should do that Amy.' She lowered herself back onto the seat.

'Why not?'

'Can't say for sure, something's bugging me; let's just say I'd like you to stick around a little longer.'

'Sorry Ian but I don't think I can do this.'

'Please, just a little longer.'

'Why should I?'

'There's the possibility you were set up, someone may have used you as a decoy to keep me at the Lord Nelson while they entered my apartment, may even be still there.'

'Someone used me, uh uh, - no way. '

'Perhaps not, but I would like the chance to establish that.'

'How?'

'Sorry Amy, but I'll need to first of all check you out, see if you are who you say you are.'

'Excuse me, - save yourself the bother. - I intend to head back to Oxford, right now, give Professor Atkins his money back and forget about the whole thing, job as well, if there ever was one.' She stood up and made to leave.

'Well the guy must have second sight or something; I've only just decided that we could do with another Programmer. But I would have to undergo a personal check into anyone I may consider hiring.' Ian said as she headed to the door. 'Sure you wouldn't want to be considered for the post?'

She hesitated, just for a moment, relieved that Ian was trying in some way, to stop her. For irrespective of the crazy circumstances she was being faced with and the job on offer, she was quite taken with him. Ian for reasons other than the dire situation he was in, didn't want her to go, in truth he rather fancied her.

'Please sit down Miss Pendleton, - Amy.' She turned to face him. 'Please.' He said pleadingly. A hardly discernable smile turned the corner of her mouth and Ian's heart skipped. 'I'd really like you to stay.'

She sat back down. 'In that case, I would like you to consider me for the position of Programmer with your company.- I have here my CV,' she rummage in her hand bag and withdrew three folded sheets of paper, 'together with a reference from Professor Michael Atkins.' She slid the papers over the desk to Ian.

'Thank you.' Ian took the papers, unfolded them, sat back legs crossed and read each of them intently. Amy took a sip of her coffee and waited.

'Hum, quite impressive.... I'd like to offer you the job here and now, subject to a personal check of course.'

'Er, er, good. I mean thank you. Don't you need to ask me some questions or something?'

Ian pursed his lips and shook his head. 'No I don't think that will be necessary. Do you want to ask me something?' Ian said enquiringly.

'I don't think so, to tell the truth I'm a little dumbfounded.'

Ian smiled leaned forward and pressed the intercom button. 'Maureen, would you arrange to have Amy's, Miss Pendleton's, records on file, employees register and set her up for a finger print and retina scan, within the next ten minutes please.'

'Will do, what about authenticity and security checks?' Maureen's voice came back.

'I'm just about to take care of that.' Ian turned to his computer and tapped in a set of commands. 'You wouldn't happen to know your National Insurance number by any chance?'

'Sure I do.' She said in a surprising manner, as if everybody should have this number tattooed on their forehead. 'It's AR 67 84 45 B.'

'Thanks, saves me looking.' He tapped in the number and within seconds Amy's life history flashed on the screen, nothing had been left out, there was a recent photograph and even a description and location of her birth mark. Ian turned the screen so that she could see.

'Wow! She said Big Brother or what. How on earth did they get my photo?'

'Passport I would presume. Seems clear that you are who you say you are, but to be absolutely sure I will need to see your birth mark.'

She looked aghast. 'But my ... er,– is—er.'

'On your bottom.' Ian finished for her. 'Left lower cheek, it says here.' A smile cut across Ian's face. 'Suppose we can get to that later.'

At that point Maureen wrapped on the door and walked in. She had a bunch of papers which she set down in front of Amy. 'I'll need you to take a look at this lot when you've read them, please sign and date them here, - here, - and here, then I'll take you to security for the scans.'

'What are there?'

'Official Secrets Act.' Ian chirped in. 'You will need to read it, understand it and fully comply with it before I can permit you to see TEOSY.'

'Tea – oss - ee?'

'Yeah, yeah, I know it sounds tacky, but I created the name Telecommunication Enhanced Observation System, before I considered the initials.'

'Oh, I s-e-e.'

CHAPTER TWENTY-SIX

It was getting late by the time Ian and Amy made their way up the staircase to the first floor office. All the rest of the staff, apart from a couple of security guards, had left for the weekend.

At the far end of the first floor office, was an area bounded by a solid wall which had a centrally positioned stainless steel access door. As they arrived at the door, Amy noted the sign stencilled on it, 'Authorised Personnel Only.' *Looks like the entrance to a safe.*

Ian did the card swipe and finger print scan which allowed him into the outer room of the chamber. He told Amy to do the same as the computer controlling the door would admit only one at a time. It was a small room with lockers and a bench seat along one wall and at one end there was a toilet and washroom. And immediately to the front of them, was another security door.

Donning white coveralls and polythene shoe covers, they repeated the procedure with a retina scan to access through this door into the inner sanctum. A dust free environment in which rows of computer column stacks stood on a galvanised steel panelled floor. Each stack had rows of various coloured flashing lights blinking at random intervals along the number of trays on each column. The air in the room was maintained at a constant temperature by air conditioners purring intermittently to satisfy the thermostat.

'This is TEOSY.... Are you impressed?'

'I'll say, looks like a powerful bit of kit.' Then she added rather naively. 'Does it have any specific function?'

Ian looked at her. 'Before I answer that you must first promise me that you will never repeat what I'm about to tell you to no one and I mean no one, after all none of my staff know the real function of this machine.'

She shrugged her shoulders. 'For what it's worth, cross my heart, hope to die.....But please don't feel you've got to tell me.'

'Well from what I'm about to do in here, it'll probably become obvious, but I would feel better about it with a more sincere promise from you.'

'Okay I promise most sincerely, that what I'm about to learn in this room, remains here.' Emphasizing her promise by making an X sign over her mouth.

'Thanks, - well what you see here is the worlds, as far as I know, most advanced computer in surveillance technology. It's a very sophisticated dedicated satellite system using laser and micro wave's technology that I've developed. It'll search for and pick up any communication device.'

'Hum-m,' she drawled, why use a silly name like tee-os-see. Why don't you call it something simple like Searcher, or Listener, or Seeker?'

Ian stared blankly at her. 'Right then....I rather like the sound of Seeker....So I guess that's what we'll call it from now on.'

'Good,' she said, 'glad to be of help.'

'I can tell you that Seeker is the proto-type of the computer now installed in the bowls of the earth, eight floors down below GCHQ Cheltenham, with a few additions. It links up to an independent satellite system unique to HM Secret Services, - and me of course.

'Is what you're doing, with this awesome piece of kit, - legal?' She turned to face him.

Ian pursed his lips and slowly shuck his head. 'Probably not, but what alternative do I have, this machine probably has the potential to save my life.'

She nodded understandingly. 'Okay, I can live with that, but before you go any further showing me things and digging me deeper into a hole, perhaps you would be good enough to tell me where all this is leading?'

'Let's sit down.' Ian pointed to the consol at the other end of the room and they walked over and sat down in front of a large terminal. 'This Haverton Hill business, I need to sort things, if only for the sake of my own protection.'

'Sorry Ian, I really don't think I should be getting involved, much as I feel for you.'

'Please Amy; I just need you to be here for support.'

She realised that no matter how she felt, she was basically locked in and didn't really have a choice, but to comply. Amy nodded slowly in compliance.

'As I told you earlier it all started innocently, I was with Colin Hatton while he was researching Billingham ICI for a new book. I became more involved when a lady showed up claiming that her family had been wiped out by fallout from a mystery plant'

'The one that produced the chemical weapon?' She interrupted, Ian nodded.

'An old friend of Colin's gave us a link to the guy in charge.'

'Dr Miles-Johnson.' She interrupted again.

'Simply because Miles-Johnson worked at Porton Down and I lived near, I volunteered to try to find him, that's if he was still alive. Which I did and he was. He told me one hell of a story.'

'Which you got on tape.'

'Please Amy, let me tell the tale.'

'Sorry.'

'What I'm getting to is, that while I was with the doctor, someone faxed Colin, from America, warning him that he was under surveillance and that if, I went to see the doctor both of us would be eliminated.' Ian paused to pat the terminal. 'When Colin got in touch and told me about the fax, I came here, to TEOSY, sorry..Seeker ...Broke my rule and scanned the Secret Service network for some sort of clue, and oh boy, did I get a clue.'

Amy moved to the edge of her seat and leaned forward. 'Go on, I'm intrigued.'

'It turned out to be a CIA operation with the help of a Mark Prichard from MI5 dirty tricks desk. We know now why the Americans wanted to keep the lid on it.'

'The toxic fallout.' Amy chirped in. Ian nodded.

'Well it turned out to be more involved, but that's not important now. With Seeker, I infiltrated Mark Prichard's system, that's when I discovered that termination of the doctor had been completed and that I was next. Shortly after that I discovered I had an ally. The head of BISS no less and he-,'

'Who?' Ian ignored her, not wanting to elaborate on the matter.

'-went ballistic. Apparently this Prichard fellow had acted without authority.'

'And the ally was this BISS head guy, right?'

'Correct.' Ian nodded. 'I guess I was somewhat fortunate really, as it turned out.'

'How?'

'Because this BISS director awarded me the contract to build this.' Ian swung his arm to emphasize the large computer. 'It seems he informed MI5 that I was a northerner living in the Tees area. I suppose that was his way of buying me some time.'

'He probably sent you that note.'

'That's what I was thinking.'

'Well that explains a lot, now what do we do?'

Ian booted the system. 'Let's check out this 'Zest Inc.' See who we're dealing with.'

'You think Zest Inc, are the assassins?' Ian nodded.

Ian ran 'Zest Inc', which came back with a slogan, -- *Eliminate a pest and contact Zest.* 'How tacky is that.' Amy said.

'Yeah, but intriguing, contact without a number.'

'Probably works on a response to the site user on the internet.'

'Probably - that means we have little chance of making contact.'

'Couldn't you try tapping this guy Pritchard's line, if, as you say he got into bother hiring the assassin, he still might be trying to make contact to call it off.'

'Good thinking, worth a try I suppose.' Ian tapped a few keys, but the line was dead. 'Probably gone home.'

'Can't you check his calls?'

'Only with prior knowledge, Seeker will record anything and everything on Mark Pritchard, from now until kingdom come if necessary, -- providing I ask it to, -- unfortunately I didn't.'

'What about his computer, can you access that?'

'Y-e-a-h I sure can and no doubt all his browsing history.' A few more taps on the key pad and. 'Bingo.' The screen filled with lists of Mark Pritchard's internet communications. Paydirt! Prichard made contact with Zest a couple of days ago,'

'Will you be able to trace it?'

'Me no, but Seeker will be able to pinpoint the location of the port where the transmit was opened.'

After several minutes Seeker eventually concluded its search. They both looked at the screen and slowly turned to face each other, it read. *Location of download, Corpus Christi College, Oxford.*

'I don't know anything about it, -- I swear,' she protested, Ian sat there in stunned silence. He turned back to the screen and hit a few keys.

'Ian I swear, I am not the assassin.' Then she started to sob, as women tend to do when there seems little else to say. It wasn't a definite tearful cry, but more or less a sharp intake of breath accentuated with a stuttering sniffle *sniff.* I don't know how I got into this mess.' She said as she dabbed at her eyes with a tissue *sniff.* I was set up.'

Ian reached out; put an arm on her shoulder. 'Amy, its okay, that terminal is an intercept, not the receiver.'

'What? *Sniff.*'

'It means that whoever has that terminal he has Seeker capabilities and can only be Secret Service.'

'Your guardian angel?'

Ian nodded, tapped a few more keys. 'It's in room 36, but--.'

'That's Professor Atkins room, the one who sent me here.'

'This Professor of yours is probably not all he seems. Let's do a check on the guy, what did you say his name was?'

'Michael Atkins must have a doctorate I believe in computer science and technology, but I'm not sure.'

Ian started to tap at the keys with vigour, Amy sat back in her seat and worked hard to pay attention and just to keep her eyes from closing, she failed on both accounts. The eventual lolling of her head as her chin slipped off a supporting hand, snapped her back into a waking state. She yawned and dozily squinted at her watch.

'It's well after ten, how you doing?'

'Nearly there,' he said as he frantically hammered away at the keyboard with speed and dexterity. The screen flashed like a faulty neon light and the text scrolled through endless lists of data changing instantly from site to site, page to page, in response to Ian's command. *'Buried that lot well, didn't we professor, but then again, you would not have expected to encounter someone of my calibre.'* Ian muttered to himself.

A moment later Ian shot up, his legs propelling the seat backwards. 'Got you!' He shouted and threw his arms in the air as if he'd just scored a goal. Amy, until that moment was slumped and almost at the point of dozing again. She shot bolt upright in her seat and patted her well rounded bosom exaggerating the shock. 'Phew, scarred the hell out of me then. – What've you got?'

'I'll tell you on the way, can't stay here all night,' he said, as he shutdown the system.

'Where're we going?'

'Got to get you into bed.'

'Thought you'd never ask.'

They looked at each other, holding the thought in their minds for just a moment, and then they laughed.

They jumped into Amy's car. 'Which way?' She said.

'Take a left out the main gate, down the hill and onto the main road towards Poole.'

Amy followed Ian's directions.

'Well?'

'Well what? ....Take a left here onto the slip road.'

'You know, what you found out.'

'Oh that,' Ian smiled keeping her in suspense as long as possible. 'It turns out that your professor has been moonlighting. Wads of tax payers' money have ended up in a Swiss bank, not traceable, you understand, but it seems Professor Atkins has purchased a villa in the South of France and a luxury yacht which he keeps in St Tropez. We're talking serious sums of money here Amy, money that has not come out of the professor's regular accounts, or from any tutorial fees......Straight on at this roundabout.'

'That could mean he's a secret agent, or something.'

'I agree. That's why so I thought I'd lift his photo off the satellite cameras and run through the agency lists.'

'And?'

'Make a right here.... Nothing -.'

'So he's not a secret agent.' She interrupted.

'Amy let me finish. ..Nothing on the video, it's apparent that my location in Poole has not been targeted on the satellite.'

'Hang on, am I missing something? I thought you wanted a photo of him.'

'My apartment, remember, someone had been in....Straight on next roundabout....I assumed it was him, while you and I were in the Nelson.'

'And it wasn't?'

'Not that I could see, even checked the CCTV that covered the front entrance....Only a couple of women and an old man that I didn't recognise as tenants.'

'Oh....You're certain that someone was.....?'

'Ninety-nine per......'

'Ian,' she put in, 'I think we're being followed.'

'Take the next slip, to Upton.' Ian turned in his seat so that he could see the headlights of the vehicles behind. 'Which one?'

'About three cars back. Been with us just after we left your car park.'

'Okay, head up the slip, go right around the roundabout and drop back down onto the carriageway on the other side.'

'Heading back the way we've come?'

'Yep.'

As Amy's car topped the ramp, the assumed pursuer indicated and pulled onto the slip. Amy rounded the island and took the exit to return back to the carriageway in the opposite direction. As her car dropped down the ramp, Ian lost sight of the other vehicle, but nothing followed them down. 'False alarm,' Ian declared. 'Take this next slip down and right, under the carriageway back towards Upton.'

'Could've sworn,' she said not wholly convinced that she'd been wrong, 'perhaps I'm getting paranoid.' As Amy's car was about to go under the bridge, Ian looked back up the slip. –

'Oh no, it's not!' He said as a car just came into view. 'Whoever it is must have slowed down. Do the same Amy; I want him to follow us. Left here, and again, and then take the right into Upton House Country Park. If he follows us in we've got him.' About a Hundred yards in, the park road loops around into a parking area. 'Drop me at the corner, you go and park over there, by the toilets.'

'What are you going to do?'

Ian touched his neck. 'It's about time I started to give something back.'

'Oh Ian, please be careful.'

'I'll try.' He said as he got out of the car and hid among the trees and bushes on the corner. Ian could now see in either direction. He watched as Amy parked the car near to the toilet block, the light shinning through the large open door presented a clear view of her and the car. He then turned his attention to the access road. Sure enough a car entered into the Park, turning off its lights as it came along the road. *Too late mate I've clocked you.*

The dark car, Ian determined was the one following them, turned slowly into the car park. The driver noticed Amy's car parked near to the middle of the car park, so he pulled in near to the corner and within spitting distance of where Ian was hid.

Ian waited and watched, only one occupant, a man judging by the silhouette created by the toilet block lights, he also appeared to be of a stocky build. Ian strode quickly and purposefully out of the shadows, grabbed and yanked the door open with his right hand, instantaneously thrusting out the left. His fist connected with the guys chin, then it grasped at the back of the head, pushing it hard back and forth several times each time impacting it with the steering wheel. There where groans moans and lots of blood and then the guy passed out. *Should've been wearing your seat belt mate.*

He reached in withdrew the car keys and threw them as far as he could into the foliage. Then he quickly searched the car checking the glove box and under the seats. He found nothing of any significance. A riffle though the guys pockets, produced a mobile which he pocketed, a wallet, some cash, credit card in the name of William Haynes and two photographs, one of him the other of Amy. He tore them into small pieces and threw them at the guy. Ian slammed the door shut and walked at pace over to Amy's car.

'Are you alright?'

'Never better.' And he jumped in. 'Let's go.' Amy's car completed the circuit and was about to pass the dark car on the way out, when Ian enquired. 'Would you mind taking a look at that guy, just to confirm that it's not Michael Atkins?'

'Well if, if you think I should.'
Ian nodded. 'Better make sure.'

Amy cautiously approached the dark car following Ian. Ian swung open the door, reached in and turned the man's head so it was visible to Amy. 'My god!' She said. 'What a mess.'

'Sorry Amy I didn't have a choice. Is this Michael Atkins?'

She screwed her face with distain and shook her head.

They got back into Amy's car and she set off. Apart from the directions Ian gave out, nothing was else was said.

They arrived in the Turner's drive and she cut the engine, but just sat there staring into the blackness. 'I'm sorry.' Ian said, trying to placate her.

'Leave it Ian,' she said, 'I've just about had all I can take today.'

Ian hauled himself out of the vehicle, sauntered to the door and rang the bell. Amy not wanting to burden Ian's parents with her mood stayed at least three steps behind him. It took a few minutes before the hall light came on and Ian's dad cranked the door open.

'Sorry Dad, I know it's late, but we need a place to crash, we're shattered.'

'Not a problem, we'd only just gone to bed. Come on in.'
Allan noticed Amy stood in the shadow. – 'Who have we here?'
'Amelia Pendleton, she works for me.'
'Very nice too,' Allan stepped back allowing both of them to squeeze past him into the small hallway, 'pleased to meet you Amelia.' He said holding out a hand as she passed. 'I'm Allan, Ian's father.'

She smiled mood swing complete, although not forgotten and took Allan's hand. 'I'd guessed, pleased to meet you Mr. Turner, I hope you don't mind putting—.'

At that moment Ian's Mum emerged from the bedroom, tying the belt on her dressing gown. 'Of course we don't mind. Hello, pleased to meet you Amelia, such a lovely name, I'm Alice.' With a furtive look towards Ian, she continued. 'It's only a two bed roomed house.'

'Alright Mum, I'll hit the settee, if that's alright.'

'Sure, - you hungry? There was a hesitant look on both their faces, which Alice took as affirmative. 'There's a beef casserole all prepared, I'll warm it up.' And she headed for the kitchen, at the same time holding up a hand to dispel any polite objections.

The next day just after breakfast, they all gathered in the lounge. Ian related the events of the previous day, including the missing hair from the door jamb and the incident in Upton Country Park.

'What do you reckon?'

'By all accounts there is only one assassin, this guy from zest, or wherever, who, it appears can't be stopped. The guy in the park, didn't have a weapon nor did he have any device to track your Audi to Billingham, so we can assume he's not the bad guy.....In fact you may just have clipped the wings of your guardian angel.'

Amelia cast Ian a knowing look, pursing her lips and nodding slowly, as if silently saying, told you so.

Ian nodded. 'Oh crumbs...'

'Did you get reg?'

'Nope....Guess I lost it when I found our photos...But I did get his mobile.'

'You've tried it?'

'Last night, as I lay on this sofa, trying to fathom things.'

'And?'

'Kept asking for a code, on the third attempt, it shutdown on me...If he was my guardian, I hope the guy's okay...May look worse than it was.'

'Too late for any sentiment, water under the bridge. You've got to get in touch with this BISS guy, see if he can help.

'Y-e-a-h.' Ian said thoughtfully.

CHAPTER TWENTY-SEVEN

Police Headquarters' Stockton on Tees

Detective James Munro of the Cleveland Constabulary, CID,
following up on Ian Turner's and Michelle Thompson's suggestions,
reviewed the autopsy report on Antony Davidson the Pathologist. He
discovered indentations on the back of the skull that matched the
barrel of J P Nicholson's gun. As further proof microscopic fibres
removed from the weapon matched the pathologist DNA. Before
closing the case, Cleveland CID undertook a thorough investigation
into Joseph Patterson Nicholson's life, which was documented and
archived along with the case notes. It transpired that he was an
American. He studied and graduated in Law at Yale, but never took

any bar exams, but instead opted for Accountancy in which he eventually majored. No explanation for this change was found. Despite that however, J P Nicholson considered himself to be an Attorney at Law, as the occupation listed on his visa application indicated.

Nicholson arrived in the UK about fifteen years previous and had in recent years represented, in one form or another, some of the relatives of deceased residents of the once town of Haverton Hill. Although no records could be found of his dealings, it was evident that he took no recompense for his services. On the contrary he is reported to have, in many cases, covered the funeral expenses from his own pocket. From bank records obtained by the Police, Nicholson appears to have been a very wealthy man, an exact figure was not determined because of constant moving of finances, but the figure was certainly upwards of twenty million pounds. However a day or so before the Billingham incident Nicholson's bank accounts had been emptied, and so far untraceable, except for the initial transactions to the United States. At that point in the investigation, the Cleveland force was instructed to drop the matter, no further action was taken.

Detective Munro following instruction to drop the case, without he perceived any pre-condition, decided, before he could close the file he should issue a press release. His statement would cover the murder of Anthony Davidson MD and the attempted murder of Ian Turner and Michelle Thompson. These crimes were committed, without a shadow of doubt by Joseph Patterson Nicholson a former American citizen living for the past fifteen years in the UK. I can confirm that Mr Nicholson was killed in a recent motoring accident.

The whole case centres on the alleged Haverton Hill disaster of fifty-nine and the fallout cover-up. It became apparent that Nicholson was blackmailing Anthony Davidson Senior Pathologist, Cleveland County, into falsifying cause of death reports on the victims of the disaster. It is believed that Nicholson murdered Davidson to stop him revealing his misguided activities to Mr Ian Turner a Dorset businessman who was responsible for recording Miles-Johnson's account of the biological weapon production at ICI Billingham, the explosion and subsequent fallout over Haverton Hill.

After Nicholson disposed of Davidson, he turned his attention to Ian Turner, attempting to murder both him and Michelle Thompson a local lady.

Detective Munro was convinced that there was still an assassin at large specifically targeting Ian Turner. But due to lack of evidence on the matter he made no mention of it in the press release, but before closing the case, and in hope of offering Ian Turner some protection, he sent everything he had to Police Headquarters' Poole, Dorset.

Downing Street

Prime Minister Graham Brown was alone in the cabinet office, his elbows rested on the large oak table, bridging a spread out newspaper, his hands cradled his forehead. He could feel the tension stiffening the muscles in his neck. *Overworked and overstressed,* he mused. *How the hell do I handle this now?* There was a tap on the door and it opened immediately without any beckoning from the Prime Minister.

Graham Brown raised his head from its cradle and wearily turned it to meet George Jenkins. 'Ah George, what can I do for you?'

'You've seen the news I take it Prime Minister?' Brown nodded, the lines of concern etched deeply on his brow.

'What a mess George, what am I to do?'

George Jenkins leaned across the Prime Ministers desk and picked up the red telephone, punched in a number and handed him the receiver. 'Perhaps Sir Peter can help.'

'Thank you, George, perhaps he can.' The Prime Minister placed the receiver to his ear; Sir Peter responded almost immediately.

'Yes Graham, what can I do for you?'

Peter, I, I think I could use some advise, bit of a tricky situation.'

The Prime Minister had a lengthy conversation with Sir Peter Thompson- Smythe, when he'd finished he slowly replaced the telephone in its holder and stared blankly at the desk top.

'Is everything alright sir?' George asked raising his eyebrows as he spoke gesturing his compliance to listen, should the Prime Minister wish to tell. Graham Brown lifted his head.

'Ahh yes George, Sir Peter feels I should not concern myself with these murders or the attempted cover up, just accept the fact that the Americans financed a plant in the ICI which had an accident. Leave it to the Lord Sommes inquiry to determine how many, if any, deaths in Haverton Hill could be attributed to this disaster. He also advised me, based on the Turner, Hatton findings, to determine a level of compensation and get the Americans to divvy up should the need arise.

'Sound advice sir, how are you going to play it?'

'Blame it all on the Yanks, even the murders, which in all the case isn't too far from the truth.....It was the CIA who by all accounts who instigated the MI5 contract on Miles-Johnson and it was an American who did this lot.' He said tapping the newspaper.

George Jenkins nodded. 'It was indeed sir....So why not.'

A slight smile of relief forced its way through the wrinkles and creased the Prime Minister's face. 'Why not indeed.'

CHAPTER TWENTY-EIGHT

Saturday night, the quay was still quite busy, as he and Amy left her car and headed for the apartment lift. Ian pushed the key into the Yale lock; he hesitated and looked around at Amy.'

'Go for it.' She said. Ian pushed the door open and switched on the light. He entered followed closely by Amy and cautiously inspected every room. 'Well,' she said, 'there's nobody here.'

'It's just like I left it, nothing seems to be out of place.'

'Except those.' Amy pointed her chin at the trail of clothes strewn across the bedroom floor.

'Oh packed in a hurry, I'll sort it later. Fancy a cuppa?'

'Please. Where can I put these?' She said as she lifted up her overnight bag, Which reminds me I'm running out of pants, I'll need to get back to Oxford soon..

'Check out the wardrobe.' Ian responded from the kitchen.

'Where am I sleeping?'

'You take the bed; I'll crash on the sofa. I haven't got round to fitting the other bedroom out.'

'I had noticed.' She cocked her head on one side and placed a hand on her hip and looked at Ian. 'Do you realise,' she said, 'we've been in each others company for almost forty hours now.'

'Huh huh,' Ian nodded thoughtfully. 'And?'

'And,' she said, 'that's longer than any first date I've been on.' She widened her eyes and began to unbutton her blouse. 'It's a King size bed, fancy keeping me company?'

Ian couldn't believe his luck as the blouse slipped to the floor her ample boobs stood out firmly supported, if support was ever necessary, by a low slung black cotton bra.

By the time Ian was able to squeak a response of delight, the zipper at the back of her sage green mini skirt had descended and her skirt slipped down her long legs and settled around her three inch high heeled patent leather shoes, which she proceeded to kick off as she stepped out of the skirt.

'You betcha!' He said as he pulled on the buttons of his shirt. *Wow she's gorgeous.* His thoughts reflected the excitement on his face as he struggled with an unyielding button at the waist of his Levi's. She was wearing black nylon briefs trimmed with lace that fitted snugly around the contours of her lower torso. Before Ian's Levi's hit the floor, Amy had turned and was heading into the bedroom, the material of her briefs almost disappearing in the crevice of swaying buttocks. Ian now hopping in an attempt to release his feet from his jeans and his slip-on shoes, followed as quick as he could. They came together at the edge of the bed and enfolded each other within their arms. They kissed, a long unhurried kiss, while gently caressing each other back and neck. Mouths still joined Ian fumbled for and unhooked, with ease, her bra strap, Amy assisted by letting the garment slip off her arms. He felt the warmth, the softness and the firmness of the protrusions, press against his chest; he could also detect the hardness of her nipples against his flesh. His head was swimming; he felt like he was *zinging* all over and his heart beat seemed to boom through his body. *Never felt like this before.*

Amy was also savouring the moment and she was unable to resist easing down Ian's boxers. Slowly and gently Ian laid her onto the bed as he did he hooked his fingers into the top of her panties and slid them off. He glanced but briefly at her nakedness, taking in the magnificence of her beauty, before lowering himself on top of her. *Paradise.* He sighed.

An hour later after making love, Amy laid enfolded in Ian's arms her head resting on his chest. 'Right,' she said with a smirk on her face, 'do you think we can go to sleep now?'

'Can't, just remembered, I've got to inspect your birthmark.'

'Don't you dare.' She said as she squirmed and giggled and they both rolled around the bed laughing, Ian pretending he was trying to look at her bottom, Amy pretending she was trying to stop him. The laughter stopped when their eyes met and they kissed and made love again.

They spent most of the Sunday morning in bed; eventually Amy eased herself out from under the duvet and headed to the kitchen in pursuit of sustenance. 'Could do with a good shop,' she shouted though to the bedroom, as she peered into the fridge, 'can't find anything at all to eat.'

'If needs must, there's s supermarket downstairs...What do we need?'

'Just about everything....' She said.

Just about then, the telephone rang, Ian hesitated wondering if he should pick up and stared at the instrument before curiosity got the better of him and he snatched it up. 'Hello.'

'Hi son.'

'Dad.'

'Did you get a paper this morning?'

'Nope...Haven't been up long....Why is there something I should know?'

'Guess so...Cleveland Police have released the full story on Nicholson, his involvement with the ICI fungal growth, the murder of the Pathologist and the attempted murder of you and the Thompson lady.'

'Wow.'

'Yeah wow....There's more, to be specific, they have hinted that it was you who got the Miles-Johnson tapes and what's more worrying they've announced you're from Dorset.'

'Well I guess it isn't going to long before the press discover which Ian Turner from Dorset it is.'

'Nor for that matter son....This Zest guy.'

CHAPTER TWENTY-NINE

Police Headquarters Poole

DI Cartridge and Sergeant Watts were discussing the report from the Cleveland Constabulary and Ian Turner's involvement in the case, as they pushed through the swing doors and into the CID Incident room. 'Hey Inspector.' A voice called after them. 'Chief wants to see you, like now.'

'Wonder what the hell he wants Mike?'

The sergeant shrugged his shoulders. 'Your guess is as good as mine guv, but you know what he's like, you'd better get in there, PDQ.'

DI Cartridge headed for the Chief Constables office. Knocked on the door and waited in the corridor, hands clasped behind his back until he got a response. He was hoping that there wouldn't be one, but he was not that lucky.

'Come!' A voice from within bellowed. DI Cartridge swung the door open and walked in.

'Ah Bob, do come in...Have a seat.'

'Sir.'

'This Turner case.'

'Yes sir, I was about to head over to Dolphin Quays, put some protection in place. The Cleveland lot, believe there's an assassin still on the loose intending to kill this Ian Turner....Something to do with this Haverton Hill thing. Apparently there's already been one attempt. So I intend to put a few plain clothes guys about the place. Cleveland inadvertently, or cock up more like, let slip that Turner lived in Dorset.'

'Y-e-s, quite, er ....Good work. Hum-m, we do however have a bit of a problem on this one, Bob.'

'Problem sir?

'Fraid so Bob. I want you to wrap it up.'

'But sir.'

'No buts Bob, you're off it, as of. Bring what you've got to me and forget it. Understand.'

DI Cartridge sighed. 'Everything sir?'

'Everything.'

'Very well.'

DI Cartridge walked out of the Chiefs office, shaking his head in dismay.

Dolphin Quay Poole

The old man had returned to the Dolphin Quays and had taken out a lease on a second floor apartment in the first of the four blocks fronting the waterfront. The apartment was on the corner of the block above a ground floor area leased to a shoe retailer and a first floor restaurant. The front of the balcony faced the marina and from one side it was possible to look back along Old Orchard Way and right, along the Quay and Quay Road. 'Perfect.' He said patting his hands on the balcony rail as he scanned each direction.

He stood on the balcony now, and observed the mêlée of reporters jostling for a better position, or picture, as Ian and Amy emerged from the front entrance.

'Sir ..Sir...Was it you who got the Mile-Johnson tapes?' A reporter from television network shouted, whilst trying to push a microphone in the direction of Ian's face. Ian gave an affirmative nod, held up a hand and gave out a statement. He confirmed his involvement with the Haverton Hill affair, Miles- Johnson, the murders and the attempt on his life. He and Amelia turned in unison and headed back to the apartment.

A few minutes later a taxi arrived, a lady who the old man later identified as Maureen Brownley, Ian's secretary, got out carrying a suitcase. She pushed her way through the reporters, who decided that she must know something and began harassing her.

'Hi Maureen.' Ian said opening the door wide to allow the secretary in 'How's everything?'

'Everything's OK, nothing to worry about. Quite a crowd you've got there.' She nodded towards the window.

'Yeah I know, but there'll be gone soon as another bit of news occurs.'

'As you requested, I've been to Marks'es, got a few things for you Amy.' She said as she put the suitcase down on the coffee table. 'Oh and Roger's set off for Oxford in a White van to collect your things from your flat.' Maureen unzipped the case and lifted the lid; as she pulled out one of the purchased articles,

Maureen fussed a little holding a blue floral dress up against Amy. 'What do you think?'

'Oh Maureen, it's beautiful.'

'Have you got time for a cuppa?' Ian enquired.

'No thanks boss, I've got to dash, taxis waiting. Oh by the way June 15, is favourite, I've got a pound on it.'

'For what?'

'Your wedding day. Goodbye.' She said as she hurried away.

'Did you hear that? They are taking bets on our wedding day. I haven't even asked you yet.'

'Are you going to?'

'Most certainly.'

'Go on then.'

'Miss Amelia Pendleton, would you give me the pleasure of being my wife?'

'Hummm, don't know...I hardly know you...I need a little time to think about it....The fifteenth sounds good to me; I might have a fiver on it myself.' She quietly said.

'Can I take that as a yes?'

'You sure can, lover boy.'

'Wow.'

Amelia smiled and casually began to examine the remaining contents of the case. *Oh good, knickers and bra's.* She mumbled lifting the various articles out for examination.

'Plenty of time for those.' Ian said as he came up behind her and nuzzled his nose into the nape of her neck. 'Do you realise this is the first time that I've had you to myself in an age.'

'She turned, giggled and threw her arms around him. 'What do you mean an age; it was only half an hour ago.'

'That long eh, probably forgot how to do it by now.'

'Uh uh, well you may just be in the need of a little practice. What do you think?'

'Yeah I guess I need all the practice I can get.' And they kissed, slowly and patiently as they edged their way into the bedroom.

The old man in the next apartment block, had a little giggle, blushed a little before he had the courtesy to remove the pans from his ears.

Ian and Amelia went into work as normal using the back stairway to avoid the reporters still gathered at the front of the apartment block. After several days passed, without incident, the press had dwindled to that of the occasional reporter keeping his option open just in case no new story broke.

Life had returned to normal, Ian and Amelia, besides work, were making plans for their forthcoming wedding.

Nothing seemed to be happening regarding the Haverton Hill situation and they both wondered from time to time, why the police had not made any contact in respect of the attempts on his life knowing that the assassin was still at large.

CHAPTER THIRTY

Some weeks later, Sunday, the reception desk in Dolphin Quays apartments was unmanned, when a tall thin man with dark hair and a hooked nose walked in through the main door. No one noticed as the man approached the elevator and pressed the call button.

The door bell to Ian's apartment chimed.

'I'll get it,' Amy shouted as she emerged from the kitchen drying her hands on a towel and headed to the door. She looked through the small glass viewer in the door panel and at the same time shouted. 'Who is it?'

'Police,' came the reply and a warrant card filled the range of her vision.

Without hesitation she turned back the lock and pulled the door open. She knew instantly, she'd got it wrong, she also instinctively knew it was the assassin. And she knew it, even before she noticed the gun with a huge silencer pointing at her midriff.

'Mind if I come in Ms Pendleton.' At the same time, pushing her with some force sending her hurtling backward.

'Ian! Ian! Amy cried out, but before Ian could react in any way, the assassin was in and again pushed Amy so that she was propelled backwards and fell heavily next to Ian on the sofa.

'What the---.' Ian blurted and shot to his feet.

'Sit down Mr. Turner we have some business to discuss.' He said motioning with the weapon.

Ian got the message and slowly lowered himself back down on the sofa, feeling for and grasping Amy's hand as he landed.

'Your contact has been cancelled you don't have to kill me anymore, -- and Amy, you should let her go, this has nothing to do with her.'

'Oh I love your sentiment, a real hero...Spare the lady take me instead.' He said mockingly. 'Now you know I can't do that, it's just not in my nature to leave witnesses and as far as contracts go, mine are never cancelled.'

'But the cover up has been exposed; it's not in MI5 or the governments' interest to want me dead.'

'Really, umm, well I don't give a rat's arse for MI5 or any one else, the thing is I've been contracted and handsomely paid to eliminate you. The good lady now of course, I'll do for free.....I never renege on a contract Mr Turner, I'm sure you understand, so bad for business. Pity.' He looked at Amy who was visibly shaking with fear. 'You see Mr. Turner I don't ask who put the contract out, I take the money and do the job, I have my reputation to consider.'

'The Intelligence Services and the Police will all wash their collective hands of you. Who else would want to employ you?'

'Please Mr. Turner give me some credit, I'm a professional, I'm not concerned about local plods, I've got irons in the fire from over the water.'

The assassin slowly paced the living room floor, as if contemplating the rudiments of removing two bodies. Neither his eyes nor the barrel of his weapon, left the two frightened people, now huddled together.

Keep him talking. Ian said to himself. 'So you tagged my car; I suppose it was you who cut the brake pipes in Billingham?'

'Of course it was.' The assassin said with a touch of bitterness in his voice. His eyes seemed to go blank as he revisited the event in his mind.

Now's my chance. Ian slowly and cautiously released his arms from around Amy. The easing of Ian's arm from around her only increased Amy's shaking. The assassin continued his spiel. 'Y-e-s, I watched with a degree of satisfaction of a job well done, as your car hurtled out of control down Billingham bank. I actually though I'd done for you. Then I clocked you and pretty Miss Pendleton here leaving ---.'

At that moment Ian pounced, he didn't have any kind of attack plan other than to relieve the assassin of his weapon. He flung the full weight of his body into his adversary at the same time shooting out his left hand to grab the wrist holding the gun. The assassin was no mug and unexpectedly, from Ian's point of view, didn't resist the force, but spun his body in the same direction he was being pushed. The gun hand came away from Ian's grip and the assassin spun full circle bringing the butt of the weapon crashing into the back of Ian's head. Ian felt the sharp pain, but realised although painful he was still conciuos.

'What the hell!' And he thrust out the weapon, pressing the gun barrel against Ian's temple. Ian automatically pulled his head away and closed his eyes tight in expectation of the bang and the bullet. Amy tried desperately to scream, but nothing but a gasping sound emitted.

Spit!

It took maybe a couple of seconds for Ian to realise that he was still alive and immediately became concerned for Amy, his eyes flashed open and he instinctively looked around shouting as he did, 'Amy! Amy!'

Amy was gripped in a state of shock and was still attempting to force out a scream that remained choked and muted. Ian spun back to checkout the assassin. The assassin was no longer looking at them, but staring in the direction of the living room door, with a bemused look on his face. He dropped his chin and unbelievingly observed the growing patch of red growing on his shirt front. The gun in his hand wavered and then lifted again, this time swung around and pointed towards the door.

Spit! - Spit! – Spit!

Three more red holes, closely grouped, appeared as if by magic in the assassin's chest. The dark head and the hook nose came down again momentarily to contemplate the accuracy of the shots, lifted again and shook it from side to side, - he then fell backwards, --- dead.

'Always did talk too much Zac.' The old man said as he walked into the room, the gun in his hand was still smoking and the smell of cordite filled the air.

'Who are you?' Ian blurted, his fear exposed by the tremble in his voice. Amy was now breathing deeply desperately resisting the urge to panic.

'Your guardian angel, just relax, you're safe now, ordeal over.' At that the old man fingered behind an ear and began to peel off a latex mask. He had only partly removed the disguise, when Amy said quizzically. 'Professor – Professor Atkins?'

'The very same, sorry about the deception Amelia, I didn't count on you getting emotionally involved, I just needed you to distract Ian while I bugged the apartment.'

'What! How dare—.'

'Saved your lives, didn't it?' Michael Atkins retorted.

Ian didn't have an answer, he just stared at the professor, - gunman, old man or whatever he was, with a perplexed look.

'I'd better explain, you see, I work for, ah um, let's just say a government agency who have an interest in your well being. When we became aware that a certain person in MI5, who, I might add has been severely reprimanded, had arranged an unsanctioned D notice on Doctor Miles-Johnson and yourself, I was tasked to protect you. Initially I attempted to access the contractor's web site and tried to countermand the instruction, but to no avail.'

Ian nodded, 'I know that's why I thought you were the assassin and for a time, til I realised that you'd intercepted the message.'

'That's your assassin.' Michael Atkins pointed with his chin to the blood soaked body lying face up on the living room formerly cream coloured carpet. 'One known as Zachariah Easterman liked to express himself as Zest.'

'Zest gets rid of your pest,' Amy chimed in and Ian was relieved to note that she seemed to be back to her chirpy self.

'Quite so, Amelia. I knew Zac Easterman of old; he was kicked out of MI6 some years ago because of his over zealous attitude and his keenness to eliminate people. He liked to torment his victims before he despatched them, took great pleasure in it, - apparently. That's why I bugged your apartment, I was pretty sure Zac would turn up here at some point and that he would want to make you squirm a little before pulling the trigger, - seems I timed it just right.'

'How could you be so sure he'd turn up here?'

'Simple logic,- I knew Zac would only be concerned about where you lived and where you worked. He probably checked out your office and no doubt would discount it on the basis of your twenty-four seven security. That left your apartment, it would be a typical Zac opp, he would get in here scare you shitless, sorry, excuse the language Amy, before dispatching you.'

'Why the wait?'

'No way could he pull off another impromptu Billingham Bottoms job. His brief was initially to make it look accidental, when that failed, he would go for you disappearing and for that he would need a back up service. Probably set here.'

'Back up service?'

'Yeah, you know, like a van, couple of carpets, boat, chains and all that sort of gubbins.'

Ian nodded. 'What about the guy in Upton Park, was he back up?'

'No no, he was mine, Bill Hayes a private dick; I hired him to keep an eye on you. He wasn't very happy, - busted nose and a few missing teeth, had to spend a night in hospital, but he's okay now.'

'He had our photographs.'

'Of course he did, I gave him them. Took them while you were talking in the pub. How else would he know who he was looking out for?' Michael Atkins unscrewed the silencer from his gun unclipped the magazine and returned the weapon components back to his pocket, as he spoke. Plucking the odd bits of latex from his face, he continued. 'Anyway getting back to Zac, he, more than likely had a way figured to remove your bodies, undoubtedly from this apartment and subsequently dispose of them.'

'Well that's reassuring to know.' Ian flippantly remarked while dabbing his fingers on the back of his head and inspecting them for traces of blood. There was none but a lump, which felt like the size of a golf ball, was forming.

Atkins looked down at the body and the mess it had made. 'I need to make some arrangements to have this removed and the place cleaned. - Speaking of which,' he turned to face the two figures who were now huddled together on the sofa, ' would you and Amelia like to take break, say a couple of nights stay in

London, take in a show, dinner at the Ritz, that kind of thing, - all expenses paid?'

Ian turned to look at Amy. 'Sounds good.' He said and she nodded in agreement.

'By the time you get back everything will be back as it was, it would be as if none of this had ever happened.'

Ian and Amy looked up at Michael Atkins. 'Sure, - why not,' Ian responded.

Everything seemed to happen so quickly, from the moment Michael Atkins made the call, a limousine turned up at Dolphin Quays. They were whisked away to London, a suite in the Savoy, no less, and had had an all paid for lunch in 'Thirteen' a Jamie Oliver restaurant. Now, just twenty-four hours after the shooting, they were sat in a private box in the Prince Edward Theatre, enjoying a show *The Jersey Boys.*

When the interval came, a tall figure with greying swept back hair entered they private box and calmly sat down next to Ian. Both Amy and Ian were startled and flashbacks of their previous encounter with a tall figure, caused a little panic.

'Oh it's you' Ian said letting the air escape loudly from his mouth, at the same time squeezing Amy's hand assuredly.

The tall man leaned in close to Ian, his head pointed so that his mouth was near Ian's ear. 'Enjoying the show Ian, didn't mean to startle you.' Ian just nodded and the tall man continued. 'I do appreciate that you've been having a rough time of it lately. However you would be doing me a great service if, how shall I say, you forget everything that's happened. We don't want to drag this mess through the courts now, do we?'

'Depends—.'

'On what?'

'On whether I receive some recompense to cover all of what I've had to endure.'

'Oh I think I can arrange an adequate compensation package for you.'

'And Amy?'

'A pro-rata sum.'

'And Michelle, Michelle Thompson?'

'Yes, of course.'

'Then consider it forgotten sir.'

Thank you Ian, now there's just this little matter of your access into TEOSY to sort out.'

Ian looked hard at Sir Peter Thompson-Smythe. 'We changed its name, it's now known as Seeker and as for using it I didn't really have a choice.'

'I understand, but the access codes must be changed to restrict any further unauthorised access. Do I make myself clear?'

'As crystal.' Ian whispered.

'Ah the second half, do enjoy the rest of the show, we'll talk later.' At that the tall grey haired man got up and left.

'Who was that?'

'You don't want to know Amy, - you don't want to know.'

CHAPTER THIRTY-ONE

Almost one year later Lord Sommes had concluded his report into
the Haverton Hill Affair, with fairly damning condemnation of the
then Labour government, primarily for the attempted cover up.
There was however insufficient evidence to conclude that Doctor
Miles- Johnson had died from anything other than natural causes. So
the report on the allegation that the Doctor was murdered proved
inconclusive. All matters relating to the attempts on Ian Turner's life

had been removed from all official records, therefore there was no case to answer and was not considered by the Sommes Enquiry Commission.

Lord Sommes also strongly condemned the British and American governments of the past for the underhand way in which these biological and chemical weapons where produced and in the case of the latter, the proximity of the production to the town of Haverton Hill.

Samples of soil tests taken from various areas where the town had once stood proved to be conclusive in that traces of toxins were found to be still present.

The findings of the report began a whole series of compensation claims and numerous Law firms jumped on the band wagon with advertisements offering to represent the claimants. The American government in their usual manner threw millions of dollars into a fund which they deemed to be sufficient to cover their liability. This then put the onus on the British to consider a similar fund and the emphasis changed from one of 'cover up' and 'denial' to that of closing the flood gates in an attempt to mitigate the situation.

The fact that these biological and chemical concoctions became the 'Weapons of Mass Destruction' looked for in Iraq, was never divulged. Graham Brown distanced himself and had taken steps to have all reference to that matter removed from any and all records.

Conlan Powell never made public his knowledge of the 'Weapons of Mass Destruction,' in connection with the Iraq war, no did he ever mention or discuss the contents of the Nixon meeting and the Eisenhower U2 revelation, other than to order Jack Rosenthal to bury the data so deep that it would never be found.

Conlan Powell never again mentioned the fact that he had been handed the responsibility of the trust fund set up for the benefit of former Haverton Hill residents. Residents who it was deemed were affected by the envisaged lethal fallout from S.IX plant. He retired from government, spending millions of dollars which he poured into a ranch with a mansion in Texas.

Simon Kendal never revealed to anyone, his part in the warning of Colin Hatton and Ian Turner and he never attempted any further breach of computer security for fear of the consequence should his incursion be discovered. Simon did however benefit indirectly. In a move to distance the department away from this Haverton Hill affair and as part of Jack Rosenthal's burying operation, all the references to the chemicals and places that initiated the situation in the first instance were removed from the computer records. Because Simon had been aware of the situation from the word go, he was sideways promoted to 'Command Communication Computing Technology' as Head of Programming. An immediate benefit, Simon chuckled to himself as he thought about it, was the fact that the Security Guards saluted and waved him and the company car he was now driving, into the CIA headquarters without hindrance.

One aspect of the Sommes Report, was the number of claimants that turned up out of the blue, some genuine and some not. Many of the genuine cases had or possibly had some experience of illness which they believed was attributable to the toxic fallout, either to themselves, or as in most cases, a close family member. In many cases the family member had passed on and so numerous were these departed souls, that it was decided to hold a remembrance service as a mark of respect.

The service was held on the former site of the Methodist Chapel, on the corner of what used to be Marlborough and Collingwood Road. Ian with his now wife Amy, together with his father and mother, were among the many hundreds that attended, as was Michelle Thompson with her husband Bill.

Michelle spotted Ian and sauntered over to meet him. They took each others hand holding on for a long moment. 'Shall we walk?' Ian motioned, and the pair of them wandered away from the crowd to a quieter area.

'How are you Michelle, it been an age since Billingham?' Ian enquired. 'Oh I'm fine and I must say you still look devilishly handsome.'

Ian trying to remain nonchalant changed the subject. 'That your husband?' He said pointing with his chin.

'Uh uh, and I see you're married now.' Ian nodded. 'She's lovely; you're a lucky man Ian Turner.'

'Oh I know.'

'Still, I guess we both were that night,' she said solemnly. 'You know Ian I really wanted the world to know Nicholson's secrets and how he killed for greed. But instead I was basically told to forget it. Ended up with a couple of mil, no doubt a pay off, but I was told the payment was by way of compensation for Mum and dad and a little something for my trouble. Can't really relate it to the lives of my parents, keep thinking hush money and I find it about as satisfying as a sleepless night.'

'Oh dear Michelle I know what you mean but we have to move on. Nothing we can do now to save all those people, it's over.' Ian turned to look at the crowds. 'Just look at that lot, most of them happy with their new found wealth. Enjoy the money Michelle; forget this, leave it in the past where it belongs.'

She nodded thoughtfully, her eyes staring at the ground, ironically the very spot where her father had lived, although she and Ian for that matter would never know. However Allan, noticing where the couple were stood talking did. He turned to Colin and pointed his chin in their direction. 'Stood in the Hartley's living room, wouldn't you say Col?'

'Yeah just about I reckon, but I doubt Michelle even realises.

Ian and Michelle headed back to mix with the rest of the people; she turned her head and smiled at Ian. 'There something I would prefer never to forget.' She flashed her eyes at him. Ian reddened, but quickly recovered his composure when they met up with Colin Hatton who was talking to his dad. At that moment Colin's wife Miriam joined the group, as did Alice and Amelia. Phillip and Jack also sidled up and there was shaking of hands and knowing nods, but nothing other than noises of greetings, was mentioned.

Colin as one of the organisers of the event and exposé of the cover up; was asked to make a speech after the religious section of the service had concluded. He in turn introduced Ian, who after another short speech unveiled a commemorative stone. The stone was formed out of granite about half a metre square mounted upon a granite block cube of one metre. Engraved on the stone was written;

HERE ONCE STOOD THE TOWN OF HAVERTON HILL.

The End

AUTHORS NOTE

The facts

I, like many others of my generation I suppose, didn't really give the matter much thought and our parents were of an age that had faced many tough times, world wars, general strikes and rationing. So being subservient and respectful of authority was probably considered the norm, just as long as they had work, and could put bread on the table was all that really mattered. For us of that age, we were growing up in the fifties, the beginning of the golden age, and everything was good and getting better. Our complacency was nurtured in a 'why rock the boat' mentality, although I must confess, by the mid sixties, we were all looking for the better deal. Nay, I would say demanding it. Upon reflection, the demands made then by the working man, probably heralded the decline of British industry, so perhaps we should not lay too much of the blame on the then Government, but that perhaps is another story.

In 1917 the Right Honourable Viscount Furness, Lord Admiral of the fleet, recognised the need to build ships to replace those sunk by U-boats. An area on the north bank of the river Tees adjacent to the small hamlet of Haverton Hill became the site of the then very modern Furness Shipbuilding Co Ltd. To attract the skilled labour needed for the shipyard, initially a large hostel to house 500 men was built. By 1920 work was completed on the 'model village' of the Furness Estate, Haverton Hill. This estate became known as the 'garden city' because each house had a garden at the front with a concrete yard and a large green area (known as the backs) to the rear. The houses were built in terrace blocks consisting of four or six houses and formed in rectangles of about six blocks by two. The streets were formed in parallel lines, most of which were named after great seafarers or had a maritime connection.

The design of the houses themselves was modern with an inside loo, a bathroom and with hot water on tap heated by a back boiler behind the lounge fire place. A far cry from the cramped back to back, outside loo style of Victorian house which at that time were prevalent for the working classes.

In 1916 the unprecedented use of explosive in the First World War, led to the government forming a scientific Nitrogen Products committee to look for a site where the UK could produce its own Nitrates.

About two miles Northwest of Haverton Hill is a place called Billingham and it was there, on the site of Grange Farm that the committee decided the new Nitrate factory should be built. By the time construction started in 1918, the war was over and with it the need for explosives, so the factory was abandoned, later to be sold.

Brunner Mond purchased the site in 1920 and set up a new company called Synthetic Ammonia and Nitrates Ltd. The nitrogen products, necessary for the production of explosives, were also an essential part of much needed fertilizers. Ammonia production started in 1923 following the introduction decoking plants, an early polluter, for gas to water gas plants needed for the production of Hydrogen, which I believe was part of the process in the manufacture of Synthetic Fertilizers.

In 1926 the works was taken over by the Imperial Chemical Industry (ICI) and thus started the expansion with the construction of more

Ammonia plants along with plants for the production of Sodium Cyanide and manufacture of Paints, Plastics and Fertilizers.

As well as the now vast above ground complex, underground, ICI had a network of miles of mine workings for the extraction of Anhydrite. This was used for mixing with Ammonia to produce sulphate of ammonia Fertilizer. It was also used for Gypsum products, Cements and Nitro Chalks.

During the Second World War the various chemical concoctions produced at Billingham ICI were again used for manufacture of explosives and other chemical gas products. Part of this large chemical works was also involved in other secret wartime work, the development of atomic bombs, for instance.

In time, the chemical works at Billingham had expanded to such a degree, that a large Synthetic Ammonia plant, believed to be number 5, was built within 150 yards of the houses on the Furness estate Haverton Hill.

We lived in Drake Street between Rodney Street and Marlborough Road. Looking along Marlborough Road, I can still recall seeing this large obnoxious structure looming above the houses. The smoke and dust billowing from its stacks, spewing out its foul, 'bad egg' smelling pollution, accompanied on occasion with a fine drizzle of nitric acid, only to fallout over Haverton Hill.

Events around 1950 saw the start of the construction of a new estate in Billingham which would in time house all of the occupants once of the Furness estate, Haverton Hill.

I remember helping my mother pack up our belongings into the removal van and moving into a new house on the Billingham estate. We were not the first or the last, but part of a systematic process that would, in few short years, see Haverton Hill evacuated, bulldozed and literally wiped of the face of the earth. What I can't remember, at that time, is anyone at all, self included, asking the question. 'Why?'

Ironically the offending plants responsible for most of the pollution over the town were also bulldozed at about the same time as they pulled down Haverton Hill. The contaminated structure was believed to have been cut up and dumped into a disused section of the Anhydrite mine, and sealed with concrete.

My wife had made the journey from Poole back to Middlesbrough to help her Mum attend her dad, who at that time was ill suffering from asbestosis, contracted when he was employed; you've guessed it, in the ICI. While she was there, she spotted an article in the Evening Gazette covering the writing of a book on Haverton Hill, by Colin Hatton. Knowing of my roots, she purchased a copy of the book for me.

I was absolutely delighted with this find and immersed myself in the nostalgia of it. I knew a lot of the people that were mentioned, all of the places and the teachers at the school, some of which still give me the creeps even today, although I expect most of them have long since died. I also knew Colin the author; he then lived in Marlborough Road and was in the school intake the term before me. The newspaper article was about how Colin had come to write the book and had listed his telephone number presumably to accrue more subject matter. I wasted no time calling him and spent close to an hour in enthralling conversation going over old times and acquaintances. Above all the things we discussed, what really stuck in my mind was, according to Colin's research, the number of our mutual friends who had died at a relatively young age, invariably from cancer in one form or another. It was that fact that sent my brain into gear, asking myself the same questions that perhaps I should have asked forty-seven years ago. What chemical concoction was the ICI pushing into the atmosphere above the citizens of Haverton Hill? And was the foul air that filled our nostrils, full of cancer bearing toxins which would inevitably account for the loss before their time of so many lives?

After talking to Colin, I spent several days trying to find any reference, other than his book, on or about Haverton Hill, the Furness estate, the school or anything at all. I found nothing, other than an aerial photo on the 'planet earth' web site, where one could just discern the lines of what were once the streets. It was as if Haverton Hill had been eradicated, never existed, wiped off the map of England, - but never from my memory.

Printed in Great Britain
by Amazon